A THRILLER

THE LAST

GIL SNIDER

Best regards,

Gil Snider

This is a work of fiction. Names, characters, places, and incidents are products of the author's imagination or are used fictitiously and are not to be construed as real. Any resemblance to actual events, locations, organizations, or persons, living or dead, is entirely coincidental.

World Castle Publishing, LLC
Pensacola, Florida

Copyright © Gil Snider 2023
Hardback ISBN: 9798395562937
Paperback ISBN: 9781960076809
eBook ISBN: 9781960076816
First Edition World Castle Publishing, LLC, June 12, 2023
http://www.worldcastlepublishing.com

Licensing Notes

Cover: Cover Designs by Karen
https://www.cover-designs-by-karen.com
Editor: Karen Fuller

Acknowledgement

I wish to thank Judy, my wife and friend, for her never-ending support and encouragement, as well as for her invaluable critiquing and helpful insights.

Thanks to my sons, Nicholas and Jonathan, and their families, for their support.

Thanks to Paul and Tracy Collins for their help in putting together the courtroom scene.

Special thanks to Anne McAneny for her excellent editorial assistance, and her patience. And thanks for teaching me so much about the skill of writing.

Most of all, thanks to Karen Fuller and World Castle Publishing for making this book a reality.

I wish to dedicate this book to all of my multiple sclerosis patients, whose courage, determination, and perseverance in the face of this difficult and unpredictable disease has been an inspiration to me.

PROLOGUE

He could feel the closeness of Death, as palpable as the blasts of cold winter wind that shook the cabin to its very foundation. Samuel Morehouse accepted his early demise stoically, as his ancestors had for hundreds of years. What saddened him, though, was his wife's stubborn denial of the inevitability of his demise and the implication of his passing on their daughter's future.

Rebecca Morehouse, her face flushed from the radiance of the wood fire, lifted the cast-iron pot from the fire with a long bar and set it on the oak table that had been in the Morehouse family for generations. The heavy metal kept the water boiling while she dipped a ceramic cup in and held it there until the handle became almost too hot to hold. Then she poured in a spoonful of dried herbs and stirred until the steam carried the aroma up to her nose in a soft, warm cloud. Using a thick linen cloth to protect her fingers, she carried the cup to her pallid husband, who lay in the bed across the darkened room.

"Drink it while it is still hot. It will break the fever more quickly."

Samuel rose with painful slowness, then leaned on his elbow and held the cup with a skeletal hand, his veins painting dark blue patterns through his translucent skin. As he sipped the tea, he periodically coughed up thick wads of bloody mucus. His sunken eyes reflected his profound weakness, and several times his wife supported the cup so it wouldn't slip from his grasp. He wrapped his cold fingers around his wife's hand and gave it a gentle, loving squeeze before she set the empty cup down on the nightstand.

The sound of a heavy footstep crunching on gravel made Rebecca start. "What was that?" Her ears strained to hear through the night wind.

"I heard nothing," Samuel mumbled.

"No, I heard someone treading on the trail from Artemis's shack."

"Perhaps it is your sister and my brother come to visit."

"Why would they come up the trail? Their house lies in the opposite direction." Rebecca took a lantern and stepped onto the porch into the bitter winter night.

Their farm lay at the edge of a dense forest that covered the entire slope of Eden Mountain up to its flat crest, which had been painstakingly cleared and transformed into the Morehouse family compound over many generations. A single trail led through the trees to the settlement, and poor drunk Artemis Donnard, their neighbor, was never sober enough at this hour to make the difficult journey from his pitiful shack. At the trail's end, Rebecca and Samuel had laid a broad gravel pathway to keep their vital connection to the outside world from becoming a muddy morass during heavy rains. It was from that path that Rebecca had heard the sound, like the crunching of a single pair of boots.

Rebecca's lantern was too dim to illuminate anything beyond the porch, so she crept cautiously down the steps, swinging the lamp in broad arcs. She sensed nothing but the clouds speeding through the starry sky and the wind rustling the trees.

"Isaiah? Miriam?" she called into the darkness. Hearing

nothing, she retreated inside from the bitter cold but was stopped by an intense fit of coughing that left her dizzy. She steadied herself against a nearby chair.

"You should be drinking some tea yourself, woman," Samuel said.

"Never you mind what I should be drinking. It is your job to do the farm work and mine to know the remedies, so do not tell me how to do my job."

"For fifteen years, have I ever been able to tell you how to do anything? Why should my dying allow me any new rights?" He sank back into the bed.

Rebecca wagged her finger at her husband. "Do not babble on about dying. I will not hear such talk in this house."

"We have been married too long to be deceiving one another," he said with a sigh. "Besides, it does not matter what happens to me or to you. We must concern ourselves only with Ruth." He summoned all his reserves of energy and sat up. "She is the last."

"She is not the last," Rebecca cried. "Not yet. We are not dead, and Miriam and Isaiah are younger than either of us."

"They remain childless. Ten years of trying, and nothing has come of it. Get it through your head that it is a matter of time until our daughter is the last. She cannot be allowed to contract our illness." Samuel stopped to catch his breath, then continued. "In town, there are real doctors trained in schools in big cities. Two years ago, one of them came up here and saved her life. They can examine our blood, have machines that can look inside our bodies, and they have medicines — real medicines — not your roots and herbs. We should see if they can help us."

"It is the Lord's doing that Ruth's life has been spared so far. You know we cannot leave this mountain. Besides, I will not abandon the two of you to seek help."

As Samuel's head fell back into his pillow, a knock sounded.

Rebecca grabbed the iron poker from the fireplace and took a tentative step toward the door. "Who is there?"

"Miriam and Isaiah," said a woman's voice. "Who else would it be?"

Rebecca opened the door to a burst of cold wind that whistled over the bare mountaintop. Two dimly lit forms stood outside the reach of the fireplace's glow. "I thought I heard someone walking outside a few minutes ago. It must have been the wind. Come out of the cold. I have water boiled for tea."

"We have not come for tea," Miriam said, remaining on the porch. "We have come for the child."

Rebecca's eyes blazed. "You shall not have Ruth. Not while I or my husband still live."

"It is not your decision," Isaiah boomed. "We cannot have children, and if either of you should die, Ruth will be the last. If she does not come with us, she will die as well, which cannot be allowed to happen. It is God's will."

Rebecca retreated from the doorway and screamed at the shadowy figures. "You cannot have her. She is my child. I will not let you take her from me."

Samuel spoke out from his bed, too weak to raise himself. "Let Ruth go, Rebecca. This house holds nothing for her but death."

"It holds my love for her, and that is enough," Rebecca cried, tears streaming down her cheeks onto the rough-hewn pine floors. "I will not give her to them."

"We have talked about this many times," Miriam said. "We knew this day would come for you, as someday it will come for us. But for now, we are the only ones who can help her." She stepped toward the threshold, the firelight illuminating the concern and weariness on her face. "Please do not make me risk my life by coming in. Your daughter needs me too much."

A silence enveloped the house, broken only by the crackling of the logs burning to embers in the hearth.

"There are no alternatives," Samuel said wearily. "Let the child go."

Rebecca stood quietly and gathered herself, then called out to the back of the house. "Ruth, your aunt and uncle are here. Please come out and greet them."

A door in the back of the room opened. A pretty, slender girl with long chestnut hair and olive skin stepped into the room. Her intense brown eyes made her look years older than her twelve years. She wore a plain white linen dress, her hands clasped in front of her as she kept her eyes looking shyly to the floor.

"Good evening, Miriam and Isaiah, and may God's grace be on you. We have not had the pleasure of your visit for many days."

"Good evening, Ruth," Isaiah said, stepping into the cabin, "and may God's grace be on you as well. Your father's illness has kept us away. I am glad to see you well."

"My mother makes me stay in my room. This is the first I have seen of my father except from my doorway." Ruth gazed sadly at Samuel.

"Your parents should have sent you to us a long time ago," Miriam said, "but we did not have the heart to come here ourselves to get you. Get your coat, Ruth. You must come stay with us for a while until your father...recovers."

Ruth glanced at her mother, who nodded slowly, her face expressionless. Ruth retreated into her room and closed the door.

"You must at least let me kiss her goodbye," Rebecca pleaded.

"Sorry," Isaiah said, "but we cannot take that chance."

Ruth returned, a coarse woolen coat covering her dress, her eyes downcast. Her mother turned away quickly.

"Do not touch your mother," Miriam commanded. "Nor your father. You must not become ill with their affliction."

"Can I not kiss them goodbye before I leave?" Ruth said, seeming to fight back tears.

Miriam rushed in, put her arm around Ruth's shoulders, and hurried her out the door. "There is no time for that now. We must leave quickly."

As Ruth fought to free herself from her aunt's grasp, her uncle clutched her tightly and led her into the darkness.

The bang of the door as the wind slammed it shut made Rebecca jump. She struggled to maintain her composure as her daughter's cries faded into the night air, replaced by the crackling of the logs. She collapsed onto a fireside stool, her body convulsing with sobs.

"Is it God's will that we should die here alone, without our child?" she wept to her husband while looking for the answer in the heavens.

Samuel held his arm out and called to her. She walked over, lay down beside him, and cried herself to sleep in his arms.

***

The fire had burned down to dull red embers when a sharp knock on the door awakened Rebecca. Opening her eyes, she felt disoriented, unsure if the sound had been part of a dream. But it returned, more insistent. She jumped out of bed and shook Samuel.

"Wake up. Your brother has brought our child back. Wake up!" But so close to death, Samuel barely opened his eyes before sinking back into his stupor. Rebecca ran to the door and flung it open, surprised and frightened by what greeted her.

Alone in the doorway stood a looming dark figure dressed not in homemade linen clothing but in a manufactured wool coat and black leather gloves, like someone from town would wear. He carried an elegant black leather bag, and his face was shielded from the cold by a thick woolen scarf.

"Who are you, and what do you want?" Strangers from town rarely visited—and never unannounced—especially at this hour. She narrowed the door's opening to a few inches, partly to block the cold wind but mainly as a shield between herself and the ominous stranger.

"My name is unimportant, Mrs. Morehouse. I came to talk about Ruth."

"What do you know about my daughter?"

"I know a lot, in some ways more than you do. I know that someday she will need special care that you and your family cannot provide. But don't worry, Mrs. Morehouse. When the time comes, I'll look out for her. I'll make sure she doesn't die the way you and your husband are doing."

Rebecca's features softened, and for the first time in weeks, a smile played across her face. "Are you truthful?"

He nodded.

"Then you must be an angel. An angel from God." She opened the door to let him in.

"I suppose you could say that." He stepped through the doorway into the cabin. After looking around, he set his leather bag on the table, removed a bottle from it, and poured a clear aromatic liquid onto a handkerchief from his pocket. Then, without warning, he grabbed Rebecca and twisted her arm behind her back, forcing the handkerchief into her mouth and muffling her screams. She fought in vain to free herself, but bit by bit, she weakened, her vision darkening and her consciousness ebbing. Thirty seconds later, she fell limply into his arms.

He laid her body across the table, then strode to the bedridden Samuel and yanked the pillow out from under his head. As Samuel awakened with a start, the visitor pushed the pillow onto his face and held it fast with the weight of his body. Half dead already, Samuel's struggles proved weaker than his wife's, and he perished quickly.

After confirming Rebecca's demise, the intruder pulled the handkerchief from her mouth and set her next to Samuel, carefully positioning them as if they were sleeping in each other's arms.

Then he poured half of the bottle's contents onto them,

sprinkling the remainder around the cabin. With one smooth motion, he held the handkerchief against the embers until it burst into flame, then flung it onto the bed. The mattress erupted in a blaze, followed by a flash so intense that despite the protection of the scarf, the stranger had to shield his face as he grabbed his bag, rushed into the night, and hurried down the gravel path to the trail from which he had come.

CHAPTER I

Three Years Later

Dots floated wherever Dr. Anne Mastik looked. Tiny maroon specks so small that she might not have seen them if she didn't know they were there.

Some drifted alone like scattered flecks of dust. Some paired up as if caught in the act of kissing, while others lined up like long strings of bloody pearls. But she ignored them all as they moved quickly across her field of vision. Only when she saw them clustering did she grow concerned. And the clumps got bigger the more she looked. Initially appearing no larger than small bunches of grapes, they soon coalesced into enormous masses, exploding in size and number until they became all she could see.

Anne pulled her head up from her microscope and gazed out her laboratory window at the foothills of the distant Blue Ridge Mountains, their peaks riding on a sea of early morning fog. In her five years as an associate professor of Infectious Disease at the University of Virginia, this slide was the worst case of Staph sepsis she had seen. The telltale clumps of tiny round bacteria, tinted deep red by the Gram stain dye, told a deadly story. As a hospital-acquired infection, it would undoubtedly be resistant to the commonly used antibiotics. Labeled "MRSA," for Methicillin-Resistant Staphylococcus aureus, it required more-expensive, toxic antibiotics and had evolved into one of the most lethal infectious organisms in the United States. With no time to lose, Anne needed to switch the patient's antibiotics. When the phone on the sixth-floor Medicine Ward nursing station rang interminably, she hung up and called her friend Dr. Gary Nesmith, the staff physician, but his cellphone went to voicemail. No alternative. She had to go directly to the unit before the patient crashed.

Anne rose from her chair and turned toward the door, but her feet failed to react when her brain told them to. She stumbled, clutching the edge of the laboratory table to prevent a fall.

God, that was close. Her pulse pounded in her ears from the rush of adrenaline. She steadied herself against the table, then took off for the Medicine Ward as fast as her stiff legs would allow.

Damn this MS.

Anne made her way through the research building toward the elevator and rounded the corner just in time to see the doors closing.

She groaned. During her athletic years playing college soccer, the four-floor climb to the Medical Ward would have been considered good exercise. She would have taken the stairs two at a time and hardly broken a sweat, but spasticity in her legs caused by multiple sclerosis made maneuvering the steps a formidable task. Plus, this was the oldest and slowest elevator in the hospital, and the floor indicator showed it stopping at every floor. It would take at least ten minutes to make the round trip back to Anne's floor. If she didn't get the order to the pharmacy in the next few minutes, the patient's first critical dose would be delayed, possibly fatally. With a sigh of disappointment, Anne turned to the stairwell and started her trek.

As she struggled up the four flights of the empty stairwell,

Anne mulled over her situation. Her first attack of multiple sclerosis had occurred during her second year of medical school at the University of Virginia, two years into her marriage to Roger. She'd woken one morning with her entire left side numb. With winter midterm exams close by, she'd done nothing about it. Probably stress, she thought. Luckily, the numbness resolved after three weeks. She forgot about the episode until six months later, when the vision in her left eye blurred to the point where she couldn't read. Reviewing her brain MRI scan with her neurologist, he pointed to evidence: abundant scarring in the form of scattered white ovals. *No use in even attempting to count,* she recalled. She heard the doctor say the words "Multiple Sclerosis," but the rest of his explanations—about prognosis, treatment, and anything else that he thought a medical student would want to know—became a blur of words as her mind churned through what this meant to her life.

Anne stopped at the next floor to catch her breath. She put her foot on the first step, held onto the railing for support, and continued her climb.

Anne's original reaction to her disease had leaned toward intellectual acceptance but emotional denial. She'd become obsessively independent and even persisted in her dream of becoming a surgeon despite her adviser's cautionary counsel. But when every surgical residency turned her down, she realized that no surgical program director could possibly accept a candidate who might struggle to tie a knot, let alone perform intricate operative procedures. The stress of the rejections triggered a relapse of her MS, which affected her right arm and both legs.

Five days of complete dependency, lying in a hospital bed receiving intravenous steroids and total nursing care, proved unbearable. In her state of denial, she became a difficult patient. But reality finally hit her during rehab, when it took a week of intensive physical therapy to master a simple unassisted trip to the bathroom and another week to get back the coordination to button her blouse.

Shaking off a deep depression, Anne resolved to conquer the disease and resume life where she had left off. Who knew how much was attributable to the steroids and how much to her stubbornness, but by the time of discharge, she was well on the mend. She recovered almost completely from that relapse, but Rehab gave her plenty of time for a realistic career assessment. She needed a specialty that, if necessary, she could practice from a wheelchair. Infectious Disease, which involved studying microorganisms capable of attacking any body organ, would be perfect. It involved no medical procedures, and she would maintain her general medical knowledge while still interacting with a broad range of other specialists. She seized upon a last-minute opening at UVA to stay on as a resident in Internal Medicine, leading to a guaranteed fellowship in Infectious Disease.

On the downside, residency training was notoriously hard on marriages, even stable ones. Anne's long hours, her obsession with her independence, and the fatigue induced by her MS had opened fault lines in her marriage. It all culminated in a major split when she accepted an academic position with a tenured track at the university.

Halfway up the third flight of stairs, Anne stopped. *It would have been quicker to take the elevator.* She looked up and shook her head. *Too late to stop now.* She grabbed the handrail and pulled herself up with each step. By the time she reached the sixth-floor landing, she was winded, her legs and arms aching. She brushed back the strands of strawberry blonde hair that had slipped in front of her face and paused to catch her breath.

"Can I get the door for you, Dr. Mastik?" said a medical student descending the steps.

Anne managed a weary smile. "No, thanks. I'm okay." She opened the door and dragged herself into the Medical Ward.

At the nursing station, she half sat, half fell into a chair and logged into the records system to write the order for the new antibiotic.

"What an honor," boomed a familiar male voice behind her. "Dr. Anne Mastik herself has come from her laboratory on high to visit the poor foot soldiers here on the front lines of patient care."

Anne smirked but continued typing. "You know my laboratory is not on high, Gary. It is exactly sixty-four steps below this floor. I know because I counted them on my way here. And if you haven't seen me for the last two weeks, it's because you're home at 8:00 p.m. when I'm rounding."

As Gary rested his arms on the nursing station desk and grinned, Anne gave him a quick glance. He'd always been a bright, cheerful guy, rounder in the torso than he should have been, with curly black hair and blacker rimmed glasses. Their friendship dated back to medical school, when he had been the one male friend who stood by Anne during her MS relapses. They'd become even closer after Gary's wife, Katy, died of breast cancer a few months after Anne's divorce.

"I told you to go into Derm," he said. "Hours are more humane. There are worse ways to make a living than injecting Botox from nine to five."

"Gary, for even a fraction of a second, could you imagine me working a nine-to-five job?"

"I couldn't, but I'm sure Roger could have."

She frowned and kept typing. "That was his problem, not mine." When Anne had accepted her academic position, Roger had seen no light at the end of the tunnel. After the divorce was finalized, he moved to the West Coast and remarried within a year. Anne had been too shattered to even cry. As paralyzed emotionally as she had been physically, she self-isolated in her apartment for weeks. Finally, she'd fought back by immersing herself in her work.

"You made it both of yours," Gary said. "You had an out.

You could have been anything you wanted."

"You mean anything Roger wanted me to be. He knew what I was like before we got married. I wasn't about to be a stay-at-home wife simply because of" — Anne's face darkened — "because of some disease." *Time to end this bull session. More important things to think about than Roger.* "By the way, your patient has MRSA. He needs an immediate change of antibiotics."

"You could've called me and saved yourself sixty-four steps."

"Your phone went to voicemail."

"Sorry. I was in a conference. Haven't had a chance to check for messages."

"This couldn't wait. There's lunch break, change of shift, and any number of ways his first dose might get delayed. I couldn't take that chance, and I needed to check his status." She hit the ENTER key. "There. Done."

"I've got a problem patient for you," Gary said.

"I love puzzles. Shoot."

"Thirty-six-year-old female veterinary assistant with a combined kidney and pancreatic transplant eight months ago for end-stage diabetic kidney disease, on the usual cocktail of meds to suppress her immune system. Admitted yesterday with a fever of 105, severely low blood pressure, elevated white blood cell count, and markedly abnormal liver tests. Only finding on the exam was mild tenderness over her liver. We scanned her from head to foot. Nothing. Bloodwork for AIDS was negative. What's she got?"

"A diabetic with an impaired immune system who works with animals? She could have almost anything." Anne tapped her fingers as she pondered. *Good case.* In this one patient, Gary had the three great challenges of Infectious Disease: evolving bacterial antibiotic resistance; the bizarre infections of the immunologically compromised patient; and finally, the zoonoses, the hidden diseases that spread to humans from animal reservoirs. "Let's see. Most of the viral infections from her transplant should have shown themselves months ago. What about parasites like toxoplasmosis from the animals she works with?"

"Her transplant team covered her for toxo with antibiotics months ago, knowing she was a setup for infection."

"Tuberculosis? Fungal infections?"

"Chest X-ray, sinus CT, and spinal tap—all negative."

"What about bacterial cultures?"

"All cooking. Nothing showing yet."

"Have you done Gram stains of her body fluids?"

"Gram-positive, rod-shaped bacteria in her blood."

"Why didn't you tell me that before?"

"You said you liked puzzles."

Anne rolled her eyes. "Gram-positive rods mean the bacteria are either Listeria or Clostridium."

"My vote was for Listeria."

"The antibiotics they put her on for toxo should cover that. What about her liver tenderness?"

"Not impressed. She barely moaned when I pressed down."

"Pain sensation in diabetics is diminished. My bet is Clostridia gangrene of the gallbladder, early enough that it didn't show up on the scans. Call surgery pronto, get an ultrasound of her gallbladder stat, and cover her with chloramphenicol as an additional antibiotic before her gallbladder ruptures. For bacteria, it's a short stroll from her gallbladder to her brand-new million-dollar pancreas."

"Thanks," Gary said, nodding. "By the way, an old fraternity brother of mine is coming to town this weekend. Care to meet him?"

"I thought only women set people up for dates."

"Can't a guy do a friend a favor?" Gary said, sounding exasperated.

Anne reached out and touched his hand. "Sorry. I didn't

mean to snap at you. It's still so hard for me to believe I can ever trust someone." Roger's parting words filled her head. Halfway out the door, suitcase in hand, he'd turned and glared at Anne, whose legs were so weakened from the stress of the breakup that she'd had to support herself on the back of a club chair.

"Look at yourself," he said. "Who the hell would want you like that?" Then he slammed the door behind him and walked out of her life.

Gary's voice brought Anne back. "You ever think that maybe you need to get out of your lab and meet people? Your biological clock doesn't stop ticking because grant proposals are due."

"Babies aren't part of my life plan right now. Now you — you would make a wonderful dad if you could only find the right woman." Anne lightly squeezed his hand. Remarriage was probably a long way off for Gary, who was still shattered by his wife's death.

Before Gary could respond, Anne's beeper directed her to the hospital operator.

"Catch you later," Gary said, heading down the hall. "If you change your mind about my friend, let me know. We can all go out for a drink."

Anne waved him off as she dialed the operator.

"Dr. Mastik, you've got a call from West Virginia."

That's a new one. "Okay, put it through."

"Mornin', Dr. Mastik. My name's Matt Drisner. I'm the Public Health Service physician here in Eden, West Virginia." The voice on the line had a southern drawl and down-home casualness that Anne didn't hear much in Charlottesville. "I saw that you're speaking at the *Updates in Medicine* conference at The Omni Homestead Resort this weekend, and I was wondering if you could help me with a little problem I've got here."

Good Lord, I almost forgot about that conference. "I'll try. What's wrong?"

"I've got a fifteen-year-old girl who lives on a mountaintop with her aunt and uncle. Real country folk, live-off-the-land types. She's been pretty sick for the last week. Fever to 104. Can't get out of bed. I've cultured her up twice, but the lab keeps growing contaminants, and they're only growing from her blood. Urine, sputum, everything else is clean."

"What are you covering her with?" Anne said, referring to the antibiotics the patient was currently taking.

"We've got her on ceftriaxone, but I give it as a muscle injection. She's holding her own for now, but she's not getting any better."

"You can't manage sepsis in someone's home," Anne said. "You've got to give the ceftriaxone intravenously, and she needs to be in a hospital, in Intensive Care."

"Believe me, I've tried. This family is the last of a community that's been isolated on a mountain for generations. As far as I know, not one of them has been to town for decades. You can't pry them out of that house with a crowbar. I was hoping you could convince her family to let the girl go to the hospital."

"You're the local doc. You know them better than I ever will. If they won't listen to you, what makes you think they'll listen to me?"

"They've been at odds with the town for generations. They don't trust the local medical establishment, or anyone else for that matter. Maybe they would see you as being more...objective."

"Get a court order. The aunt and uncle are endangering the well-being of the child."

"Tried that too. This is a small town. Small, religious, and extremely conservative. The judge saw this as a First Amendment issue, and I don't have time to go to the Supreme Court."

"What happened to her parents? Can't you talk with them?"

"They died in a house fire three years ago. Her aunt and uncle are the only family she's got."

A pang hit Anne. Only ten years ago, her own parents

had died in a car crash. Her heart went out to this poor girl. "Unfortunately, I can't simply drop what I'm doing and drive out to West Virginia."

"Eden's not far from The Homestead. After the conference, you could drive there in a few hours. It would really help if you could convince them to bring her to the hospital."

"I'm sorry, but I've got a terribly busy schedule right now. I can't take time off to argue with a couple of Christian Scientists."

"They're not Christian Sci—"

"I don't care what religion they are. I'm sorry, but I can't come."

A rising urgency sounded in Drisner's voice. "Dr. Mastik, you have no idea how important this girl's life is. I can't explain why, but I can tell you she is…unique." Drisner's voice cracked at the word. "I really, really need your help."

Anne paused. *He's holding back on something that makes this deeply personal for him. And she's an orphan.* That broke Anne's heart.

"Okay, let me speak to my chairman. I'll see what I can do."

"I'll be at the conference this weekend." He sounded pitifully hopeful. "Can you let me know then?"

"I make no promises, but I'll do what I can."

***

Anne finally made it home at 10:00 p.m., her legs fatigued to the point where she simply fell back on the living room couch. She kicked off her shoes and reflected on the day. Gary's MRSA patient had improved, her lab experiment was on autopilot—at least for the next week—and her conference lecture was packed away on PowerPoint. Life was good. All that remained was to call Bob Rothberg, which she dreaded, especially at this late hour.

"Bob, this is Anne Mastik. Hope I didn't wake you." Dr. Robert Rothberg was chairman of her department and her boss.

"I was getting ready for bed. Everything okay?" He

sounded mildly annoyed.

"Everything's fine, but I need to discuss a situation that came up. I got a call today from a West Virginia doc. He asked me, actually begged me, to consult on a patient."

"So, what's the problem?"

"It's not a phone consult. He wants me to see the patient personally."

"What! Isn't that stepping over the line a bit?"

"At first, I told him no way, but he was desperate. It sounded personal."

After a heavy silence, Rothberg sighed. "You really are a softy, Anne. You've already made up your mind, haven't you?"

"I might be able to wrap it all up this weekend. Besides, I'm already late for my monthly natalizumab, and it's the only thing that keeps my MS under control. I'll definitely be back Monday."

"But...?" Rothberg said, suspicion edging his voice.

Anne steeled herself and spoke. "Everybody but you is at the Chicago HIV conference, and I need someone to cover consult service until I get back." Bob had been hired as chairman based on his research and administrative abilities, not his clinical or teaching skills. This was no small favor.

"You've got a pair, Anne, calling me at ten at night for this."

"Bob, this guy's Public Health Service. I'm sure he sends his sick patients to Morgantown. What if the university could establish a solid referral base in West Virginia? Isn't that why you wanted me to give a lecture at the conference—for the referring PCPs?" *Nothing like the prospect of more patients to whet the appetite of a department chairman.*

A protracted silence filled the other end of the phone as Anne held her breath.

"All right, all right, I'll do it. But you owe me one. And no dawdling, understand?"

"Thanks, Bob. You won't regret this."

"I already do." But then he added, "Oh, hell. Have a good time."

As Anne climbed into bed, images of the sick, lonely orphan girl on the mountaintop filled her mind. She lay down and allowed herself a long gaze at the photograph of her parents on her nightstand before turning off the light.

CHAPTER II

Anne left the Shenandoah Valley and threaded her way over the meandering country roads that ran along the stretch of the Blue Ridge Mountains between Virginia and West Virginia. As the dramatic ending of Mendelssohn's "Reformation" Symphony playing on her car's audio and came to a close, Led Zeppelin's "Stairway To Heaven" popped uninvited into her head.

Of course, it did. Over the years, whenever she and Roger had driven to The Homestead, their favorite getaway, they'd fight over the music. How typical that the two of them could transform the most scenic, romantic spot in Virginia into a subject of contention.

The Homestead was Virginia's venerable resort, tucked in an out-of-the-way corner of the state known for its scenic beauty and natural hot springs. Since Revolutionary War days, it had been the playground of the rich and famous, but when American vacation spots lost their appeal to the beach playgrounds of Europe, South America, and the Caribbean, the resort fell into decline. However, in recent years The Homestead was staging a comeback, fed by American passions for golf and skiing. As the red-brick and white-limestone tower of The Homestead came into view over the tops of the surrounding hills, Anne dreaded confronting the memories she had so carefully exorcised.

She got out of her car after pulling up to the hotel entrance and gazed around. Here in the mountains, the elevation tempered the sweltering heat of summer that usually sapped her strength. *At least here I won't be held prisoner to central air conditioning.*

Coming out to greet her was a lanky bellhop, barely out of his teens. "Take your bags, ma'am?"

"No, thanks. My bag's got wheels. I'll take it in."

He looked crestfallen.

Uh-oh, poor kid needs the tip. "Actually, I could use some help. You take the bag. I'll take the laptop."

"You hurt your leg, ma'am?" he asked as they entered the lobby, with its vast expanse of plush carpeting and elegant leather chairs. The ornate trayed ceiling was flanked by two long rows of Corinthian columns echoing the Greek revival architecture of nearby Charlottesville.

"No. I...walk funny, that's all."

"We get a lot of people here with arthritis that goes to the spa. The hot springs does 'em a lot of good. You might give that a try, ma'am."

Anne nodded politely but didn't want to embarrass him by telling him the spa would only make her symptoms worse. The hot water would raise her body temperature and make her so weak that she couldn't get out of the tub, a reaction so predictable that decades ago, it was a diagnostic procedure for multiple sclerosis.

"Are you from around here?" Anne asked.

"West Virginia, ma'am. Right across the border."

"Ever hear of a town called Eden?"

"Yes, ma'am. Beautiful place. That's why it's called Eden."

"How would I get there?"

"Drive up the road to Warm Springs and make a left onto Route 39 until you get to the Monongahela National Forest. That's when you'll be in West Virginia. Keep driving, and right about the time you think you're lost, you'll be out of the Forest, and you'll see a sign that'll direct you to Eden. Here's the reception desk, ma'am. Need me to take your bag upstairs?"

"No, thanks. I'll handle it from here." She handed him a ten-dollar bill.

"Have a nice weekend, ma'am." He pocketed his tip and sauntered away.

***

Pasting her *Hello. My Name Is*…nametag to her jacket lapel, Anne took a deep breath and entered the reception hall.

She was late, having intentionally spent more time than necessary deciding which suit to wear to the reception. A substantial crowd was already milling around the bar, which she skirted in favor of the deserted vegetable platter. As she grabbed a carrot, a stocky, bespectacled man approached her, bald except for a ring of graying hair encircling a head slightly too large for his body.

"Dr. Mastik, I'm so glad you could come. It's been years since we could convince an Infectious Disease specialist to give one of our lectures."

"No problem, Doctor…?" Anne's eyes trailed to find his paper nametag, but in its place was a plastic tag festooned with a blue ribbon and thin, illegible letters.

"Langston. Martin Langston, from Roanoke. I'm the conference organizer."

"I guess I should be thanking you for the opportunity. I haven't been to The Homestead for a long time. It holds a lot of memories."

"Good ones, I hope."

"Of course," she lied. "I'm looking forward to taking some nice long walks in the woods."

"Or a nice long walk on a golf course."

"I'm not much on golf."

"This is a wonderful place to learn the game, and I know precisely the person to teach you. Let me introduce you to one of your fellow lecturers." He called to a tall, dark-haired man who was chatting with a group of physicians on the other side of the room, "Evan, come over here for a minute. I want you to meet someone."

Anne squirmed. *This was not at all what I had in mind.*

"Evan Garaud," Langston whispered. "He's absolutely brilliant. Moved around academically in the past few years but was heading the stem cell and transplant research team at West Virginia University when a biotech firm snared him. Big loss to the university."

Dr. Garaud broke free of the cluster of physicians and strolled over, holding a drink. Handsome, meticulously dressed, and half a head taller than most of the attendees, he projected a poised confidence that set him apart. He gripped Dr. Langston's hand and shook it firmly. "Marty, you must have done an excellent job arranging the meeting this year if they gave you the blue ribbon."

Langston ran his hand over his bare scalp. "I certainly didn't get it for 'Best of Show.' Evan, I want you to meet the young woman who was kind enough to come from Charlottesville to—"

"You must be Anne Mastik," Evan said, shaking Anne's hand. "I enjoyed your review article on opportunistic infections in allograft recipients. Very professionally researched, beautifully written."

Anne blushed, and despite Evan enfolding her hand a few seconds more than etiquette required, she made no attempt to withdraw it. Dr. Langston quietly slipped away.

"Thanks for the compliment, Dr. Garaud. It's always nice to know that someone, somewhere, is reading your work. What are you lecturing on?"

"Please, call me Evan. I believe we're both on the docket for tomorrow morning. I'll be discussing recent advances in cultured tissue transplantation. As I recall, your topic is tuberculosis."

"You seem to know a lot of people. Do you lecture here

often?"

"I've managed to wrangle a lecture out of Marty every year for the past five conferences. I started giving these talks before I was even at WVU. Now that I'm out of academics, it gives me an excuse to come back and hobnob with old friends."

"Where do you work now?"

"Northwest corner of North Carolina, near the Blue Ridge Mountains. It's the headquarters for Regen Corporation. We do front-line research on stem cell and organ transplantation. You wouldn't believe the breakthroughs we're about to make. It's amazing what can be accomplished when you don't have to waste time writing grant proposals."

"Don't I know it. Is that why you gave up academics?"

"One of many reasons. The pace is glacial. Meeting after meeting, departmental politics, red tape. Takes forever to get anything done."

"Oh, come on. Stop being so cynical. All of that happens at UVA, but things still get accomplished, and it's exciting to be part of scientific progress."

"In business, time is money. If something needs to be done quickly, we take shortcuts. It's a different life."

Uh-oh, I can see where this is going. "Dr. Langston told me you play golf."

"I dabble. Especially when I'm here. Beautiful courses. Do you play?"

"Used to. My ex-husband would drag me along when he and his friends needed a fourth, but I could never understand the fascination with ten minutes of walking followed by fifteen seconds of hitting a ball."

"A common over-simplification. If you really learned to play, you would see the game in a different light. Particularly on the courses here. Perhaps we could go for a round tomorrow afternoon." He grinned. "If you don't like it, I'll buy you dinner."

"And if I do like it?"

"I'll still buy you dinner."

Wait till he sees me walk. How am I supposed to hide my condition on a nine-hole course?

"Sounds like a win-win to me," she said. "But only nine holes." *More than enough time to make an ass of myself.*

"Okay, but you don't know what you'll be missing if —"

"Dr. Mastik, I presume."

Anne and Evan both turned to see a casually dressed physician with sandy-blond hair and light blue eyes who shook Anne's hand with the strong, vigorous grip of a man raised in the country.

"I'm Matt Drisner, the guy who called you yesterday. About the girl."

"Oh, yes." She turned to Evan. "Evan, this is Dr. Matt Drisner. He's asked me to consult on a difficult case. A young girl with an undiagnosed immunodeficiency disease and an opportunistic infection."

Evan's eyebrows rose. "Right up your alley, Anne. Do you practice near here, Matt?"

"Not far. A small town called Eden."

"I've heard of it. Hidden treasure, from what I understand. Well, I'd better get going. I've got an early lecture. See you tomorrow, Anne, and nice meeting you, Matt."

"Sorry if I busted up the party," Drisner remarked.

"No party. Not yet, at any rate."

"I was eager to see when you'd be able to come to Eden."

"Would Sunday morning work?"

He cocked his head. "It's a tricky drive to Eden. I'm leaving tomorrow after dinner. If you'd like, I can drive you out there."

"No, thank you. I'm sure I can find it myself."

"The little girl is quite sick, and I was hoping you would be able to get to Eden before Sunday. The mountains of West Virginia are not a place to get lost late at night."

"I'll be there, Dr. Drisner, on Sunday morning as early as

I can make it. I promise. Now if you will excuse me, I have a lecture to prepare for."

"If you change your mind, let me know. I'm on the eighth floor in the Tower."

God, the man is obstinate. If that's what I was like, no wonder Roger divorced me.

***

Anne settled down on the bed in a cotton terry robe and allowed herself the rare pleasure of a glass of wine while reviewing her slides. Since contracting MS, she mostly shunned alcohol. She had problems enough with balance, and even a small glass of wine could impair her coordination enough to embarrass her. But what the hell — she was on vacation, and the longest distance she would walk tonight was to the bathroom.

Wine often made her mind wander but tonight, for the first time in months, not to her research or Roger. Instead, it made a beeline for Evan: the lingering touch of his hand, the gentleness of his eyes, his sense of humor, and the respect he'd shown for her as an academician.

But what about that six-hour drive from Charlottesville to the North Carolina Blue Ridge? Oh well.

She set her wine on the nightstand and blessed her foresight in ordering a single glass from room service. Otherwise, she might have been tempted to down a whole bottle and really make a fool of herself at tomorrow's conference.

She set the alarm and turned off the light. *Maybe Evan won't pick up on my MS. At least the weather is cool, so the fatigue might not get to me.* She closed her eyes and let the wine have its effect as she drifted off to sleep.

***

In his room at the top of the Tower, Matt was awakened by the insistent dinging of his cell phone. He knew the caller by the specialized ringtone; besides, nobody else would call at this hour.

He answered and listened for several seconds.

"Yes, sir," he answered. "I convinced her to come, but she won't leave until Sunday morning…. Nothing I could do. She wouldn't leave earlier, and I said all I could without raising suspicion…. Yes, the girl will be okay. Good night, sir."

CHAPTER III

Anne finished showering before her wake-up call. A feeling of anticipation had awakened her before her usual six o'clock arousal and stubbornly prevented her from going back to sleep. *Nothing to do but get up early, go to breakfast, and hopefully run into Evan before the start of the conference.*

Arriving at the dining room shortly after it opened, she picked up a croissant and coffee—about all her nervous stomach would tolerate. She sat facing the door and placed her laptop conspicuously on the chair next to her. As the seats at her table filled, she made small talk while her eyes searched the room. When a waiter announced the start of the conference, she gave up on meeting Evan and headed in.

Dr. Langston greeted her at the dais. "You're up first, Anne."

"I didn't see Evan at breakfast," she said. "Isn't his talk following mine?"

"I'm sure he slept in. He told me he would be up late making phone calls. Are you set up? We're ready to go."

Anne's lecture, "Re-Emergence of Antibiotic Resistant Tuberculosis as a Public Health Concern," went smoothly. She ran through it with time to spare, perhaps too much time. When she asked if there were any questions, only the whirring of her laptop fan broke the silence.

She turned, somewhat dispirited, and was surprised to find Evan occupying the seat next to hers on the dais.

"Tough crowd," he whispered as she sat.

"I could swear I saw them drinking coffee at breakfast."

Evan chuckled. "The first slot's the roughest. It's like standup comedy. Someone's always stuck as the warm-up act."

Langston briefly introduced Evan, who stood up to a smattering of applause.

"Good morning. I've been asked to talk on recent advancements in stem cell and tissue transplantation. I have spent my career chasing the Holy Grail of safe and effective tissue grafting into diseased organs, my particular interest being neural tissue. I would like to devote this talk to some general principles."

Evan's continued with a wrap-up of basic science and did little to rouse the crowd, but their interest seemed piqued when he cited stem cell transplant research in diabetes, cancer, Parkinson's disease, and Alzheimer's disease. And when he mentioned the use of stem cells to treat spinal cord injuries and multiple sclerosis, Anne detected a brief glance her way.

From there, Evan listed the challenges with the clinical use of stem cells, such as the need to suppress the immune system to avoid transplant rejection.

"For grafts to function, transplant recipients need immunosuppression, which requires the administration of highly toxic drugs. These drugs expose the body to attack from foreign agents, a subject that our previous lecturer"—he gestured to Anne—"is all too familiar with. Although we are developing less-damaging drugs, we are still left with the inescapable problem that stem cell recipients lead a life in which the family cat, a plate of spoiled tuna salad, or a coughing child could expose them to potentially lethal infections.

"It is my belief that we are on the cusp of developing

an immunologically neutral cell line that will fool the immune system into ignoring the implanted tissue. Our ability to treat disease and trauma will only be limited by how many of the two hundred and ten human tissue types can be coaxed into stem cell conversion. So far? Over one hundred and rising fast.

"I believe that within our lifetimes, we will see the development of new techniques that will help conquer the ailments of trauma, aging and disease that have plagued mankind since the days of Adam and Eve."

Evan sat down to hearty applause and a rush of physicians to the microphone.

"Thanks for warming them up," he whispered to Anne.

"You certainly had the livelier talk."

Dr. Langston took the podium and observed the quickly lengthening line behind the floor mike. "We will now entertain questions for both speakers."

The first questioner leaned into the microphone. "To Dr. Garaud. Funding for stem cell research has been a political football for decades. The Federal government is very restrictive about the use of funds. How can you do research without a reliable source of grant money?"

"Our corporation is privately funded and owned," Evan said. "Many of our private investors have intensely personal reasons for seeing our research succeed. If we show them results, they tend to leave us alone."

"Is your corporation ever going public?"

"Right now, we're a small fish in a large pond. We have a strong research program, particularly in stem cell treatment of diabetes and neurologic diseases. However, we are currently in development of an immunity-neutral cell line. If we can patent it, we will have a clear competitive advantage, which makes an IPO viable, perhaps as early as next year. Our corporate name is Regen."

Anne smirked internally as almost everyone in the room

jotted down the company name. *Note to self: The key to a successful lecture is to end it with a stock tip.*

A young physician, dressed in jacket and tie despite the casual dress code, stepped up next. "My question is for Dr. Garaud. Could you respond to ethical concerns about stem cell research on embryonic tissue?"

"Our technique calls for cloning embryos. We use a process called parthenogenesis, which literally means 'virgin birth.' This gives us more control over the result's genetic composition and creates a life form that could only exist in a laboratory environment. In essence, we are dealing with a hypothetical life. It is as manmade as a toaster oven or cell phone. I have no ethical conflict about using these cells to save lives and reverse disabilities."

"But Dr. Garaud, against God's divine laws, you are creating monsters in the lab."

Anne could swear she saw the hairs on the back of Evan's neck bristle as his shoulders rose. "Doctor, when were you appointed God's authorized interpreter?" he said acidly.

"God never intended man to create life in this manner," the physician shouted.

Evan remained calm. "A hundred years ago, it was said that if God had intended man to fly, he would have given us wings and that the internal combustion engine was the work of Satan. Now, not only are we flying, but we've gone to the moon and other planets. God didn't need to give us wings. He gave us infinitely greater gifts: opposable thumbs and a brain with 100 billion nerve cells. And He told us to have dominion over all the earth and to subdue it. If we'd been complacent and not used those gifts, *that* would be against God's will."

Evan sat down to loud applause, and Dr. Langston quickly returned to the podium.

"This would be a good time to start our coffee break. Please be back in your seats in fifteen minutes for the cardiovascular section of the conference. I would like to thank Dr. Mastik and Dr. Garaud for two fascinating and informative lectures."

***

A half-hour later, Anne met Evan at the first tee. To her surprise, he was sitting in a covered golf cart with two sets of clubs and a cooler in the back.

"I thought we'd play in style."

"Isn't a cart against the rules?" Anne asked.

"This isn't the PGA, and I'm not a purist. Go ahead and tee off."

Anne picked a driver from the bag, nervously approached the ball, and gave it a solid hit that hooked sharply and landed near a stand of trees to the left of the fairway. Evan's drive went down the middle of the fairway, coming to rest a dozen yards short of the green.

"You handled that fellow back at the conference very well," Anne commented during the drive.

"I get at least one religious fanatic at each lecture. After a while, you learn to deal with them on their own turf. I can fight them with the Bible, verse for verse, if they want to. In fact, I've got a Biblical quote app on my cell. You should download it. You might find it useful."

"You're very convinced of what you're doing."

"It's almost a crusade for me. When the techniques for stem cell implantation are perfected—and they will be within the next few years—it will revolutionize medical practice. We will only be limited by our imagination. We could replace dead heart tissue after heart attacks, repair retinal cells for blindness, do nerve and brain cell transplants for Parkinson's disease and multiple sclerosis, and pancreatic cell transplants for diabetes. We're only beginning to investigate a whole host of disorders: cystic fibrosis, sickle cell anemia, and muscular dystrophy. Give us some time, and they'll be a thing of the past. The cures are within our reach."

Evan dominated the game, but Anne could see he regarded it as nothing but a game. There was none of the intense competitiveness that Roger used to show. Conversation came easily, and Anne felt a sense of comfort that she hadn't experienced with a man for some time.

As she prepared to tee off at the seventh hole, Evan sidled up next to her.

"May I make a suggestion?"

"Sure."

"I've figured out why you hook your shots. You might want to change your grip for this shot. Here, I'll show you."

He stood behind her and reached around to the club. His chest pressed softly against her back, his breath wafting against her cheek. Meanwhile, she concentrated on keeping her breathing under control as he enfolded her hands in his.

"Turn your right hand around a little and twist it slightly on your follow-through like this." He guided her through a practice swing, and as she turned her head in follow-through, she noticed Evan's eyes fixed on her. For a moment, a palpable silence hung in the air.

"Perfect. Loosen your legs when you swing."

"I...I'm a bit nervous right now."

He backed away. "I'm sorry. I didn't mean to be forward."

Anne reached out and touched his arm. "You weren't. I was feeling a little flustered, that's all." She didn't want to admit it, but long-dormant feelings had risen within her.

"Then no offense taken?"

"None at all."

The next two holes flew by. Anne sat close to Evan as he drove the golf cart, and she once dared to let her hand rest on his forearm. But with the early afternoon sun high in the sky, she was exhausted after eight holes.

"Here we are," Evan said as he got off the cart. "The notorious ninth hole."

They stood at the top of a fifty-foot rise above the green that lay off in the distance. A few yards away, the rise dropped precipitously to the level of the green.

Anne eyed the steep embankment with a sense of foreboding. "What do I do here?"

"The trick is to make sure your drive goes past the base of the hill. If it lands on the slope, there's no way of predicting which way it will roll. Remember what I told you. Keep your legs loose, and you'll do just great."

Anne took a practice swing. The driver felt heavy, like a sledgehammer instead of a golf club. She addressed the ball, drew back, and swung as hard as she could. At the last second, a surge of spasticity caused her legs to stiffen. Her driver topped the ball, and she watched in frustration as it skittered from the tee over the edge of the escarpment and rolled halfway down the slope before coming to rest.

"Want to take a mulligan?" Evan offered.

Anne shot him a hard look. "No, I'll play it where it lies."

A puzzled expression crossed his face. "Be my guest."

Anne stumbled down the slope carrying her nine iron, her legs feeling like two long strips of rubber with stiff steel springs for knees. She stabilized herself as best as she could on the steep incline. No elegant way to hit this one. Starting tomorrow, she would take up shuffleboard instead.

Evan made his way down. "If you must play by the rules, take the shot, and we'll put the ball at the bottom of the hill."

Anne ignored him and addressed the ball. "I'll play it here, thank you." She took a swing, but the head of the club dug into the ground, throwing her off-balance. As she fell, Evan grabbed her around the waist and drew her close, anchoring his feet to prevent them both from tumbling downward.

"What the hell was that all about?" he said. "I think you owe me an explanation."

Anne caught her breath. "Can we get back to the cart first?"

They only had to climb a short distance up the hill, but Anne was encumbered by her spasticity. By the time they reached the cart, she had only enough energy to collapse into the seat.

"Why was it so damn important for you to make that shot?"

"No favors granted, no favors asked."

"Pretty hard-assed approach to a game, don't you think?"

"Same way I approach life. Play the ball as it lies. I've been doing that for years, and I don't intend to stop now."

Evan looked her in the eyes. "Is it possible your multiple sclerosis denial is ruling you more than your actual disability?"

"Who told you I had MS? Langston?"

"When you've seen as many spinal cord patients as I have, it's hard to miss spasticity. That's why I ordered the golf cart. I can add two and two together, you know."

Anne shook her head. "I'm too tired to get angry."

"Clubhouse, then? A frozen margarita will cool you off, and after you're rested, we can fight about whatever you want."

"You make it difficult to stay angry at you."

Evan leaned closer. "Am I forgiven?"

"Perhaps."

"Would dinner and an evening stroll make that more definite?"

"Let me think about it."

"Then think about this." Evan kissed her, and she responded by placing her hand behind his head and drawing him closer.

***

From the wrought iron chair on his Tower balcony overlooking the golf course, Matt Drisner had kept track of Anne Mastik for the last three holes. As she and Garaud locked lips, he set his binoculars down on the cocktail table and took a sip of his bourbon on the rocks.

So that's why she couldn't leave tonight. I suppose what happens in Hot Springs stays in Hot Springs. He picked up his laptop and Googled "Dr. Evan Garaud." *Better to be safe than sorry.*

CHAPTER IV

Route 39 turned out to be a twisting two-lane road that followed the contours of the Alleghenies. This ancient mountain range rippled through West Virginia in parallel waves that ran through the Monongahela National Forest, an enormous park that followed the boundary between West Virginia and Virginia for miles. The old-growth woodlands lining the mountains created a dense green curtain, broken only by trailer homes or small ranch houses placed in carved-out clearings. Anne knew parts of the Forest from hiking and camping trips many years ago, but the park was vast, and she was driving through a section she had never seen before.

The picturesque drive turned monotonous after an hour, and Anne's thoughts drifted to Evan. The evening had turned romantic, starting with a long stroll through a rose garden, the intermingled scents perfuming the cool breezes. They talked into the night, particularly about her MS and the divorce, but also about her research on infections in immunodeficiency diseases. Evan was guarded about his research—for proprietary reasons, as he explained. But how refreshing it was to converse with a man more interested in talking about her life than his own.

The time had passed too quickly for Anne, but she'd needed to retire early to go to Eden. To her relief, Evan had agreed that the girl's illness sounded like a life-or-death issue and that Anne needed her rest to be at the top of her game. He'd pledged to call her within a few days.

A burst of wind from a passing eighteen-wheeler shook Anne's car and refocused her attention. She couldn't remember when she'd last seen a road sign or a turnoff, and it had been a good forty-five minutes since she had passed a gas station.

"In two miles, turn right onto Eden Mountain Road," her GPS chimed in. She grinned as she recalled the bellhop's directions.

A mile after she turned right, the woods on either side of the road gave way to broad expanses of farmland, bounded to the north and south by parallel chains of foothills rising several miles apart. But as she drove on, the foothills closed in on her like a vanishing point in a drawing. When the two ranges were about a mile apart, she entered Eden.

Eden was situated in a narrow valley flanked to the north and south by heavily wooded hillsides. On its north side, a narrow river paralleled the base of the hill, separating it from the town proper and from any commercial or residential development. However, on the south side, the streets angled upward, and the hillside was dotted with elegant turn-of-the-century Victorian houses, which clung to the slopes with admirable determination. One incongruous contemporary-style house jutted from the hill, far above the level of the others. *Wonder what egomaniac built that one.*

Closing the valley off on its eastern end and looming directly in front of her was Eden Mountain, one of the tallest peaks Anne had ever seen in West Virginia. The river seemed to flow from its base, its origin probably from a spring somewhere on the mountain slope, and thick stands of ancient maples and oaks sprang from its slope, hiding the leveled top from view.

At the town limits, Eden Mountain Road became Main Street, which ran through the center of the valley and comprised the business district. Neat rows of modestly constructed two-story brick buildings from the 1950s had been well maintained, although the thick layers of paint on some of the window frames testified to their age. From the looks of things, mass culture hadn't yet arrived in Eden—no McDonald's, Taco Bells, or 7-Elevens. Not even a supermarket or large chain hardware store. In fact, the only recognizable corporate names belonged to an auto parts store and the sole gas station, which was servicing a line of well-used pickups, apparently the favored mode of transportation. Some were old enough to be antiques. Maybe the major limitation on residential zoning was the ability of a fully loaded pickup to safely negotiate an icy hillside driveway in winter.

If the number of houses of worship was any indication, religion ran strong in Eden. Most of the churches were unassuming storefront tabernacles or small free-standing buildings. *Probably never held more than a score of families, even on Easter Sunday.* However, one church stood out, its steeple towering commandingly over the town. The centerpiece of a cluster of aristocratic houses, of all the churches in town, it alone boasted stained glass windows and a paved parking lot.

Anne drove almost completely through town before she reached Eden Community Hospital. By far the newest building in town, it was small enough that even on one of her bad days, she could walk around it in ten minutes. She parked and headed inside.

"Excuse me," Anne said to the woman behind the reception desk. "Can you please tell Dr. Drisner that Dr. Anne Mastik is here? He's expecting me."

The receptionist appeared startled.

Out-of-towners must be a rare sight here.

"He's in his office, third door on the right. Go on in."

Anne found Dr. Drisner typing on a computer at his desk, his shirtsleeves rolled up, and his mismatched tie loosened at the collar. *Looks more like a first-year resident than a practicing physician.*

"I don't see many physicians use the hunt-and-peck method nowadays," she said.

Drisner looked up. "Never learned the normal way. Daddy always said typing was for girls. Now, the girls are engineers and attorneys. All I can say is, thank God for computerized voice transcription." He stood and shook Anne's hand. "Thanks for coming."

"You were very persuasive."

"You mean to say pigheaded, but I appreciate your diplomacy." He glanced at his watch. "I'd love to show you around, but we'd better get up the mountain. It's best we use my pickup."

Five minutes later, Anne climbed into Drisner's well-worn Ford F-150. "What can you tell me about this family?" she said.

"Everyone around here knows about the Morehouses," Drisner began as they pulled out of the hospital parking lot, "but no one actually knows them. Their ancestors settled this area three hundred years ago, established a settlement on top of the mountain, and they've been isolated up there since."

"Must be quite a lot of inbreeding. Is there any family history I should be aware of?"

"The community's been dying off for the past fifty years, and nobody knows why. The only ones left are the girl, Ruth, and her aunt and uncle, Miriam and Isaiah."

"Is your inpatient unit up to handling a complicated patient like Ruth?" Anne asked as he turned onto Main Street toward Eden Mountain.

"We've got forty beds for routine care and a fully equipped lab and Radiology suite."

"What if she needs Intensive Care?"

"State-of-the-art. Four-bed unit and each room can be converted into a complete isolation unit. Full battery of monitoring equipment, except for neurosurgical. Head patients go to Morgantown. Nursing is one-on-one."

A mile outside of town, Matt swerved onto a steep gravel and dirt road. Anne was thrown backward against the window. She tightened her seatbelt and grabbed the safety bar over the door.

"What about subspecialty coverage?" she asked.

"Limited. We have a full-time cardiologist and gastroenterologist. I'm the hospitalist and intensivist, and I manage the ventilators. Anything else, you got to call in from Charleston or Morgantown. We've got a general surgeon that'll do anything but a craniotomy, and orthopedics is on call."

"How did you end up…here?"

"Born and raised in Kentucky. The Feds paid for my training, so I had to give them two years in an underserved area. I'm from a real small town, and I'm a simple sort of guy, so I chose Eden. That was four years ago, and it's either the local beauty or inertia that keeps me here." He shot her a playful glance. "It's certainly not the wild nightlife, I can tell you that much. The people here are good people, and I feel needed. And believe it or not, Eden Community is the medical hub for a radius of thirty-five miles."

The gravel road disappeared, replaced by a simple mountain trail. The truck made its way over rocks and roots while Anne clung to the overhead bar with one hand, bracing her other hand against the dash. "I noticed the upscale houses on the mountainside. And the church."

Drisner turned on the wipers as the front wheels dove into a sizable puddle, spraying the windshield. The wipers only smeared the mud, obscuring the view. "Ah, yes," he said. "The church. Sometime I'll introduce you to Reverend Wainstock. He's an interesting character. Wields a lot of power locally."

After fifteen minutes, the road widened into a small clearing surrounded by trees that allowed a narrow column of light into the clearing. Just past the edge of the column, blending in with the shadows of the forest, stood the most decrepit shack

Anne had ever seen.

Drisner stopped the truck and turned off the engine. After thirty minutes of a transmission grinding in first gear, the silence was bliss to Anne's ears. After a few seconds, the high-pitched buzz of cicadas, probably frightened into silence by their arrival, began a gradual crescendo.

"Is this it?" Anne asked anxiously, scanning the neglect that surrounded her.

"Not quite. I've got to make a social call first. Wait here. I'll introduce you."

Matt strode up to the shack and banged his fist repeatedly on the door.

"Artemis, wake the hell up! You've got company." After a minute, the door opened on bitterly complaining hinges and a man stepped out.

Anne approached hesitantly. Artemis was every bit as slovenly as the shack he lived in. Bare-chested, his abdomen protruded over the top of a pair of dirty jeans, barely supported by suspenders. His face was pallid, but his cheeks and nose were bumpy and ruddy, colored by an advanced case of rosacea. His jowls were ringed by at least a week's worth of stubble, and a crop of hair exploded from the top of his head in a matted grayish-brown tangle. Completing the picture, a pair of reddish eyes squinted at the sunlight between puffy lids.

Please don't tell me I have to go in there, Anne thought. As dark as the forest was, it was probably a blaze of glory compared to the inside of the shack.

The man cleared his throat and spat, the color of his phlegm blending invisibly with the soil. "Christ, Doc. Why the hell you makin' such a racket?"

"Mornin', more or less. I need you to take my friend and me to the Morehouses." Matt turned to Anne. "Anne Mastik, meet Artemis Donnard."

Artemis squinted in Anne's direction, then snorted and

walked toward her, arm extended. Anne eyed the outstretched hand with a touch of apprehension. *Oh well, it couldn't possibly harbor more dangerous organisms than those in my lab.* She reached out and shook it gingerly.

Artemis ambled back to the shack, mumbling to Drisner. "Ah'll be out in a minute. Jes' wait here while I git my shoes an' shirt."

"Charming," Anne said after the door closed.

"His social graces are a bit rusty," Drisner said dryly.

"What is he doing here?"

"The Donnards are a big local family, and Artemis inherited this tract of property a while back. The family supports him, so he doesn't sell it." Drisner shook his head. "There are some interesting real estate issues about this mountain that I'll explain sometime."

Artemis reemerged after a few minutes, thankfully wearing a flannel shirt. He headed up a dirt trail and motioned them to follow.

The path at times seemed to disappear into the brush, then reappear after several yards. *It'd be easy to get lost in this,* Anne thought. After ten minutes, they reached another clearing, which contained the old, charred remnants of a cabin of some sort. All that remained was a blackened fireplace, a chimney, and a stone foundation.

"That was the house of the girl's ma and pa," Donnard said. "Burned to the ground three years ago, a few hours after the aunt and uncle got hold of her. They say the parents was dyin', prob'ly too weak to do anything when some embers caught the wooden building. Place went up" —he snapped his fingers— "like that. Sad thing. Parents was real nice folks. Kept to themselves."

The surrounding land—what once must have been a farm—had been reclaimed by a dense overgrowth of weeds. Across a large open field bordered by more woods sat the ruins of several deserted farmhouses. "This is desolation," Anne muttered to Drisner. "Heck of a place to raise a child."

They came to a large bronze bell hanging from a thick tree branch a short distance from a tidy cabin surrounded by well-tended gardens.

Donnard picked up a large stone. "Doorbell," he explained and struck the bell with it a half-dozen times. "Isaiah, you got visitors," he yelled. "I brought that doctor fella, and he's got a lady doctor with him."

A tall, lean man with hair down to his shoulders and a beard stippled with grey stepped out of the cabin. His face was weathered, and he was simply dressed in a linen shirt and pants. His feet were shod in sandals made of a woven bark-like material.

"May God's grace be on you, Artemis Donnard, and to your companions."

"This here's Matt Drisner, an' the lady is Anne Mastik," Donnard introduced, then turned to Anne. "They don't much believe in titles here."

Isaiah's eyes lit up as he shook Anne's hand. "You cannot imagine how glad I am to meet you."

"How's yer niece doin'?" Artemis inquired.

"She fares poorly. It is my prayer that our visitors can assist us."

Artemis shook his head sadly, then turned and held his hand out until Matt put a twenty-dollar bill in it. Then he grunted his thanks and shuffled back down the trail.

As they walked to the cabin, Anne looked around her. The Morehouse residence was an ancient structure of rough-hewn logs, which seemed to be meticulously cared for. It was surrounded by a garden of wildflowers, and a variety of crops grew over several acres of land terraced along a nearby embankment. The coziness of the cabin contrasted sharply with the disrepair Anne had seen on the remainder of the mountaintop.

The inside was homey. A central area served as kitchen, dining room, and family room, with two bedrooms extending off the central main room. The furniture was wooden and likely handmade, almost Shaker in its simplicity. But something was missing, and it took Anne a minute to realize what: There was nothing electric in the house, not even a light bulb. No radio, television, or phone. Artemis Donnard must be their sole connection to the outside world. Anne's heart sank. *Would the poor girl die on this bleak, lonely mountaintop, having never talked or played with anyone even remotely her own age? Something had to be done, and I'm the person to do it.*

Isaiah came out of a bedroom accompanied by an attractive woman with light brown skin and brunette hair tied neatly back in a tight bun. She wore a simple linen skirt and blouse despite the July heat.

"This is my wife, Miriam."

"May God's grace be on you," Miriam said. "I hope you will forgive my rudeness in not greeting you earlier."

"Love for a child is not a cause for offense," Anne replied.

Miriam nodded politely but said nothing.

"I thought Anne might examine Ruth now," Drisner said.

Miriam led Anne and Matt into the bedroom. Curtains were drawn across the windows, a candle on a nightstand provided the only illumination.

Taking charge, Anne opened the curtains and flooded the room with sunlight. A bed with a feather mattress and down comforter filled the center of the room, and nestled in its midst was a teenage girl, her long brown hair disheveled and matted with sweat. She scarcely seemed to be breathing, and her face had the pallor of death. Anne's breath caught as she feared she had come too late, but the girl unexpectedly inhaled sharply and licked her crusted lips with a dry tongue.

Anne sat at the bedside, slipped her hand under the comforter, and drew Ruth's icy hand out. *Peripheral vasoconstriction. The blood vessels in her extremities must be clamping down to shift blood flow to the essential internal organs.* Ruth's hand was a mottled purple. Anne pressed lightly on a fingernail. It turned pallid and showed no returning blush of pink after Anne released the pressure. *Ruth's circulation was seriously impaired. She's going into shock. There isn't much time.*

After the pressure on her fingernail, Ruth moaned, her eyelids parting laboriously. Then her eyes flew open, and she panicked at seeing a strange face in front of her.

Miriam flew to the bedside. "Fear not. This is Anne Mastik, a doctor who has come to help. She will not hurt you."

The words seemed to calm Ruth. "Welcome, Anne," she said in a weak voice, "and may God's grace be on you."

"Time for examination," Anne said. "All those of the male persuasion, out, please."

She pulled down the comforter and examined Ruth under the watchful eyes of Miriam. Ruth gasped when the cold stethoscope touched her chest, but otherwise, the exam proceeded uneventfully.

Back in the main room, Anne updated the Morehouses. "Your niece is seriously ill. She has an overwhelming infection and is going into septic shock, the body's final reaction to a severe infection. The blood pressure drops and the pulse gets weak. Eventually, she'll go into a coma, the brain and heart will lose their blood supply, and she'll die. Frankly, she's only survived this long because she's young and otherwise healthy."

"What can be done for her?" Miriam said.

"She needs antibiotics, intravenous fluids, and monitoring of her vital signs, plus special medications to keep her blood pressure up until the infection passes. I hope we aren't too late. Ruth is an extremely sick child."

"Then you may bring your medicines here to treat Ruth," Miriam said.

"That's impossible. Everything would have to be carted up the hill and over that path, and I don't even know what the proper antibiotic is for her until tests are done. She needs full-time nursing care, X-rays, lab work, and monitoring equipment. You don't even have electricity. There is no alternative to Ruth being hospitalized."

"She cannot leave here," Miriam said. "Years ago, when she was sick as a child, the doctors brought the medications here, and we treated her at home."

To Anne's left, Drisner sighed, probably having been through this same conversation multiple times.

"She must not have been this sick. I understand you're concerned that Ruth will not be treated properly, but I'll take full responsibility for her. I'll do everything I can to protect her."

"I trust you, but I cannot let Ruth leave this mountain. That is God's will."

Anne recoiled at the proclamation. "It can't be God's will. God would never ask for the death of a child."

Miriam's arms and shoulders stiffened, her brow creased, and her hands balled into fists. "He will not allow Ruth to die. I know it. His grace is upon her. She will not die."

"No, she will die. I can say that for a certainty. You're praying for a miracle, and believe me, I'm praying for one, too. But I've seen hundreds of cases like this. They do not get better without appropriate medical treatment. They all die. And it has nothing to do with God's will."

"You are wrong." Miriam's hands shook, and her voice cracked. "It has everything to do with God's will."

The woman was clearly struggling with some terrible internal conflict. If Anne challenged her on legal or medical grounds, she might only dig her heels in deeper. *Only one thing to do, and this child's life lies in the balance.*

Anne picked up her cell phone and opened the app that Evan had recommended. From her childhood Sunday school days, she recalled a passage that still held a terrifying fascination for her and read it aloud. "And the angel of the Lord called unto him out of Heaven, and said, Abraham, Abraham: and he said,

Here am I. And He said, 'Lay not thine hand upon the lad, neither do thou any thing unto him: for now I know that thou fearest God, seeing thou has not withheld thy son, thine only son from me.'"

Anne closed the app and approached Miriam. "God knows that you would not withhold Ruth, but He would not want her to die at your hand any more than He wanted Isaac to die at the hand of his father. Please, let me take Ruth to the hospital."

Miriam stood stone-faced for an agonizingly long moment. "I must talk alone with my husband. Will you please excuse us?"

Anne nodded. Unable to sit, she paced back and forth in the main room.

"That was a master stroke," Matt said. "Where did that come from?"

"Something Evan told me at the conference. I hope it works. She was right on the edge and needed something she could accept as part of her value system. I don't know where this 'God's will' thing came from, but it seems to rule their life. How else can you argue with God, if not with the Bible?"

The Morehouses returned. This time, Isaiah spoke. "You may take Ruth to the hospital. There are conditions. No one is to lay hands on her but you, Miriam is to stay with her at all times, and she is to return home as soon as her health allows it."

"I accept your conditions," Anne said. *And how am I going to explain this to Rothberg?*

"Good. Give us a few minutes to get ready."

Anne fell into a chair, her legs weak from the tension. Drisner gave her a respectful nod.

CHAPTER V

The trip back to Matt's pickup made the trip up the mountain seem like a jaunt. Ruth needed to be carried to the truck by Isaiah and Drisner, who used a stretcher of tree limbs and blankets. The late-afternoon mosquitoes and flies were out in full force as they struggled against the rocky terrain, helpless against the endlessly biting insects and the punishing branches that flew into their faces with each step. Both men seemed exhausted by the time they laid Ruth on the mattress that Matt had put in the truck bed.

Anne climbed in and positioned herself next to Ruth. "Miriam, you can ride up front with Matt."

Miriam nodded and turned to her husband. "You care for yourself. I will worry about you, being alone up here."

"What could possibly happen to me that I would need the assistance of a frantic woman and a sickly child?"

"Do not mock me. For all our lives, we have never been farther apart than the width of this mountaintop. I will feel alone without you next to me."

Isaiah held Miriam to his breast. "And I without you. But we will have all the more to talk about when you and Ruth return."

"Not to worry," Drisner said. "I brought you a cell phone, Isaiah." He pressed it into the old man's hand.

Isaiah looked with consternation at the object.

"If it makes a sound," Drisner said, "push this button and talk. Keep it on, and always keep it with you. The battery will last for a few days."

"I'll call you when we reach the hospital," Anne said. "Now, could we please get moving? I need to get Ruth to the hospital. Pronto."

***

By evening, Ruth lay in her bed in isolation in the Intensive Care Unit, where she would stay until Anne could stabilize her. Rhythmically beeping monitors flashed tracings of red, blue, and green as they tracked Ruth's vital signs. Miriam's eyes were wide with astonishment at the complexity surrounding her, even jumping at the alarms until she realized they merely indicated the need for a minor adjustment. Overall, though, she seemed to take everything in stride because Artemis had apparently kept the family connected to the world by bringing magazines and books from town. Miriam made herself at home within the close confines of the hospital room, which didn't entail much. Other than her clothes and a few jars of herbs, her sole possession was a hand-copied Bible.

Anne made good on her vow to be the only one to touch Ruth, to the point of inserting all the arterial lines and catheters and personally checking Ruth's vital signs. She even did the spinal tap to make sure Ruth's fever wasn't due to meningitis. Through all of it, Miriam remained a silent observer, asking no questions. But peering over the obligatory surgical mask, her eyes intently followed Anne's activities.

An hour after Ruth's admission, Anne was paged to the lab. When she got there, she found the technician hunched over an antiquated microscope with a single eyepiece rather than the stereo binocular eyepiece Anne was accustomed to.

"Your patient is very anemic," the technician said. "You might want to look at this Gram stain."

Anne squinted to see through the eyepiece. "How come you only have a monocular microscope?"

"All our regular scopes are in the shop. This was the only loaner we could get."

Anne shook her head and looked back into the eyepiece. *Lots of white blood cells. Must be a hell of an infection.* Scattered amongst the cells—mere dust specks to an untrained eye—were the villains: tiny oblong bacteria, with the barest hint of red coloration, unlike the deep red of the Staphylococcus she'd seen at University Hospital. These were Gram-negative bacteria, so called because they didn't pick up the dark maroon Gram stain and would likely be resistant to the antibiotics that Anne had ordered for Ruth.

Anne thanked the tech and rushed back to the ICU to rewrite her antibiotic orders. Nothing to be done after that, but sit tight until the final sensitivities came back as a double check on her antibiotic choice.

***

After the initial chaos of admission, Miriam settled down to read her Bible. Ruth remained stuporous, but her vital signs were stable, color had returned to her cheeks, and her extremities felt warmer.

Anne picked up a journal and tried to read, but the small print blurred and became illegible, no matter how she rubbed her eyes. *God, I must be exhausted.* She threw the journal down. *No sense in forcing the issue.* She slipped a pillow under her head, leaned back in her recliner, and dozed off to the monotonous beeping of the cardiac monitors.

She hadn't been resting long when the strident tone of the blood pressure alarm disturbed her. She took a quick look at the monitor. Ruth's pulse was racing as her blood pressure plummeted.

Anne cranked the IV pump to maximum flow and yelled for the nurse, who arrived promptly. "I need a Levophed drip up here and fast. Get a liter of lactated Ringer's solution and run it in wide open as soon as it gets here."

She felt Ruth's hands and feet—icy cold. *What the hell! She's going back into shock. Must be the wrong antibiotic.*

Once the nurse hooked up the drips, Ruth's vital signs normalized precariously. Anne kept her eyes on the monitor, following the roller coaster ride that was Ruth's vital signs and fine-tuning the various infusions as necessary. Her urine output was dropping, however, which meant that her kidneys were failing, and unless Anne could find the right antibiotic, things would rapidly go downhill.

She raced back to the laboratory. "I need a preliminary report for the blood culture on Morehouse."

"It's kind of early, Doctor," he said. "Could you come back in the morning?"

"No! She'll be dead in the morning. I need that prelim—now!"

The tech brought the agar plate out from the microbiology lab. "Looks like Listeria to me, probably monocytogenes, but it's too early to tell."

Anne paled. "It can't be Listeria. That's Gram-*positive* bacteria. The slide I saw today was Gram-negative. I'm sure of it. Unless the day tech screwed up the stain."

"I don't know, Doc. She's meticulous with her staining technique."

He handed the blood sample slide to Anne, who pored over it a second time. *Dammit!* The solvent had been left on the slide for too long. Too much of the stain had been removed from the slide, washing out the color. Even the white blood cells that should have picked up the stain looked too pale.

"Your tech over-decolorized the slide," Anne said. "Look at this."

The tech peered into the scope and screwed up his face. "Looks Gram-positive to me," he said, "but I'll get the manual."

He pulled open a cabinet drawer and pulled out a booklet, which he flipped through page by page.

God, these people are inept. Do I have to stain the slide myself?

"Here you go, Doc. It's a pretty good match to me."

Anne looked at the color illustration in the manual. The picture of the Gram-positive bacteria looked exactly like the slide, but the words were so blurred she could hardly read them. She rushed back to look at the slide again. The bacteria no longer appeared as sharply defined bits of dust but as fuzzy, indistinct blobs, regardless of how she focused the eyepiece or rubbed her eyes. Finally, she pressed her other eye to the eyepiece and gasped.

Not only was the image on the slide clearly focused, but the bacteria and white blood cells were dark red—clearly Gram-positive.

She drew away from the microscope in shock. She covered one eye, then the other, while gazing at the bright red EXIT sign above the door. It looked like two different signs, with the left eye brilliant red and the right eye bleached and pale.

She fought back panic. The day tech had done her job perfectly. Anne's MS was at fault. The disease was attacking the nerve connecting her right eye and brain, stripping its fatty insulation and slowing the electrical impulses, just as it had done to her left eye years ago. She had missed the first sign: impairment of color vision.

And so, she had put Ruth on the wrong antibiotics.

She rushed back to the ICU nursing station. "Tell the pharmacy to switch my patient's antibiotics to ampicillin and gentamicin. Hook up another bag of lactated Ringers as fast as it will run. I need to draw some labs."

"I'm so sorry," Anne said to Miriam as she returned to Ruth's room. "I made a mistake, a serious one. I put Ruth on the wrong antibiotic this afternoon. We've lost valuable time."

"She will do well," Miriam said, gazing calmly at Anne. "I

know it. I have prayed."

"Tonight will be critical, Miriam."

"Then I will pray harder."

***

It proved to be a long night. True to her pledge, Anne spent the night varying the IV rate to maintain Ruth's urine output and tweaking the various drips to regulate her blood pressure and heart rate. At times, when Ruth's fever shot up to a point that the cooling blanket and acetaminophen couldn't keep it down, Anne wiped her face with a washcloth dampened with iced alcohol. She drew the blood work and, when necessary, restarted the IV lines. By midnight, Anne felt more exhausted than she had been since her internship. To make matters worse, her physical fatigue not only aggravated her long-standing leg weakness, but the vision in her right eye became so blurred that it seemed like she was viewing the world through a frosted window.

In a quiet moment, Anne sat by the bedside and looked at Ruth, a beautiful girl despite her pallor. In the glare of the room's fluorescent lights, her skin had lost its mottled appearance and taken on an almost translucent quality, as delicate and fragile as fine china. Then Anne touched Ruth's hands. Practically frozen again. The monitor showed Ruth's blood pressure, previously hovering at the bare minimum, dropping dangerously low, and her heart was racing. But even as it raced, there were frightening bouts without a heartbeat, followed by a pattern of bizarre electrical activity for several beats before reverting to normal. Time to call Matt.

He answered on the first ring.

"Ruth's in trouble. She's going into shock, and her heart is giving out."

"I know. The nurses alerted me already. I called Dr. Marcus Stendahl, our cardiologist. He should be there in a few minutes."

Anne frowned. "Are you keeping tabs on me?"

"That girl is my responsibility too. How are you holding

up?"

"If I had the time, I would collapse. I'm surviving on adrenalin right now."

"Call me if you need me. I'll be there first thing."

Anne hung up just as a nurse brought in the lab report. Reading the lab sheet, Anne panicked. Ruth had grown more anemic since admission. The toxins produced by the infection were clearly destroying her red blood cells and causing her blood pressure to plummet, thereby putting her heart under enormous strain. If the shock progressed, her heart would give out completely.

"I'll need a type and cross for two units of blood immediately," Anne called out to Ruth's primary nurse. "Keep the IVs wide open and get the cardiologist over here, STAT. This girl needs a pacemaker."

"What is wrong?" Miriam said, setting down her Bible. "Tell me what is happening."

"This is a crisis. We must move quickly, or we'll lose Ruth. She needs a blood transfusion."

"No!" Miriam's voice echoed loudly throughout the ICU. "She will not get any blood. I forbid it!"

"You don't understand. If she doesn't get blood, she will die."

Miriam stood, her arms stiffly at her side, her hands drawn into fists. "It cannot be done. It will not be done. There will be no blood."

"Is this part of your religion?" Anne demanded.

Miriam didn't answer, but her forehead wrinkled, and her eyes narrowed into a hard glare. "This is an absolute. There will be no blood. Not now, not ever. Not under any circumstances."

As stern as she had looked in the cabin, that was nothing compared to the fire that burned in her eyes now.

"I'll do what I can," Anne said, "but she may die."

"I hold you blameless. It is God's decision."

For the next twenty minutes, Ruth's vital signs teetered on the brink. Anne loaded Ruth with saline, plasma, albumin—whatever fluids she could to keep Ruth's blood pressure up. But every time Ruth's heart stopped, the interval between beats lengthened, her pressure dropped lower, and her recovery more uncertain. She needed a pacemaker and quickly, or she would arrest.

A nurse called Anne to the nursing station. Standing there was a tall, athletic, middle-aged man in green scrubs, who greeted her in surprisingly good spirits, considering he'd probably been dragged out of bed at 1:00 a.m.

"Matt told me you're the lucky stiff who gets to take care of the Morehouse kid," he said, shaking her hand. "I'm Marcus Stendahl."

"It appears my patient is something of a local celebrity. How do you know her?"

"We're neighbors, in a way."

"I thought Artemis Donnard was their only neighbor."

"The Donnards own the property ringing the base of the mountain. My grandmother was a Donnard, and a portion of her property was passed down to me. We can chat about this later. Now, can someone explain to me why a fifteen-year-old needs a pacemaker at one in the morning?"

"Septic shock with intermittent heart block," Anne said. "If you don't get a pacemaker into her pronto, she won't make it to morning."

Anne led Stendahl to Ruth's room, where Miriam turned to greet him.

"Sorry we have to meet under these circumstances," Stendahl said to Miriam as he glanced at Ruth's monitor, "but I'm your neighbor, Dr. Marcus Stendahl. Looks like I'll be putting a pacemaker into your niece tonight."

"You will put what into my niece?"

"A pacemaker. A small electronic device that will deliver

a tiny shock to the heart if—"

"You will put nothing into my niece. I have an agreement with Anne that only she will touch my niece."

"Miriam," Anne said, "this is a highly specialized procedure. I'm not qualified to do it."

"Then this doctor can teach you how to do it. But I will not allow him to touch Ruth."

"Please hear me out, ma'am," Stendahl said. "Dr. Mastik is absolutely right. This is a dangerous procedure for someone with no experience. One slip and Ruth could die. I'm not questioning Dr. Mastik's clinical skills, but you don't want someone practicing this procedure on your niece."

"I trust Anne and nobody else. I will have no one touch Ruth but her. That is our arrangement. I will take my niece home before I let anyone else touch her."

Stendahl began to object, but Anne motioned him to follow her to the nursing station.

Stendahl shook his head. "She's as loony as they say. I hear the whole family is wacky, but she takes the cake."

"I don't think we're going to argue her out of this."

"You want to learn how to put in a pacemaker?"

"Don't joke. I don't have much of a sense of humor at this hour."

"I'm not joking. Have you ever put a catheter into the heart to monitor cardiac function?"

"A Swan-Ganz? Sure, but not since residency."

"Well, if you can put in a Swan-Ganz catheter, you can put in a pacemaker wire. After it's in place, we hook it up to an external pacemaker, and, voilà, it's done."

"But I've got multiple sclerosis. When I get nervous or tense, my legs stiffen, and my right hand shakes." She raised her right hand, her fingers visibly trembling. "This girl's sick enough to die while I swab her arm, let alone jam a wire into her heart."

"Would a shot of whiskey settle your nerves then? Because

as I see it, we're out of options." Stendahl strode into Ruth's room and addressed Miriam. "Do you at least agree to my overseeing Dr. Mastik?"

"I do, as long as she is the only one touching her."

Stendahl cast an inquiring glance at Anne, who glumly nodded her assent.

"I'll get the pacemaker tray ready," he said. "Anne, you have her sign the consent."

Anne sat down next to Miriam and started to speak, but Miriam held up a stern finger to silence her. "I know my ways are strange to you, and you may think me mad, but I will do what is best for my niece according to my beliefs. I will not bend on that."

"God's will again?"

Miriam's silence spoke for her.

"I don't think I can do this," Anne said. "If Ruth dies, I'll never forgive myself."

"If she dies, you will forgive yourself because I will forgive you, and God will forgive you. But Ruth will not die." Miriam grasped Anne's hand and gazed into her eyes. "It is not her time."

Stendahl burst into the room. "I've got the pacemaker tray. We're ready to go if you two are finished chatting."

Miriam scanned the consent, using her finger as a guide. She stopped when she reached the section outlining possible complications, including death. Then she closed her eyes and mouthed what seemed to be a brief prayer before signing.

"May God's grace be on you," Miriam said to Anne, then left the room.

Stendahl unwrapped the sterile pacemaker set on a bedside tray while Anne gowned and gloved and prepped Ruth's arm with iodine solution.

"You psyched for this?" Stendahl said.

"I've never been so scared in my life."

"You'll do terrific. I'll be right behind you."

Anne smiled wanly as she prepped Ruth's neck with a

sterilizing solution.

"The first step is to get the needle into the right jugular vein." Stendahl pointed to the large vein in Ruth's neck, its color deep blue against the pallor of her skin and almost collapsed from her declining blood pressure. "Oh! And be careful. You really don't want to puncture the lung."

Anne picked up the pacemaker guide wire, which was attached to an IV needle that looked too large to fit in the vein. Bending over Ruth's neck, she felt for the jugular with her left index finger and held the needle with her quivering right hand as she approached. The closer she got, the worse she trembled. She backed away and tried again. *No go.*

She straightened up and shook her head. "I can't do this. I couldn't even start an IV anymore."

"Then let me do it. Miriam will never know."

"No," Anne said firmly. "I'll try again."

As her hand wobbled, she grabbed her wrist with her left hand, dampening the tremor slightly. Then she grasped the hand itself, but it still wasn't enough.

Anne straightened up again, her legs heavy and sweat soaking her mask. Stendahl wiped her forehead with a gauze pad.

"Need a break?" he asked.

"No." *For God's sake, if I could relearn to feed myself after total paralysis from my last attack, I can do this.*

She interlocked the fingers of both hands as if in prayer and grasped the needle between her thumb and index finger. As the two fingers wavered, she gripped the needle even more tightly. She held her breath to quiet the movement of her body and plunged the sharp steel point into Ruth's neck.

Inky blood rushed up the catheter, and Anne exhaled gratefully. She'd hit the jugular. *Thank God, but no time for celebration now.*

"Tape," she called. She gripped her hand again, advanced

the needle, and secured it with the tape Stendahl handed her. Later, she would secure it with a suture, but she didn't want to think about that now.

"Terrific," Stendahl said. "So much for the easy part. Now advance the catheter through the needle. Whatever you do, once you push it in, don't pull back. The sharp edge of the needle may catch on the catheter and slice it off. If that happens, the free piece will float into the heart, and it's a bitch to fish out."

"You're trying to make me feel good, aren't you?"

"Push the guide wire in a few inches at a time."

Anne gripped the wire with her left hand and gingerly slid it an inch further. *Easy-peasy.* The wire had enough slack to absorb her shaking, and the shaft of the needle eliminated any wiggle once it got into the vein.

"At that rate, she'll be dead by the time it reaches her heart," Stendahl said.

"Sorry. I'm still a little nervous."

"As long as it slides smoothly, you're okay. Now watch the monitor."

Stendahl had hooked the wire up to the cardiac monitor so the blood pressure wave coincided with Ruth's heartbeat. As Anne advanced the wire further toward the heart, the wave grew larger. But the pauses between heartbeats had grown longer and were more frequent.

"Marcus, do you see —"

"You've got to speed this up. Keep advancing the wire."

"I can't. It feels like it's stuck."

"Probably jammed against the wall of the blood vessel. Pull the needle back about a half inch."

Anne clasped her hands together and pinched the hub of the needle, straining to pull it back slightly, but her hand jerked involuntarily, pulling the needle completely out.

"Oh, God. What do I do now?"

"Don't panic. We don't need the needle anymore, but

you've got to hurry. Push the wire in. Is it still stuck?"

"No, I can feel it move, and if I can turn it...."

The EKG monitor blared an alarm, not the usual rhythmic beep that alerted the nurses to a needed adjustment but a high-pitched scream that drew the attention of everyone in the unit. Anne looked up. The EKG tracing was flat, the bright green line interrupted only by a regularly spaced sequence of tiny blips, the futile attempt of the heart's own pacemaker to initiate a contraction. *Come on, come on, do something, dammit.* But for the next ten agonizing seconds, there was only the wail of the alarm. Suddenly, a single bizarre-shaped contraction appeared, then nothing more. Ruth was in complete heart block, the heart muscle unresponsive to the electrical stimulation from the atrium. If they didn't get the pacemaker to work, it might not beat again.

"We've got to move," Stendahl shouted. "Thread the guide wire. Fast."

"There's nothing. Call a code blue?"

"We are the code blue. Keep going. We're almost there."

The pressure tracing jumped.

"What happened? Did I do something wrong?" Her right arm trembled so hard that her entire body shook. She let go of the wire, afraid she might perforate the lung.

Stendahl groaned. "You were perfect. The wire was in the right atrium. You've got to get the wire through the pulmonary valve into the right ventricle, and then we're golden. But hurry. She's only had one heartbeat in the past twenty seconds."

"I'm shaking too much. I can't do it."

Anne's hand went into overdrive, but Stendahl grabbed her right arm. Emboldened by his support, she clenched her hands together and pinched the wire between her thumb and index finger as hard as she could.

"Okay, one, two, three," Stendahl said, pushing her hands until the wire would go no further. He rushed to the tray, hooked the free end of the wire to the pacing unit, and turned it on. A small spike appeared on the screen, but no heartbeat. Stendahl turned a dial. The spike was larger, but still no beat. He turned it again. This time, every line on the monitor jumped as the heart gave a massive contraction and a jet of blood pulsed through Ruth's body. Contractions followed every two seconds, then every second, and then every three-quarters of a second as Stendahl adjusted a dial. Stendahl set the pacemaker down.

"Nice job. I have to tell you, for a moment there, I was on the verge of pushing the wire in myself."

"I'm glad you didn't. They have a belief system that dictates every aspect of their lives, and apparently, they stand by it even if it literally kills them. If I had broken that trust, Miriam would have taken Ruth out of the hospital to die at home."

"But you can't do three shifts a day for very long."

"I'll get some rest here after you leave."

Stendahl shook his head. "I feel a little responsible myself, being their neighbor. I'll check in later and see how you're doing."

"Thanks. Could you send Miriam back in?" Anne looked at the clock on the wall. *Three hours before shift change.* She crumpled into her recliner and fell asleep to the comforting metronome of the monitor.

***

"Morning, ladies!"

Anne snapped to full alertness. "Matt, don't ever sneak up on me like that. It's 4:00 a.m. A little early for rounds, don't you think?"

"Couldn't sleep. I was wondering if I could help."

"Not really." She glanced over at Miriam, who was just stirring in her recliner. "We women have things under control. Don't we, Miriam?"

"That is so," Miriam said.

Matt turned to Anne. "Can I steal you away for a quick coffee break?"

Miriam nodded her approval, and Anne and Matt walked

to the hot drink dispenser at the nursing station. Anne kept a watchful eye on the monitors while she sipped a welcome cup of coffee.

"How's Ruth?" Matt asked.

"As well as could be expected, considering my royal screw-up."

"The nurse told me about switching her antibiotics. How's Miriam taking it?"

"Calmly. I know she's worried, but she seems very much in control of her emotions. A little too much if you ask me. Her relationship with teenage Ruth must be interesting."

A piercing scream from Ruth made Anne spill her coffee. She rushed back to the room, Matt at her heels. Miriam was gripping Ruth's wrists as the girl struggled to get out of bed.

"She thinks she is home," Miriam cried. "I have never seen her like this."

Two nurses carrying wrist restraints ran in.

"No!" Miriam cried out. "She is only a girl. I will not let you tie her down."

The nurses wavered, looking at Anne for guidance.

"No restraints," Anne ordered, "and get me two milligrams of lorazepam for IV push, stat."

"What are you giving her?" Miriam asked.

"Something to quiet her down."

"No. Please, no more medicines. She is getting too much already."

"I have to. Otherwise, she'll climb out of bed."

"I will keep her in bed myself. No more medication. Please."

"She's delirious, and you're only making her more agitated." As Anne spoke, Ruth struggled harder, and Miriam responded by shaking her in frustration.

"Let me try," Anne said, leading Miriam away from the bed.

She sat on the bed and clasped Ruth's hands. Ruth calmed down briefly but then burst into renewed thrashing. While Ruth struggled, Anne clutched her tightly and stroked her hair. After a minute, she pressed her own face against Ruth's until she calmed down and limply fell back onto the bed.

"Nice work, Dr. Mastik," Matt said.

"Thanks," Anne replied calmly as her arms trembled.

"Thank *you*," Miriam said, touching Anne's hand, then turning her head away.

"You were right," Matt said, glancing at Anne. "You ladies do seem to have everything under control. But would you mind coming to my office after the shift change?"

"Sure thing."

Ruth settled down into a fitful sleep, and at times Anne had to reach over and touch her arm to quiet her down. But after her fever broke, she seemed to be over the delirium. Shortly after daybreak, Anne sat down to rest. Miriam looked up from her Bible and spoke for the first time since Matt left.

"You care for Ruth."

"There's been a lot to do tonight. She almost died."

"No. I do not mean you are caring for Ruth. I mean, you care for Ruth."

"She's extremely ill. I take it seriously when a patient of mine is so close to dying."

"You still do not understand. I see the way you look at her, how you touch her. I'm sure you are an excellent doctor and are concerned about your patients, but I sense there is something about Ruth that draws you to her."

"I've never seen your niece before yesterday. Of course, I'm concerned about her, but only as a patient."

"There is a link between the two of you. You are meant to be here."

Anne started to speak but thought better of it. *Another one of her "God's will" kicks. No use in arguing.*

"I have a favor to ask of you," Miriam said. "Promise me that you will always take care of Ruth."

Anne knit her eyebrows together. "I don't think she'll need an infectious disease specialist again."

Miriam spoke firmly. "Promise me that you will always take care of Ruth."

"I really don't see the need —"

"Promise me, Anne."

"What's so important about this?"

"I can't explain. Please, this is all I ask of you."

Too exhausted to argue, Anne blurted out, "Okay, okay. I promise I'll always take care of Ruth."

As the obligatory words left her lips, Anne felt something within her inexplicably change. Although she couldn't put her finger on it, she felt the relationship between the three women had just decisively altered.

A smile flickered across Miriam's face, then quickly disappeared. It was the first one Anne had seen since they'd met.

She certainly is an odd one.

CHAPTER VI

Dawn found both women sound asleep, Miriam with her Bible open in her lap and Anne with her head resting on the bed. The bustling activity during the nurses' change of shift woke both.

Anne was afraid she might have slept through a crisis, but the monitor beeped reassuringly. She slipped her hand under Ruth's blanket. To her surprise, Ruth's fingers were warm, and the color returned to her face. Ruth grasped Anne's hand.

"Good morning, Anne. Good morning, Miriam," she said weakly. "May God's grace be on you both. I'm hungry."

"We'll get you some breakfast," Anne said, scarcely hiding her excitement.

Miriam approached the bedside. "When can she go home?"

"She'll need several more days of antibiotics, and she's too weak to go home."

"Can you give her pills? The nurses and I can care for her at home."

"No. She needs intravenous antibiotics."

"But look at her. She is well. Her fever has broken."

"If we stop the antibiotics, she'll relapse, and the organism may become resistant."

"Resistant?"

"The medicines may not work again if we stop them too soon."

"Then give me the bags of medicine. I have seen you attach them to the tubes. It is not difficult."

How do I get through to this woman?

"I believe I should stay," Ruth interjected.

"Hush, child. This is between two adults."

"I will not hush. It is not only between two adults. It is my life."

"I am your guardian. I make all decisions regarding your welfare."

"I am old enough to make my own decisions. Besides, who ever made you my official guardian? I have seen no legal writ proposing such."

"Legally," Anne said to Ruth, "since Miriam and Isaiah are your only next of kin, they are your guardians until you reach eighteen."

"That," Ruth murmured, "will come not a moment too soon if you ask me."

Miriam glared at Ruth. "Mind yourself, child. I will not tolerate any disrespect."

"And I will not tolerate your making decisions about my life. I choose to stay, and I will stay."

"Stop it, you two," Anne yelled. "Ruth needs her rest. Miriam, why do you feel it is so urgent to discharge Ruth?"

"We must get back to the homestead. Ruth understands that."

"She wants to shut me up on the top of that mountain, that's why."

"It is not by my choice," Miriam said stiffly.

"Well, it certainly is not by *my* choice," Ruth said in a huff. "As far as I'm concerned, you can take your silly prophecy and drop it down the deepest well in West Virginia."

"Ruth Morehouse!" Miriam shouted so loudly that the

nurses turned their heads.

Ruth's face blanched. She yanked the covers over her head and hid beneath them.

"What prophecy?" Anne asked.

"Family business does not concern you," Miriam said.

"If it involves discharging a patient of mine before she's well, it does concern me."

"It is not something I wish to discuss."

Anne turned to the mound under the covers that was Ruth. "Can you tell me about this prophecy?"

No reply.

Anne turned to Miriam. "Does your wanting to take Ruth home today have anything to do with this prophecy?"

Miriam hesitated. "Yes. I can say no more."

"Then how about a compromise? If Ruth stays here another week and remains stable, perhaps we can arrange further treatment at home."

"A week! That is far too long."

"It would usually be at least two weeks, and getting nursing care and medications to your cabin isn't practical. One week is my minimum."

After a long pause, Miriam answered. "I agree to your conditions."

Anne turned and talked to the lump in the bed. "Ruth, is that okay with you?"

Ruth gave a sullen grunt from under the covers.

Anne smiled. *Not perfect, but I'll take what I can get.* "Then it's a deal. But I must be free to care for Ruth without interference. From anyone."

Miriam squirmed. "Agreed."

"Good. I'm going to the on-call room for a shower and breakfast."

"What about Ruth?"

"Her nurse can take care of her while I'm gone."

"But you promised—"

"Her nurse can take care of her, Miriam," Anne said firmly. "You call Isaiah and tell him Ruth is much better. I'll be back soon."

Anne couldn't remember a shower she had enjoyed quite so much. After she dressed, she gave in to the luxury of a cup of coffee in the solitude of the doctors' lounge.

"Mind if we join you?"

Matt stood in the doorway, accompanied by a tall, strikingly attractive brunette in a business suit far too elegant for the West Virginia hills.

"Anne," he said, "allow me to introduce Lillian Petrillo, assistant administrator for Eden Community Hospital."

Lillian shook Anne's hand. "Please don't get up. Matt told me you were coming to town, and I'm so happy you could make it."

"Don't let her title fool you," Matt said. "Lillian is assistant to no one. Everybody knows she manages this hospital, but nobody will acknowledge it publicly, least of all Lillian. If John Buckram would get off his ass, this hospital wouldn't be in the financial trouble it's in."

"Hush," Lillian said in a stage whisper. "Are you trying to get me in trouble?"

Matt ignored her protest. "The Board's afraid to put a woman in charge, so they've got their good ol' boy sitting in the CEO seat while Lillian drives the bus."

"John deals with the politics and fundraising. That's as important as what I do."

Matt turned to Anne. "I told you she wouldn't admit it."

"I'm just doing my job," Lillian said. "We both know what that's like, don't we, Dr. Mastik?"

Anne nodded. *Proving myself as a woman in a man's world? You bet I do, sister.* "By the way, everyone seems pretty informal here. Please call me Anne."

"Now that you two ladies have been introduced, I hope you'll excuse me. The office beckons."

"Matt told me you brought the Morehouse girl in," Lillian said as Matt left.

"You know her?"

"The Morehouses are a local legend. Carved out their homestead and hid away for three hundred years. You'd have created less of a stir if you brought in Bigfoot. How's the girl doing?"

"Very well. I didn't expect her to make such a dramatic turnaround."

"So you think she'll recover?"

"Sure, if I can coerce Miriam into letting her stay." *And keep those two from tearing the room apart.* "By the way, do you know anything about a prophecy?"

"No. Why?"

"Miriam mentioned it. Is there anyone in town who might know more about it?"

"Try Reverend Lucius Wainstock, the minister of the Church of the Righteous Disciples. It's the biggest one in town."

"I know which one you're talking about. Why would he know anything?"

"His congregation controls over eighty percent of the wealth in this town. Some say his power extends all the way to Charleston. He keeps his fingers tightly on the pulse of this town, and I can tell you he has a definite opinion on any topic you care to bring up."

"Thanks." Anne stood up. "Got to go. Coffee break's over."

"Nice talking with you. Why don't we have a girls' night out sometime?"

"As soon as Ruth's stable. That's the deal I made with Miriam."

"Where are you staying?"

"Don't know. I thought I'd find a hotel."

"Good luck. Hotels are nonexistent in town. How about I fix you up in a nice, homey bed-and-breakfast? Courtesy of the hospital."

Anne felt more relaxed just thinking about it. "That may take some convincing with Miriam, but it sounds delightful."

Returning to the ICU, Anne was gratified to see that Ruth's vital signs were stable and she was resting peacefully. Anne turned to Miriam. "I'm afraid I've got to excuse myself for the rest of the morning."

"But—"

"Sorry, Miriam, no buts."

Against Miriam's vigorous but futile objections, she promised that she would be instantly available by cell phone and would call Isaiah later that afternoon with an update.

The Church of the Righteous Disciples was as magnificent on the inside as it was imposing on the outside. It could seat several hundred, both on the main level and in a mezzanine section at the back. The choir loft, altar, and pews were of hand-carved mahogany, while stained glass windows depicting scenes from Christ's life encircled the interior. The pulpit, heavily cantilevered, seemed to float above the assembly. *Quite a show of opulence – they probably pass a hell of a big hat around on Sundays.*

"May I help you?" boomed a voice obviously accustomed to filling the vast recesses of the church.

Anne turned to see a tall, slender elderly man with a head of thick gray hair marked by a prominent widow's peak. Bright, searching eyes dominated his gaunt face, and even in the July heat, he was dressed in a formal black suit.

"I'm looking for Reverend Wainstock."

"Seek and ye shall find; knock, and it shall be opened unto you."

Sheesh. "Pleased to meet you. I'm Dr. Anne Mastik."

"I don't recognize the name. Are you from these parts?"

"Dr. Drisner invited me here to consult on a patient. But

I'm in need of information about local lore and was told you were the person to see."

Wainstock seemed to glow at the recognition. "Glad to help if I can. My family goes back many generations in this area, and I have more than a passing knowledge of local history."

"I've heard something about a Morehouse family prophecy. Know anything about it?"

"I know the Morehouses," Wainstock snapped. "Heretics and blasphemers, the whole ungodly bunch of them, sitting up on their damned mountain for the last three hundred years. I'm surprised you got them to come down."

Anne's eyes widened in surprise at Wainstock's reaction. "Does this prophecy have anything to do with their isolation?"

"Why don't we talk in my office?" While Anne took a seat in a large leather chair, Wainstock closed the door behind them even though the church was empty.

Wainstock took a seat behind his desk in a large mahogany leather wingback executive chair. "You'll never meet a more secretive bunch," he began, leaning over and resting on his elbows, fingers interlaced. "The Morehouses were some of the earliest settlers in this state, sometime in the early 1700s, supposedly chased out of New York and Pennsylvania for their outrageous beliefs and eventually finding their way to Eden Mountain. And there they stay."

"Their community doesn't seem to have been very successful. There's only three of them left."

"At one point, Morehouses covered the top of the mountain and then some, like a colony of ants. But over the last fifty years, they've died out."

"Not enough converts?"

Wainstock shook his head. "They never looked for converts. Always kept strictly to themselves. From what I understand, their beliefs exclude outsiders."

"What could possibly be the purpose of sequestering

yourself on some mountaintop?"

Wainstock huffed out a weary sigh. "They're waiting for the Second Coming of Jesus Christ. They believe He will not come down from the clouds of Heaven but will be born from" — he raised his brows— "a sinful act."

"Oh, come on. Nobody sits on top of a mountain for three centuries waiting for the Second Coming. Religious cults like that fizzle out quickly."

Wainstock leaned back in his chair. "I've told you everything I know."

Anne stood to leave. "At least this gives me something to work with. One last question, Reverend. Do you believe the Morehouses' prophecy?"

He narrowed his eyes to slits. "I believe that unless they repent of their sacrilegious beliefs, they will burn in Hell for all eternity."

That's a conversation stopper. Anne excused herself and hurried out of the church.

***

The drive back to the hospital gave Anne time to think. The Morehouses had secluded themselves for over ten generations. In isolated communities with such a restricted gene pool, defective genes could develop and eventually kill off the community, probably by impairing their immune systems. It might not be long before Ruth's guardians died off, leaving Ruth as the sole survivor.

Oh no. Hadn't she sworn to Miriam that she would always take care of Ruth?

She slammed on the brakes. *Was Miriam anticipating that she and Isaiah would die soon — so she'd chosen Anne as Ruth's future guardian?* Anne was struck by the absurdity of the situation and gave a nervous laugh in the solitude of her car.

As Anne got out of her car at the back of the hospital parking lot, a thin twenty-something man in a cheap, ill-fitting suit ran up to her.

"How do you do, Dr. Mastik. I'm Bryan Dunmore of *The Eden Guardian*."

Anne looked at him quizzically.

"Uh, that's our local newspaper," he added. "I'm a reporter. For the newspaper. I was wondering if I could ask you a few questions about your patient, Ruth Morehouse."

"I'm sorry, Mr. Dunmore, but I can't discuss her case. Patient confidentiality."

"I understand that, but isn't there anything you can tell me about her condition? How serious is it?"

"No comment, Mr. Dunmore. Now if will you excuse me?" Anne stumbled on a crack in the asphalt, and Dunmore held her arm until she regained her balance.

"There are lots of handicapped spaces next to the ER entrance," he said. "I'm sure nobody would mind if you parked there."

Anne pulled her arm from his grasp. "I prefer to walk, thank you, and save those spaces for the disabled." She walked off.

As soon as she entered the Emergency Room, Matt ran over. "I've been looking all over the hospital for you. Where've you been?"

"Doing research. By the way, did you know that a reporter from the newspaper wanted to interview me?"

"I'm not surprised. Ruth's the hottest news around here since a school bus rolled into a drainage ditch. Why don't you come to my office?"

Anne shook her head. "I'm really too busy right now."

"No, you're not. The lab tech told me about you misreading the Gram stain. I think you're in the middle of an MS relapse, and I'm the closest thing to a neurologist you're going to find for a two-hour drive in any direction. Meet me in my office. Now."

***

Wrapped in a grossly oversized paper gown, Anne sat on the exam table in Matt's office, looking at the bright red copy of the Physician's Desk Reference he held in front of her.

"This really isn't necessary, Matt. I'm doing fine."

"You told me a few hours ago that you had an attack of optic neuritis. That is not 'doing fine' in my book. Now, does the red look the same in the left eye" — he covered her right eye with his hand — "as it does in the right eye?" He switched his hand to cover her left eye.

"Duller in the right eye. And I can't read the title on the cover."

"That means you're worse than 20/400." Matt checked her pupils, looked into her eyes with his ophthalmoscope, and tapped her knee with a reflex hammer. Her leg jerked out and kicked him in the shin.

"Believe it or not, that wasn't intentional," Anne said, repressing a chuckle. "My reflexes have been that way since my second relapse. My exam is pretty much unchanged from my neurologist's last exam. Except for my vision."

"You've had an attack of optic neuritis in the right eye. You know the drill."

"One thousand milligrams of intravenous steroids every day for five days," Anne said wearily. That was the standard regimen for an MS relapse. She'd been through it too many times. "What about my natalizumab? I'm a week overdue already. Needs to be done at an approved infusion center."

Matt pecked away at his computer. "Closest one is in Summersville. A good three-hour drive through the mountains. Scenic, but not easy."

Anne sighed. "Then I'll wait until I get back to Charlottesville, but I'll go ahead with the steroids."

"Great. You'll get your first steroid dose tomorrow morning. Oh, and by the way, I got a call from Lillian. John Buckram wants to meet with us."

"The CEO? About what?"

"She didn't say, but I'll bet it has something to do with money."

***

As a secretary escorted Anne and Matt into a richly appointed office in the administrative suite, a large, stocky man in a well-tailored dark gray pinstripe suit rose from his desk and introduced himself as Dr. John Buckram, the Chief Executive Officer and Chief Medical Officer of Eden Community. He motioned for them to sit.

"First, Dr. Mastik, let me tell you how honored we are to have a doctor of your academic caliber visiting our hospital. We're off the beaten path and don't get visitors very often."

"It's been a pleasure," Anne responded warily.

"Your time is valuable, and I'll get right to the point. How long will your patient be here?"

"I'm not sure. Possibly another week until she finishes her course of antibiotics."

"We were hoping you could find a way to discharge her sooner. Perhaps in a day or two."

"I don't see how I could do that without significant risk to her."

"Could she be put on oral medication?"

"That wouldn't be appropriate. The IV route is much more reliable, particularly for sepsis."

"Then perhaps we can arrange for a visiting nurse to deliver the antibiotics."

"Not practical. She lives on the top of a heavily wooded mountain without electricity. Some of the antibiotics must be administered every six hours. And she's still in danger of a relapse. What's the problem with keeping her where she is?"

"This is a small community hospital, Dr. Mastik. Our financial resources are limited, and we're not accustomed to having a patient who requires such an intensive level of care."

"Then why have an ICU? Ruth's type of infection generally attacks people with impaired immune systems. She needs an isolation facility, and she needs close monitoring of her vital signs and intravenous drips. Besides, I don't see how her level of care has been different than any other patient in the unit. For God's sake, she's not even on a ventilator."

"Perhaps we can transfer her to a lower level of care."

"Not now," Anne bristled. "She will stay where she is until she is out of danger."

"You're being very unreasonable, Dr. Mastik."

"I'm defending my patient's best interests, Dr. Buckram. I'm sorry if that inconveniences the hospital, but I assure you her current level of care is necessary. If it weren't, I wouldn't have been up all night with her."

Buckram stiffened. "I had hoped it wouldn't come to this, but the hospital board authorized emergency privileges for you at Dr. Drisner's request. I'm afraid I must recommend that these privileges be withdrawn pending additional documentation of your qualifications and official confirmation of your licensure from the Board of Medicine of the State of Virginia."

"You can't do that!" Matt roared. "That'll take weeks."

"I will do whatever is necessary to protect the reputation of my hospital."

Anne's legs stiffened as adrenalin intensified her spasticity. "I don't know what your game is, but I can have a reporter from *The Guardian* in your office in five minutes."

"Don't try to bluff me. Whether you know it or not, I hold all the aces. Good day, Dr. Mastik. You'll be notified of your status after tomorrow's board meeting."

"This wouldn't be happening if Ruth Morehouse had insurance, would it?" Anne said.

Buckram's face showed no expression. "I said, good day, Dr. Mastik."

***

Anne's blood boiled as they left Buckram's office.

"Do you see what he's doing? He's trying to kick Ruth out of the hospital. Over insurance coverage, of all the nerve."

"It's all bull," Matt said as they walked down the hospital hallway. "This area is dirt poor, and hardly anyone is insured. The state gives us tons of money to care for them."

"Then what's the problem?"

He seemed to shy away from Anne before continuing. "Let's just say the Morehouses aren't winning any popularity contests."

"So they stay to themselves — so what? That's no reason to deprive a young girl of medical care."

Matt shifted uncomfortably. "It goes a bit beyond that."

Anne peered at Matt. *He's hiding something, and I'll bet it's big.* "What do you mean?"

"It involves money. Lots of money."

"And?" Anne was not finished digging.

"The Morehouse homestead is a valuable piece of real estate. It takes up the entire crest of the highest mountain for miles."

Anne pulled a confused face. "Why would anyone want that property? It's practically impossible to reach."

"It'd be easy by ski lift."

Where the hell did that come from?

Matt continued. "Developers want to turn the mountain into a ski resort, but the Morehouses refuse to sell. This is a very depressed region, Anne. The mines have closed, and there are no industries for miles. As sports tourism booms in West Virginia, we're watching it pass us by. But with no Morehouses around, the property is up for grabs."

He can't possibly mean what I'm thinking. "Did you say 'with no Morehouses?'"

Matt said nothing.

"My God, Matt. Are you suggesting that the hospital

board wants Ruth dead? That's insane."

Matt's voice took on a dead serious tone. "Some townsfolk have been lusting after the Morehouse property for decades, ever since the group started dying off." He looked at Anne. "Only three to go."

"Wouldn't the property go to the state?"

"They'd probably auction it off. I'll let you in on another secret. You remember Artemis Donnard?"

"Sure." *If nothing else, Artemis was certainly unforgettable.*

"The town is full of Donnards, by birth or marriage. They control the hospital board. One owns *The Guardian*, and Reverend Wainstock is another. They're one of the wealthiest and most well-connected families in the state. They've got big land holdings, which would be worth a whole lot more if Eden becomes a resort town. And since he owns the adjacent property, Cousin Artemis gets first dibs. That's why the family supports him and keeps him well-saturated. He ain't much to look at, but Artemis Donnard could be the key to a megamillion-dollar real estate deal."

"But Ruth has her aunt and uncle."

"For the time being. Three years ago, Ruth's parents died in a fire. Ruth was rescued by her aunt and uncle, and she's been their ward since. The fire was classified as accidental, but the investigation was cursory at best. Isaiah and Miriam suspect arson, but it's too late to prove it now."

"And while Ruth is here in town...."

"Whoever got to her parents can probably get to her."

"So this prophecy business is only part of Miriam's issues?"

"I suspect she breaks out the prophecy to keep Ruth from getting frightened."

Anne smacked her head. "That's why she doesn't want anyone to touch Ruth but me. I've got to get back to the ICU!"

***

The charge nurse approached Anne as soon as she entered the

ICU.

"Thank God you're back. Ruth's nurse is ready to tear her hair out. Mrs. Morehouse won't let anyone touch Ruth, so we haven't drawn labs or gotten vital signs since you left. Now she's overdue for her antibiotics. Also, Dr. Stendahl wanted to remove the temporary pacemaker, but Mrs. Morehouse wouldn't let him. We can't take care of the child if the aunt won't let us near her."

"It's my fault," Anne said. "I shouldn't have been gone so long. I'll make sure this doesn't happen again."

Miriam was pacing when Anne walked into the room.

"You have been gone a very long time, Anne. I was worried."

"Sorry, Miriam. How is Ruth?"

"I'm doing well, thank you," Ruth chimed in. "It is my aunt who needs to be in a bed."

"Hush." Miriam glared at Ruth, then turned back to Anne. "We had a promise. I expect you to abide by it."

"May I talk with you? Outside the room?"

Miriam nodded, so Anne led her to a small conference room.

"Is your urgency to get back to Eden Mountain about the prophecy, or do you think someone is trying to kill Ruth?" Anne asked.

Miriam's hands gripped into fists as her eyes hardened. "With whom have you been speaking?"

"Answer my question."

"You are delving into matters that do not concern you."

"I've taken on the responsibility of your niece's health and well-being. I have to be prepared for all eventualities."

Miriam scanned the area to see if anyone was listening, then spoke in a hushed voice. "It is for both of those reasons — the prophecy and the threat to Ruth's life. I do not understand all that goes on in this hospital. Medicines are being given to Ruth that I know nothing about by people I do not know. Ruth is trusting, but I cannot afford to be so."

"You think someone is trying to kill Ruth?"

"Perhaps. And Isaiah and me, as well. They have already killed my sister and her husband."

"Do you have proof?"

"One can never be sure of anything, but I have my suspicions. My sister Rebecca and her husband had a sickness like Ruth's, so Isaiah and I took Ruth to safety not an hour before they died." Miriam's eyes welled up with tears. "That same night, right before we arrived, Rebecca heard someone walking outside her home. I could see no one in the dark."

"Who do you think killed them?"

Miriam wiped her eyes, resumed her stoic stance, and shook her head. "It is a wise man who knows his enemies. It is a fool who thinks he knows them all."

"Why don't you go to the police?"

"They will not help. They think we are mad, and they side with the townspeople."

"What will happen with Ruth?"

"God will provide for her."

"You can't trust Ruth's life to miracles."

"We have lived three centuries trusting in miracles."

"Your family is dying out. You've used up all your miracles."

"There is still one left."

Anne hesitated before speaking. "Miriam, do you really believe in the Second Coming?"

Miriam's face tightened. "Lucius Wainstock told you that, did he not? He knows nothing. I will tell you all that you need to know at the proper time."

***

Ruth continued her recovery unimpeded. It was more important than ever to keep her in the ICU. She needed not only isolation facilities but security. Granted, an electronic door and closed-circuit video guarded the entrance, and nurses were within full view, but it didn't feel like enough. For Anne, keeping her there had also become an issue of either principle or personal pride, and she couldn't say which.

Ruth's heart had been back on autopilot all day. Time to pull the wire.

"Ready to get this wire out?" Anne asked Ruth.

"You will not pull anything out with it?" Miriam asked.

"Nope. Easy as pie." Anne disconnected the wire from the external pacemaker. "Ready?"

Ruth looked fearful but nodded.

Anne clasped Ruth's hand and looked into her eyes. "Do you trust me?"

Ruth nodded hesitantly.

"Okay. Here we go. One…two…three." Ruth's mouth and eyes opened wide in disbelief as Anne pulled the foot-long wire out of her neck in one continuous motion. *Thank God removing it was easier than placing it!*

***

Miriam and Ruth seemed perfectly happy to read their well-worn copies of the Bible, but Anne was interested to see that both read news magazines and newspapers avidly. Miriam wouldn't allow television in the room, although Anne was surprised to find that she did allow a radio. Anne quickly exhausted the reading material of interest to her in the hospital's small library when the intercom crackled with the voice of the desk clerk. "Dr. Mastik, there's a personal call for you on the family conference room phone."

Puzzled, Anne rushed to the empty conference room and closed the door.

"How is your mystery patient doing?" a familiar voice asked after she picked up the phone.

"Evan, is that you? How did you find me?"

"Where else in the town of Eden would you look for an

Infectious Disease doctor taking care of a patient with an immune deficiency disease and an opportunistic infection?"

"I didn't think you remembered."

"Don't keep me in suspense. How is she?"

"She's over the hump medically, but she'll need two weeks of antibiotics, and the hospital administration is getting ugly about keeping her here."

"Why?"

"Money and politics. The CEO is threatening to play hardball if I don't get her out of the hospital within the next two days."

"Can you transfer her to your hospital in Charlottesville?"

"The girl's aunt won't agree to it. I've stumbled into a very bizarre situation."

"What is that?" Evan asked.

"I'll explain someday. It's complicated."

"Sure. So listen, I called to tell you what a wonderful time I had the other day. I haven't forgotten you gave your word that we would go out again, and I wanted to make sure you were serious."

"Name the day—after I finish up here, that is."

"Great. By the way, I work in a lab with state-of-the-art isolation facilities and medical support, so there would be no problem keeping your patient here—and it might make our date happen sooner."

Anne blushed and felt grateful they weren't FaceTiming. "Thanks, but that would be a lot of money."

"I have my means. Don't worry about it. Call if you need me."

"I will." Anne glanced at her watch. "Sorry, but I've got to go back to Ruth's room."

"Hey, one more thing."

"What's that?"

"I'll be thinking about you."

"Ditto." Anne grinned as she hung up. *Nice to have at least one uncomplicated thing in her life.*

CHAPTER VII

What had been a series of near disasters and critical hair-trigger decisions had settled down into the tedium of hospital routine: vital sign checks, switching of sterile bags of intravenous antibiotics, and the occasional tearful blood drawing. Even the periodic monitor alarms had become so routine that Miriam no longer looked up from her Bible when a nurse came in, pushed a button or two, and left.

Anne observed the Morehouses' singular eating habits: strict vegan. All fruits and vegetables had to be cooked or, if fresh, Miriam washed them with soap and water. Listeria was contracted by eating contaminated foods, usually dairy. But they didn't eat dairy products, and they washed their food. *So how in the world did Ruth get infected?*

Anne filed the question away. More urgent problems loomed. Whether or not she agreed with Buckram, she would never be able to keep an otherwise healthy teenager in the hospital for two weeks. If she didn't worm her way out of her vow to Miriam, she'd be spending the next seven days doing scut work. As she mulled over possible solutions, an aide informed her that she had a call from Lillian Petrillo at the nursing station.

"How are things going?" Lillian asked when Anne picked up the receiver.

"Ruth seems to be bouncing back, and Miriam's been a lot easier to deal with."

"How about that girls' night out then?"

"I've got four hours until the next bag of Ampicillin is hung. Is that enough time?"

Lillian laughed. "Sure! We could see the town, have dinner, and take in a movie with that much time. I'll meet you in the lobby."

***

Lillian hadn't exaggerated. Within an hour, she had shown Anne the entire town, throwing in sordid behind-the-scenes points of interest, including the home of John Buckram's mistress, where Buckram's BMW sat in the driveway. Shortly before sunset, they ended up at a cozy restaurant perched high on a mountain overlooking the town. It had once been a private residence and, according to Lillian, was the only restaurant that didn't keep ketchup on its tables. The hostess seated them by the window as the last rays of sun disappeared behind the mountains. Lillian insisted they split a bottle of wine, and after a few sips, Anne felt herself slowing down for the first time since arriving in Eden.

"You seem like more of a city person," Anne said. "How did you end up here?"

"The job hunt was rough, so when I found a position here, I snapped it up. But to tell you the truth, I never intended to stay as long as I have."

"Country life grew on you?"

"Not really. More a combination of laziness, job security, and…love interest."

"Matt?"

Lillian waved that suggestion away. "We're just friends. I met a guy a few years back, but he's paranoid about keeping our relationship secret."

"Is it working out?"

"Kind of. Y'know, I really love the guy. Oh, crap. Who am

I trying to kid? It sucks. If I had anything more substantial in line, I'd drop the whole thing. I mean, what can a girl do in a town where every eligible bachelor owns a pickup truck with a gun rack and a beer cooler? What about you?"

"I was married once already, and we now define 'irreconcilable differences' in the legal dictionary of Virginia. While I'd like to blame it all on his reaction to my MS, it went deeper than that."

Lillian grabbed Anne's hand. "I'm sorry. I didn't realize you had MS."

"I thought Matt would have told you."

"He's actually a pretty quiet guy."

"Matt? Matt Drisner? Are we talking about the same person?"

Lillian laughed. "I know. He's loud in public, but he takes in a lot more than he gives out. He'll let you know a few things about himself, but he pulls back before you find out too much. On the other hand, in a small town like this, it's nice to have a friend who can keep a secret."

Intriguing. Dr. Matt Drisner, Man of Mystery. "What does your boyfriend think about this?"

"It's none of his damn business. Besides, how do I know what he's doing?"

The vehemence of Lillian's last statement caught Anne by surprise until she realized that the wine bottle was practically empty, while Anne wasn't even halfway through her first glass.

"Enough about me," Lillian said. "Is being a woman in academia as much of a pain in the ass as being a woman in hospital administration?"

"It has its moments. Sometimes, it's nice to lock myself in the lab with my phone on voicemail. Then, I'm alone with my thoughts — and my ever-loving bacteria."

"Here's to bacteria," Lillian slurred, raising her glass and taking a long swallow. "And here's to yeast, too, while we're at it." She drank again. "I'll bet Matt had a tough time convincing you to come here."

"He can be very persuasive. Ruth's condition is fascinating, but I've painted myself into a corner. Miriam expects me to stay with Ruth until she can be discharged, but that won't be for a week. At least my chairman did me a favor by giving me a weekend off."

"No kidding. What does Dr. Big Bucks have to say?"

"You mean Buckram?"

Lillian rubbed her fingers together to indicate money. "He loves that cash."

"I believe it. He wants Ruth and me gone. He'd kick us out now if he could."

"Oh, he can do it, all right. The hospital board will back him on whatever he wants to do."

Anne slammed her fork down. "If they force Ruth out and she dies, the family could sue for a fortune."

"The Morehouses? Sue? The word isn't in their dictionary. They'd view the board's decision as God's will. Your best bet is University Hospital."

"You're probably right, but I'm not looking forward to confronting Miriam on that. Flexibility isn't her strong suit."

By the time dessert came, Lillian had already downed a second bottle of wine. Helping Lillian out to the car, Anne managed to swipe her keys and driver's license from her purse before setting her in the passenger seat, where she promptly passed out. It was rough going, but Anne drove her home and assisted her all the way to bed, which left one major problem. She called Drisner.

"Matt, could you do me a favor? Lillian and I went out to dinner and—"

"And she got drunk, you drove her home, and you're wondering if I can drive you back to the hospital. No problem."

"This is a regular thing?" *How the hell does the woman get to work every morning?*

"I'll tell you about it in the car."

***

"Lillian isn't happy here, is she?" Anne asked Matt.

"Not really. The hospital administration is a 'good ol' boy' network, and Lillian is definitely not a good ol' boy. She was trained to do a job and does it damn well, but Buckram gets the credit, and she gets the shaft. She's in a dead-end job and lacks the willpower to leave. So, she drinks. A lot. But only after work."

"What about this relationship she's in?"

Matt shrugged. "She tells me it's with an out-of-towner, but my theory is she's having an affair with someone local. In my opinion, Lillian needs a complete change of venue, but she's afraid of change, so she's trapped here waiting for Mr. Wrong to propose. By the way, I stopped by to see Ruth. Any chance of switching her to oral meds?"

"No way. She'd relapse within a few days. Listeria is uncommon. Most people who get it have an immune deficiency disorder, but I'm not smart enough to know which one she has."

Matt pulled up to the hospital entrance to drop Anne off. "Lillian probably showed you the town's haute cuisine, but if you want a home-cooked meal, grilling's my specialty."

"Thanks, I'll keep that in mind."

***

Anne entered Ruth's room to find Bryan Dunmore, the reporter who'd accosted her in the parking lot, getting an earful from Miriam. He turned and gave Anne a "gotcha" grin. "Hello again, Dr. Mastik."

"This boy claims you told him to talk to us," Miriam said. "Did you do so, Anne?"

"I said no such thing." She glared at Dunmore. "What are you doing in my patient's room?"

Dunmore shrugged. "My boss always says 'get it right or get it first'. I'm trying to do both."

"You're not allowed in here. Please leave."

Ruth sat up in bed and straightened her hospital gown, which had slipped partway down her arm, leaving her shoulder bare. When it slipped again, Ruth made no attempt to lift it. "I do not want him to leave. I enjoy his company."

Anne shot her a stern look. "This is a matter for Miriam and me to decide."

Ruth's eyes flashed. "I am the patient, and he is interested in what I have to say." She tossed her hair from her face and smiled at Dunmore. "Is that not so, Bryan?"

Anne knew that smile well. She had seen it on the faces of scores of teenage girls at dances, at beaches, and on street corners, all in the hope of meeting boys. *If I don't do something now, this could go south fast.*

"You can't barge into a patient's room like this," Anne said. "Now get out before I have Security throw you out."

"Call if you want." He waved a slip of paper. "I've got a pass from Administration. Read it and weep."

Anne grabbed the pass. Typed on official hospital letterhead, it had been signed by Buckram. She stormed out to the nursing station and called the hospital operator.

"This is Doctor Mastik. I need to speak to Dr. Buckram."

"Ms. Petrillo is taking Dr. Buckram's calls this evening," the operator responded.

"No, I need to talk to Dr. Buckram. I happen to know that Ms. Petrillo is unavailable right now."

"I'm sorry. He left instructions that he is not taking any calls tonight."

"Then please pass a message to him. Tell him I know where he lives and where his mistress lives, and I'll be knocking on both those doors within the next thirty minutes, accompanied by a reporter from *The Guardian* — unless he calls the ICU in the next five minutes."

"I...I'm not allowed to interrupt Dr. Buckram on his

evening off, ma'am. I have specific instructions in that regard."

"Your name, please?"

"Edith...Edith Lapeer."

"Listen to me, Ms. Lapeer. You've wasted thirteen valuable seconds of those five minutes. If necessary, I will look up the requisite phone numbers myself and call. I'm trying to spare Dr. Buckram a lot of embarrassment. Please page him to this number. Now."

"But I—"

"Four minutes and twenty-eight seconds, Ms. Lapeer."

"Yes, ma'am. Right away."

Anne paced for four minutes before the call came. "You cut things a bit close, Dr. Buckram."

"I was...occupied."

"I'm sure."

"I don't appreciate your heavy-handed attempt at blackmail."

"Well, I don't appreciate your giving a reporter access to Ruth's room. Have you shared any other medically privileged information with the press?"

"I've told him nothing, not even your patient's condition. I merely allowed him to interview her if she wished to be interviewed. Her hospitalization is of great interest to the community, and I've been besieged by phone calls for the past two days. I felt that any information should come directly from the Morehouses."

"I suspect there's another event of community interest going on as we speak, Dr. Buckram."

"Don't waste your time. *The Guardian*'s owner is on the hospital board and goes to my church. You won't get anything past him."

Anne slowed her breathing to calm down. "You've got your bases covered, don't you?"

"Good night, Dr. Mastik. And tell Lillian to lay off the

sauce before her mouth gets her into any more trouble."

Back in Ruth's room, the scenario had changed. Dunmore was seated and wearing a bemused expression while Ruth and Miriam screamed at each other.

"He is here to talk to me, not you," Ruth cried, "and I want him to stay."

"He is prying into our personal affairs, and I will not allow it."

"I am the patient. He is only asking me how I feel." Ruth turned to the young man. "That is not a family matter, is it, Bryan?"

Miriam raged on before he could answer. "Look at you— half undressed in that gown. Cover yourself up."

Ruth pulled the sheets up over her exposed legs but took her time doing it.

Anne waded in. "This girl is a minor, Mr. Dunmore. Her aunt may not understand the legalities here, but I do. If you do not leave now, then pass or no pass, I'll have you thrown out."

Dunmore threw up his hands in mock self-defense. "Say no more. I'm leaving."

"Bryan, please stay," Ruth wailed.

"Mr. Dunmore, go. Now."

As Anne escorted him out, Ruth cried and beat the pillows with her fists.

"I hope you're happy, Mr. Dunmore," Anne said. "Is that how you were taught to get a story? By playing with a young girl's emotions?"

"Hey, that whole scene wasn't my doing. Those two have been stuck together on that mountain too long. To tell you the truth, I'd hate to be stuck up there with them. So long, lady. I'll get my story from Administration."

Anne suddenly remembered Isaiah. He hadn't been updated all day. She pulled out her cell phone and dialed but got no answer. She tried three more times. Same result.

"Miriam, I'm worried," Anne said when she entered Ruth's room. "Isaiah isn't answering his phone."

"As long as I have known my husband, his snoring would drown out any sound that phone could make. Call him in the morning. He rises with the sun."

Anne curled up in a bed in the doctors' on-call room. But a sense of unease kept her awake. *He might be a heavy sleeper, but if he doesn't answer in the morning, I'm going up there.*

CHAPTER VIII

Clearing his mind from the fog of sleep, Drisner was confused until he figured out that it was his cell phone, not his alarm clock, awakening him at 5:00 a.m. He glanced at the Caller ID.

"What is it, Anne? Is Ruth okay?"

"She's fine, but I'm worried about Isaiah. I called him last night and again this morning, but he's not answering."

"He's probably out in the fields."

"But we told him to keep the phone with him at all times. I don't know, I've got a bad feeling about this."

Drisner sighed. "You want me to drive you up to the mountain?"

"Pick me up in a half hour. I'll be at the main entrance."

By seven, Matt was honking his horn in front of Artemis's shack. When that proved unproductive, he rolled his eyes at Anne, dismounted from the cab, and pounded on Donnard's door until he heard muffled cursing.

"I guess he's awake now," Matt yelled to Anne. If at all possible, Artemis Donnard was even more sullen and uncouth than he had been on Anne's first visit, and the hike proceeded in silence. When they arrived at the bell, Artemis gruffly waved them on and turned back to his shack, presumably to jumpstart his usual noon drinking time.

Anne picked up a rock and rang the bell. No response. She rang it over a dozen more times, and when Isaiah still hadn't appeared, she and Matt exchanged an apprehensive glance. They dashed to the house, but their knock went unanswered. Matt threw open the door, and they rushed in.

A stifling odor hit Anne's nostrils as soon as she entered the dark cabin. She looked around the room: Cell phone on the table, battery light on, nothing disturbed. *Where's Isaiah?*

"Isaiah, are you here?" Matt called out. "It's Anne and Matt."

A low moan seeped out from the bedroom. Anne charged the door, and the two of them burst in to find a haggard-looking Isaiah reaching out from his bed.

Anne rushed over to give him water. "I'll get a stretcher together," Matt yelled as he dashed out.

"Ruth?" was all Isaiah could get out.

"Ruth is okay," Anne said. "She's feeling much better. What happened to you?"

"Our illness...killed my parents...killed my brother... almost killed Ruth."

"We've got to get you to the hospital."

"Die here."

"You won't die. Ruth survived, and she's doing very well." Isaiah shook his head. "Die here.... God's will."

"We're not going through this again. Matt and I are bringing you into town if we have to carry you."

"Does not matter. I am...no longer...important."

"You've got to take care of Ruth. You're her uncle."

"You...you care for Ruth."

"Don't be ridiculous. Where did you two get this crazy idea that I'm going to take care of Ruth?"

For a moment, Isaiah's gaze cleared, and he focused directly on Anne. "God's plan."

"Stop it," Anne yelled. "I won't listen to this anymore."

Isaiah lay back on his bed. His eyes were smoky, his breathing labored, and his hands were ice cold. He didn't have long.

"Ruth...end of lineage.... She is...the last."

"Does this have anything to do with the prophecy?"

Isaiah looked surprised but continued haltingly. "From her shall come the Savior of humanity."

Anne's jaw dropped. "Wait, you really think Ruth will give birth to the Savior?"

He nodded.

Pure crazy. How do I argue with that? "Okay, then that's all the more reason to live. You're the one who must protect her. Stay with me."

Isaiah's lids drooped, and his eyes rolled up briefly before they flicked open, staring right at Anne.

"Swear! Swear you will care for Ruth."

"I already promised Miriam."

"Promise *me*."

Exasperated, Anne started to blurt out a promise, but the words stuck in her throat. This was no idle schoolyard pledge. She felt something sobering about Isaiah's deathbed request.

"You hesitate," Isaiah murmured.

"Are you asking me to be her doctor, or is this something more?"

Isaiah's eyes spoke for him.

Anne uttered each word carefully. "Do you expect me to take care of Ruth if you and Miriam die?"

He nodded deliberately.

Anne shuddered. "I can't do that. I've got...a condition. I'm not up to it." Roger's hurtful words blared in her head: *You want a kid? You don't even have time to put into our marriage. How the hell are you going to take care of a kid?*

"You are," Isaiah said. "Trust yourself. We trust you."

"I'm the first stranger your family has had contact with for three hundred years. What makes you so sure I'm trustworthy?"

"Chosen. By God. Promise."

Anne was stunned into momentary silence. "God couldn't have chosen me. I'm not religious. I don't even believe in God."

"Not now, but you will." He coughed. "Promise.... Please.... No time."

Anne spoke carefully, weighing each word. "I swear I will do my best to care for Ruth."

"Forever?"

Anne paused. "Forever."

Peace washed over Isaiah's face. "Then God's grace be on...."

And he breathed his last.

***

There were questions that had to be answered before Anne left the mountain. She called Miriam.

"Isaiah is very ill," Anne lied. "I'm afraid he might not make it. Matt and I are trying to help him, but you must tell me everything you can about the prophecy."

"What did Isaiah say?"

"He made me pledge I'd take care of Ruth forever."

Anne could hear Miriam's steely reserve cracking over the phone. "Then he is dying."

"I'm so sorry."

"It is God's will."

"Miriam, both you and Isaiah have made me swear to care for Ruth. Your whole family is susceptible to an infection that's been killing you off for years. If I'm going to figure this out and help Ruth, I need all the information I can get. Please, tell me whatever you can."

"You will think us all mad."

"I promise I won't."

"Our ancestor, Joshua Morehouse, and his followers fled to America three centuries ago; we know not from where. They were persecuted for their beliefs and were driven out of many communities until Joshua found the mountaintop. There, we have been free to live our lives according to his interpretation of the Laws of Moses. Joshua said that if we followed those Laws faithfully, our lineage would eventually die out, and the last of us would be a woman who would give birth to the Savior of humanity."

"What are these Laws?"

"We eat no meat or product of any animal, we keep our bodies uncontaminated by blood in any form, and we stay away from those who are not of the community."

"Why?"

"To maintain our sanctity before God."

"How do I fit into this?"

"Someone must care for Ruth after we die. It was foretold that a woman healer would be the final protector."

Now things are falling into place. "Why must you die?"

"It is our fate to die young. As the generations pass, our age of death gets younger and younger. I feared that Ruth would not reach her childbearing years. Then you came and gave me hope."

"But if Ruth is the last Morehouse alive, and you can't marry outside of the family, how will she conceive?"

"God will provide."

I can see where this is leading. "If you can't consume animals, why do you have a horse and sheep up here?"

"For work and clothing."

"If Ruth is so important, I need to take her to Charlottesville with me. Eden doesn't have the facilities to properly diagnose her condition."

"No. Our agreement is that she stays here until she is better then home. She is better, and she needs to go home. Now."

"If she goes home now, she'll probably get re-infected unless I find out why she can't fight this infection."

"I am afraid for her. None of us has even gone this far from the mountain before. To go to Charlottesville—I cannot allow it. I will soon lose my husband. Are you now asking me to lose the only other person I have left?"

"You won't be losing her. I'll bring her back home as soon as she is well enough. I promise."

"If Ruth leaves, rest assured that I will never see her again." Miriam hung up and didn't pick up when Anne called back.

***

Neither Anne nor Matt said a word on the long ride back to the hospital. Anne mulled over a dozen different ways to break the news, but she always came back to the central question—Why?—for which she had no answer.

Anne walked into Ruth's room, steeling herself for what was to follow. "There's something I have to tell you both."

Miriam sat, Bible closed on her lap, and stared stone-faced out the window, expecting the worst. Ruth sat up in bed, looking back and forth between the two women's faces, bewilderment showing on her face.

Miriam hasn't told her that Isaiah was dying. Poor girl.

When Anne told them Isaiah had died, Miriam held her grief in as much as she could. Even as she continued to stare straight ahead, hands immobile in her lap, the tears rolled down her cheeks, but she made no effort to wipe her face.

Ruth, however, seemed shattered. She fell back into her bed and buried her face in the pillow, soaking it with tears, her body shaking with sobs.

Anne glanced at the impassive Miriam. *Can't you see the girl needs comforting? Is that not in your repertoire?*

Anne sat next to Ruth, who sat up and sobbed onto Anne's shoulder. Anne again looked at Miriam, hoping she would take over and comfort Ruth, but she continued to stare out the window. Finally, Anne let Ruth go and approached Miriam.

"Go to Ruth," she whispered harshly. "She needs you."

Miriam turned her face to Anne, her expression pitiful. "I cannot."

"For God's sake, stop thinking about yourself and your prophecy. You're no longer an aunt to this girl. You're her mother, whether you want to be or not. Start acting like one."

Miriam put her hands to her face and sobbed. "I don't know how."

"Go. Hold her. It's the only way you'll learn."

Miriam dried her eyes and stood up hesitantly.

Anne shook her head. *Miriam's faith might bring her closer to God, but it distances her from those she loves.*

Miriam sat on the bed and put her arms around Ruth, stiffly at first but then drawing her close. As if having waited years for this level of comfort, Ruth hugged her aunt. Finally, Miriam's façade cracked, and they broke down in each other's arms.

As Anne headed out the door, she almost collided with a pretty teenage girl with short, pink-streaked blonde hair.

"Excuse me, ma'am. Is this Ruth Morehouse's room?"

"Yes, but I don't think she wants any visitors right now. She just learned that her uncle died."

The girl's hands flew to her mouth. "Oh my God, I'm so sorry. Please tell her Mary Beth came to say hello and tell her how sorry I am that Isaiah died."

"How do you know Ruth?" Anne asked, suddenly suspicious. I didn't think the Morehouses knew anybody in town."

"I'm Mary Beth Stendahl. Ruth is my best friend."

"You're the cardiologist's daughter?"

The girl nodded. "My dad told me Ruth was in the hospital. I wanted to see her."

Anne held up a finger. "Give me a minute."

Anne went back into the room and closed the door behind her. Miriam and Ruth were teary-eyed but calmer, still clinging to each other.

"Ruth, you have a friend outside—Mary Beth. Do you want to see her?"

Ruth's face lit up, then she dried her tears on her hospital gown. "Oh, yes, yes. Please."

Miriam knit her brows. "Who is Mary Beth?"

"A friend." Ruth's offhand tone contained an edge of nervousness.

"You have never told me about this friend."

"I did not think you needed to know."

"Perhaps this would be a good time to be introduced. Let her in, Anne."

Mary Beth wore cutoffs and a pink spaghetti-strap top, her bare midriff displaying a pierced navel, and her makeup straight out of *Seventeen*. She looked like a typical teenage girl, making the contrast between her and Ruth even more striking as the two embraced.

"I should like to meet your friend now," Miriam interrupted.

"I'm Mary Beth, Mrs. Morehouse. Dr. Stendahl's daughter."

"How long have you two been friends?"

Mary Beth looked at Ruth and beamed. "It seems like forever. I know it was before, um, before Ruth's parents died. We usually get together in the woods where the properties meet."

"What do your parents think about you socializing with one of us?"

"I told them once when I first met Ruth. They didn't think we should be friends, so I never mentioned it again."

"At least Ruth is not the only one disobeying her parents."

If Mary Beth was offended, she didn't show it, but Ruth's face colored as she addressed Miriam. "How do you think I feel, all alone on that mountain? I am not a child. I need someone my own age to talk to."

"What do you two talk about?" Miriam asked stiffly.

"Things," Ruth said, shrugging.

"What sorts of things?"

Mary Beth and Ruth glanced at each other, but neither answered.

"Ruth Morehouse, what do you talk about?"

"Clothes, music, books. Things."

Miriam shook her head and sighed. "I suppose you are right. I cannot expect you to be satisfied solely with the company of elders."

Ruth grinned, but if Miriam expected a thank you, she didn't get one.

"Well," Anne said, "why don't Miriam and I step out for a minute?"

***

"She is becoming defiant," Miriam exclaimed as she and Anne entered the visitors' lounge.

"She is becoming a teenager. That's a reality you must face. Sooner or later, whether you like it or not, Ruth will come down from that mountain." Anne squeezed Miriam's hand and put her arm around her shoulders. "Don't be afraid of Ruth growing up."

As the two women sat quietly together, Anne received a call from University Hospital's main number. She excused herself and walked out into the hallway.

"Anne, this is Dr. Robert Rothberg."

Boy, am I in trouble now! Rothberg never referred to himself as Robert. Unless he was pissed.

"Bob, I meant to —"

"For the past four days, I've been managing the consult service, plus taking care of the department, plus covering your research without knowing what the hell I'm talking about."

"Bob, I'm very sorry, but — "

"Plus," he continued, "I've been worried sick about you. I'd have no idea at all where you were if Dr. Garaud hadn't called and — "

"Evan called? When?"

Rothberg paused. "It's Evan, is it? Mm-hmm," he muttered. "Do I sense a touch of romance in the air?"

Anne was glad that Bob couldn't see her blush. "We're friends, that's all. What did he say?"

"He was looking for you, but *he* had to tell *me* where you were. Now please explain why you've spent the last three days taking care of one patient out in the boonies."

Anne summarized the last few days, which seemed to calm Bob down.

"If the aunt won't allow a transfer," he said, "get Protective Services involved."

"That would destroy her trust in me."

"Well, do something and do it soon. I'll cover for another three days, and that's it."

Something had to be done. Anne walked back into the visitor's lounge.

"I can only stay another three days. I'm needed back in Charlottesville," Anne said as she closed the door behind her.

"And you think Ruth should go with you, of course."

Anne nodded.

"You are right. Ruth must go with you."

"You agree?"

"I now realize there is no alternative."

"I want you to come with us. I'll need your consent for any procedures, even to admit Ruth to the hospital."

"I will sign whatever forms you need, but I must stay and bury my husband. I will not leave our home." Miriam lowered her eyes. "I mean, my home."

"But Ruth will need you. She'll be alone in Charlottesville."

"She'll have you."

"I'm not her mother."

Miriam scowled. "Neither am I. For the past three years, I have tried to be her mother. Three years of anger, fighting, and tears. She hates me for what I am, and she hates me for what I am not. One thing I am not, and never can be, is her mother."

Anne reached out and touched Miriam's shoulder. "You're learning. You just need more time."

"There will be no more time. I shall stay here."

Anne started to speak, but Miriam held up her hand and cut her off. "My mind is made up. We must talk to Ruth."

***

When Miriam and Anne returned, Ruth seemed animated and contented as she and Mary Beth held hands and chatted.

Poor Ruth, Anne thought. Forced by centuries-old tradition to live sequestered from children her own age, but at least she had found a soulmate in Mary Beth.

"Anne and I have talked," Miriam began. "She has responsibilities in Charlottesville and cannot stay here much longer. She feels that you need specialized care that is unavailable here. It is a difficult decision for me, but I believe you should go with her to Charlottesville."

Mary Beth squealed and hugged Ruth, but Ruth was strangely quiet. *For all her talk about independence, Ruth was probably terrified of leaving Eden Mountain.*

"Will you go with me, Miriam?" Ruth asked.

"I must stay here and bury Isaiah."

"Later then? Please?"

"I'll be with you," Anne said. "You'll be fine."

"But it is so far away, so many people."

Mary Beth clapped her hands together. "Think of it as a big adventure. You'll love Charlottesville."

Ruth looked down, rubbing her hands nervously on her legs. "I have never had an adventure before. How long will I be away?"

"A few days," Miriam said. "Perhaps a week. Then you will come home."

"I need to talk to Mary Beth," Anne said. "Alone. It would

be best if the two of you talked as well."

Anne and Mary Beth convened in the visitors' lounge.

"Now that Miriam isn't around," Anne said, "can you tell me how long you and Ruth have been friends?"

"Swear you won't tell?"

"Cross my heart and hope to die."

Mary Beth gave her a confused look.

"Sorry," Anne said. "An expression from when I was little. Yes, I swear I won't tell."

Mary Beth's eyes glistened. "Since we were five."

"That's a long time to keep a secret. You two seem very close."

Mary Beth thought for a moment before she spoke. "Dr. Mastik, when you were little, did you have an imaginary friend?"

Anne was taken aback by the directness of the question. "I haven't thought about her for a long time, but I did. I called her Tamara."

"What was she like?"

"Pretty, blonde, and —"

"Not like that. What was she like as a friend?"

Anne recollected details of her childhood she hadn't thought about for decades. "We played house, or hide-and-seek, or anything else I wanted to play. She was never mean, never argued with me, always laughed at my jokes."

"Did you tell her your secrets?"

"Every one of them."

"You knew she would keep them all to herself?"

"Of course. She was imaginary."

"Did your parents know about her?"

"I never told them, but I'm sure they knew. There was a table in my room with a little tea set for two. They must have overheard our conversations."

"Was it fun having a secret friend that nobody knew but you?"

"It was wonderful," Anne said, a wistful smile playing across her face. "I would hide under the blanket with a flashlight so we could talk without anyone hearing. I never felt alone as long as I had Tamara."

"How old were you when she went away? I mean, when you stopped believing in her."

"Maybe six."

"That's what Ruth and I are like. We play together, and we tell each other everything, and no one else will ever know our secrets. But there's a big difference. Ruth is real, and she'll never go away."

"You two are way out in the woods. What do you do out there?"

"When we were little, we played games. Sometimes we switched clothes. It was fun to wear Ruth's homemades, and she liked trying on my stuff. But now, we just talk. I lend her some of my books, and we discuss them. I really like that. The girls in my school don't like to do that."

"You ever talk about boys?"

Mary Beth nodded. "Ruth asks a lot about boys. She wants to know what it feels like to, you know, be with a boy."

"Sex?"

"Oh my God, never." Mary Beth blushed. "She would never, you know, do anything like that. Neither would I. She's never even talked to a boy. She just wants to know how it feels to, like, hold hands, what guys and girls talk about, what we do together, stuff like that. Lately, she's been asking what it's like to be kissed. It's kinda cute. Like having a little sister, but one who's my age."

"Does she talk about the Bible?"

"Sometimes. But she's not, like, a fanatic or anything. We talk about God and why we're here. We never get too heavy about it, although Ruth seems to think there's something special about her." Mary Beth cast her eyes down. "I'm worried about her, Dr. Mastik. I've never seen her this sick. Is she going to be okay?"

"She's turned the corner. But I'm worried she could get reinfected. For some reason, her body can't fight off this infection."

"Can I get it?"

"I don't think so. Besides, it's not transmitted from person to person. You get it by eating contaminated food."

Mary Beth squirmed. "What kind of food?"

"Usually spoiled milk and cheese."

Mary Beth stood up. "Um, I've got to go."

Anne grabbed her hand. "What's wrong?"

"I can't tell you."

"If this is about Ruth's illness, you've got to tell me."

"I can't. I promised. Please, let me go."

"You can't keep a secret if it means Ruth might die. That's not what a friend would do."

Mary Beth wavered for a moment, then sat down, her eyes moist. "I didn't mean to hurt her."

"Of course you didn't," Anne said soothingly. "What happened?"

"When we were little, Ruth told me she was a vegan. She wouldn't eat meat or milk or eggs, and that was cool. But when we got older, sometimes we'd talk about going out on dates for, like, pizza or hamburgers or ice cream and stuff. Well, Ruth didn't know what any of that stuff was 'cause she wasn't allowed to eat it. This past year, she kept asking me to bring her, you know, like a slice of pizza."

"What about hamburgers?"

"No way. She would never, ever even *touch* meat, and she wouldn't eat pizza if it had pepperoni or sausage on it."

"But she ate cheese?"

"Yeah, but it's supposed to be a secret. She'd be so mad if she found out I told you."

"That's okay, Mary Beth. This is important. Did she ever

eat ice cream?"

"She likes ice cream, and she really, really likes chocolate ice cream. Even if it's melted, she'd drink it right out of the container."

Anne's jaw nearly fell open. "Did she do that recently?"

"Maybe a week ago."

That was it! Everything! Ruth's illness, the family's isolation, and maybe even the prophecy itself.

"Mary Beth, you've been a tremendous help."

"You won't tell Ruth I told you?"

"No, but I have to tell her aunt."

"Oh, no! Please don't do that. She'll be furious."

"Don't worry. You go home. I'll handle Miriam."

Mary Beth's awkward smile betrayed her trepidation as she turned and walked away.

Anne raced to the phone. "Matt, it's Anne. We must talk. Now. Where can we meet?"

***

There was nothing special about the interior of Belle's Diner. It looked like all the other family-owned diners in thousands of small towns all over the United States, with revolving red vinyl stools lined up in front of a faux marble laminate countertop, behind which harried waitresses yelled orders to the harried owner and assistant cook. Next to picture windows clouded with ages of accumulated grease and cigarette smoke were booths with matching tables and benches, the ripped seats patched with silver vinyl tape.

Matt and Anne sat in one such booth, where Matt absentmindedly picked up a plastic-covered menu, scowled at the all-too-familiar choices, and signaled Belle for a cup of coffee.

"I've got a lead on the significance of the prophecy," Anne said.

"Really?"

"Ruth's family has some sort of hereditary immune

disorder. They can't fight off bacterial infections because their immune systems don't recognize the bacteria as foreign invaders. Miriam told me about the group's founder, Joshua Morehouse. He must have figured that out and set up the rules to keep them isolated from infection."

"Who knew about immunity three centuries ago? The pathogen theory of disease didn't exist for another hundred and fifty years."

"Joshua probably saw his kinfolk dying in towns and cities — breeding zones for infectious disease — but when they were quarantined, they survived."

"Don't be ridiculous. Bacteria are everywhere. How could he hope to keep them segregated from the entire world?"

"By shutting them up on a mountain and telling them it's God's will. By telling them that being vegan was God's will and that if they followed God's Laws faithfully, one of their descendants would birth the Savior. Read Deuteronomy. It's full of so-called Laws of God that were developed for health reasons. Cattle with tuberculosis get hardened lymph nodes in their necks. If you butcher them by slitting their throats like the Bible says, the knife gets stuck, the meat isn't kosher, and you've got to throw it out. Shellfish transmit hepatitis, pork carries trichinosis, and rabbits and rodents carry the plague and tularemia. All those are forbidden foods. Not to mention the animals that carry brucellosis. The list goes on. There are dozens of zoonoses — diseases carried by animals — that people can avoid simply by being vegan."

"So by sticking them up on the mountain — "

"It keeps them away from human contagions: smallpox, polio, bubonic plague, typhus, influenza, measles — all diseases of large concentrations of people. They exist in societies where people rapidly move from one urban center to another. Stay away from urban centers, start your own commune in the mountains, and you avoid the infections."

"Then what went wrong? Why'd they die off?"

"Without crossbreeding to dilute harmful genes, the Morehouse immune defect became more prominent over the generations, and they lost resistance. Now it hardly takes anything at all to tip them over. They succumb to diseases that most of us would shrug off." Anne made sure Matt was looking at her before she continued. "If we don't pinpoint the genetic defect, Miriam and Ruth will die. Maybe not tomorrow or next year, but soon enough."

"If these traditions keep the family from infections," Matt said with a smirk, "how did Ruth get sick?"

"Mary Beth Stendahl has been sneaking her forbidden food for years. Most of the time, it was cooked enough to kill any bacteria, but Ruth recently swigged down a container of melted chocolate ice cream—a prime source of Listeria."

"Then, the prophecy—"

"Has nothing to do with divine intervention. It's a rational solution to a problem of survival, made by a man of great intelligence and observational power."

Matt sipped his coffee, then set the cup down. "What are you going to do?"

"Ruth needs an academic evaluation so we can figure out her disorder. I've got to talk to Miriam."

"Going to tell her your theory?"

"Yes, but I must be careful. To her, the prophecy is a matter of faith, not rationality. If I set science over God, I'll lose her." Anne stopped to catch her breath. "I've got to go."

"What about our barbecue date?" Matt called out as she left.

She spun around. "Soon. I promise."

***

During the trip back to the hospital, Anne focused on what to say to Miriam and Ruth. Miriam would be furious that Ruth had disobeyed the prophecy, so Anne would have to defuse that issue. But no matter what, she had to make Ruth understand the importance of the prophecy's dietary guidelines. Adolescent rebellion was always dangerous if it led to risk-taking. In this situation, it could be as deadly as reckless driving.

Her phone rang as she was about to enter the hospital.

"Dr. Mastik, this is Reverend Wainstock. We need to talk about Ruth Morehouse."

"I'm sorry, Reverend, but I can't tell you anything about her case. Privacy issues."

"I understand, but I've filed a petition with the court for a restraining order against Miriam and Isaiah Morehouse for child endangerment and neglect. You've probably committed malpractice by not pursuing such charges earlier."

Anne stopped short. "I beg your pardon. What makes you think Miriam has been neglectful?"

"In spite of repeated efforts by Dr. Drisner and yourself, she delayed hospitalization of the child."

"Ruth's admission was delayed, but only by a few days."

"Vitally important days. By the time she was hospitalized, she was critically ill. Her condition had advanced into septic shock, and she could have died as a result."

"Who told you that?"

"I have my sources. The girl needs to be made a ward of the court, and the sooner, the better."

"I seriously believe it is not in the best interests of the child, who is recovering from a life-threatening illness, by the way, to throw her into the middle of a court battle. I have spoken at length with Miriam, and I know her to be genuinely concerned about Ruth's welfare. Her objections to treatment are of a religious nature. Surely a man of your background can appreciate the significance of that."

"The girl is a minor. Her aunt cannot make a decision, religious or otherwise, that puts the girl's life at risk. What if she makes another decision that jeopardizes her life?"

"I assure you, Reverend, that I will take all steps necessary to make sure that doesn't happen. I can also assure you that as Ruth's guardian, Miriam is making the best decisions she can for Ruth."

"Ha! What makes you think she is Ruth's guardian?"

"She's her aunt." *This man is impossible!*

"I checked at the courthouse. She's never signed guardianship papers."

"But she's Ruth's only living next of kin."

"Nonetheless, she has no legal right to make crucial decisions on Ruth's behalf."

"Well, someone has to." If Anne could have reached through the phone and strangled Wainstock, she would have.

"I have petitioned the court to become her ward. At least until this issue is settled."

"That's crazy! What possible interest do you have in Ruth's well-being? You've never even met her."

"I have an important interest. I am concerned about her immortal soul. That poor girl has spent her life as a prisoner, trapped up on that mountain with an incestuous cult of blasphemers and heretics. I toss and turn at night, worried about her being condemned to eternal damnation for the foul lies with which they are filling her innocent, naïve head. To me, there is nothing — absolutely nothing — more important than the salvation of that young girl's soul. Good day, Dr. Mastik."

Dumbstruck, Anne drifted into the elevator, pressed the button, and stared blankly as the doors closed in front of her.

***

"That Paulist!" Miriam snarled so vehemently that three nurses turned to stare. "I knew he was up to something."

Anne ushered Miriam into the family conference room, then shut and locked the door.

"Why do you call Wainstock a Paulist?"

"All I can say is that my people have...differences...with

the reverend and his church."

Another mystery, but there were more pressing issues.

"Miriam, we need to talk. I have the answer to Ruth's illness. But you must agree to something."

"What?"

"That you won't get angry with Ruth."

"What did she do?" Miriam's mouth drew up tightly as her brow wrinkled.

"I need you to promise."

"Why?"

"Because forgiveness is part of love."

Miriam's face softened. "That girl let me hold her in my arms for the first time since the funeral of her parents. I will do nothing to jeopardize her affection."

Anne took a deep breath. "Ruth ate some dairy products. Mary Beth gave her cheese and ice cream."

Miriam fell into a chair. "Why would Ruth do that? She knows it is wrong."

Anne sat down and put her hand on Miriam's shoulder. "She's only a child. She doesn't understand right and wrong the way we do.'

Miriam looked at Anne. "She disobeyed God's Law."

"And she suffered for it. She doesn't need you to punish her too."

Miriam appeared lost in thought, then she turned to Anne. "I cannot believe God would punish a child thusly."

Anne was shocked. *Was Miriam's faith wavering?*

"Ruth's illness is more complicated than a punishment from God," Anne said. "It may be the key to the origins of the prophecy."

Anne recounted her theory of the Morehouse genetic disorder and the prophecy's origin. When she finished, Miriam sneered.

"That may have been true if the prophecy were three

hundred years old," Miriam said, "but the origins of our beliefs do not go back centuries; they go back millennia."

"But you told me —"

"I didn't want to tell you earlier, but we are an ancient religion." Miriam glanced about the room. "Are you certain that no one can hear us?"

"This room is designed for private conversations between physicians and patient families. It's soundproof. Even someone right outside the door can't hear us."

"There is nothing I can tell you about myself and Ruth that will be more confidential than this, but my only choice is to trust you. What I am about to say has not been breathed to another soul outside of our family."

"Whatever you say will stay between the two of us."

"There is a scroll, an ancient holy manuscript. It is our most precious possession and the reason we have spent two millennia on the run. It is our own Gospel, written by James the Just, the brother of our Lord, in Aramaic and Hebrew, not in any false translation. It holds the secrets of the prophecy spoken from his own lips. Since its writing, it has been sealed in a clay vessel, its contents passed on, mouth to mouth, for two thousand years."

"Miriam, there are historians and archeologists who would consider that book to be a valuable historical treasure."

"It must be kept a secret until the prophecy is fulfilled. The Paulists would destroy the scroll if they knew of its existence, which is the reason we keep the prophecy itself a secret. You will speak no more of this to anyone."

"Okay, okay. I get it."

"Good. Let us go back to Ruth's room. I believe she has learned her lesson."

As they rounded the corner from the family conference room, Anne noticed the ICU clerk wheel her chair away from the phone bank. The clerk smiled sweetly and nodded. *Hmm, that's a first.*

With her hand on the door latch, Anne peeked over her shoulder and saw the clerk wheel her chair back to the phone bank, pick up the headset, and dial.

CHAPTER IX

Isaiah's funeral began as the summer sun set, the Appalachians casting their broad shadows across the treeless mountaintop, where a small party of mourners had gathered to lay his body to rest in the family graveyard already filled with his ancestors.

Anne had worked hard to organize the service. After Miriam objected to using local ministers, Anne had enlisted a group of Mennonites from a nearby town to dig the grave and preach the service. Ruth was still too ill to be discharged, so Mary Beth and Lillian had agreed to stay with her, leaving Anne as the only woman present to comfort Miriam.

As Isaiah's casket was lowered, Anne grasped Miriam's arm, and the two women drew closer. As the first shovelfuls of dirt fell onto the casket, Anne put her arm around Miriam's shoulder, and they both wept.

After the ceremony, Miriam led Anne past the far corner of the cemetery, away from the fields and deserted farmhouses.

"There is something that you need to see, but it is part of our secret."

Miriam brought her to the highest point on the mountain, marked by a towering granite outcropping that was split by a two-foot-wide fissure. Miriam pointed to the fissure. "We are going in there. You first."

"No way. I can't fit in there."

"Of course, you can. Go sideways."

Anne shook her head but reluctantly obliged, advancing inch by inch. Three or four feet in, the narrow path made a sharp turn. Anne could no longer see outside, and the cleft narrowed so that she had to hold her hands in front of her face to protect it from scraping against the rock. Mere inches now separated the back of her head and shoulders from the jagged edges. Then she bumped into a waist-high projection. "I can't go any farther. There's a bulge in the rock blocking my way."

"You are almost there. You can get past it if you draw in your stomach. I'm coming in."

Anne shuddered, sucked in her stomach, and pushed past the protrusion. She found herself in a roughly circular chamber no more than six feet in diameter, with a smooth floor that sloped gradually toward the cleft. Far above, through a vertical continuation of the fissure, she spied a tiny slice of indigo sky.

Miriam bumped into Anne as she pushed through the opening, the two of them almost filling the chamber.

Damn. This is what it must feel like in a mausoleum. Anne began hyperventilating.

"Slow your breathing, and the feeling will pass," Miriam reassured her. "We will be out in a few minutes. I must show you something."

Miriam put a candle on a small ledge and lit it using a matchbook from her skirt pocket. The flickering light illuminated the rock face, which faded to blackness where the rock met the sky.

"There's nothing here," Anne said. "Can we leave now?"

Miriam pointed to a hollowed-out vestibule at their feet, protected by the small overhang. "Reach in there."

Anne extended her arm warily, afraid of disturbing any animal that might be nesting in the recess. Then she touched something smooth and hard. "I feel something."

"Take it out carefully."

Anne pulled out a two-foot-tall clay jar so heavy that Miriam had to help her. The vessel was capped by a heavy clay cover, sealed on with a thick layer of wax. The jar was unadorned except for archaic lettering scratched into its surface.

"Inside are the writings I told you about, sealed inside shortly after being written. We know their contents only through the oral history passed down over generations."

"Can we peek inside? It might be nothing but powder by now."

"It still exists because God has willed it. There will come a time when its existence will be known only to you. You must keep this knowledge to yourself."

"Does Ruth know about it?"

"She is still a girl and does not mind her words. If she knew its message, she might tell the wrong people. She has been told that the prophecy is the reason we stay on Eden Mountain, nothing more. We have been its guardians for two millennia, and when Ruth is the only one left, it will be time to show it to the world. There is something else."

Miriam took two envelopes from her blouse and gave one to Anne. "After I die, this letter will make you Ruth's guardian. I will leave another copy here in case that one is lost." Miriam pushed the clay pot back into the vestibule and slipped the envelope behind it.

"Miriam, I—"

"Say nothing more. It has been agreed upon. Now go. I will follow."

No point arguing. Anne sucked her stomach in and slipped back through the cleft, which turned pitch-black when Miriam blew out the candle.

"The contents of that jar are more precious than any treasure you can imagine," Miriam said as they trekked back to the funeral site. "There are people who would kill to get their hands on it. I believe some already have."

"You mean your sister and brother-in-law?"

Miriam nodded. "And Isaiah."

"But Isaiah contracted a disease. He wasn't murdered."

"You yourself said this disease is not borne from person to person but by contaminated meat, poultry, and milk. Except for Ruth's indiscretion, we do not eat those foods. When we brought Ruth to the hospital, Isaiah was alive and healthy. How did he die so quickly?"

The thought stunned Anne. "I don't know."

"I believe he was poisoned."

"Then let's stop the funeral. I'll order an autopsy."

"It is against our law. His body must not be desecrated."

"Let me at least draw blood for testing. If Isaiah was murdered—"

"I will not stop this funeral."

Anne stopped in her tracks. "Miriam, if there is suspicion of murder, it's the law. There has to be an investigation."

"I obey God's law. There is no law in this town for us." Miriam gestured for Anne to keep moving. "You see what Reverend Wainstock is doing."

"He's bluffing. There's no way he can get custody of Ruth."

"The corruption in this town would astound you."

"Don't be ridiculous. He'd never win if you appeal."

"That would take time and money, neither of which I have. I would be forced to sell the mountain, which might expose the scroll's existence."

"You think this is a plot to gain possession of the mountain?"

"Powerful people covet our property. The town has been trying to take our property for as long as I can remember. Once I die, they will try to gain control over Ruth, which is why I want you to care for her." Miriam turned to Anne, her eyes pleading. "You must take her away from here if I die."

Anne started to speak but was cut short by Matt's arrival. "We've almost finished with the burial. Where'd you two go?"

"I was not feeling well," Miriam answered.

"Come on. I'll drive us all back to town."

"I must stay here tonight."

"Are you sure you want to be up here alone?" Anne asked.

"I still feel my husband's spirit. I need to spend this night with him."

"Then I'll stay with you," Anne said.

"No. Ruth cannot be left alone," Miriam said. "Someone must stay with her."

"I could sleep in the on-call room," Matt said, "and Lillian and Mary Beth could stay in Ruth's room."

Miriam turned to Anne. "I don't think so. What if something happens to Ruth?"

"I have my cell phone," Anne said, "and Matt can handle any emergencies as well as I can."

"I will not make good company," Miriam said apologetically.

Anne grasped her hand. "I won't mind. You shouldn't be alone tonight."

***

Anne wandered onto the field next to Miriam's house. The darkness surrounding her was almost palpable. The sky was thick with stars, silhouetting the trees at the forest's edge. Anne closed her eyes to focus on the smells of the forest that surrounded her.

She hadn't felt this sensation since camping with Roger when they were still in love. Hiking through the woods had been so easy before MS, before she grew fearful of the summer heat, before every rock and root was a trap waiting to be sprung on her clumsy legs. They used to crawl naked into their sleeping bags, too roiled by passion to bother pitching a tent, and then they'd make love under the stars until the fire turned to embers. That life felt so close tonight but was a million miles away.

Anne strolled back to the cabin and sat down on the porch next to Miriam, each in her own rocking chair, between them a big bowl of fruit. The fire offered barely enough light for Anne to make out Miriam's face.

"You never told me why you called Reverend Wainstock a Paulist," Anne said.

"We are a community of Ebionites, the original followers of Jesus. For us, Jesus was flesh and blood, born of man and woman. Because of His perfect righteousness, He was chosen by God to teach the world His laws and was sacrificed on the cross for the sins of the world. We follow strict veganism and avoid the ingestion of blood to show respect for the sanctity of all life, and we adhere to the teachings of Moses. Paul and his followers — the Paulists — betrayed us."

"How did they betray you?"

"They brought forth a new religion, not based on the words of Jesus but on those of Paul. And they disparaged the Law."

"How long were you and Isaiah married?"

"Almost twenty years."

"And before Ruth's illness, you never spent a day apart?"

"Not one." Miriam wiped a tear from her eye. "That is why I cannot go to Charlottesville. I must stay here with Isaiah."

***

Miriam lay in bed, staring at the ceiling and listening to the sounds of the night.

Anne was right. This was the first night in twenty years I sleep alone, the first night in this bed without Isaiah by my side.

The sadness and emptiness pressed down on her so hard that it made her heart ache. After an hour, she quietly got out of bed and walked outside.

The darkness didn't frighten Miriam. To her, it was an old friend, as familiar as her furniture, perhaps more so because the furniture, like everything else made by man, changed with time.

But the darkness remained immutable, unchanging, as close and as comforting as the presence of God.

She walked with confident steps. Even though the newly risen moon dimly illuminated the mountaintop, she knew every path, every root, every rock. She looked up at the familiar patterns of stars as they wheeled around the sky. *From somewhere up there, Isaiah is looking down on me.* She could feel his presence outside more so than in the house, which overflowed with painful reminders of his absence.

Miriam stopped. Something had changed. She knew the sounds of the forest, especially in the dark when her ears were focused. Holding her breath, she ignored the accelerated beating of her heart and tried to determine what was different. The wind still blew through the trees, gently rustling their leaves, but—Miriam realized what she *didn't* hear.

The crickets had ceased chirping.

She looked around wildly, eyes straining to see in the blackness. *Was a human form moving toward her?*

"Isaiah, is that you? Isaiah?" But then came the crunch of shoes on gravel, footsteps coming closer. *There is nothing spectral about this!*

Miriam screamed and ran. But running in the dark was not the same as walking, and she tripped on a rock, falling headlong to the ground.

"Who are you?" she called to the specter. "What are you doing here?"

The intruder picked up a large rock, heaved it over his head, and advanced toward her.

"Miriam!" Anne called. "Are you hurt?"

"Anne! Help me!" A heavy thud followed as the man dropped the rock. Then his footsteps rapidly trailed off toward the forest.

"Miriam, keep talking. I can't see you."

Miriam saw the dim light of a kerosene lamp advancing

from the house. "I am over here. Help me. I have fallen."

Anne ran towards Miriam's voice. "What happened? Are you alright?"

Miriam pushed herself up to her knees. "We must get back into the house. Quickly."

"Let me help you up. You're still too unsteady."

"There is somebody out here. We must get back to the house."

As soon as they got into the house, Miriam set about shuttering the windows and barring the doors. Only when the house had been secured did she stop and sit next to the fireplace with Anne.

"It must have been him, the one who killed Isaiah."

"Don't worry. He's gone now."

"He will come back. Maybe not tonight, but he will return."

"What are you talking about?"

Miriam looked at Anne squarely. "He wants to kill me. I saw him pick up a rock, a heavy one, by the sound it made when he dropped it. He was prepared to crack my skull with it when you chased him away." She gripped Anne's arm anxiously. "Ruth is in terrible danger."

Anne grabbed her phone and dialed. "Lillian, is all well there?"

"Everything's great. The girls have been chatting and playing cards all—"

"Ruth is okay?"

"She gets teary, but Mary Beth will give her a hug and let her cry for a while until she feels better. You sound upset."

"Are you in Ruth's room now?"

"I'm right outside the door."

"Can Ruth hear you?"

"No. What's wrong?"

"Someone just tried to kill Miriam."

"Oh, my God! Is she okay?"

"She fell and hit her face, but no serious injury."

"You two need to get out of there."

"Too dangerous to drive around here at night. I'll have Matt pick us up first thing in the morning."

"Do you at least have a gun?"

"No. But the cabin's locked up tight. I think we're safe for the night."

"Is there anything I can do?"

"Just stay with Ruth—and do *not* let her leave that room."

"Will do."

"And Lillian?"

"Yes?"

"Please keep everyone away from her except the nurses. And I mean everyone."

"Of course."

"You're the best. Good night."

***

Lillian glanced down the empty hallway. The only nurse in sight was busy charting at the nurses' station, her back turned. Lillian slipped into the family conference room and locked the door. She fell back onto a couch, drew a small flask from her purse and took a long swig.

"That Goddam sonofabitch," she swore, then took another swallow from the flask before she put it back in her purse and walked back to Ruth's room.

CHAPTER X

The emergency department physician hung his ophthalmoscope on the wall unit, then turned back to Miriam and Anne as he finished writing his note. "I don't see anything that an ice pack and some rest won't cure. A little lower, and you might have fractured your orbit or damaged your eye. How did it happen?"

"It is my own fault. I was outside at night and tripped on a root. When I fell, my face hit a rock."

"Miriam," Anne said, "how can you—"

"I tripped on a root and fell against a stone," Miriam said firmly, her eyes fixed on Anne. "I am sorry my foolishness has caused so much trouble. Please do not embarrass me further."

Anne frowned and turned away. "Whatever you say."

The room went silent as the doctor scribbled a prescription and handed it to Miriam. "One every four hours if the pain gets severe. Call me if you experience headache, dizziness, or any change in vision." He looked at Miriam eye-to-eye. "Or if you have anything else, you need to tell me."

"Thank you," Miriam said as he left the room. Then she tore up the prescription and threw it in the trash.

"Why did you tell him you tripped?"

"I have my reasons."

"But you lied to save someone who tried to kill you and

probably killed your husband."

"I do not want Ruth any more upset. She has enough sadness without worrying about some crazed maniac trying to kill us."

"She'd want you to be protected, though."

"Nobody in Eden will protect me, and I will not leave my house. There are more important considerations than my life."

"You can't be talking about —"

Miriam put her finger to her lips to shush Anne.

"...the scroll," Anne finished in a whisper.

Miriam nodded. "Things have changed. You must now take it with you to Charlottesville."

"Why?"

"It is no longer safe here. I fear that whoever attacked me was after both Ruth and the scroll."

"How can I carry that jar? The two of us could hardly lift it. I don't know who got it into that cave, but I do know that the two of us can't get it out. Maybe Matt could help us."

"No. I do not trust anybody from town to know it exists."

"My friend Gary would help, but I don't think he'd fit. Maybe this man I met a few days ago? He might be willing."

"No," Miriam said flatly. "Not if you've only known him a few days."

"You're not leaving us many options."

"Then we will take the manuscript and leave the jar."

"But you said it's ancient. In this humidity, it will rot in less than a week. It's too risky."

"I don't see any alternative. It is a risk we will have to take. There must be someone in Charlottesville who can care for it."

"The university has a Department of Religious Studies, and I know a professor specializing in ancient biblical languages and manuscripts. I'm sure it will be safe with him."

"Then it is settled. Take Ruth to Charlottesville, and when she is secure in the hospital, bring it to your professor. It will only be out of the jar for a short time."

"I'll call and make arrangements for Ruth's transfer."

"What arrangements?"

"I have to reserve a bed and arrange an ambulance transport."

"You cannot drive her yourself?"

"Not with her IV line, and not right out of the ICU. She needs the safety of an ambulance in case something happens."

Miriam shook her head. "I do not trust an ambulance. Too many people I do not know. Cannot Ruth take the antibiotic as pills?"

"Not absorbed well enough by mouth to treat an infection like this. She could relapse."

"But Ruth gets her medicine every six hours. That is more than enough time to drive her to Charlottesville."

"I still don't feel comfortable transferring her without medical transport."

"What could be worse than what she's already been through? When you came here, you were willing to take her to Charlottesville yourself. The only difference is that she is stronger now."

Drat! Beaten at my own game. "I've got to go." But as Anne turned to leave, she practically bumped into a police officer.

"Morning. Which of you ladies might be Miriam Morehouse?"

"I am she."

"Are you the parent of...." —he scanned his papers—"a minor female, Ruth Morehouse?"

"I am her aunt. Her parents are dead."

"Ma'am, I'm here to serve you a court order remanding Ruth Morehouse into the temporary custody of the Domestic and Juvenile Court of Calhoun County."

Miriam glared at the policeman. "On what basis do you intend to take my child?"

"A complaint's been lodged against you alleging child neglect, ma'am."

"I have always restrained my hand against this girl. Her discipline has always been of a gentle nature."

"I'm sorry, ma'am. I don't know the details of the charges."

"Who has made these charges?" Miriam asked.

"That's privileged information."

"You cannot say who has accused me nor the nature of the allegation, but you wish me to surrender my child? I will do no such thing."

"Officer," Anne said, "I'm Ruth's physician. She is too ill to leave the hospital, and the trauma of forcing her to leave her family would send her into a relapse."

"Ma'am, I'm here to serve the papers. If you have a problem, tell it to the judge."

Miriam seemed ready to say something, but Anne gripped her arm and spoke first. "I understand, Officer. Thank you."

After he left, Miriam jerked her arm from Anne's grasp. "Why did you hold me back? He wishes to take my child away."

"He's only the messenger. This is Wainstock's doing."

Miriam's face tensed. "I told you Ruth was in danger here. That man is evil, and he wields a lot of power."

"Don't worry. He won't be able to make this stick."

"I will not let him try. You will take Ruth away. Quickly."

"We're dealing with a court order, Miriam. Taking Ruth across state lines is tantamount to kidnapping."

"There will come a time to do what must be done," Miriam said, and stormed out of the Emergency Department.

Anne rubbed her temples in a vain attempt to stall off a burgeoning headache. Miriam's request went beyond her usual level of obstinacy, and Anne wasn't about to commit a Federal offense that could land her in jail and get her medical license revoked. Charlottesville would have to wait.

***

Although only early morning, the July sun already heated the concrete as Anne made her way up the dozen steps to the Church of the Righteous Disciples. Between the blazing sun and her multiple sclerosis, she felt like she had lead shackles on. Halfway up, she paused and gathered her energy. She would need all of it when she confronted Wainstock.

Three minutes later, Anne's footsteps echoed noisily against the empty pews as she approached the altar, beyond which lay the administrative offices. As she stopped midway for her body to cool down, Wainstock emerged from his office.

"Hmph," he said with a sneer. "I didn't expect to see you here."

"We need to talk."

He ushered Anne into his office.

"Why are you doing this?" Anne asked. "You have no relationship to the Morehouses. No court will grant you guardianship, even on a temporary basis."

"Perhaps not, but the court can assume guardianship if I prove that the family is not acting in the best interests of the child. Mrs. Morehouse has repeatedly resisted therapeutic intervention by the hospital staff, and she has tried to discharge Ruth against medical advice."

"As guardian of the child, she has every right—indeed, every obligation—to request an explanation for any procedure or treatment offered to Ruth, with a discussion of risks and benefits. I don't know how you got your information, but it's covered under doctor-patient confidentiality. Whoever disclosed it has committed a Federal offense."

"Nobody has broken any laws, Dr. Mastik. My pastoral privileges at the hospital allow me to receive information from hospital staff about possible neglect, and it is my legal responsibility to report it."

"I can't believe you would stoop to this level to get Ruth away from her aunt." Anne glared at him. "What's your game,

Reverend? You're not investing this much time and energy into Ruth because of her soul. It's Eden Mountain, isn't it? You're trying to drive the family off the mountain for that ski resort. Who put you up to this—the Donnards?"

"This has nothing to do with any ski resort. My business is the Lord's work."

"Your objectives coincide pretty closely with those of the business community in this town. As I understand it, if the Morehouses are kicked off that mountain, it would make a lot of people in this town very wealthy."

"I have no financial interest in anything that happens with that mountain," he said stiffly.

"You have parishioners that contribute heavily to your church, and your salary is dependent on the level of contributions, and yet you say you have no financial interest?"

The color rose in Wainstock's face. "You have no idea of my motives. Those people are apostates of the worst kind. God Almighty Himself will cast them down to the deepest levels of Hell."

"This country has more Christian sects than even God can keep track of. What makes you think He would single out the Morehouses? And why would He make *you* His authority?"

"You are obviously not a woman of God, or you would realize that the Morehouses' heresies are not about minor theological points or Biblical interpretation. Their doctrines go against the fundamental tenets of Christianity, including that our Lord Jesus Christ is the only begotten Son of Almighty God, who died on the cross to save us from eternal punishment for our sins. They imagine that our Lord will be reborn through sinful sexual relations rather than by descending from Heaven at the end of times." Wainstock shook his finger to the sky. "And to back up this blasphemy, they claim to have a document written by James, the so-called brother of Jesus." He pounded his fist repeatedly on the desk. "In this church, in full witness of our Heavenly Father,

I say that such a document can only be Satan's handiwork, and those who believe in it will be cursed for all eternity and cast into a fiery pit from which there is no escape. I wish nothing less than to save Ruth from eternal damnation while her innocent mind can still be turned to the light of the Lord and away from the darkness of Satan's lies."

Anne's face flushed with fury, but she held her tongue. She recalled the incongruous smile of the ICU clerk, rolling her chair back and forth from the phone bank. *Wainstock has eyes and ears all over the hospital. Miriam was right. They had to get Ruth out of this town – and soon.*

Anne glowered at Wainstock. "You will never get your hands on that manuscript," she spat out. Then she turned to leave, but her rage had intensified her spasticity, so she was forced to half walk, half stumble out of the church, grabbing clumsily at the pews for support, certain that Wainstock was smirking behind her. Once inside her car, she blasted the air conditioning and stayed put, too afraid to drive.

As she cooled off physically and emotionally, she took some time to think. *Could last night's intruder have been one of Wainstock's minions? Was Isaiah's death fortuitous, or had he been murdered? No alternative. I need to speak with Artemis.* She wrinkled her nose in disgust.

***

As Anne and Matt bounced their way up the now-familiar road to Artemis's shack an hour later, Anne filled him in on her conversation with Wainstock, omitting any mention of the scroll.

"I guess his interest in Ruth has nothing to do with his FCC filing for a televised evangelical hour?"

Anne jerked her head left. "What! He didn't mention anything about that."

"That's odd. He talks about it every Sunday in his sermons. He wants to save souls, all right. But it appears that there aren't enough souls in Eden, so he's set loftier goals. He already has a Sunday prayer hour on the radio, but there's no way a small church like his could afford a televised hour. Electronic equipment and licensing fees are expensive, and Wainstock's having a hard time prying open his congregants' wallets. There'd be a lot more gratitude on Sundays if Eden Mountain were in someone else's hands."

"That conniving, self-righteous…. He's not actually that devious, is he?"

Matt's mouth curled into a cynical smile. "Of course not. He's doing the Lord's work."

***

By late morning, they reached Artemis's shack, and Anne stepped out of the cab of Matt's truck to a sultry blast of warm, humid air. Anne couldn't wait to get this over with and go back to the air-conditioned hospital.

Matt knocked on the shack door. "Artemis, open up! We need to talk to you."

After a few raps with no response, Matt banged with his fist. "C'mon, Artemis. Wake the hell up." Matt looked back at Anne. "Damn, he must really be plowed."

Matt opened the door and beckoned for Anne. She followed him in, only to be greeted by air dank with the odor of sweat and spoiled food. Flies buzzed in swarms as she and Matt walked through what passed as a living room and kitchenette, stepping around dirty clothes and empty liquor bottles. A cluster of half-empty food cans, several with utensils sticking out of them, sat on a decrepit Formica and aluminum table.

"What a life. Couldn't his family keep him in better shape?" Anne asked.

Matt shrugged. "His choice. Do you smell something?"

Anne wrinkled her nose. "It's coming from behind this door." She held her breath and pushed the door open.

A wave of fetid air washed over them as they entered the bedroom. The buzzing of flies, which had been a barely audible hum, swelled to a loud crescendo. Anne held a handkerchief to her face and stepped into the room, totally unprepared for what she saw.

The bedroom was a sparse affair. A small wooden chest of drawers sat in the corner. A half-open curtainless window — the panes so smudged they were almost opaque — provided the only light. In the center of the room sat a rickety wood-framed bed topped by a food-stained mattress, its stuffing pouring out of several large tears. Filling the bed, so bloated with decay that the skin on its arms and face had split, lay Artemis's purple corpse.

Anne bolted from the room, her head swimming, and vomited outside the front door.

"What do you think?" Anne asked Matt on her return. "Aspirated on his vomit?"

"Could've drunk himself to death. No signs of struggle, no wounds on the body." He scanned the surroundings. "Well, well, what's this?" He bent over and picked up one of the bottles littering the floor. "Wild Turkey. Artemis was moving up in the world."

Anne took a mental inventory of the bottles scattered around the cabin floor. "You're right. Not a lot of top-shelf brands lying around."

"All Artemis wanted was to get from here to there as quickly and cheaply as possible." Matt poured a drop of the booze onto his finger.

"Ew, you're not going to — "

Matt stuck the glistening finger into his mouth, then withdrew it and spat on the floor.

"Oh, God! I might puke again. I hope you're not going to do that with every bottle."

"Nope, only the good stuff. You like bourbon?"

"Not enough to drink it out of *that* bottle."

"Well, I'm a good ol' Kentucky boy, and I've ordered plenty of Wild Turkey in my day, and if a bartender served me this, I'd spit it in his face."

Anne cocked her head. "That's not Wild Turkey?"

"Yeah, it's Wild Turkey, but it's tainted. Artemis was poisoned. Someone must have brought him a special gift spiked with something toxic. Probably knew that Artemis would knock it down right away."

"Artemis must have known him."

"Let's bag the bottle and bring it back. Maybe the police can get prints off it. But who would want to kill Artemis?"

"Probably the same person who tried to kill Miriam."

***

By the time Anne and Matt reached the Morehouse homestead, Anne was exhausted, but she had work to be done.

"We're here," Matt said. "Now what?"

"We need vegetables from Isaiah's garden."

"You dragged me up here to pick vegetables? Why?"

"I've got a hunch."

Anne led him to the garden behind the cabin. *The intruder certainly wanted Miriam dead, but why did he have to improvise by picking up a rock? He must have come to the cabin anticipating that Miriam was already dead or dying and was surprised to find her alive. The answer is somewhere here, staring me in the face.* She pulled two pairs of latex gloves and a box of large sealable plastic bags from a knapsack. "I need samples of each plant, except for roots and tubers. Be on the lookout for signs of spoilage."

"Why?"

"I'll tell you later." Anne handed him gloves and bags. "Get picking."

As Matt busied himself with squash and green peppers, Anne realized she couldn't possibly bring all the vegetables to her lab. Even if she could, it would take forever to test them all. She needed to think like the killer—and simultaneously like an Infectious Disease doctor: What if Miriam was right? What if Isaiah had been poisoned with Listeria, the same bacteria that attacked Ruth? If so, it couldn't be a coincidence. Listeria was generally contracted by eating contaminated milk products, like Ruth's melted ice cream, but Isaiah would have gotten it elsewhere. So how did the killer know that Isaiah would eat the poisoned food? Would he have dusted the entire garden? If so, many of the plants would have shown signs of spoilage, and a good rain would have washed it off. Plus, the Morehouses washed their food before they ate it. So how did one distribute Listeria to vegans? Some vegetables, like tomatoes and rhubarb, were too acidic for Listeria to survive, so they were out. And it wouldn't be a veggie likely to be cooked. Maybe a salad item, one that was protected from the rain, already washed, and soon to be eaten.

That's it!

"Matt, stop! I know what I'm looking for."

Matt painfully straightened his back. "Wish you could have told me that before I picked three dozen peppers."

Anne put on her gloves and strode to the porch, where a bowl of fruit had been sitting between two rocking chairs. She placed each fruit and the bowl in separate bags then sealed them.

"We're done," she said, throwing her gloves into a bag. "Let's go."

***

Anne hurried back to her B and B and, with gloved hands, picked up a peach. Flashlight and magnifying glass in hand, she set about examining it. No grossly visible evidence of contamination, but that didn't mean much. The Morehouses would have washed that away. She pushed away the stem's small leaves and — *aha!* — spotted something suspicious. A few millimeters from the base of the stem was a minute discolored spot no larger than the head of a pin, a puncture mark in its center. *Gotcha!*

Anne examined the other fruits. Same telltale spot, same inconspicuous location. She estimated the angle that a needle would have to travel to avoid contacting the pit. Then she picked up a scalpel and sliced.

A triumphant smile crossed her face as she cut out a small wedge of fruit. The scalpel blade had sliced right through a thin brown needle track that ran deep into the peach and ended in a tiny pool of brown liquid. If this was a tiny drop of pure Listeria culture, Isaiah had been poisoned with a biologic agent.

But Anne now found herself in a delicate situation. Whoever had killed Artemis had also murdered Isaiah and tried to kill Miriam. Were the local police capable—or even willing—of running the investigation? Matt was on his way to the police with the Wild Turkey, but what to do with the fruit? She picked up her phone and dialed.

Twenty minutes later, Anne opened her door. "Thanks for coming, Lillian. I didn't know who else to call."

Lillian entered and sat on the bed. "I came as quickly as I could. Is this about Ruth?"

"Sort of. Isaiah's death wasn't accidental." Anne pointed to her delicious-looking lab experiment. "These fruits have been injected with something; my hunch is Listeria. I need to have them cultured as soon as possible, and if anyone in administration knows that I'm behind this, they'll have the cultures destroyed."

Lillian did a double-take. "Why?"

"Because someone local, well-connected, and dangerous is behind this. Can you bring them in for me?"

"Sure. But what do I tell the lab?"

"Tell them it's a public health issue. Tell them your dog ate the fruit and got sick. But don't tell them you got it from the Morehouse farm."

"I've never been a good liar, but I'll think of something."

Anne hugged Lillian as she departed. "Thanks. I owe you one."

**

After Lillian left, Anne called Gary Nesmith.

"What's up?"

"I've got a problem, Gary. A big one." She gave as brief a synopsis as she could about the Morehouse situation.

"The only person I know that would have access to Eden Mountain and have that degree of medical acumen would be Marcus Stendahl. But I can't believe it would be him. He saved Ruth's life. Perhaps he's part of a town conspiracy to take over the property."

"What's your next step?"

"I've got to get Ruth out of here, and I need your help. I may have to smuggle her out of town and lie low in Charlottesville for a day or two. Can we stay at your place until I straighten this out?"

"Sure. When?"

"I won't be able to drive directly to Charlottesville." Anne paced as she thought. "If you'll bring us each a change of clothes, we'll meet you somewhere out of the way two days from now. I'll let you know exactly where and when the night before." Anne hesitated before asking the next question. "Also, Ruth needs antibiotics daily, or she'll relapse. Can you get her a few doses of ampicillin?"

"Might be tricky, but I'll try."

"When the Listeria culture results come back in a few days, it will prove Isaiah was poisoned. The court should be more forgiving then, so figure on three days max, four doses a day."

They said their goodbyes, and Anne called Matt. "Guess what?" she said. "I found puncture marks in every piece of fruit. I'll bet they're each a tiny injection of bacterial culture."

"Damn," Matt said. "I've got an out-of-town lab we can use."

"Already gave the bag to Lillian. She can get it cultured without our names on it."

Matt sighed. "My lab is more reliable than the hospital's."

"Sorry. I wanted to get it in ASAP."

"I know, Lillian. She'll handle it."

***

Following the short drive to the hospital, Lillian parked in a remote end of the visitors' lot. After scanning the deserted lot, she got out of her car and tossed the bag of fruit into a dumpster. Then she jumped back in the driver's seat, cleaned her hands with a sanitizing wipe, and drove off, humming a hymn from last week's church service.

CHAPTER XI

Anne paced outside Buckram's office. Ironically, the man might be her best hope to get Ruth out of the hospital and away from this crooked town.

"Mr. Buckram will see you now," the secretary said. Anne took a deep breath and entered the lion's den.

"Dr. Mastik, good to see you again." Buckram rose from behind his desk and offered her a chair. "How is our star patient doing?"

"That's what I want to discuss. Ruth has made a remarkable recovery, and I've rethought your suggestion about discharging her."

"Really! Go on."

"Ruth receives her antibiotics every six hours. Matt can discharge her to my care. Then, instead of a costly ambulance ride to Charlottesville, I could transport her by car, admit her to University Hospital in time for her next dose, and have her evaluated there for her immune problem."

His eyes became dangerous slits. "A very generous offer, Dr. Mastik. But until the issue of her guardianship is settled, she can't leave."

"The court will know her whereabouts. It's in her best interest to be transferred, and she'll return once her antibiotics are finished."

"Until the judge makes his decision, she can't leave. My hands are tied on this, Dr. Mastik."

Anne could see that further protest was futile. *Time for plan B.*

***

Anne rushed back to the ICU and dragged Miriam to the visitor's lounge. But this time, she turned on a music app on her phone and held it against the intercom before they spoke.

"It is as I feared," Miriam said when Anne told her about the fruit.

"Whoever killed Isaiah was trying to kill you, too." Anne reached out and held Miriam's hand. "Don't worry, we'll find him."

Miriam gave Anne a hard look. "I despair of justice in this town."

"Dr. Drisner is working on this. He has evidence that may lead to Artemis's killer, and I'm sure that's the same man who killed Isaiah."

"Poor Artemis. A rough man with a good heart, but he could never conquer his demons. May God's grace be on him."

"We have other problems, though. They won't let Ruth out of the hospital, at least not until the judge makes his ruling on guardianship."

Miriam slammed her fist against her palm. "They cannot hold us against our will."

"Right now, they can do anything they want."

"Is there no way to get back to the mountain? I fear for Ruth's safety." Miriam's voice subsided to a whisper. "And I fear for the scroll."

"So do I. Somehow Reverend Wainstock found out about it."

"I knew that devil was up to something. What can we do?"

"He doesn't know where it's hidden. I'll go back to check

on it tonight, and I *will* get Ruth out of here. No matter what."

Anne entered Ruth's room to find Ruth and Mary Beth laughing together. Ruth had on Mary Beth's hot pink lipstick and green eye shadow, making her look five years older.

"Does Miriam know you've been doing that?" Anne said.

"She said I could, as long as I washed it off before bed."

"Mary Beth, would you give us a moment?"

Mary Beth headed out, and Ruth turned sullen. "When can I get out of here?"

"Soon, I hope. I'm working on it. You really adore Mary Beth, don't you?"

Ruth nodded, a wistful look on her face. "Sometimes I wish I could be her. She is so free. She can do what she wants, eat what she wants, make friends, and travels. She tells me about the places she goes, the people she meets. It must be amazing."

Anne felt a surge of deep pity for the teenager. *She bears the weight of two thousand years of prayers and expectations on her slender shoulders. Hope she doesn't break under the load.*

Anne put her arm around Ruth. "Someday you'll have lots of friends and go lots of places. Who knows? Perhaps Mary Beth will wish that she were you."

Ruth hugged Anne. "Perhaps one day you will be the one who takes me everywhere?"

Anne felt a momentary pang as she recalled her oaths to Miriam and Isaiah. "Maybe. Now get back in bed. You'll be in a regular room in a little while. Then, maybe I can take you outside in a wheelchair. It's not everywhere. But it's a start."

***

Anne sat down at an empty table in a quiet corner of the hospital cafeteria. She eyed her tray dubiously, but a few bites proved more rewarding than she'd expected — or maybe she was hungrier than she'd thought. As she raised her soda to her lips, Marcus Stendahl approached her table, food tray in hand.

"May I join you?"

"Be my guest." Anne gestured to the seat across from her. "It's about time we had a chat. That is, when no one's life is at stake."

"You think you know your daughter. Then she becomes a teenager, and all bets are off," Stendahl said with a sigh as he sat down. Anne cocked her head and raised a puzzled eyebrow. Stendahl continued.

"Years ago, when Mary Beth was starting middle school, my wife and I thought she should spend time with kids in town. Mary Beth was always charismatic and well-liked in school, so we envisioned her hanging out with the popular crowd. Now I find out that her best friend is the ultimate outsider."

"I think Mary Beth values Ruth's honesty and simplicity. With Ruth, what you see is what you get. There's no pressure to conform, to be something you don't want to be. So as much as your daughter enjoys the trappings of society, I suspect she secretly yearns for a simpler life."

"Seems you've learned more about my daughter in three days than I have in fifteen years."

"Just girl talk. I'm sure your wife knows all of this."

A dark cloud spread over Stendahl's face. "Afraid not. She died six years ago," he said, staring at his drink glass.

"I'm sorry. I didn't mean to upset you." For the first time, Anne noticed the ruddiness in Stendahl's face. *I'll bet he wishes there were something stronger than iced tea in that glass. No wonder he didn't know about the girls' friendship. Time to change the subject.*

"Do you ever visit the Morehouses?" Anne asked.

"Not really. It's too rocky and overgrown to get there directly, and we'd have to pass Artemis's place to get to the path. Even though he's sort of family, I'd as soon have as little to do with him as possible. Besides, I don't think the Morehouses wanted company."

Ah, the opening Anne had been waiting for. "Matt and I went by Artemis's place this morning. Did you know he died?"

She observed Stendahl's face for any change.

"I'm not surprised," Stendahl said, his face impassive. "He's been hospitalized for liver failure umpteen times. Just a matter of time before he drank himself to death."

"I guess you heard that Isaiah Morehouse died recently." Anne steeled herself for the next question. "Do you know anyone who would want to kill him?"

"Kill? No. Why would you think that?"

"He died so unexpectedly. He was healthy just two days ago."

"There's nothing mysterious about his death. Everyone in that family dies early. He probably got whatever Ruth has."

Best not to pry further. "Nice talking to you, Marcus," Anne said as she stood to leave. "By the way, your daughter is a wonderful girl. You must be proud of her."

Stendahl beamed. "Thanks. You can thank my wife for that." Then as quickly as it had come, the light disappeared from his face. He looked down at his tray and aimlessly pushed his food with his fork. "Good luck with Ruth."

Even with my MS, perhaps it was for the best that I was holding the pacemaker wire, not him.

***

Back in the room, Miriam addressed Anne. "Will you be coming back here tonight?"

"No. I was planning on spending the night at the B and B."

"Good," Miriam answered, to Anne's surprise. "You have been working hard."

"You're not concerned about Ruth?"

"We will do well. You need to get some rest. There is much yet to be done."

"Anne," Mary Beth said, "can you take me home? Dad's working late, as usual."

***

"I met your father in the cafeteria," Anne said to Mary Beth as she drove her car along the now-familiar road that led up the mountain. "I didn't know your mother had died. I'm sorry."

Mary Beth dropped her head. "She had cancer. Breast cancer. That's why I put pink in my hair, so whenever I look in a mirror, it reminds me of her. It was real hard on me but worse for Dad. He had to pull out of his practice for a while. Still has a hard time talking about it."

"He drinks, doesn't he?"

"A little. Well, more than a little. We don't talk much anymore. That's why Ruth is so important to me. She lost her parents, and you can see that Miriam doesn't talk much."

"She and Miriam seem to be getting closer now."

Mary Beth brightened. "I know. That makes me happy. Oh, we're here."

Anne stopped the car and looked for a house but saw only trees.

"You see that trail?" Mary Beth said, pointing to the forest. "Right by the pile of rocks over there. That's my secret path. It leads up to a clearing where it crosses another path. If you turn right, it leads to my house, go straight ahead, and it leads up to Ruth's. We always meet at the clearing."

Anne eyed the trail warily. "Aren't you afraid of getting hurt?"

"It's kinda steep in places and a little rocky, but it's not too bad. Nobody but us knows about it. You won't tell Dad?"

"Nah."

"Swear it."

"I swear. Just don't go there at night. It's not safe."

Mary Beth rolled her eyes. "Of course not. I'm not stupid."

She gave Anne a hug and got out of the car, waving before she disappeared into the woods.

***

Anne headed to the town pharmacy on Main Street, almost deserted in the heat of the summer afternoon. She found a clear cylindrical plastic spaghetti container with a screw-on plastic lid that suited her purposes perfectly. Then she grabbed several small bottles of vitamins and stopped at the checkout.

"Health nut?" the clerk asked when she saw all the vitamins.

"Yeah. Traveling through, and I left my vitamins at home."

"You should try our special vitamin shake at the soda fountain."

"No, thanks. I noticed you have a poster for a church barbecue in your window. You belong to the Church of the Righteous Disciples?"

"Ha! I ain't rich enough. They don't let just anybody into their congregation, y'know. But if they hear you come into some money, a bunch of them church ladies is sure to come by your place, cake and lemonade in hand."

"You know Reverend Wainstock?"

The clerk glanced around nervously, then leaned forward and spoke in a hushed voice. "Everyone knows the reverend. Follows the first five Commandments to a tee and makes damn sure everybody knows it. Not so strict about the other five, although I can't say as how he's killed anyone. Not as I know of, at any rate."

"What have you heard about the ski resort being built here soon."

"Not unless someone gets rid of the Morehouses. They been at the top of that mountain since before this town was built, and I don't see them movin' anytime soon. But I'll tell you somethin'. Every time a piece of property in town goes up for sale, someone from that church snatches it right up. Sometimes, the bankers in town will lean a bit on the owners to sell cheap, know what I mean? Ain't no coincidence they're all in with the reverend." The clerk nodded her head and looked toward the door as a customer walked in. "Have a good one."

***

Back in her room, Anne dumped all the vitamins onto the bed. Then she sorted the dehydration packets that kept the pills fresh and dry, dropped them into her spaghetti container, and swept the pills into a wastebasket. Now she was ready.

CHAPTER XII

The road up Eden Mountain was pitch black, and even though Anne had been on it earlier with Mary Beth, it had taken on an air of foreboding. She slowed as she passed the path that led to Artemis's house, knowing that Mary Beth's path lay only a few dozen yards farther. After her headlights reflected off the rockpile that marked Mary Beth's trail, she drove until she had enough of a shoulder to park on. Then she got out of her car and took a backpack and flashlight with her.

Even as her flashlight illuminated the asphalt directly in front of her, it did nothing to dispel the gloom of the lonely road. The dense canopy of branches arching overhead obscured the sky and formed a narrow tunnel that swallowed up the flashlight beam within a few yards, making it impossible to know what dangers lay beyond the narrow confines of the light.

Anne's heart jumped at a rustling in the bushes not fifteen feet away. After a few seconds, a raccoon sauntered out of the woods and stopped in front of her to stare, its eyes gleaming like two burning red coals. Apparently convinced of Anne's harmlessness, it resumed its trek across the road and disappeared into the woods.

After her heart slowed, Anne found the trail marker close to where the raccoon had emerged from the woods. She listened for any stray sound that might indicate she had been followed. Hearing nothing, she ventured onward.

Although the first few yards only inclined slightly, things quickly changed. She had to clamber over clusters of rocks and support herself against boulders as she struggled for air. *Only a fifteen-year-old would consider this a path!* With a terrible chill, she recalled her fears about the trail near Artemis's shack. *What if I'm already headed the wrong way? Could I be lost in the woods?* But then she recalled Mary Beth's admonition that the trail was "a little rocky." *Yeah, right! Like I'm only "a little scared."*

After several minutes, the rocks gave way to a steep incline crisscrossed with tree roots that acted as stairs. Anne assessed every step, often grabbing random branches for support when she lost her balance.

Eventually, the tree root staircase leveled off. She caught her breath and shone her flashlight around.

The large round clearing was exactly as Mary Beth had described, about fifty feet across, with two plastic children's chairs facing each other. What first drew Anne's attention was an empty chocolate ice cream carton, now washed clean by the rain. Investigating further, she saw lipstick tubes, clothes hangers, plastic bags, empty cans of soft drinks, and old pizza boxes. Anne smiled as she imagined the girls trying on each other's clothes, putting on make-up, and fixing each other's hair.

Suddenly, a flashlight shone back at her, blinding her with its glare. She dropped to the ground and stifled a scream.

In the split second it took her to reach the ground, the light disappeared, and the clearing returned to its eerie, dead stillness. Anne cautiously let the flashlight beam creep up a tree near the other beam's source, and once again, the clearing became bathed in shimmering light—which was reflecting off a long mirror nailed into the tree trunk.

Anne took a deep breath as her heartbeat slowed. *Of course, the girls needed a mirror! No matter their upbringing, girls would be girls.*

There were actually three paths that led from the clearing. One headed right to the Stendahl home. A second, narrower path, almost obscured by the forest underbrush, veered left. Probably led to Artemis's house, but it wasn't the one she and Matt had taken, which must lie farther up the mountain. *Hmm, Mary Beth hadn't mentioned this path.* She shone her flashlight at its entrance. *What's this?* Adult male shoeprints imprinted in the muddy ground. Someone evidently knew about this clearing. But who? Artemis? Stendahl?

Anne shuddered — the killer?

The third path headed to the Morehouse homestead, so Anne hoisted her backpack and headed up, but the climb proved harder than expected. Finally, as her endurance ebbed, the forest cleared, and the path leveled off, ending in a broad field at the entrance to the Morehouse homestead. A clear sky bursting with stars and a brilliant moon brightened the setting. She took a minute to steady herself, thankful that the return trip would be downhill, and set off for the cave.

***

The ancient, dilapidated farmhouses that populated much of the homestead, each lit only by moonlight, gave Anne the creeps. She moved on quickly until she reached the granite outcropping, which stuck up from the field like a gigantic fist. Anne removed the spaghetti canister, a butane lighter, and a pocketknife from her backpack, which she then set on the ground by the fissure. She aimed her flashlight into the crevice, the beam hitting the stone wall at the bend. At night, the opening appeared even tighter than it had in daylight. Anne tried not to think about the creepy crawlies lurking inside as she swallowed hard and edged her way in.

Closing her eyes so she wouldn't see the terrifying proximity of the rock face, she sidled along until she bumped into the protruding shelf. Then she sucked in her stomach and squeezed by into the central chamber. Entombed in the blackness, with only a few stars visible in the skyward cleft, she broke into a cold sweat, hyperventilating in the suffocating air of the chamber. Remembering Miriam's cautionary words, she tried to slow her breathing.

After a minute or two, she had calmed down enough that she could set her flashlight on the ground and painstakingly edge the clay jar out of the vestibule. On an intuition, she took several pictures of the jar with her cell phone, hoping the flash wouldn't draw any lurking killer's attention. Then, with her pocketknife, she scraped away as much of the wax seal as she could, but the lid wouldn't budge. Igniting her butane lighter, she gradually heated the wax, cutting away pieces as they softened. After repeated softening and scraping, the lid finally budged and, with a hiss of air, gave way. Anne switched off the lighter and peered into the jar with her flashlight.

What the hell!? She pulled out a tightly coiled scroll wrapped in linen and bound by a strip of leather. Brown around the edges, it looked fragile but amazingly was in one piece. She looked again into the jar to see if there were any broken scraps of parchment, but the jar was empty. She placed the scroll into the spaghetti container—a snug but perfect fit. Screwing the lid onto the container and holding it to her breast, Anne pushed the jar back into the vestibule and turned to leave.

Then she heard the scrape.

Windblown tree branches rubbing against one another? Couldn't be. No trees near the outcropping. She extinguished her flashlight. In the pitch-black, her other senses became hyperacute. The scratching recurred. *Footsteps on gravel...only a few yards away!* She was trapped but at least obscured. *Thank God for the bend in the fissure. They probably didn't see my light.*

She clutched the container close, not daring to breathe. Drops of sweat trickled down her back as the dankness of the rock enclosure seeped into her body and soul. With no way out, she struggled against her surging panic and the sense of entombment within the huge granite mass. The ponderous weight seemed to close in, pressing the air out of her lungs.

Outside, the footsteps grew louder and sharper until they stopped directly outside the entrance. Then stillness and silence — until the ripping of a zipper. *Oh God! He found the backpack!* Suddenly, the blackness was pierced by an intense beam of light playing on the wall where the fissure made its sharp turn two yards away. The beam reflected off the rock face into the chamber, dimly illuminating it. At the same time, a trail of tiny prickles crossed her feet, followed by the tactile sensation of a thin wet string. A soft pattering filled the chamber, and a score of tiny, mirrored points of red light shone up at Anne from the ground.

Rats!

She pressed her hand over her mouth to stifle a scream as her heart pounded thunderously in her chest. Her other hand shook so hard she almost dropped the canister, and her legs stiffened to the point of immobility. An awful moment of silence followed as the beam searched the crevice.

When one of the more adventurous rats scuttled out of the crevice, the light abruptly disappeared, and a muffled curse preceded rapidly receding footsteps.

Anne scarcely breathed for the next several minutes. *Do I dare?* She lit the butane lighter and waved it about in broad arcs. Startled by the flame, the remaining rats scattered. Most ran out the crevice, while a few scampered up the walls and escaped through the skyward vent.

No more lab rats for me! So. Help. Me. God!

Outside, nothing but silence. *Is he gone? Or is he biding his time, waiting for me to emerge?*

Anne listened for the slightest sound that might betray his presence, but she heard only the breeze blowing over the starlit opening above. Once her tremors subsided, she inched into the crevice. But as she squeezed past the rock ledge, a paroxysm of spasticity gripped her legs. Her body jerked upward, and her lower back smashed against the projecting rock. An excruciating pain shot through her body, intensifying the rigid stiffness in her legs and forcing her back ever harder against the ledge. Again, she pressed her hand to her mouth, agonizingly pinned in the passageway for what seemed like an eternity, helpless to control her body.

I can do this. I must do this. I dealt with pain like this in rehab, and it didn't stop me. I will not let it stop me now.

She employed breathing exercises she had learned years ago to allow her spasming muscles to slowly relax, and she pushed the pain to the back of her mind. Gradually, the attack abated, her legs relaxed, and she eased her way out.

As soon as she made it through the narrowing, she supported herself against the rock wall until the pain receded. Kneeling on the ground, she slipped her hand around the rock, and felt for her backpack. With a sigh of relief, she found it in the same place she had left it.

Anne stuck her head outside of the crevice and searched for any flicker of light, any shadow in the moonlight. Satisfied that she was alone, she left the safety of the crevice, placed the container into the backpack, and slung it across her back. She dared not turn her flashlight on. Step by cautious step, she crossed the field, aided only by moonlight, to where she thought Mary Beth's trail was.

To her relief, she found the opening. She took her first steps down the incline but had no sooner reached the first cluster of rocks than the beam of another flashlight, one hundred yards to her right, appeared — moving quickly toward her!

As she struggled over roots and rocks, her legs getting stiffer and weaker with the strain, the intruder gained on her. She finally half stumbled and half fell into the clearing, her pursuer a hundred feet up the path and closing fast. She flung one of her shoes toward the trail to the Donnards' house, turned off her flashlight, and crept behind the mirror tree, gasping for breath.

No sooner had she settled herself than her pursuer burst into the clearing. She didn't dare peek, but the searching beam flashed wildly in every direction.

"Shit!" a man's voice yelled.

Gotcha! He must have been startled by the mirror's reflection. Footsteps approached her tree, stopping nearby as she cowered in the tree's shadow. The beam played up and down, left and right. Finally, the underbrush rustled as the stranger moved along the trail to the Donnards' house. *He took the bait. Time to go.*

She felt her way across the clearing, found the path, and stumbled her way down to the road. Not looking back, she threw her other shoe into the woods and ran barefoot to her car, made a sharp U-turn, and raced back to town.

***

Hearing the squeal of Anne's car tires as she fled, Matt Drisner realized he had been tricked. Whatever Anne was up to, he'd have to wait until daylight to figure it out.

CHAPTER XIII

Awakened by beams of early morning sunlight playing over her eyelids, Anne stretched lazily for a moment before recalling where she was. She instantly searched behind the bed's dust ruffle until her hand contacted the spaghetti container; she breathed a sigh of relief and grabbed her phone.

"Department of Religious and Biblical Studies," a secretarial voice answered.

"This is Dr. Anne Mastik. I need to speak with Dr. Peter Jones, please."

"Sorry. He's out of the office until tomorrow afternoon."

Damn. "Can I set up a time to talk with him tomorrow?"

"He should be available anytime after two."

Anne hung up. *Tomorrow would be tight. Very tight.*

The short walk to the bathroom proved difficult like she was dragging two sandbags instead of feet. But she had no time for rest today, let alone for her much-needed steroid injection. The summer heat would sap her energy, so she turned the spigot to "Cold." She'd need all her strength to confront Wainstock.

***

By eight, Anne sat across from Wainstock. After the most minimal of pleasantries, Anne spent several minutes presenting her arguments about how much Ruth meant to her family while

Wainstock, his face impassive, leaned back and nodded from time to time.

Wainstock finally spoke. "I do not wish to steal Ruth from her family. I only wish to protect her from her aunt's neglect. You know that she resisted getting Ruth appropriate medical care now and three years ago, when she almost died."

Anne let him have it. "Reverend, if that is your only concern, I will be glad to petition the court to make me her guardian for medical issues."

Wainstock recoiled and frowned. He clearly hadn't counted on this. "I'm not an evil man, Dr. Mastik. I know you won't believe me, but I am doing this for the girl's benefit. I don't know all the details of their…cult, but I do know that they deny the divinity of our Lord, Jesus Christ, and they deny the one true path to becoming right with God. To save that poor girl's immortal soul, it is imperative that I get her out of that household so that she might be taught the way of our Lord. For God's sake."

"The last I heard, the Constitution permits any belief, or lack of belief, for that matter, and leaves religious training to the parents. I don't see how the court could possibly object to whatever religious upbringing the family chooses."

"Then neither you nor Miriam should have any concern about letting this case run its course."

"That will take months, and Ruth should not be separated from her sole surviving family member for that long."

"I'm sure the court will grant periods of supervised visitation."

Anne resisted the impulse to reach across the table and punch Wainstock in the nose. "If you take Miriam to court, you'll bankrupt her."

"Hmph. I wouldn't worry about Miriam Morehouse's finances. Her property is an extremely valuable piece of real estate."

Anne stood up, eyes blazing and legs shaking with rage.

"So that's your plan. You're going to wear Miriam down in the courts until she's forced to sell her property, then snap it up at pennies to the dollar."

"Miriam can hold onto her property if she prefers, as long as I have Ruth. She is young enough that her soul can still be saved."

"Keep your damned self-righteousness. You want that property. That's what this whole charade is all about."

"Perhaps there's another way I could be persuaded to drop the case," Wainstock said. "The Morehouses have something else of value."

"And what is that?"

He leaned forward, his gaunt face distorted by a sardonic grin. "I want that scroll," he said in a menacing cadence.

"What possible significance could it have for you?"

"Its contents may be dangerous to the faith of millions of Christians. For those whose Christian faith is…infirm, it may be taken the wrong way."

"You want to destroy it, don't you? It's a priceless religious and historical document, and you want to destroy it!"

Wainstock glared. "You have your options. Consider them carefully and quickly. I anticipate a restraining order against Miriam Morehouse coming out of the court by tomorrow afternoon." Wainstock leaned forward again, his eyes cold and hard. "I warn you; I will move Heaven and earth to get that manuscript. This conversation is over, Dr. Mastik. Saving lives is your job. Saving souls is mine."

"A scroll for a soul," Anne sneered, and stormed out to her car.

***

Anne furiously pounded the steering wheel with her fists. "You're damn right I have my options, you pompous S.O.B.," she muttered through clenched teeth and picked up her phone.

"Evan, it's Anne. I need a favor. I've got to bring Ruth to

your facility."

"What's wrong? You sound worried."

Anne told him about her conversations with Reverend Wainstock, skipping any mention of the scroll.

"He'd never get away with it," Evan said.

"Under most circumstances, I would agree with you, but he's a powerful figure in the area. He'll keep throwing legal roadblocks in front of Miriam, and she has no money to fight him. She gave me a guardianship letter, but I must get Ruth out before the court issues a restraining order."

"I'll need a day or two to get everything ready."

"No problem. I've got business to take care of in Charlottesville first. I'll call you when I'm done."

That was easy. Now for the hard part. Anne called Matt and summarized her conversation with Wainstock, again omitting any mention of the scroll. Or Evan.

"What are you going to do?" he said.

"I'm still thinking that one out. Any news about Artemis?"

"Not really. The only fingerprints on the bottle were his and mine, which didn't look good, but luckily I had an alibi. Toxicology won't be back for a few days. For now, it looks like he drank himself to death, and nobody's going to get too bent out of shape about that."

I'm running out of time. Got to move quickly. "I have an idea. Why don't I bring Lillian to your place, and we can all talk this out tonight?"

"Sounds great. In my experience, there's no problem that can't be solved over a full rack of baby back ribs and a bottle of wine."

"And I'll even drive Lillian home."

"Much obliged," Matt said, chuckling. "You get an extra order of ribs for that one."

CHAPTER XIV

If Anne had any doubts about how Eden got its name, the view from Matt Drisner's front porch answered it. Situated halfway up the side of a hill, Anne recognized Drisner's house as the individualistic contemporary she had noted on her drive into town. It overlooked the entire valley and the river running below, with Eden Mountain towering over everything. Matt, Lillian, and Anne each sat holding a glass of wine, watching as the setting sun lit the mountain's face in a brilliant copper that contrasted with the deepening dusk behind it. Only after the sun had dropped behind the horizon did Matt get up and put the ribs on the grill.

"I can understand how you could get lulled into staying here," Anne told Lillian. "The valley is beautiful."

"This town would be great if it weren't for the people. How about a refill, Matt?" Lillian said, lifting her empty glass.

Matt swooped in and took away her glass. "That's already your second. No more until dinner. I want you to be able to taste the ribs." And he turned back to the grill.

Lillian stuck her tongue at him, then turned to Anne. "He does make the best ribs in the state. Some secret barbecue sauce his father taught him."

"Not so secret," Matt called out as a cloud of mouth-watering smoke drifted to Anne's nostrils. "Kentucky bourbon, brown sugar, homegrown herbs and spices, and 'enough cayenne to make a gator smile,' as Daddy used to say."

"Matt," Anne said, "could you do me a favor? I've got to check Ruth's vital signs, and I don't have access to the hospital's system. Could you log on for me?"

"Sure. It'll take the ribs another ten or fifteen minutes anyway." He set down his spatula. "Lillian, make sure nothing catches on fire."

As Anne followed Matt inside, she turned and caught a glimpse of Lillian pouring herself another glass of wine.

Matt's house was magnificent, an open, soaring masterpiece of wood and stone. Clearly, no expense had been spared in the furnishings, either. *At least now I know who that egomaniac was.*

"Did you build this house yourself?" Anne asked. "It's absolutely gorgeous."

"Sure did. Took out my checkbook and used it to drive in every last nail," Matt said with a smile. "I did design it, though." They passed a beautifully equipped kitchen. "It looks impressive," he added, "but take my word, the microwave and the grill are my two most valuable possessions. Couldn't survive without them. Come on, I'll show you upstairs."

Anne didn't enjoy the sixteen-step climb to Matt's study, but the view from the picture windows made up for it as the entire valley stretched out before them.

"It's breathtaking," she said, overwhelmed by the vista.

"Hard to find a view like this anywhere east of the Mississippi without spending the rest of your life in servitude to the bank." Matt sat down at his computer and pecked away. As he logged on to the hospital's electronic medical record, Anne looked over his shoulder.

"Here's Ruth's chart," he said. "Actually, her vital signs look pretty good. Maybe we should move her out of the ICU."

"I'd like to keep her there overnight. I'd feel safer transferring her in the morning."

"Good idea. Thinking about it, Buckram may have a point. If Ruth is stable, maybe we shouldn't transfer her to Charlottesville."

"I guess we can wait another day or two," Anne said. "I'm going to talk to Miriam about getting a postponement. I'll see how that pans out before pushing the transfer issue."

"You said you had a plan. Is that it?"

"I'm still working on it. I'll tell you more tomorrow, but I don't want Lillian to know anything yet. She talks too much when she drinks." Anne looked down at the patio to see Lillian popping the cork on another bottle. *Jeez, the woman is a sponge.*

Matt followed Anne's gaze. "Damn. I can't trust her alone for ten minutes. Let's get down there before the ribs catch fire."

***

Anne negotiated the winding road leading down to Lillian's house carefully. Aside from an occasional loud snore coming from the back seat, Lillian slept silently. But Anne kept the window open, just in case.

Glad she didn't eat much. I'd hate to have to clean barbecued ribs, baked beans and two bottles of wine off the leather.

The rest of dinner had gone uneventfully, and Lillian had been right. Best ribs ever! But she'd been right about one other thing, too: Matt kept his cards close to his chest. Anne hadn't learned anything new about his personal life.

She pulled up to Lillian's driveway and cut the engine.

"Last stop," Anne called to the back of the car. "All ashore that's going ashore."

Lillian stirred and groaned. "Why can't I jus' sleep here?"

"Because this is my car, that's why." Anne got out and opened Lillian's door. "Come on. Up and at 'em."

Anne didn't realize how hard it would be to support Lillian back to her house. *Look at us! I can hardly walk, and Lillian can hardly stand. If I'd been stopped by a cop, we'd be spending the night in jail.*

"I need your key," Anne said.

Lillian handed over her purse and collapsed onto Anne's shoulder as Anne opened the door, dragged Lillian to the bedroom, and sat her on the bed.

"Men! Goddamn bastards, every last one of 'em," Lillian bawled. "Try to screw you every chance they get." Her voice dropped. "'Cept when you want 'em to."

"You like Matt, don't you?" Anne asked, pulling off Lillian's shoes and stockings.

"Yeah," Lillian said dreamily, "but I messed that up a long time ago. Now all I got is Mr. 'Don't-call-us-we'll-call-you.' That sucks." Lillian pulled off her dress, threw it on the floor and settled between the sheets as Anne tucked her in. "Could you stay here for a few more minutes?"

"Sure."

"Matt's right. I gotta get outta this place. Everything about it is dragging me down." She closed her eyes. "G'night, Anne. And thanks for taking care of me."

Anne didn't say a word but turned out the light and left the room. Back in the living room, she rifled through Lillian's purse.

This really stinks, but there are no other alternatives.

She bit her lip as she took Lillian's hospital ID badge and put it in her purse. Then she left, making sure the front door was locked behind her, and took off in her car.

So far, everything was going according to plan.

CHAPTER XV

"Sure you want to check out at this hour?" said the clerk at the B and B. "The night's already paid for. And the roads around here are right dangerous in the dark."

Anne nodded. "I've got to get back to work tomorrow morning. By the way, could you help me with my suitcase?"

"Sure thing. While I'm at it, would you like me to carry your tote bag?"

"No, thanks." She reflexively tightened her grip on the bag. "It's not heavy at all."

The clerk heaved her suitcase into the trunk while Anne secured the tote in the passenger seat with the seat belt. She wasn't about to take a chance with the scroll's safety. Despite her precautions, she drove with one hand on the tote's strap, her breath catching with every pothole and rough patch.

***

Anne parked at the back of the empty hospital lot, close to the Radiology department delivery entrance, then transferred the tote bag to the trunk. The short walk to the hospital entrance fatigued her, reminding her not only how overdue she was for her monthly infusion but that she had never gone for any of the intravenous steroids Matt had ordered. *Too late to do anything about it now.*

Up in the ICU, Anne found Ruth resting in bed while Miriam, as usual, sat reading her Bible.

Anne closed the door, pulled the curtains closed, then taped a wad of gauze bandages over the intercom to make sure they weren't overheard.

"Wainstock may get temporary custody of Ruth tomorrow. We've got to get Ruth and the scroll out of here tonight."

Ruth's hands gripped her sheets in fear. "He cannot do that, can he?"

"I don't know, but it will take a lot of money to challenge him." She turned to Miriam. "Money that you don't have."

"And where do you intend to take us?" Miriam asked.

"You'll find out. Trust me."

They were interrupted by a knock on the door. "Dinner," a woman's voice called out.

"Just a second." Anne tore the gauze bandage from the intercom. "Come in."

As the kitchen aide set down the meal, Miriam inspected it to make certain it was vegan.

"Very good. Ruth, you eat your dinner. Anne and I are going downstairs to the cafeteria. We must talk for a while."

***

Anne and Miriam sipped tea in the cafeteria, as far away from others as possible.

"I cannot go with you," Miriam whispered. "You and Ruth must go alone."

"That's ridiculous. Why?"

"When you leave, the hospital will notify the police. They will be looking for a young girl in the company of two women, not one. If I am not with you, it will be easier for you to escape. Besides, my appearance and my speech would give us away, and I would slow you down."

"But you're in danger if you stay alone on that mountain. You do remember what happened two days ago?"

"I have lived my entire life on that mountain, as have my ancestors for hundreds of years before me. I do not intend to leave it. For many generations, my family has carried the seeds of our destruction within our bodies, and many have died at a far younger age than I, so I have no fear of death. What I fear is the destruction of the manuscript—and Ruth succumbing to our affliction before she fulfills the prophecy."

"Ruth loves you. She needs you. She'll be devastated if we leave without you."

"She will not need me. She has you to care for her. You have knowledge of the world that I lack, and you can give her the warmth and affection I have never been able to give her." Miriam brushed a tear from her cheek.

Anne reached over and held Miriam's hand. "But you gave her every bit of the love you had. Ruth knows that, and she'll always love you for it. Come, you can say goodbye until you see her again."

***

Anne spoke into the intercom in Ruth's room. "Nurse, we're going to need some private time. Can you hold vital sign checks for a few minutes?"

"Certainly, Dr. Mastik. By the way, Dr. Drisner wrote an order to transfer Ruth to the floor in the morning."

"I know. I've discussed that already with Dr. Drisner. Thanks." She taped the gauze back onto the intercom as Ruth cried in Miriam's arms.

"I do not want to leave without you," Ruth sobbed. "I do not know what I will do without you. Who will protect me?"

"Anne will protect you. And you will see such a big, exciting world that you will not miss me at all."

"That is not true. I will miss you terribly. Are you leaving me because you are angry at me? I swear I will never give you any trouble again. Please."

"No, no, no," Miriam said, holding Ruth's face in her

hands. "I am not angry at you at all. I love you very, very much. That is why I am letting you go. If you stay, you will be in terrible danger. But do not worry. Anne will bring you back to Eden Mountain as soon as she can, and we will be together again."

Ruth turned to Anne. "Do you promise?"

Anne nodded. "As soon as it's safe."

Ruth gave her aunt one last hug. "Then may God's grace be on you."

Miriam kissed her niece on the forehead. "And may God's grace be on you, too."

"Come," Anne said. "We must go quickly."

***

"There is still time to change your mind," Anne said to Miriam as they made the bumpy trip up the mountain. "You'll be all alone up here. It's dangerous."

Miriam stared resolutely ahead. "I will not be alone. I will have Isaiah's spirit, and I will have the spirits of all my ancestors to keep me company. Only in the hospital did I feel alone." But then she smiled. "Except for Ruth."

Anne pulled up to the clearing in front of Artemis's shack and turned off the ignition, leaving the headlights on. She reached into her purse and took out a box.

"This is Isaiah's burner phone. You can call me or Dr. Drisner if you're in any danger. I wrote our phone numbers on a slip of paper inside. I also wrote down the numbers of Dr. Stendahl, Mary Beth, and the hospital emergency department. The battery won't last forever, but it should work until I can get back here…I hope. Want me to walk you to the house?"

"I will be fine. Keep your lights on the path, and I will ring the bell when I am safe."

After Miriam got out of the car, she turned back to Anne. "You will take care of her?"

"As I promised you and Isaiah."

"Then you may do anything you need to protect her.

Absolutely anything."

"What do you mean?"

Miriam gave her the resolute look Anne had seen so many times. "You will know when the time comes."

Miriam walked silently to the path that led to her cabin, then turned and waved. Anne waved back, then waited until the familiar sound of the bell rang out in a single tone, which echoed around the mountaintop. She paused, hoping Miriam would change her mind. After five minutes, she turned the key in the ignition and drove down the twisting trail off the mountain.

***

As the rumble of Anne's car faded to silence in the dense forest, Miriam strolled to her house. After she climbed the ancient wooden steps to her porch, she lit the oil lamp between the rocking chairs of her and Isaiah, which she could not bear to remove.

Inside the house, she marveled at the phone. What a wonderful device, able to send voices across so many miles so clearly that you could hear every inflection. She set it down on the brick hearth, then took the slip of paper Anne had given her and used it as kindling. Once a fire was well started, she picked up an iron poker and stirred up the logs, prompting a shower of brilliant orange sparks. She threw the phone onto the burning logs, held the poker up as high as she could, and drove its iron point through the phone, smashing it to pieces.

It had been a long day, and she was too tired to eat. She changed into her nightgown, crawled into bed, and fell fast asleep.

CHAPTER XVI

Close to midnight, Anne stopped at the ICU's physician-dictation desk, tucked in a corner away from the nursing station. She logged on using Matt's username and password, which she had memorized when he'd pecked his way over the keyboard earlier. *You would think that a man who could design a house as beautiful as his would be more original than Password123.* She typed in an order for an MRI of the abdomen and clicked "STAT." Then she electronically signed the order and logged out.

Ruth was sound asleep when Anne walked into her room and turned on the reading light over the bed. Anne taped the gauze pad over the intercom, sat on the bed, and shook her shoulder.

"Ruth, wake up. We have to talk."

Ruth stirred, and Anne gave her a moment to fully arouse.

"We've got to leave. I have my car ready, with a change of clothes for you in the back."

The night nurse knocked and spoke through the door. "Dr. Mastik, Dr. Drisner ordered a stat MRI of the abdomen. Do you want us to call and see if we can put that off until tomorrow?"

"No, don't wake him." Anne opened the door a crack to speak with the nurse. "Tonight will be fine."

"They called the tech, but it takes an hour for the machine

to warm up. We've got a transporter to bring Ruth to Radiology if you leave now before change of shift, but we don't have anyone that can sit with her."

"No problem. I'll sit with her. Give us enough pillows and blankets so she can take a nap and not get chilled. Can she take her clothes with her? The hospital gown's pretty thin, and they keep the scanner room cold."

"Sure."

"How long until the gurney gets here?"

"Five minutes, plus minus."

"We'll be ready."

***

"Hi, I'm George, the MRI tech," said a short but husky guy in scrubs. "I'll have to leave you here for about an hour while I get the machine ready." Anne noted the "EXIT" door a few yards away, its electronic proximity sensor pad blinking red.

"Sorry to ruin your evening," Anne said.

"No problem. That's what I get paid for. If you need anything, push that button on the wall, and I'll come runnin'."

"I'm sure we'll be fine."

Anne waited until George closed the door.

"Ruth, get up. Quickly. We've got to move."

Ruth jumped off the gurney, fully dressed. Anne arranged the extra pillows and blankets to give the appearance of someone asleep under the blankets. Then she gave a short prayer, held her breath, and passed Lillian's ID card over the proximity sensor.

The moment of truth!

The red blinking light turned green. Anne exhaled as the electronic door slid open. No alarms. She gestured to Ruth, and the two slipped out into the cool night air, the door closing soundlessly behind them.

No time to waste. They ran to the car, Anne motioning Ruth into the backseat where a change of clothing awaited. Then she drove down the deserted Main Street, stopping at the last cross-street out of town.

"All set?" Anne asked.

Ruth nodded and gave a thumbs-up.

Anne turned on the headlights and stepped on the accelerator.

They were on their way. Anne had one hour to put as much distance between them and Eden as she could.

CHAPTER XVII

Anne sped down Route 39, the same road she had taken from Hot Springs and the only way out of town. But she couldn't stay on it for long. She turned on her GPS for only a moment, worried that once the word of their escape got out, the police might use it to track her car.

After a few miles, she turned south on a two-lane country road that traversed the back country toward Virginia. Navigation was harrowing. The road turned unpredictably, and every so often, the shoulder dropped off precipitously into drainage ditches. But at least she was driving through a valley, mainly farmland, and didn't have to worry about falling off the side of a mountain. The vision in her right eye was still blurred from her attack of optic neuritis, and the excitement of the escape from the hospital had aggravated the spasticity in her legs, slowing her reaction time. Fortunately, at this hour, she had the road to herself.

Ruth was asleep, curled up under a blanket in the back seat. Anne turned on the radio, searching for news but finding only bluegrass, gospel, or country-western stations, all of which faded in and out until the Amber Alert came through loud and clear. It described Ruth, Anne, Anne's car, and "possibly another adult female."

The Amber Alerts kept coming at regular intervals on every station she turned to, and they were looking for her car. They would never make it to Charlottesville in this thing.

They would have to walk. She called Gary.

"I've been waiting for your call. Where are you?"

"Do you remember the back road we took into the Monongahela National Forest when we used to go hiking?"

"Yeah. What about it?"

"I need you to pick me up at the turnout where we used to park, a mile from the border on the Virginia side."

"Why?"

"Believe it or not, I'm an Amber Alert. I can't risk crossing by car. Ruth and I are going to hike across the border."

"That's a helluva hike. What time should I pick you up?"

"I don't know, and I won't be able to use my phone. Be there by two o'clock with a change of clothes for each of us. It's going to be a long and dusty hike."

Anne rolled down her window and tossed the phone into a drainage ditch. They were on their own now.

***

After another two hours of driving, much of it on the heavily wooded roads running through the Monongahela National Forest, Anne was in familiar territory. In happier days, she and Roger hiked and camped here with friends, including Gary and Katy. Though most of the park was mountainous and far beyond Anne's current capabilities, she knew of secluded trails running through flat terrain in the valleys.

Anne steered down the unpaved forest road leading to one particular trail, praying that the parking lot—a glorified clearing—had space available. *Yes!* Not only was there space but there were no other cars in the clearing, which made it unlikely they'd encounter other hikers.

"Where are we?" Ruth asked. "Are we lost?"

"No, we're not lost. A long time ago, I used to hike through this park with my husband. I know a trail that will lead us across to Virginia, where my friend Gary will be waiting to take us to Charlottesville."

"What will you do with the car?"

"Good question. For now, I'll leave it here."

"What are we going to eat?"

"I packed some PB and J sandwiches and juice in a backpack. You carry that, and I'll take the tote bag."

Ruth put on the backpack. "Shall we go for a hike?" she exclaimed.

Anne eyed the wooded path with disquiet.

"I guess we shall," she muttered as they opened the wooden gate and stepped onto the trail.

***

"What the hell do you mean I ordered an MRI of the abdomen last night?"

For Matt, the morning had started out terribly and was getting worse by the minute. It started at 2:00 a.m. when he was awakened by the hospital switchboard telling him Ruth and Anne had disappeared. Then Lillian called, half-drunk and sobbing hysterically. Her hospital ID badge was missing, and Buckram demanded to know why she had allowed Anne and Ruth to escape by opening the emergency exit to Radiology.

By three, Matt had arrived at the ICU. The police had already interviewed nursing staff, but no one knew anything due to the shift change. That left only him and the MRI tech—and what Matt was learning did not make him feel hopeful.

"The logs indicate that you ordered an MRI of the abdomen at"—the officer checked his notepad—"ten minutes after midnight, during shift change."

"Where was the order logged?"

The officer pointed. "At that computer in the corner."

"Impossible. I was asleep at home."

"Anyone else know your password? Specifically, did you

tell Dr. Mastik?"

"Of course not. I don't give anyone my—" Matt stopped short. *Oh crap! She was standing over my shoulder when I logged on. And she must have stolen Lillian's badge when she put her to bed.*

"Doc? You okay?"

"Sorry, I have no idea how she got my password."

"Do you have any suggestion where Dr. Mastik could be taking Ms. Morehouse?"

"I would imagine Charlottesville."

"We've got her apartment under surveillance, and we've spoken to her boss, but he hasn't seen her for a week."

"Sorry, officer. I can't think of where she would go. I can tell you she was upset about the guardianship situation with Reverend Wainstock and said she had some sort of a plan. That's all I know."

"We've spoken with Reverend Wainstock. If you think of anything else, here's my card."

"Sure thing." As soon as the officer left, Matt threw the card in the trash. He'd screwed it up; he had to fix this now.

CHAPTER XVIII

Not a breath of wind stirred the forest as Anne followed Ruth down the hiking trail, constantly mindful of booby traps lying in wait to send her tumbling. As the morning sun made its steady climb toward its noon zenith, the forest warmed. At first, Anne welcomed it because it dispelled the lingering cold and dampness that had accumulated overnight on the forest floor. But as it continued its ascent, it seemed to trap the heat and humidity beneath the forest canopy, and Anne's body reacted as it always did: stiff legs that slowed her down.

"Wait up," Anne called to Ruth, five yards ahead.

"Sorry. I thought you were right behind me."

"I was, but I'm not as accustomed as you are to this terrain," she lied.

"Would you like me to take your arm?"

"Not necessary. But perhaps you could carry the tote bag."

"Of course. And I will walk alongside you."

Hiking along the heavily wooded footpath, Ruth chatted excitedly about their upcoming adventure while Anne simply listened, conserving her energy as she could see that the farther they walked, the greater the gradient. Gradually, the dense woods thinned out until the trail was fully exposed to the sun. Anne trudged on as the trail inclined sharply up the side of a hill, its grassy slope leading down to a broad meadow, obscured by fog, a hundred feet below the trail. *Odd, having fog in this heat.*

"Isn't that beautiful?" Ruth exclaimed, pointing down to the meadow. "Look at the colors of all of the flowers."

Anne looked down at the foggy, featureless meadow. Closing her right eye, all she saw was green grass. Struggling to focus, she eventually made out a few bland yellow and pink flowers, their hues washed out and indistinct. She closed her left eye—nothing but fog. *Damn!* The heat had affected her optic nerves, blocking nerve impulses not only to her right eye, where she'd had her attack but also impairing her left eye, already vulnerable from the attack she had years ago.

"Beautiful," Anne said. *Can't tell her I'm going blind. She'll panic.* Anne assessed the upcoming path with apprehension. *Don't even want to think about the rest of the climb.*

***

Fifteen minutes later, as the trail reached its summit, the full heat of the late morning sun beat down on Anne's body. Ruth seemed totally unaffected and chatted on as any teenage girl might. But to Anne, each step proved harder than the one before. The air itself felt dense, like wading in a swimming pool full of hot water. As the incline steepened and Anne's legs weakened further, the air took on the consistency of syrup, like straining against a river of molasses.

Then Anne's legs buckled. Struggling to maintain her balance, she teetered to the edge of the path, and her foot slipped over the edge. Rolling down the grassy slope, she came to a stop halfway down.

"Anne!" Ruth shouted, running down to where Anne lay. By the time she got there, Anne had pushed herself up to a seated position, her legs straight out in front of her.

"Are you hurt?"

"I'm fine. Just let me get up."

"I can help you."

"No! I said I'm fine. I can get up by myself."

She tried. And tried. Pushing herself from side to side, battling to get up, her legs refused to move. She crumpled back to the ground, winded and exhausted, while Ruth gaped helplessly. Grunting with the effort, Anne propped herself up once more, but her legs lay as inert as two logs.

Anne blurted out curses so loudly that a flock of birds took off from the surrounding trees, then she balled her hands into fists and beat her legs continually.

"Stop it!" Ruth cried. "Stop it! Stop it!" She grabbed Anne's wrists and held them tightly, but Anne shoved her aside and pummeled her fists against her immobile legs as if pounding on a door that had barred her from a life of her dreams, howling the curses she wished she had yelled at Roger when he walked out on her.

Anne felt Ruth's arms wrap around her from behind, pinning her arms to her body.

"Let me go, dammit!" Anne shrieked. But Ruth held fast. Anne fought until, physically and emotionally drained, she collapsed into Ruth's grasp, her body wracked by the pent-up sobs she had suppressed for the past five years.

Ruth loosened her hold after several minutes but still hugged Anne until she calmed down.

"You've got to go," Anne said quietly. "Take the tote bag and meet up with Gary."

Ruth got to her feet and stood directly in from of Anne, her eyes fierce. "And why would you have me do that?"

"I can't move my legs, which means I can't walk. And my vision is so blurred I can hardly see. You need to get yourself and the scroll to safety."

Ruth crossed her arms and shook her head. "I will not leave you here." Her voice was reminiscent of Miriam's, resolute and stubborn. "You came this far. Why can you not make it the rest of the way?"

"Heat drains my strength. After you're safe, Gary can send help to pick me up. Don't worry, I'll be fine."

"You are stronger if you are cooler?"

"Yes. And since this park isn't air-conditioned, I'm stuck here until after sunset. Which is why you must go."

Ruth cocked her head, reflecting. "Then go, I shall." And with that, she left.

As Anne watched, Ruth strode off, first through the border of ferns that edged the meadow and then into the forest. When she had disappeared, Anne lay back in the grass, but her head bumped against something hard — the plastic canister in the tote bag, which held the scroll.

Anne screamed Ruth's name repeatedly, but Ruth was apparently beyond the sound of her voice. She cursed in frustration and clutched the canister to her breast. *Come nightfall, help will arrive. Until then, there's nothing I can do.* She lay back and fell asleep as the noonday sun sucked the last vestiges of energy from her.

***

Anne awoke to her shoulder being roughly shaken. In her first seconds of confusion, all she saw was a blurry shadow outlined against the sun, and her name was being called over and over... in Ruth's voice.

"You frightened me," Ruth said. "I thought you were dead."

Anne's mind cleared, but her vision didn't. "Did you come back for the scroll?"

"I came back for you. I told you I would not leave you."

"I told you to leave and —"

"You are not in a position to tell me what to do," Ruth said firmly, her brow creased and her lips tightened. "I will say this once more, and you will not question me further." She grabbed Anne's shoulders and stared into her eyes. "I will not leave you here. I will not leave you. Ever."

"But—"

Ruth put her hand over Anne's mouth. "I noticed a brook as we entered the park. It ran alongside the trail for a while, then turned into the forest, so I went to find it. It is but a ten-minute walk from here. If you get into the water, it will cool you off, and you will get your strength back. Then we will walk out of this park together."

"But I can't walk, not even to the stream."

"Then I will carry you. We had best get started."

Ruth arduously pulled Anne to her feet, then placed her arms around Anne's waist.

"Can you stand?" Ruth asked.

"For a few seconds, no more."

"That is time enough." Ruth picked up the tote bag, supporting Anne with her other hand. Then she turned her back to Anne and braced her legs. "Put your arms around my neck."

"But I—"

"Clasp your arms together around my neck," Ruth commanded, and this time Anne obeyed. "Now, hold tight." Ruth bent forward, lifting Anne off the ground and staggering forward.

***

The journey proved a good deal longer than ten minutes, but Ruth managed to carry and drag Anne through the forest. Twice, Anne tried walking by herself but couldn't do it for more than a few steps, so Ruth constantly supported her. By the time they arrived at the brook, Anne was spent, and Ruth was panting.

The crystal-clear water of the stream rushed down from mountain springs in the foothills of the West Virginia Appalachians before it mixed with other waterways downstream that carried mine tailings and coal dust. The rocks on the bottom of the stream had been worn smooth, and tiny silvery fish darted among them, reflecting the sunbeams that flashed through the trees.

"Come," Ruth said, holding out her hand. "You need to get into the water. I will be with you."

Ruth led Anne into the water, and they both screamed and laughed at its coldness. As they reached the middle of the stream, Ruth lost her footing on the slippery river rocks and fell unceremoniously bottom-first into the brook. For the first time in years, Anne broke out into uncontrollable laughter as she crawled on her knees to mid-stream.

Ruth sat down cross-legged on the rocks, the water a few inches above her waist, and pulled Anne over so that she was almost completely submerged, only her head above water, with Anne's shoulders on her lap.

"How do you feel?" Ruth asked.

"My legs feel stronger already."

"You will feel even better with your head in the water. Come, I will not let you drown. Tug on my sleeve when you are ready, and I will bring you up." Ruth gently lowered Anne's head into the water.

Anne held her breath and eased her head onto Ruth's lap, her hands clasping Ruth's arms. Underwater, she heard nothing but the beating of her heart and the gentle tinkling of water rushing over the stones as the invigorating current coursed over her face and body. Then she opened her eyes and gazed up through the rippling surface at the spectral, wavy outline of Ruth's head and body silhouetted against the sun. She relaxed into an almost spiritual state. Holding her breath became effortless, her body weightless in the rushing water. It felt so peaceful she wished she could stay under the water for hours.

Then Ruth yanked her up.

"Are you all right?" Ruth asked, panicked.

"Of course. Why?"

"You were under a long time. I was afraid you had drowned."

Anne glanced around. The fog in her right eye had

disappeared, and the flowers alongside the brook burst into full color. Her vision was back! She stood up on the rocks, the water flowing around her ankles as her legs held her up with new strength.

"I'm perfect," she beamed. "Never been better. I feel like a new person. Let's find Gary."

***

By three o'clock, they arrived at the trail's end, where Anne was overjoyed to see Gary's car.

"It's about time," he said with a scowl. "I see you had enough time for a swim. Why not a picnic lunch?"

Anne introduced Gary and Ruth and explained what happened in the park. Then she displayed the container with the scroll. "*This* is why we had to sneak out of town. Handle with extreme care."

Gary backed away, his hands up. "Don't worry, I'm not touching it. What is it?"

"A two-thousand-year-old sacred manuscript."

He nodded reverently and handed them each a dry change of clothes. "Here's your stuff. I will never, ever shop for a teenage girl's clothing again. Anne, some of your clothes were Katy's; she was about your size. I also picked up a burner phone for you and brought some of Katy's wigs."

Gary had given Anne a floral print summer dress and low-heeled sandals. He gave Ruth a sleeveless white blouse with designer jeans and light blue sneakers. To hide her long brown hair, Gary had bought a navy-blue newsboy cap. Anne chose a dark brunette feathered look with bangs to best disguise her strawberry blonde bob. Ruth was a different story.

"These make me look like an old woman," Ruth grumbled after trying on several wigs. "Besides, I cannot fit them over my hair."

Anne groaned. "We'll worry about your hair later. Just keep the cap on."

As the two changed in the privacy of the woods, Ruth chatted excitedly about their outfits, giving Anne a glimpse of the camaraderie that must have existed between Ruth and Mary Beth. By the time Ruth finished changing, her speech and mannerisms were transformed. She seemed more like Mary Beth than herself...no longer a throwback to the nineteenth century, but a twenty-first-century teen. All she needed was some cover-up for her olive skin, which Anne applied over Ruth's vigorous protest.

As Gary drove from the park, Anne picked up the burner phone and called the Department of Religious and Biblical Studies at the university.

"This is Anne Mastik. I called yesterday. May I speak with Dr. Peter Jones?"

"I believe he's still in his office. One moment, please."

A brief pause followed. "Dr. Jones speaking."

"This is Dr. Anne Mastik. I'm a physician at the university, and I have a matter of critical importance to discuss with you. I'm...out of town right now, but I'm driving in. May I see you this evening?"

"Dr. Mastik, it's Friday afternoon, and—"

"This *cannot* wait over the weekend."

"How about now, over the phone?"

"We must meet in person. I promise you won't regret it."

"I don't understand what sort of issue—"

"I have an artifact. An extremely delicate and valuable historic artifact that needs safekeeping. If not treated properly, it may deteriorate, even over the next few days."

Dr. Jones held an edgy wariness. "Under no circumstances will I accept stolen or illegally obtained relics."

"I assure you the owners gave it to me freely, and there will be no money involved. Please. You're my only hope. Can we meet tonight?"

During the ensuing pause, Anne's heart pounded, and her

hands shook.

"I'll be in my office until six," Jones said flatly. "This had better be legit."

***

As they drove through Charlottesville, Ruth and Anne in the back seat, the town was just getting started on the evening's activities, which might present a problem. By contemporary standards, Charlottesville was considered a small, quaint college town. University academics and architecture aside, it resembled any number of similar-sized towns around the country. However, to Ruth, whose only familiarity with the outside world was from the window of the Intensive Care Unit, Charlottesville embodied an intoxicating, bustling metropolis full of diverse sights, sounds, and people. For most of the ride, Ruth plastered her face to the window like a five-year-old peeking into a toy store at Christmas. She excitedly pointed at people who strolled past until Anne pulled her back in her seat.

"Ruth, keep down until we get to Gary's house."

"But look at all the people, and the buildings, and the—"

"The police are looking for us. If they find us, I'll be put in jail, and you may have to live with Reverend Wainstock. We can't attract attention. Is that understood?"

Chastised, Ruth nodded silently, eyes downcast. Anne gave her a quick hug. "You can look out the window, but do it quietly."

Two minutes later they pulled up in front of a two-story Colonial fronted by a long porch, whose columns echoed the Greek Revival architecture for which Charlottesville was famous.

Anne hadn't been inside since Katy's death, and not much had changed. The interior was spacious but not overwhelming, and the furniture was attractive but utilitarian. But the kitchen appliances were modern and spotlessly clean, not likely due to Gary's meticulous cleaning but rather because Gary's current concept of a home-cooked meal entailed a well-beaten path from freezer to microwave to garbage compactor, interrupted by a brief stop at the kitchen table. Anne trailed her fingers over the back of the dining room chair where she used to sit, briefly reminiscing of long-ago dinners with Katy cooking, Gary serving, and a table full of friends chatting and laughing together.

Anne knew that Gary's bedroom was the real Gary, and Anne was relieved that the closed door hid its chronic messiness from Ruth. Gary led them past it to the bedroom where Katy had lain bedridden for months before her death.

"Ruth," he said, "you can stay in here." Gary had kept the room unchanged from when Katy died, and Anne's mind flooded with terrible memories of sitting on that bed for hours, holding Katy's frigid hands and feeling helpless to do anything but watch her struggle with the pain. Anne was glad Ruth, and not she, would bunk there.

"And Anne, I hope you don't mind the pull-out sofa in the living room."

"Sounds great."

"You ladies freshen up. I'm off to the hospital. I have a friend in the pharmacy who managed to set aside some recently expired ampicillin for me, no questions asked." He turned to Anne. "I might be able to get you a gram of steroids, but no promises."

"Gary, you're a doll." She gave him a hug.

"The guest bathroom is down the hall," Gary said to Ruth. "It's still got Katy's stuff in it if you need anything. I'll be back in an hour or two, so you two relax."

After Gary left, Ruth picked up Gary's tablet, flopped down on the bed, and tapped away.

"How did you learn to use one of those?"

"Mary Beth." Ruth looked up at Anne with a look of supreme annoyance. "I am not clueless," she huffed, and turned back to the tablet, leaving Anne pondering at Ruth's transformation into a typical American teenager.

"Ruth, I have to meet someone about the scroll. Can I trust you to stay put and not let anybody in until Gary comes back?"

Ruth stayed glued to the screen. "I will go nowhere."

Although Anne was curious to see what a teenage girl brought up in a log cabin would find of interest on the Internet, she didn't have time to find out. She grabbed her tote and raced through the back streets toward Dr. Jones's office as fast as her legs could carry her.

***

"You do realize, Dr. Mastik, that this is highly unusual," Dr. Jones said as Anne sat down and handed him the canister. "No biblical text has ever come to light by being found in a West Virginia cave, which makes the legitimacy of this document highly suspect, to say the least. If you're trying to sell me this as an artifact, it would take months to verify its authenticity, not to mention an investigation to ensure it hasn't been stolen."

"I understand. I know for sure it's authentic, and I don't want a penny for it. I brought it to you for safekeeping and, if possible, to translate it and tell me who wrote it."

"How long has the owner had it in their possession?"

"As near as I can tell, it's been passed on through the generations for two thousand years."

Dr. Jones's eyebrows lifted. "That's almost as old as the Dead Sea Scrolls, and they survived only because they were kept in caves in the arid Judean Desert, not on a mountaintop in West Virginia."

"I know, but please have a look. We can submit it for tests of authenticity in the future, but I need the translation as soon as possible."

"If — and I do mean if — this document is as old as you say, it must be handled extremely carefully, or it will disintegrate. Unrolling it will be a slow and painstaking process. It may take years."

"I've been as gentle as possible, but it's been through some rough treatment in the past day or two, and it seems to be holding up well so far."

Jones removed his glasses, picked up a magnifying glass, and scanned the document through the plastic.

"It is in remarkable condition. Appears to be written on vellum. Very expensive to produce. Most unusual for anything but the most important documents. It must have been treated with something to keep it from decaying."

"It was kept in a clay jar, which was sealed with wax and never opened until two days ago."

"Do you have a picture of the jar?"

Anne showed him the pictures she'd taken.

After examining them, his attitude seemed to soften. "If this is a hoax, you've certainly done your homework."

"Meaning?"

"This jar is a singular type, only found in one specific location from one specific time period. If the age of this jar is verified, this document would be priceless."

"I told you, I'm not interested in the money. I need you to keep it safe and tell me what it says. Please, a girl's life may depend on it."

"I'll do what I can. Can you tell me who the original owner is?"

"For now," Anne said after some hesitation, "they would like to remain anonymous. But in due time, I can let you have any information you need to verify its legitimacy."

Dr. Jones stared at her suspiciously, then nodded. "So be it. I'll do my best."

Anne thanked him and breathed a deep sigh of relief as she left his office.

CHAPTER XIX

Anne carefully navigated the dark side streets on her return to Gary's house, avoiding the busy Downtown Mall District where she might be recognized.

"Ruth, I'm home," she called as she entered the living room. Hearing no answer, she knocked on Ruth's door. "Are you okay?" Still no answer.

Anne threw open the door. The room was empty, though the bed still had the impression of Ruth's body. Anne felt the blanket—still warm. She ran through the house, frantically shouting Ruth's name. Finally, Anne found a note on the dining room table: *I MUST go out to see this amazing city. Please do not worry. I swear I will be careful. I shall be back by sunset. - Ruth*

Anne's fingers and hands shook as she dialed her phone. "Gary, she's gone."

"Who? Ruth?" Gary asked.

"Yes, Ruth, dammit. And I mean gone, as in 'she left the house, and I have no idea where the hell she went.'"

"Didn't she hear anything you said?"

"She's a teenage girl. Disobeying authority is part of her job description. All I've got is a note that she's gone to explore the town. Are you still in your car?"

"Yeah, I'm close to the house. You want me to pick you

up?"

"No. We need to search separately. You check around campus. I'll cover the Downtown Mall."

***

Anne knew the Downtown Mall well. It was a picturesque pedestrian shopping area, typical of the national trend toward renovating downtown areas that had become focal points of moderate-sized towns that could afford redevelopment. Lined with an eclectic mixture of restaurants, small independent bookstores, high-end clothing stores, and antique shops, it also boasted renovated turn-of-the-century theaters and outdoor concert venues that catered to the middle-aged, hippie-turned-yuppie-turned-academician crowd. During most days, residents and tourists casually wandered from shop to shop, taking their pick of the restaurants' streetside tables. But in the evenings, particularly on weekends, the tempo shifted into high gear. And on summer weekend evenings, the pace grew frenetic.

***

It was into this bustling, shifting, noisy flood of humanity that Ruth had been drawn and then pushed about, the pandemonium initially acting on her like a stimulant drug, but the turmoil soon grew disorienting and frightening.

She struggled to free herself.

Propelled involuntarily down the street, Ruth finally broke loose in front of a quiet alleyway, where a weathered, elderly Black man in a well-worn suit and crumpled hat played guitar for the passing crowd. Periodically, he sipped from a small bottle wrapped in a brown paper bag, and his guitar case had coins and dollar bills scattered over its bottom.

"I have no money to give you, but I like your music," Ruth said. "I have never before felt music" — she put her hand over her heart — "here."

The old man's face lit up, his eyes wrinkled into deep crow's feet, and his mouth flashed a broad tobacco-stained smile punctuated by a single gold tooth.

"Young lady, if you feel the blues here" — he put his hand over his own heart — "you can listen for free as long as you like."

Ruth sat down on the pavement and watched the guitarist's fingers fly over the strings of his guitar. After several songs, she clapped, thanked him, and then stood up to leave.

"You be careful, young lady. Have a blessed day."

"May God's grace be on you," she said as she walked away.

Eventually, Ruth made her way to the far end of the Mall. There were few stores and fewer people, with a small park that offered some benches and a large empty tent for summer concerts. Ruth took a break on the first bench, grateful for the quiet and solitude. She needed to get back to Gary's house before sunset, when the Sabbath began, but she had been spun around so many times that she had no idea how to get there.

As she pondered her predicament, a scrawny young man was walking, or rather stumbling, toward her. Like Artemis Donnard, he staggered as if the earth were moving randomly underneath him. He wore tattered jeans and a muscle shirt, with tattoos covering his arms and the visible parts of his chest. His hair was as blond as Mary Beth's, but unlike hers, it had decidedly dark roots and was arrayed in long spikes that exploded from his head. As he got closer, Ruth was astonished by the innumerable piercings on his lips, nose, ears, and even eyebrows. She couldn't help but stare at him as he fell, rather than sat, next to her.

"Whatcha lookin' at, gorgeous?" he inquired, his breath yeasty.

"I have never seen hair like yours. May I touch it?"

"Sure," he said, shrugging. "I never seen a hat like yours. You 'shamed of your hair?"

"No, I like to wear my hat." She gingerly touched the tips of his hair spikes, which gave way with a slight crunch, and she worried that if she touched them harder, they might break off.

"You live 'round here?" he asked, resting his arm on the back of the bench, his hand dropping within inches of her shoulder.

"No, I am far from home," Ruth answered, unable to keep a touch of sadness out of her voice.

"You with your parents?"

"My parents are dead." Her eyes misted. "I live with my aunt and uncle, but I had to leave them."

"You're a runaway?" The young man's voice brightened.

"Yes, I am running away," Ruth answered, wiping away the tear.

"It's your uncle, right? Did he beat you?"

"Oh, no, no! He would never do that."

"I get it. You don't have to tell me what he did. Where you stayin'?"

"I am not sure where it is that I am staying. I am lost."

He became more animated. "I live with a buncha guys. We're all crashin' a few blocks that way." He gripped Ruth's shoulders with both hands, turned her slightly, and pointed off in the distance. As he edged closer, their bodies touched. Ruth tried to pull away, but he gripped her more tightly and dropped his arm, letting his hand rest on her knee.

"I do not think I should stay with anyone. I need to find my way home." Alarm bells sounded in Ruth's head, and she strained against his grip to stand up, but he pushed down on her shoulder and slid his hand up her leg.

"You wouldn't call a cop, would ya?"

"No, please." She remembered what Anne had told her about avoiding the police. "No police."

His mouth broadened into a smirk. "Hey, don't worry about being sent back home. No police, I promise. You can crash with us. We could do a little weed, maybe a few lines, knock down a coupla beers. Y'know, have a little party. My friends would be glad to listen to what your uncle did to you. They'd be real…sympathetic."

Ruth tried to wriggle away, but he wrapped his arm tightly around her and pulled her closer. She was helpless as he moved his face alarmingly close to hers.

"Hey, doncha wanna be friends?"

"Get your hands off her, pervert," a woman's voice said from behind them. A second later, Anne stood in front of them, arms crossed, eyes fiercely blazing.

"Mind your own fuckin' business, lady," he snarled.

"I'm her guardian, and she *is* my business, so get your grimy paws off her, creep. Now! And before you get your hopes up, Romeo, I've got two words for you: jail…bait. Get it? I'm giving you to the count of three to get your sorry ass off that bench and put at least one hundred yards between us before I call the cops, who would certainly be interested in that plastic bag sticking out of your pocket."

The man looked stunned as he loosened his grip. He stared open-mouthed at Anne, then back at Ruth, who instantly slid away.

"One," Anne bellowed.

"Wait a minute. I didn't know she was—"

"Two."

"Damn." He looked at Ruth. "You are one crazy chick!"

"Three." Anne took in a deep breath as if to yell.

"Screw you!" He took off at a run. When he got about thirty yards away, he turned and shrieked, "You two bitches are both nuts." Then he disappeared into the crowd.

***

"Now do you understand why I told you to stay inside?" Anne said as they headed back to Gary's house.

Ruth's eyes were downcast. "Yes," she replied sheepishly.

"You're lucky I found you when I did. That man meant you no good."

"I wanted to see people. I have never seen so many people

before. They are all different. Different clothes, different hair, different faces, even different colors. It was so exciting."

Anne put her arm around Ruth's shoulder. "I know, but there's a lot of danger out there too. For now, you must stay close to me." A chill ran down her spine. "If it weren't for that guitar player back there, I don't know how I would have found you."

Ruth nodded and slid her arm around Anne's waist as they climbed the steps to Gary's house.

***

"I hope you realize you scared the—you scared me to death," Gary said while hooking up Ruth's IV.

"I am deeply sorry. I will not do that again."

"We'll have to think of a new way to hide you," Anne said to Ruth. "With that Amber Alert out, the whole town will be looking for you. At least your hair is hidden by that hat."

"She'll have to wear long sleeves," Gary said, "and we can cover her face with makeup. But we've got bigger problems. I could only get four doses of ampicillin. That's enough for today and tomorrow. Then we're screwed. And I couldn't get any steroids for you, Anne. Sorry."

Anne frowned. Her vision was clouding up again, and her walking slowing down. "I need to make a call. In private."

"Yeah, sure. Use the study."

Anne's pulse quickened as she waited for Evan to pick up his phone. She hadn't felt this way since shortly after she and Roger wed. Finally, he answered.

"Evan, it's Anne. I need your help. Badly. No questions asked."

"Sure. Where are you?"

"I'm…I'd rather not say."

"Just tell me what you need."

"I need a place to stay—with medical facilities, possibly isolation capability, and access to antibiotics."

"I have exactly the place. Can you get to Gethsemane,

North Carolina?"

"Never heard of it."

"It's in the northwest corner of the state. Use your GPS, and I'll meet you in front of the bus depot whenever it works for you."

Anne checked the time. "I can be there by 4:00 a.m. Sunday."

"Wow, this is urgent."

"Evan, please don't tell anybody."

"Of course not," he said.

Anne breathed a sigh of relief. "I can't thank you enough."

"You already have. See you Sunday."

Anne went to check on Ruth, whose infusion should be almost done. She knocked.

A long silence followed. "Yes?"

"May I come in?"

Another long silence. "You may."

Anne found Ruth on her bed, reading a book written in a language Anne couldn't identify. A tear trickled down the young girl's cheek.

"What's wrong?" Anne said, sitting next to her.

"It is the Sabbath. Isaiah is dead, and I should be home with Miriam." Ruth burst into tears. "I miss them so much. I want to be home."

Anne hugged her. "Sometime soon, it will be safe to go home."

"I am afraid. Imah and Abbah are dead. Isaiah is dead. What happens if Miriam dies? I will be all alone. Who will take care of me?"

"I'll take care of you. I made a vow to Isaiah and Miriam that I'll always take care of you. But Miriam's healthy. You'll see her again."

Ruth wiped her eyes. "I want to tell you something. The night my parents died — the night Miriam and Isaiah came to take me—I heard them all saying that I was 'the last.' But I do not know what that means. They always mentioned a prophecy, but when I asked about it, they only said that I was special and that the most important thing in the world was that I have children. Can you tell me what the prophecy says?"

Anne busied herself removing the IV. "I'm trying to find that out myself, and when I do, I'll tell you. Or Miriam will tell you. But for now, don't worry. You've had a long day. Lie down, and I'll stay here until you're asleep."

Ruth put her head on the pillow, and Anne stroked her hair. "You said Imah and Abbah were dead. Who were they?"

"That means 'mother' and 'father,' in the language my parents used when they did not want me to understand them. But Uncle Isaiah had taught it to me, so I knew what they were saying."

"What language is it?" Anne asked.

"Aramaic, the language that Jesus spoke," Ruth answered, and closed her eyes.

CHAPTER XX

Lillian steered her car down the long gravel road to her house after the most horrific day of her life. It had started an hour after Ruth's early-morning abduction when an infuriated Buckram woke her and forced her to fight through a horrendous hangover while he screamed at her over the phone. She had tearfully reviewed the events of last evening with Matt, then explained to the police how Anne must have stolen her ID card and sneaked Ruth out of the hospital. To make matters worse, upon arriving at the hospital, she'd been forced to deal with the press snapping at her like a pack of wolves, and before she could even sit behind her desk, Reverend Wainstock had barged in, ranting for a full half hour before she could get security to show him out.

It had only gotten worse from there.

Lillian couldn't wait to pour herself a big glass of Cabernet and relax on the couch. Maybe two glasses. No, today was definitely a four-glass day. Minimum.

She stepped inside, locked the door, and switched on the living room light.

"I was wondering when you would get home," said a familiar and welcome voice, but Lillian was so startled that she dropped her keys and purse. Even after she saw her lover sitting on the couch by the fireplace, it took her a moment to collect herself.

"I didn't see your car outside," she said.

"I parked around back." He stood and approached her with a glass of red wine. "You look like you could use this."

Lillian ran to his arms, grabbed the wine, and gave him a long, full kiss. She gazed into his eyes and ran her fingertips gently over his lips. "You know what I could really use, don't you?"

"Let's have a drink first," he said, pulling her to the sofa, where they sat and kissed again.

"I heard about the kidnapping," he said. "How's the girl?"

Lillian took a long swallow before answering. "I've been dealing with that situation all day. How about we talk about something else?" She took another lengthy sip, set the glass on the coffee table, then entwined her arms around his neck. "How about we talk about us?"

"I'm wrapping things up at home," he said. "It should be very soon."

"It's always very soon," she pouted, pouring herself more wine. "Very soon, any day, right around the corner. Blah, blah, blah."

"Darling, you know I can't do anything until the divorce is final."

"I'm tired of slinking around. I can't make plans, and I hate my job. I want to leave it, but you won't commit to me."

He held her hands and brought them up to his lips. "On my honor, I swear that soon we'll make this public."

"How soon?"

"If things go as planned, my attorney says no more than three weeks."

Lillian broke out into a smile. "You swear?"

He raised his right hand. "I swear."

Lillian hugged him as her eyes welled up. "I never thought I'd hear you say that."

"Are you happy?"

She wiped her eyes and nodded.

"Then let's drink to it. To us," he said, raising his glass.

"To us," she said, draining hers.

As they both got up, Lillian glanced at the table. "Darling, you hardly touched your wine."

"You know I don't hold it as well as you do."

Lillian frowned. "But we made a toast," she slurred, "to us. You must drink."

"Bring the bottle to the bedroom. I'll drink while I watch you undress."

Lillian stumbled as she picked up the bottle. "Whoo! That's potent stuff."

"A special wine for a special occasion."

Before she could take another step, her eyes rolled up, her legs buckled, and she fell into his arms. He deftly grabbed the wine bottle, cradled her in his arms, and carried her to the bedroom. But instead of laying her on the bed, he carried her into the bathroom and placed her in the Jacuzzi.

Moving quickly, he undressed her, folded her clothes, and set them on the bed. Then he turned on the faucets. As the water splashed over Lillian's naked body, he took her wineglass, wiped it clean, and wrapped her fingers around it before placing it by the side of the tub. He then poured the rest of the wine down the sink and stashed the empty bottle in a plastic bag.

Lillian sluggishly opened her eyes as the water reached her shoulders. "What am I doin' in th' J'cuzzi?" she mumbled sleepily. But as she tried to get out, he pushed her back down and turned on the jets, splashing water in her face. She sputtered and tried to stay above the rising water level, but he held her down, one hand on her chest and another on her face. Even as she kicked and thrashed, her breathing gave way to strangled coughs as he plunged her beneath the foaming whirlpool. After a minute, her struggles weakened.

When her eyes opened in a fixed stare, and all movement had stopped, he walked back to the living room, grabbed his wine glass and the open bottle of wine, and poured most of the wine into the bathroom sink, flushing it copiously with water. He poured what was left into Lillian's glass, wiped the bottle clean, and wrapped her fingers around it before he lay it down next to the glass and cork.

From the foyer, he retrieved her phone and deleted her call history. Then he wiped the device clean and placed it under the pile of clothes. Finally, he slipped his glass into the plastic bag, which he took with him as he left the house, wiping the knobs and locking the door with the key that Lillian had provided him long ago.

***

Miriam sat alone on her front porch, rocking in the darkness as a cool night breeze blew through her hair. It was a beautiful night, the stars standing out against the pitch-black sky and only visible here, far away from the town lights that masked their brilliance. She'd missed the mountains while at the hospital, but Anne was now caring for Ruth. She could trust Anne, whose motives were beyond reproach and whose knowledge would keep Ruth alive to fulfill the prophecy.

Only when the breeze subsided did Miriam heard the ominous sound of shoes crunching on gravel. She recognized that tread. She had heard them before, on the night she and Anne had been here alone, the night of Isaiah's funeral. More than likely, her sister Rebecca had heard them, too, just before she and Samuel perished in the fire.

They were the footsteps of Death.

But tonight, they held no fear, only hope. Ruth was now protected by a woman healer, as had been foretold by the prophecy. With Miriam's death, Ruth would indeed be the last, and the salvation of humanity would follow. Miriam kept rocking as the footsteps grew closer and stopped in the darkness a few yards from the porch.

"She is not here," Miriam said to the darkness. "She is gone."

"I know. I came to tell you I don't wish to hurt her. I only want to protect her."

"Is that what you told her parents? Before you killed them?"

"Yes. And it is a guarantee that I make to you."

"Before you kill me." Miriam said this as a statement rather than as a question.

He paused. "Yes."

"I have no fear of death. Isaiah and I have fulfilled our purpose, as you are fulfilling yours. Ruth is all that matters now."

"Yes, Ruth is all that matters. And I cannot risk you interfering with my plans for her."

The steps came closer. Miriam closed her eyes as she heard them ascend the creaky wooden steps. She opened her eyes but saw only the outline of his body against the background of stars.

A strong, gloved hand grabbed her neck, and she smelled an overwhelmingly pungent odor as a wet cloth covered her nose. Miriam struggled reflexively, clutching and scratching against her assailant, to no avail. As her consciousness receded, her body slumped forward.

The attacker picked up her limp body and carried it inside to the bed, then pressed a pillow to her face. Every few minutes, he touched his hand to her neck, checking for a pulse. When he could feel it no longer, he put the pillow under her head and covered her lifeless body with a blanket.

Guiding his footsteps with a flashlight, he walked several yards from the house before turning around for one last look at the homestead. No need to burn the house down this time. There were no longer any obstacles.

CHAPTER XXI

After Anne awoke, she found Ruth up and dressed, reading from a book she had brought with her.

"What are you reading?" Anne asked.

"This is my Bible. I had to leave my Old Testament back home because it was too big to carry in my pocket."

"May I see it?"

Ruth nodded and moved over to make room for Anne in her bed.

Once settled, Anne glanced at Ruth's head. "You don't have to wear the hat when we're in the house, you know." She reached for the newsboy cap, but Ruth pulled her head away.

"I want to keep it on. I...like it on."

Anne shrugged. "Whatever you like. Tell me about your Bible."

"I copied it myself. That's how Isaiah taught me Aramaic."

Anne flipped through the limited pages. "It's not very big."

"We only have one Gospel, and we have no need for Paul's teachings."

"Your aunt doesn't approve of Paul, I know."

"He is the reason we must live on the mountain."

"Soon, we will go back and live up there."

Ruth looked into Anne's eyes. "You said 'we.'"

"Did I? I guess I did."

"Does this mean you will no longer live here in Charlottesville?"

Oh, no! I promised Bob Rothberg I'd be back at work today, and if he calls my phone, all he'll get is an "out of service" message. Anne cringed. "You know what? I'm not sure that will be an option. But come. My nose tells me that Gary's been cooking."

By the time they reached the kitchen, Gary had already laid out breakfast.

"Coffee, two strips of bacon, and two sunny-side up eggs for Anne, and two pieces of toast, oatmeal with raisins, and a glass of OJ for the young lady. Milk, anyone?"

"No, thank you," Ruth said. "I have already gotten into enough trouble for eating ice cream. Peanut butter and jelly for my toast, please, and a glass of water."

"Eat up," Anne said. "We've got a big day ahead, and we're leaving town tonight."

"Where are you going?" Gary asked when he returned to the table.

"Can't tell you. The less you know, the better."

"Look, this Amber Alert is a bunch of crap. Everything will blow over in a few weeks."

"Maybe, but I can't bet Ruth's life on that. She's going to need sophisticated medical care."

"You'll send me a Christmas card?" Gary said with a touch of edginess.

"Maybe. We'll see."

***

Matt negotiated the twisting road to Lillian's house, as he had done countless times in the past, but this time he didn't slow down on turns, and he was steering with only his left hand as he redialed Lillian's number with his right.

Why isn't she answering?

For some reason, Artemis Donnard's fate filled his head, and he hoped Lillian wasn't in any danger. With a renewed urgency, Matt pushed on the accelerator as hard as he could and still make the turns on four wheels. His brakes screeched as he turned into Lillian's driveway, then took the steps with a single leap, unlocked the door, and bounded inside.

"Lillian, where the hell are you?" He raced through the house, but her purse and keys were in the entryway, while a fresh wine stain decorated the living room carpet. Then he entered her bedroom.

Laid out in a neat pile were the clothes Lillian had worn yesterday. The bathroom light was on, and the door ajar. The sound of churning water gave him a chill. He dashed into the bathroom and gasped at the sight of Lillian's submerged nude body, her eyes open in an unblinking stare. Grabbing her by the arms, Drisner hauled her out of the water and draped her body over the edge of the tub. When he pushed on her chest, water poured out of her mouth and spilled over the floor. Resuscitation was out of the question.

Drisner sat next to her on the bathroom floor and buried his face in his hands. *I could see this day coming. With Lillian's long, slow downhill trajectory, if death weren't by alcohol poisoning, it would have happened when her liver and vital organs refused to repair themselves any longer.* He returned to the bedroom and took out his phone. But before he dialed, he paused.

Something was wrong.

He stared at the neat arrangement of Lillian's clothes. *Odd.* When drunk, she usually threw her clothes around randomly as she staggered to bed — or in this case, the tub — or she simply slept fully dressed.

Matt reentered the bathroom. Lying next to the tub was a partially filled wine glass and an empty wine bottle, the cork still impaled on a corkscrew. There had to be another bottle. Lillian could down several glassfuls without even slurring her speech.

To get this smashed, she must have drunk at least one more bottle.

Matt ransacked the house for the other bottle, not in the refrigerator, the cupboards, or any of the trash cans. He was about to go outside to check the garbage can when something caught his eye: a second cork under the coffee table. He sniffed it and picked up a persistent wine aroma; it must have been freshly uncorked. On a hunch, he headed back to the bathroom. The living room cork bore the brand of the bottle, which had obviously been opened in the living room, but the one on the corkscrew was a different brand. It didn't make any sense. There *must* be a second bottle.

Unless someone had taken that bottle away.

Matt ran outside. The garbage can was empty. He searched the bushes. No bottle. He searched Lillian's car. No bottle. He combed through the backyard. Still no bottle. But he did find something else: Tire tracks. Fresh tire tracks. From a different car than Lillian's.

He needed to call the police, but first, he grabbed a slide-lock plastic sandwich bag from the kitchen and searched until he found Lillian's cell phone under the pile of clothes on her bed. He turned the bag inside out, used it like a glove to pick up the phone, then zipped the bag shut. Pressing the screen through the plastic, he opened her Recent Calls. *Dammit*. The memory had been wiped clean of all incoming and outgoing calls — something Lillian would never do because she liked to have a record of each day.

He made a call from his own phone.

"Federal Bureau of Investigation. How may I direct your call?"

"This is Agent Matthew Drisner. I need to speak to Agent Steven Armstrong in Science and Technology."

"One minute, please."

While Matt was placed on perpetual hold, his thoughts wandered to childhood. It wasn't for nothing that Daddy had taught him to shoot squirrels and rabbits in the woods behind their house. Being the best shot in his high school Rifle Club and winning the Kentucky State Junior Championship in rimfire and long-range categories, he'd been recruited by the FBI, which paid for a free ride through college and medical school. After five months of training at Quantico, he'd been considered the perfect agent to look after the government's most valuable medical asset.

And now, she was in the wind.

"Digital Forensics. Agent Armstrong speaking."

"Steve, it's Matt. Remember I told you about my friend Lillian?"

"The hospital administrator, yeah. What about her?"

"I think she's been murdered. And the girl's gone."

"Gone? How did that happen?"

"Um, a physician I consulted kidnapped her."

"Jee-suss! You gonna tell El Sid?" Sid Antonucci was the department chief and Matt's boss.

"Not yet. I need you to dig out all recent numbers on Lillian's phone. Pronto."

"I'll try," Steve said, with obvious reluctance, "but if you don't locate the girl soon, I'll have to pass this on to Sid."

"I know," Matt said wearily. "Just hold him off for a day or two, would you?"

"I'll try, but when he finds out the girl is lost, the shit's gonna hit the fan, and I don't want to be standing in front of it."

"Got it. See you tonight."

Matt shook his head and dialed 911. "This is Dr. Matt Drisner. I'd like to report a homicide."

***

"Ow," Ruth whined as Gary skillfully started an IV line in her arm. "I hate this medicine. Can't you give me a pill instead?"

Anne stroked Ruth's hair. "Sorry, Ruth, but it's got to be given in a vein. Don't worry, Gary's the best IV starter in Virginia, aren't you?"

"Well, I was in my med student days, but I'm a little rusty now."

"You did great," Anne said. "Couldn't have done better myself."

Gary watched Anne's hands fumble as she packed a suitcase. "I know. That's why I'm the one starting the IVs, right? Wherever you're going, I hope you'll have someone else to stick her."

"She'll be well cared for."

"How many more times will I need this medicine?" Ruth asked.

"A few," Anne lied. With her defective immune system, Ruth would need a full two-week course.

"But I feel fine. Why do we not stop?"

"Because then the infection will return, and you wouldn't want to go back into the hospital."

Ruth pouted and played with Gary's tablet.

Anne locked the suitcase, then she and Gary left Ruth to rest. "Come on, Anne," he said, "why don't you just tell me where you two are headed?"

"For the fourth time, you need plausible deniability, or you'll be aiding and abetting. Ruth and I must be untraceable. That's why I got rid of my phone. I've got a safe place to go, and that's all you need to know."

"Terrific. And how do you intend to get there without waving a red flag for the cops?"

Anne gave Gary her best puppy-dog look.

"Oh, no! Uh-uh!" Gary shook his head. He knew exactly what Anne had in mind.

"Please?" she begged. "Pretty please?"

He sighed. "Jeez, what I do for a friend."

He led her outside, where a black Ford F-150 sat in the driveway.

"I don't know if I can drive a pickup," Anne said.

"I'll need that one to get to work. Here." Gary pressed the garage door opener, and the door lifted, displaying a beige SUV next to a bright red muscle car.

"You're lending me the Barracuda!" Anne shrieked and clapped her hands together in feigned excitement.

"Whoa! Wait just a minute! Nobody, and I mean nobody, drives my '69 Barracuda but me!"

"Gary, I'm joking. Of course, I'm taking Katy's car."

Gary muttered something under his breath and calmed down. "I only use it for shopping, so it's still in great shape. Can't bring myself to sell it."

Anne gave Gary a hug that was cut short by Gary's phone ringing. "It's for you," he said, puzzled that anyone knew she was with him.

"Dr. Mastik, this is Dr. Peter Jones."

Anne detected underlying agitation in his voice. "Good morning, Dr. Jones. Any luck?"

"We have to talk. Not on the phone. In my office."

"Just a second. Let me get inside."

Anne entered the house, and Gary followed.

"How is the scroll?" she said into the phone. "It hasn't been damaged, has it?"

"Don't worry, it's in remarkable condition. I've managed to unroll a small portion. It's...it's.... I can't tell you more over the phone. Meet me in my office right away." Jones hung up.

Anne held the phone, her hand tremulous.

"What's wrong?" Gary asked.

"I don't know. Dr. Jones needs to talk to me in person. Can you drive me to his office? I'd take the SUV, but I can't really duck from policemen if I'm driving."

Gary nodded. "Ruth's IV will be finished in a few minutes."

They both turned to the bedroom and glared at Ruth, who'd clearly overheard.

Ruth raised her right hand. "I have learned my lesson.

Besides, it is the Sabbath. I swear to God I will not take one step from this house."

***

They made the drive in silence, Anne slouching low and running through half a dozen disaster scenarios, not to mention worrying that this could be a trap.

"Relax, Anne. I'm sure everything is okay."

"Jones sounded disturbed. Why meet in his office unless something's wrong? It's damaged. I know it's been damaged, and he didn't want to admit it. Maybe the letters have faded, and it's illegible."

"Don't go charging in there like a bull in Pamplona. Here we are." Gary circled the building looking for police cars, then pulled up to the rear entrance. "When should I pick you up?"

"I'll call when I'm done. We can meet in The Virginian. If you get there first, grab a booth near the kitchen, as far in the back as you can, and order takeout for Ruth."

Anne paused in the empty hallway outside Dr. Jones's office, gathered her courage, and knocked.

The door cracked open an inch. Dr. Jones eyed her briefly before opening the door.

"Come in. Quickly." He shut the door behind her and locked it. "I must know the truth. Where did you get this?"

"I told you everything. As far as I know, it's been sitting in a cave at the top of a mountain in West Virginia for three hundred years. Before that, I have no idea."

"How do we account for the other seventeen hundred years?"

Anne was stunned. "You think it's real?"

"It's certainly real. Or it's an extraordinary forgery. About the clay vessel. Could you go back and get it?"

"I'm afraid I'm not in a position to do that. Why?"

"This is the exact type of jar in which the Dead Sea Scrolls were found in the caves of Qumran. This style of jar is only found in those caves and nowhere else on earth."

"Hold on! For us non-biblical history majors, could you explain what you're talking about?"

"From the second century B.C.E. until just prior to the destruction of the Second Temple in the year 70, a sect of ultra-Orthodox Jews maintained an isolated Community near the Dead Sea called Qumran. High in the surrounding cliffs were a cluster of caves where the Community stored hundreds of documents, many of them in clay jars exactly like yours. Several were copies of Old Testament books, but some outlined the bylaws of the Community, and others predicted an imminent battle between the forces of good and evil, with the Community leading the forces of good. Collectively, these are called the Dead Sea Scrolls, and they are the most significant biblical find of the twentieth century."

"Is the scroll undamaged?" Anne asked anxiously.

"For its age, it's in extraordinary condition. It's written on vellum, a specially processed calfskin, very expensive to produce and only used for extremely important documents. I took the liberty of having a piece analyzed. We traced it to a variety of cattle found only in the Eastern Mediterranean, and the skins were soaked in a solution with an extremely high salt concentration, which is probably why it's been preserved so well. I had that analyzed as well. It contains a unique mixture of minerals characteristic of only one place on earth: The Dead Sea. I compared it to published mineral analyses done on the Dead Sea Scrolls from the early part of the twentieth century, and they're identical. Because Israelis have been mining the minerals in the Dead Sea for the past fifty years, the chemical composition has changed, so you couldn't fake the vellum if you tried. And the chemical composition of the ink is characteristic of the late Second Temple period in Judea."

Anne started to ask a question, but Dr. Jones held his hand

up.

"There's more. Come into my study."

The room next to Jones's office was pitch-black—lights off, and blackout blinds were drawn over a solitary window. Jones flipped a switch, bathing the room in a dim red light from a single bulb. In the center of the room, on top of a simple wooden table, sat a small black box. Through a slot at the box's base, the first few inches of the scroll were drawn out onto the table and covered by a quarter-inch-thick sheet of tinted tempered glass. In the corner, a piece of electronic equipment hummed constantly, with occasional variations in pitch.

"Climate control," Jones said. "I need to keep temperature, humidity, and light levels within strict limits to avoid degradation of the parchment. Here, let me show you something."

He lit up a portion of the text with a pocket flashlight.

"There are two types of writing on this page. Do you see this part here? That's Aramaic. There are very few surviving Aramaic documents, usually just fragments, and that will take some time to translate. But this section is written in Hebrew. There's a field of biblical studies called paleography, which classifies the exact way scribes wrote the letters—their handwriting, if you will—according to the place and time in which the documents were composed.

"These letters here…and here…and here," he continued, aiming the flashlight over different sections of the text, "are characteristically from Judea in the middle part of the first century." He straightened up. "Dr. Mastik, every single bit of evidence I have points to this document being genuine, having been written near the shores of the Dead Sea in the decades after the crucifixion of Jesus Christ, and sealed into that clay jar two millennia ago, as unbelievable as it sounds."

"Were you able to translate anything?" Anne asked desperately.

"It's been difficult. I don't want to risk damaging it, so I've only translated a part of this page. The Aramaic section is the end of some sort of Gospel, but not any Gospel I'm familiar with. I must work on this further because some of the script is faded. But what's fascinating is the paragraph before the Gospel portion."

"Is it a prophecy?"

Jones stared at Anne, astonished. "How did you know?"

"The owners have been living under the instructions of an ancient prophecy for two millennia. It has something to do with a girl giving birth to the Savior of humanity if they follow the teachings of Moses."

Jones stayed silent for a moment before he spoke. "Then I'm certain you'll find this interesting. First, the portion I referred to isn't Aramaic. It's in Hebrew, generally reserved for sacred texts." Jones translated for Anne, illuminating each word with the flashlight.

***

"These words are from the mouth of Yaakov, brother of the Lord, written down by the scribe Eliezer, son of Yehudah, to be given as an augury to those who are descended from my brothers and sisters, our Lord's family. There will soon come a time when Jerusalem shall be destroyed. Before then, those who believe in our Lord shall take safe refuge in the city of Pella. If you and your descendants follow the Law as God gave it to Moses, foreswear eating of any part or product of any animal, especially the blood, and shall live separate from other nations so that you remain holy to your God, then know that at the end of times, your bloodline will die out, all but one last woman. As a foretelling, she will be safeguarded by a healer, a woman sent to you by God. And from the womb of this last woman shall come the salvation of humanity, and she shall be called blessed above all other women on earth."

***

"Dr. Jones, are you sure about that last line? I distinctly remember being told that the prophecy said, 'from her shall come the Savior of humanity.'"

Jones reexamined the document intently. "No. What's written here is clearly *g'ulah,* salvation. *Goel* would be the word for Savior. The two words have the same root, but there's a switch of a letter in Hebrew. I imagine the two words became conflated in oral transmission over generations."

"I guess it doesn't make much difference in context," Anne said.

"You'd be surprised at how significant minor biblical mistranslations can be. What people believe is written can be more important than what is actually written."

"Who was this 'Yaakov,' and what does this all mean?" Anne asked.

"Jesus had siblings. They and their offspring were called the *desposynoi*—belonging to the Lord—and they were especially revered in the early Christian community."

"I thought Mary was a perpetual virgin."

"Jesus definitely had brothers, the most significant being James the Just, whom Paul and the early Christian historians recognized as the first leader of the Jerusalem Christian church. His Greek name translated as James, but his Hebrew name was Yaakov. Jude and Shimeon were brothers, or at least half-brothers, of Jesus and became leaders of what Paul called 'the Judaizers' after James's death. They were thereby related to Jesus, and because they were of the bloodline of King David, they theoretically had a claim to kingship over Israel, so the Romans hunted them down and crucified them as traitors."

Anne was puzzled. "How did this family get here?"

"Can't say. A few years before the destruction of the Temple, the *desposynoi* and their followers, the Ebionites, fled from Judea to the city of Pella, across the Jordan River. The Ebionites faded from the historical record but were considered to be heretics by the early Christian fathers."

"Why?

"They didn't believe in the teachings of Paul. The Ebionites believed...."

"I've heard the Ebionite story already," Anne interrupted, and waved her hand dismissively.

Jones had a bewildered look. "How?"

"It was told to me...," Anne hesitated, then made a snap decision to fully trust Jones. "It was told to me by the girl that the family believes is the prophecy's fulfillment."

"You mean she's the last woman?" Jones asked, incredulous.

Anne nodded. *I could knock him over with a feather right now.*

"Dr. Mastik, do you really think the possessors of this manuscript are descended from the family of Jesus?"

"It sounds crazy, but everything I know goes along with that. They obey a Jewish Sabbath, they won't accept blood transfusions, and they speak and write Aramaic."

"What! Aramaic has all but disappeared as a spoken language. If they speak the ancient form, that would be invaluable to researchers of biblical history. Any chance I can meet them?"

"I'm afraid that's not an option right now." Anne glanced at her watch. "I'm late for another appointment. Please keep the scroll safe, and for now, you must swear to tell absolutely no one."

"Tell no one? This may be one of the greatest finds in biblical literature. Think of its impact on Christianity."

"That's why I'm giving it to you. It may be a dangerous document to possess."

***

Anne kept a low profile as she entered The Virginian restaurant and scanned the single row of high-backed wooden booths. She spotted Gary in the last booth.

"How's Ruth?" Anne whispered as she slid into the booth.

"No idea. Haven't had a chance to go back home yet."

Anne glanced at the menu, then threw it back on the table.

"You okay?" Gary said.

"The last twenty-four hours have taken a lot out of me. I'm worried about taking the trip tonight."

Gary leaned forward and spoke in a hushed tone. "As well you should. Turn around slowly and check out the TV over the bar."

Anne turned and saw her own face on the screen, with closed-captioning saying that she was wanted for kidnapping. Fortunately, the picture was a seven-year-old photo from her UVA badge, when her hair was longer, and she wore glasses.

"May I recommend that we leave post-haste?" Gary said quietly. "I've got a takeout salad and an order of fries for Ruth. I had to park in the Downtown Mall lot. It'll be safer if I pick you up in ten minutes in the cul-de-sac by Varsity Hall."

***

Anne reached Varsity Hall in three minutes. The deserted cul-de-sac was the perfect place to meet Gary and to make a phone call while she waited. She picked up her phone and dialed.

"Microbiology Lab. Cheryl speaking."

"I'm calling from Dr. Drisner's office," Anne said. "Lillian Petrillo dropped off some contaminated fruit for bacterial culture three days ago. Are the results available?"

"Oh my, wasn't that a terrible thing that happened to Miss Petrillo?"

What the...? "I don't know about it. I've been out of the office until today."

"I hate to tell you, but Miss Petrillo was found deceased in her house by Dr. Drisner. Hasn't he told you?"

The blood drained from Anne's face. "No, he...he hasn't come to the office yet."

"Very sad. The police say she drowned in her own tub after drinking too much."

"Sorry to hear that. I'll have to get the details from Dr. Drisner. I don't mean to sound insensitive, but do you have those culture results?"

"I don't recall any fruits being brought here. Give me a minute, and I'll check the records."

Gary drove up and gestured her into the car. She hurried into the backseat and slumped down low as Gary drove off.

"Ma'am, are you still there?" Cheryl said through the phone.

"Yes."

"I checked the records going back all week. I'm sorry, but no fruit or any other foodstuff was brought in for culture. May I have your name, please?"

Anne hung up.

"What's wrong?" Gary asked.

"Lillian never brought the fruit to the lab, and now she's dead. I have no proof that Isaiah was murdered."

***

When Anne and Gary arrived home, the living room windows were wide open.

"Ruth, are you all right?" Anne called out.

"I'm fine," Ruth called curtly from her bedroom.

"Why are the windows open?"

"I needed some air."

"We brought you some dinner," Anne said. "May I come in?"

Ruth opened the door barely enough to stick her arm out, grabbed the takeout bag, and shut the door without saying a word.

"A 'thank you' would be nice," Anne said.

Ruth grunted a brusque 'Thank you' between mouthfuls of fries.

"Remember, we leave in a few hours," Anne said loudly. "Pack anything you need in the suitcase. We'll be traveling light." She waited for an acknowledgment, but all she got was another grunt. *Teenagers.*

"I don't envy you traveling with Miss Sweetness in there," Gary said as he closed the windows and drew the blinds.

"She's stressed out. This week has been horrendous." She gave Gary a peck on the cheek. "I can never repay you enough for all you've done."

"Just get her where she'll be safe—and I wouldn't mind you coming home in one piece either."

***

Matt stood in Lillian's living room, watching the police fumble the investigation while he collected his thoughts.

With a missing bottle of wine and a suspicious drowning, he was potentially dealing with the same *modus operandi* as the poisoning of Artemis. No sign of forced entry, so Lillian had probably known her murderer, just as Artemis had. And Lillian's murder coincided with the disappearance of Anne and Ruth, a fact that seemed to escape the police but weighed heavily on Matt.

Time to revisit Eden Mountain.

***

Five minutes before sundown, Drisner parked his car near the path that led to the tree mirror. He hurried up the path to take advantage of what little daylight was left.

He smiled at Anne's clear footprints: shoes on while ascending, shoes off coming down.

The clearing interested Drisner, with its empty ice cream container and various artifacts of the girls' secret visits strewn about. He was about to start up the trail to the Morehouse home when something caught his eye. Bending down, he examined the path to Artemis's shack. There were large shoeprints, not made by Artemis's clunky work boots, but a refined, smooth leather sole. *Looks like Marcus Stendahl knew about the path to the Morehouse cabin after all.*

It didn't take long to reach Miriam's house, but when he got there, he felt a heavy silence hanging over the farm.

"Miriam," Matt yelled, "we need to talk."

He called her name repeatedly, with a growing sense of alarm. Across the field were the Morehouses' horse and sheep, their only animals. But the horse was feeding in the vegetable garden, something Miriam would never allow.

"Miriam!" he called out with a new urgency. "Where are you?"

He walked up the porch steps. Between the two rocking chairs, on a small table, sat a bowl of fruit. Remembering Isaiah, Drisner inspected them carefully, but there were no signs of injections.

The farmhouse was eerily silent. He stopped outside of the bedroom and steadied himself as he opened the door.

Miriam was lying in bed, the covers up to her neck. He tentatively approached, calling her name but expecting no answer. Even in the fading light of dusk, he could tell she wasn't breathing, her face the ashen color of death. He reached under her hair to feel her carotid pulse. Nothing.

It had been his job to protect them, and he had failed. Now only Ruth remained. *How does Anne think she can provide the care Ruth needs with a two-state Amber Alert out for them?*

He smelled something vaguely familiar, a pungent odor that hearkened back to his medical school days. It filled the room but was strongest coming from Miriam. He noticed a faint red rash surrounding her face and eyes. He carefully lifted the edge of the pillow and sniffed. The odor was so strong it made him dizzy. He ran outside for air, finally recognizing the smell.

Diethyl ether. Miriam had been anesthetized and probably smothered with the pillow while she was under.

Matt made a call.

"Toxicology. Agent Bartlett speaking."

"Phil, this is Matt Drisner. You get anything out of that bottle of Wild Turkey I sent you?"

"It's an opioid. The prelims look like fentanyl, the drug of choice in West Virginia nowadays, and in most of the country, I might add."

Drisner swore under his breath. *Fentanyl was so available that even little old ladies could get it.* "Any idea how much was in the bottle?"

"The quantitatives are still out, but in nonscientific terms, 'a shitload' would be more or less correct. My guess is a thousand mics, maybe more. Real overkill, if you'll forgive the pun."

"Christ. Thanks, Phil. Any fingerprints on the bottle?"

"Only from the deceased."

"Thanks anyway. I may have more samples coming your way."

"Anything in particular?"

"Blood. And wine."

"Wine, huh? Sounds like the same M.O. to me."

"Me too. Later."

***

Matt had to think. His investigation had hit a wall. *What was Anne doing up here that night, and why was her empty backpack outside that crevice?*

By the time Matt made the short uphill walk to the outcropping, the sun had set, so he pulled out his flashlight. The chunk of granite's only distinguishing feature was the vertical crevice, not deep enough for Anne to have hidden in, and he'd investigated it thoroughly the other night. But then there was that rat that had run out, unseen when Matt had originally shone his flashlight into the crevice. *There might literally be more to this than meets the eye.*

In he went. A couple of yards deep, the crevice made a sharp turn, so he continued until he was blocked by a waist-high projection. If he sucked in his stomach, he could push past it, but was it worth risking being trapped in a rock when nobody knew where he was? Then he shone his flashlight past the projection, surprised to see it shining against a wall six feet away.

Matt sucked in his stomach, said a prayer, and squeezed past the obstruction into a small chamber, with the remains of a burned-out candle melted onto a small ledge in the rock.

As he inched backward, his heel hit something that made a hollow clunk. Looking down, he saw a tall clay jar in a small recess, its cap lying a few inches away. *Could this be what Anne had been looking for? If so, whatever it had held was important enough to risk her life.*

Matt looked closer. The rim and the cap were covered in a thick layer of wax. He lifted the jar a few inches. Much too heavy for Anne to carry out, even with Miriam's help. As he set it down, something brushed against its side. He reached into the narrow space and pulled out a white envelope. After scanning the contents, he let out a low whistle of astonishment before tucking the envelope in his back pocket and starting the laborious squeeze out of the tomb-like enclosure.

CHAPTER XXII

Gary threw the suitcase into the back of the SUV and slammed the trunk door shut. "All packed. Everybody geared up?"

"Ruth's putting on her makeup," Anne said, adjusting her own wig. "But I'm a little worried about her. She hasn't left her room since we came home."

"I've been thinking about what you said. Her uncle's dead, she hasn't seen her aunt for days, and now she's going on a trip with no idea of what's at the other end. Poor girl's been through a lot."

"I know." *Just wait until she learns about the prophecy.* "Ruth, Sabbath's over. We need to get going," Anne yelled as she threw a snack bag into the back seat.

The door to the garage opened, and Ruth approached the SUV, her eyes downcast. She wore a long-sleeve blouse and her newsboy hat, which hid as much of her as possible.

"Here, let me smooth out your makeup," Anne said. She ran her fingers over Ruth's forehead, but Ruth brushed her hands away. "Stop. I am fine."

Anne and Gary briefly exchanged knowing looks.

"I guess we're all rarin' to go," Gary said, giving Anne the keys and closing the passenger door as Ruth sat down. "Registration's in the glove box, tank's full. You sure you won't tell me where you're going?"

"If anyone asks, you never heard about the Amber Alert, and I asked to borrow the car for a camping trip with my niece because my car was in the shop."

"But—"

"I know, it's pretty lame. But the less you know, the better. Don't worry about us."

"You'll call when you're safe?"

"Sure." They hugged one last time before Anne got in the car and buckled up.

Gary opened the garage door, then Anne backed the car out, stopping just long enough for one last wave before driving off.

***

Gary watched the SUV until it made the turn toward the interstate, then went back inside the house, grabbed a beer from the fridge, and sat down on the living room couch. He leaned over to pick up the TV remote from the coffee table but stopped short at what he saw next to the remote.

Anne had left her burner phone.

***

As soon as she turned onto Interstate 64, Anne put the car on cruise control. The less she had to do with her stiff legs, the better. The highway was almost devoid of traffic on Saturday night, but she kept the car at just a mile or two above the speed limit. No sense in risking a traffic stop, and she didn't have to worry about traversing any backroads until she got close to the Cherokee National Forest.

Meanwhile, Ruth was napping in the back seat, her head resting against the window. Anne took advantage of the quiet to rethink her future.

Charlottesville held nothing for her anymore. Bob Rothberg would not take kindly to her irresponsibility in making no attempt to explain why she hadn't come back to work. She certainly had no job waiting for her, probably not even a polite but non-committal letter of reference if she applied elsewhere — assuming anyone would hire an accused felon.

Accused Felon. She hadn't even considered the label until now, but that's what she was. Surprisingly, it didn't bother her. Simply put, she'd kidnapped a minor and transported her across state lines. But Miriam would testify on her behalf. She wouldn't get prison time, but the charges would certainly be a black mark on her record. *So much for her medical license.*

Then there was Evan. Anne was surprised at the ease with which she'd fallen for him. While she wouldn't mind falling in love, and this certainly presented the opportunity, that was no reason to make some crazy road trip to the middle of nowhere. She glanced in the rear-view mirror at Ruth and realized how fiercely protective of the girl she had grown in the past few days, which only reinforced the decision to divert her life in a totally different direction. Anne hadn't realized until now exactly how much she had bonded with Ruth, a girl who had lost both parents like she had and who reminded Anne so much of herself — headstrong and determined and something of an outsider.

At the very least, it will be interesting to see if Ruth fulfills the prophecy. And leaving the burner phone at Gary's had irrevocably cut the last slim thread that connected her to her old life.

Ruth roused. "Anne?"

"Yes?"

"You keep saying you will tell me about the prophecy sometime. Is it time yet?"

Why not? "I guess this is as good a time as any. Do you remember that scroll we carried through the park?"

"Mm-hmm."

"Well, your people have been protecting it for the past twenty centuries."

Ruth looked startled. "Are you being truthful?"

"Yes. It includes a prophecy that if your community follows

the Laws of Moses, lives apart from other people, and doesn't eat meat or anything that comes from an animal, especially the blood, then there will remain one last woman, which is you, and from this woman will come the salvation of humanity." Anne shot a quick glance at Ruth and smiled. "And she shall be called blessed above all other women on earth."

Ruth rested her head back on the window and said nothing for several minutes, although her eyes stayed open in thought. "I want no part of that prophecy," she finally declared.

It was Anne's turn to be startled. "Why wouldn't you want the prophecy to be about you? The whole world would remember you forever. I'd think you'd be excited about that."

"To be chosen by God is to suffer. The Hebrews were enslaved bitterly for four hundred years in Egypt and wandered for forty years in the desert. The Prophets suffered. Job was a favorite of God, but he suffered terribly. The Jewish people suffered in exile in Babylon and have suffered still more for two thousand years. Mary watched her Son die horribly, all because God chose him. All I want is to go back to Eden Mountain, marry a good man, have happy children, and keep to ourselves on our farm. Charlottesville has been quite enough of the world for me, thank you. Good night." Ruth closed her eyes to go back to sleep.

Wow! Definitely did not see that coming.

***

A little after two in the morning, Anne turned off the interstate onto the two-lane road that would eventually take them to Gethsemane. Ruth woke up and stretched.

"Where are we?" she asked.

"Eastern Tennessee, heading to the Carolina Smoky Mountains, I think."

"I'm hungry."

"There are snacks on the back seat."

Ruth rummaged through the backpack. "I am tired of peanut butter sandwiches. Can we stop and get some food?"

"We're trying to lie low."

"We are no longer in Virginia. Can we stop? Please?"

Good Lord. "We'll stop at the next diner. I suppose I could use a stretch and a cup of coffee." The twisting mountain roads were playing havoc with her spasticity, anyway.

Finding an open eatery proved to be quite an undertaking, but as luck would have it, they stumbled across an all-night roadside diner somewhere out in the sticks.

Anne turned to Ruth. "In case anyone asks, we can't use our real names. What do you want me to call you?"

"Mary Beth," Ruth said with a grin. "And I'll call you Rebecca, Imah's name."

"I think 'Mom' would sound better. Let's get some grub."

Anne sat across from Ruth in a small booth. A stocky square-built waitress, her leathery, wrinkled face a testament to a two- or three-pack-a-day habit, approached with pad and pen in hand.

"Don't usually see folks here at this hour unless they're goin' huntin'," she commented. "Griddle won't open for another hour."

"Can we please have two oatmeals, a piece of cherry pie, a cup of coffee for me, and a glass of water for my daughter?"

"Sure thing. You passin' through?" she asked, a touch of suspicion in her voice.

"Trying to get to my parents. We're in a bit of a hurry."

"Comin' right up," she said, nodding. Then she headed behind the counter.

Anne and Ruth had their breakfasts a minute later— finishing them in five. They were about to leave when a police officer sauntered into the diner. He held a brief whispered conversation with the waitress before ambling to their booth.

"You two lost? Don't usually see folks driving through at this hour."

"Heard last night that my mother is ill. Kind of an

emergency."

"Uh-huh," the officer grunted, looking down at his notepad. "How about you, young lady? Could you take off your hat, please?"

"I do not want to," Ruth replied, eyes averted.

"I didn't ask whether you wanted to. I asked you to take off your hat. Please." His voice rose sharply at the last word.

Ruth continued looking down. "I would rather not."

The officer's voice rose further. "Listen, young lady, you can either take your hat off now, or I can take you and your mama to the station, and you can take it off there."

Anne perspired under her light summer blouse. "The officer asked you to take off your hat, Mary Beth. Take it off. Now."

Without lifting her head, Ruth reached up, pulled off her newsboy cap, and threw it onto the table. Anne stifled a gasp.

Somehow, Ruth had chopped her long brown hair in a grotesque approximation of a pixie cut but more closely resembling a ragged, chaotic punk style. She must have tried to bleach it too, but she'd left the dye on too long. Her hair was pale blonde, almost white, all the way to the roots.

The officer noticed Anne's reaction and smiled before putting his notepad back in his pocket. "I got a teenager too. Don't worry. It's a phase. She'll outgrow it in a year or two." He waved to the waitress on his way out and drove away.

***

"What on earth did you do to your hair?" Anne asked after they got on their way.

"I wanted to look pretty, like Mary Beth," Ruth said quietly, avoiding Anne's eyes in the mirror. "I found a bottle in the bathroom, so I cut my hair and did this while you and Gary were out." She finally looked at Anne, eyes moist. "It did not turn out the way I thought it would."

Anne almost burst out laughing, but poor Ruth was so

distraught she stifled her laugh and turned it into a cough.

"Is that why you opened the windows? To get the smell out?"

Ruth nodded. "Are you angry with me?"

"Of course not. Sometimes you have to see what it's like being someone else before you're happy being yourself."

"I am sorry I have been so much trouble to you," Ruth sobbed. "You are not going to leave me, are you?"

"No, I will not leave you. Ever," Anne said gently.

***

Drisner paced. Time was passing, and he was no closer to tracking down Ruth and Anne or to determining the identity of the murderer who might be after them. *What am I missing?*

His phone rang. He picked it up before it finished its first ring. "Drisner. Who's this?"

"It's Steve. I've been working all day on Lillian's phone. You wanted the results ASAP."

"What did you find?"

"Lots of calls to Eden Community Hospital, but I guess that makes sense."

"Anyone in particular?"

"All to the hospital operator. Can't tell where they were routed from there. Then there was a whole mess of calls received yesterday, most from local media."

"Yeah, that was when the news got out that Anne and Ruth were gone. What else?"

"Several interesting numbers kept popping up, all from burner phones. All incoming, none outgoing."

"Lillian's boyfriend, I bet. She complained that he would call her, but she couldn't call him. He may be our prime suspect because I suspect Lillian knew her murderer. Anything else about those calls?"

"No, but the guy was smart. He'd use one burner for a few calls, then switch to another. By now, he's probably on a totally different burner."

"Where was he calling from?"

"Can only run a trace while the phone's being used. No chance of that now."

Matt swore. *Another dead end.* "Anything I can use? Anything at all?"

"I traced Lillian's phone records back five years. There were a lot of calls to and from one number in Morgantown, West Virginia. And I mean a lot. At least a few a week, sometimes every day. Some calls were long, too. Then, bingo, they stopped a few years ago."

"An old boyfriend?"

"Maybe not so old. A few days after those calls stopped, Mr. Burner started — with the same pattern. Lots of calls, some long. Never missed a beat. But that's when all the calls were in one direction. In, not out."

"So, unlikely to be a new guy."

"Mr. Morgantown probably got spooked, didn't want to be traced, and started using burners. I'll bet he never told Lillian his number."

"Do you have a name?"

"Not yet. I've got to get ahold of the service provider, and they're closed. I'll call first thing in the morning. Oh, and in case you were curious, the only prints on the phone were Lillian's."

"Thanks, Steve. Let me know when you find anything new."

"Sure thing."

Things were looking ominous. In less than a week, the peaceful town of Eden had four murders, with no way to solve them. The murderer was on the loose, possibly focused on Ruth and Anne, and they were out somewhere in the night, unreachable and untraceable.

Would Anne go to Charlottesville? The cops had already tried the Infectious Disease Department and gotten nowhere. She wouldn't dare go to her apartment. And if she was staying with a friend, he had no idea how to find them.

There was one clue he hadn't explored yet: Anne's last talk with Wainstock. She'd always been angry about the guardianship battle, but after her last conversation with Wainstock, she'd developed a desperate edge. Perhaps Wainstock was the key.

He made the call. "Reverend Wainstock, this is Dr. Matt Drisner. Sorry to wake you, but I need your help. It's important."

"You haven't been to church for years, Matt. Can't this wait until morning? I can meet you before services start."

"It's not that kind of help. I need information. About Dr. Mastik and Ruth."

Wainstock's voice suddenly became animated. "Where are they? What happened to the girl?"

"I'm trying to find them. Listen, Anne had a conversation with you two days ago. What was that about?"

"We discussed the importance of saving that poor girl's soul from the false religion she and her family practiced."

Matt rolled his eyes. "There must have been something else."

Wainstock was silent. Matt could practically hear his brain churning.

"We talked about a document that the family has been hiding for two thousand years."

That's what was in the clay jar. "Why is it so important?"

Another long pause. "It's Satan's work. It needs to be destroyed. I can tell you no more."

"Please, what is in it? What does it mean to Anne or the Morehouses?"

"Goodnight, Dr. Drisner."

Matt refrained from throwing his phone across the room. There was a document important enough to the Morehouses that they had kept it safe for two thousand years. Anne had risked her life for it, and it was dangerous enough to Wainstock that he was willing to destroy what was probably a valuable ancient artifact. Where would Anne take that document and keep Ruth safe? It had to be Charlottesville. There must be some contact at UVA that she knew could safeguard it.

Matt checked the University of Virginia website for the Department of Religious and Biblical Studies. Most of the faculty's specialties were of no relevance, and many were out of the country on sabbaticals or archeological digs. But one faculty member stood out: Dr. Peter Jones, an expert in Second Temple Jewish and early Christian literature as well as Middle Eastern languages. Matt ran down Jones's impressive list of publications. They all pertained to the late Second Temple into the early Christian periods. Anne would surely trust him to interpret and protect the document.

Dr. Jones wouldn't be thrilled about being called at 1:00 a.m., but Matt had no choice. Five rings later, Jones answered. "Who the hell is this?"

"My name is Dr. Matt Drisner. I'm a physician in Eden, West Virginia, and I'm a friend of Dr. Anne Mastik. I have reason to believe that Dr. Mastik is in imminent danger, but I can't reach her by phone. Do you know of any way I can get in touch?"

There was a good ten seconds of silence at the other end of the phone.

"What makes you think I know her?" Jones asked warily.

"She had an ancient historical document, and she was going to bring it for safekeeping to someone at the University. I figured it had to be you."

"What do you want with this manuscript? *If* I had seen it, that is."

"I don't care about the manuscript. I need to find Anne. She may be in danger."

That seemed to loosen Jones up. "She gave me a phone contact here in Charlottesville. I don't know whose number it is, but she was going to stay at this residence for a few days. Dr.

Drisner, is this about the girl?"

It was Matt's turn to be cautious. "She told you about Ruth?"

"She told me about a girl who spoke Aramaic. I know about the Amber Alert. I can't imagine she'd put that girl in any danger."

"She wouldn't, but someone else might."

"Let me know if there's anything else I can do to help. Dr. Mastik seems to be an extraordinary woman."

You don't know the half of it.

Immediately after hanging up, Matt dialed the number.

"'Lo. Who's this?" a sleepy voice answered.

"Dr. Matt Drisner. I'm looking for Anne Mastik and Ruth Morehouse."

The voice snapped to alertness. "Who is this? And what do you want with Anne and Ruth?"

"I'm Dr. Matt Drisner," he repeated deliberately. "A week ago, I asked Anne to come to Eden, West Virginia, to treat my patient Ruth Morehouse, and now she may be in danger. I got your number from Dr. Peter Jones at UVA. He said you might know where Anne took Ruth. Who am I talking to?"

"Gary Nesmith. I'm a friend of Anne's. What kind of danger?"

Pressed for time but knowing that Nesmith was probably protecting Anne, Matt continued. "In the past week, four people have been murdered here: Ruth's uncle and aunt, and two that have connections to Ruth and Anne."

"Ruth's aunt is dead too?"

"Yes, and whoever killed her might be after Ruth."

"They're not here anymore."

"Where did they go?'

"No idea. I lent them a car, but Anne refused to tell me where she was going. It was somewhere Ruth could be safe and get her antibiotics. Sorry, but that's all I know."

Drisner had one glimmer of hope. "Did Anne make any phone calls while she was there?"

"A few to Dr. Peter Jones, a few to my cell. Oh, and one more that she made in private the night before she left, but she didn't say to whom."

"Do you still have the phone she made that call from?"

"Yeah, right here."

"Check recent calls. Is there a name listed for that call?" Drisner's heart pounded violently against his ribcage.

"Let's see…. Recents…. Here it is. Nope, no name, just a number and a location, Gethsemane, North Carolina. They'll be okay, won't they?" Gary asked.

"I hope so," Drisner answered, and hung up.

Why the hell is she heading there? Matt pulled up Gethsemane on his laptop, and a red dot popped up in the middle of the foothills of the Carolina Blue Ridge. *Not much of anything there except…. Jesus Christ! Regen Corporation!*

Evan Garaud!

Matt smashed his fist repeatedly into his forehead. How could he have missed it?

Gethsemane was twenty miles from the nearest sizeable town and over a hundred miles from an academic hospital. In fact, the single most distinguishing characteristic about Gethsemane was its isolation. The surrounding area was barren except for a few scattered rural routes that traced twisted paths through the forests and peaks of the Blue Ridge Mountains.

The perfect spot to hide a kidnapped girl.

CHAPTER XXIII

Matt was in big trouble. But at least now he had a lead.

He tossed a tent, sleeping bag, and toolkit into a knapsack. He unlocked his gun case and considered what he needed to take, settling on a Beretta 92FS and a 300 Winchester Magnum with a sniper scope.

As he threw his gear into the backseat of his Silverado, his phone rang. Caller ID showed "El Sid." *Dammit, Steve, I told you to buy me some time.*

"Drisner speaking."

"What the hell is going on there?" said Sid Antonucci.

"There's been a problem, Sid."

"A problem? The kid's aunt and uncle are dead, she skips town, and nobody knows where she is—that's what you call a problem? A problem is when your faucet's leaking on Christmas Eve, and you can't find a plumber. This is not a problem. This is a disaster."

"Take it easy. I've tracked her to Gethsemane, North Carolina, and I'm on my way there now. She's with an Infectious Disease doctor and, at least as of ten o'clock last night, was healthy. I'm sure she's safe."

"Correction. She is not safe until she's back in our sights, and that means finalizing Operation Gene Pool."

Matt's gut twisted. "You can't finalize Gene Pool yet. She's only fifteen."

"Old enough. Now that she's been off the mountain, we can't risk losing her again. I'm sorry about her family, but we have no choice."

"But Sid—"

"Drisner, this protocol was decided on long ago. Find the girl and bring her back, whatever it takes. And I mean back to Bethesda, not West Virginia. Is that understood?"

"Yes, sir. Understood."

"I want progress reports every six hours. You have until dawn Monday. If the girl's not in a secured van on her way to D.C. by then, I'm sending a full task force to Gethsemane. We'll find the girl ourselves, and we'll do it the hard way if we must. Is that clear?"

"Yes, sir. On my way."

"Make no mistake, Drisner. Your ass is on the line. Do not screw this up."

***

Anne guided the SUV down what passed as the main street of Gethsemane. In front of a drugstore at the end of the street was a green wooden bench with the words "BUS DEPOT" painted boldly in white. Anne parked the SUV in front of it, then she and Ruth got out and stretched. They were up in the mountains, and even in July, an early morning chill turned their breaths to clouds of white vapor that rose into the air and blended into the foggy mist enveloping the entire town. They stood at the edge of what must be the business section. Anne counted a total of four streetlights and perhaps eight stores, including a drugstore, a diner next to it, and a gas station and service mart across the street, but no cars. Anne sat on the bus depot bench.

"Well, we're here," she said as cheerfully as possible.

"Wherever 'here' is, there is not much of it," Ruth moaned. "I am cold."

"There should be someone coming any...."

Before she could finish, a black Cadillac Escalade turned onto the street and pulled up in front of them. To Anne's delight, out stepped Evan. She rushed into his arms, and they embraced.

Anne was breathless. "I was worried you weren't coming."

"Sorry, my research complex is way out of town. It's tough to negotiate those mountain turns in my tank." Evan held her at arm's length. "It's good to see you again." Then he pulled her closer and gave her a long kiss, which Anne happily returned.

Ruth loudly cleared her throat.

"I'm sorry," Anne said, breaking away. "Ruth, this is Dr. Evan Garaud. Evan, meet Ruth Morehouse, the young girl I spoke to you about."

Evan extended his hand. "I've been looking forward to meeting you, Ruth."

Ruth mumbled an incomprehensible greeting and briefly shook his hand.

"She's tired," Anne said. "We had a long night."

"Of course. It's a long ride to the complex, so follow my car."

***

As dawn broke, the Escalade slowed and turned off the main road, its tires grinding on a narrow gravel road leading through a forest thick with pines.

Ruth stirred and opened her eyes when Anne touched her shoulder.

"Time to get up. We're here."

The Escalade came to a stop in front of a small guard house and an electronic gate. A tall chain-link fence stretched across the road and was topped by razor wire as it disappeared into the forest on either side of the road. A security guard shined his flashlight at the Escalade and waved it and Anne's car through the gate.

A series of small wooden barracks-like buildings made

up two neat rows on either side of the road. They gave way to a series of attractive houses with well-manicured lawns and gardens of azaleas, hydrangeas, and hollies. As Evan and Anne drove farther, they came to a broad cul-de-sac encompassed by an imposing two-story brick building with a curved façade that stretched halfway around the cul-de-sac. Evan stopped at the last of several entrances and got out of the Escalade.

"Last stop," Evan called out. "Everybody out."

"Quite a setup you have here," Anne said as Evan helped her out of her car.

"A work in progress. Let me show you to your quarters."

"Where is everybody?" Ruth asked as Evan held his ID badge up to an electronic proximity lock at the building's entrance.

"It's Sunday. There's only a skeleton crew overnight. The morning shift hasn't come in yet." He led them down a long hallway.

"Will Ruth be able to get her antibiotics?" Anne asked. "She needs them soon."

"Nursing staff will be here in an hour, and I've been able to sneak a vial of natalizumab for you. You'll both be getting infusions later this morning."

"How'd you manage that? Do you run an authorized infusion center?"

"No, but I pulled some strings and told them it was for animal research."

"I am hungry," Ruth wailed. "When do we eat?"

Anne put her finger to her lips, but Evan smiled patiently. "Don't worry. I'll have room service send breakfast in a few minutes."

"Ruth has some particular requirements," Anne said. "She's strictly vegan."

"No problem. And…here we are." He stopped in front of a door at the end of the hallway and ran his card over an electronic lock.

The door opened into a spacious suite. They stepped into a great room with vaulted ceilings. A U-shaped tan leather sofa, flanked by a matching love seat and recliner, faced a stone fireplace. Over the fireplace hung a seventy-inch television, its speakers embedded in the walls. To the rear was an opening into a cozy but fully equipped kitchen and a dining area with a maple wood table set for two. Ruth stared open-mouthed.

"Come. Let me show you to your bedrooms," Evan said. "You each have your own bathroom, television, and Wi-Fi, and I've outfitted Ruth's bedroom with full medical monitoring."

"I can't believe all this," Anne gushed. "It's magnificent."

Evan touched her arm. "I hope this will convince you to stay." He pressed his lips against hers. Anne responded by wrapping her arms around his neck and drawing him closer. For a long moment, they kissed passionately.

"I really must go," Evan whispered, moving his eyes briefly in Ruth's direction and smiling. "I have a lot to do, and you both must be exhausted."

Anne touched his cheek. "See you later."

"Of course. I'll take you both on a tour of the grounds."

After he left, Anne sat on the sofa next to Ruth.

"It would appear to me there is a great deal of affection between the two of you," Ruth commented matter-of-factly.

"Yes, so it would appear." Several clinks sounded in the hallway. "Ah, that sounds like our breakfast arriving."

Sure enough, after a knock on the door, a white-clad server let himself in, pushing a rolling service tray.

"Good morning, ladies," he said. "May I set your breakfast down on the table?"

"Yes, sir," Ruth said, wide-eyed.

The server lifted the cloches from the breakfast plates and set them on the table along with a pitcher of orange juice, a carafe of coffee, and a silver sugar bowl and creamer.

"I hope you find this satisfactory. Feel free to pick up the phone if there's anything else you need. The operator will be glad to direct your call." With a quick nod, he left.

Ruth practically squealed with delight as she devoured her bowl of oatmeal with raisins and nuts. "Anne, this is like a dream. I wish Aunt Miriam were here to see it all."

"Slow down. We have all day," Anne said, gratefully sitting down to her Eggs Benedict. "I can't wait to see the rest of the facility."

"How do you know Evan?" Ruth asked between mouthfuls.

"I met him shortly before I came to Eden to take care of you."

"He is very nice. I like him." Ruth paused a moment, then looked directly at Anne. "Do you love him?"

"That's a rather personal question, don't you think?"

Ruth shrugged. "I do not know much about love. When Mary Beth and I sometimes talked about boys, she would say she was in love, but that did not seem to last very long. Miriam and Isaiah never talked about love, and I do not remember my parents talking about it either. Other than God's love, that is. But I do not think that is the same thing."

Oh God, is The Talk part of the deal I made with Isaiah and Miriam? Ruth is getting to that age, though. Better to have it sooner than later.

"To answer your question, I like Evan. A lot. But it's a bit too soon to say whether I love him."

"What is the difference?"

Choose your words carefully, Anne. "Liking someone can happen very quickly. You can like someone because they're fun to be around, they're easy to talk to, and they make you laugh. I'm sure that's how you feel about Mary Beth. Love…that's different. It takes time."

Anne spoke unhurriedly as she struggled to recollect her

feelings from the early years of her marriage. "There's a closeness that develops, a feeling that you're completely safe, that you can trust that person totally with your innermost feelings, thoughts, and dreams. But it's even more than that. It's seeing that person walk through the door at the end of the day, and you feel your heart leap, and you can't stop smiling. It's the feeling that the rest of the world could disappear, but you could still be happy spending the rest of your days with that one person."

Ruth looked awed. "Have you ever been in love?"

"Yes. Once." A tear rolled down her cheek.

"Oh, Anne, I am so sorry." Ruth ran around the table to hug her. "I did not mean to make you cry."

Anne hugged her back. "Sometimes it's good to cry. Come, finish your breakfast. We've got to start our infusions."

***

When the nurse arrived to start the intravenous lines, she told Ruth and Anne to go to their separate rooms, but Ruth successfully begged the nurse to let them remain together. Five minutes later, Ruth sat up in her bed, hooked to the telemetry unit as the antibiotic dripped into her vein. Meanwhile, Anne settled into a leather recliner to surf the internet for the four hours the natalizumab infusion would take. Occasionally, as Ruth perused a Bible she'd found in her nightstand, a scowl would cross her face, and she'd skip through several pages.

"What's wrong?" Anne asked.

"This is so different," Ruth said. "I recognize most of this Gospel called Matthew and portions of Mark and Luke. And John talks a lot about Jesus, but it is different than what I am used to. Most of the rest talks about what Paul said and did more than it does about what Jesus said and did. Abbah, Imah, Isaiah, and Miriam all talked about Jesus, but I don't remember them saying much about Paul."

"Christianity has changed quite a bit since your ancestors wrote down their Bible." Anne recalled her conversations with

Dr. Jones and Reverend Wainstock. "I was lucky to get your scroll to an expert for safekeeping."

***

Matt had just exited the interstate in Tennessee on his way to Gethsemane when his phone rang. He eyed the twisting mountain road warily and put it on speaker.

"Hell of a time to take off on a vacation, Drisner," John Buckram said angrily. "How am I supposed to run the ICU without a doctor?"

"Sorry, John. Personal business."

"With Lillian's death and the Morehouse kidnapping, the whole hospital is a mess right now. Do you have any idea of the chaos going on? When will you be back?"

"A few days at most."

"What if the police need you?"

"I've given them my statement and told them everything I know about Artemis, Lillian, and Miriam. They've given me the thumbs-up to leave town."

"Just get the hell back ASAP. My ass is hanging in the wind."

"You're a big boy, John. I'm sure you can handle it. If you're not sure what to do, think of how Lillian would've handled it." Matt turned off his phone. He had more important business right now.

CHAPTER XXIV

Matt parked his truck at Karl's Kwik Korner Market and Gas, got out, and stretched his back and legs, stiff from the long drive. Aside from the cluster of cars gathered by a nearby diner, the street was deserted. From the looks of it, the diner was filled with families dressed for church. Meanwhile, in a voice he could hear clear across the street, a waitress shouted orders to the cook.

Matt strolled into the market. A clerk sat behind the counter, chewing Red Man and reading a Hollywood tabloid.

"Mornin'," Matt said with as much animation as he could muster. "I'm looking for someone who might have been passing through last night."

"Don't open on Sundays 'til eight," the clerk said without looking up. "Ain't seen no out-of-towners since then, 'cept'n you."

"Is there a medical facility near here?"

"Nearest hospital's in Boone, but if I were you, I'd keep drivin' 'til I got to Winston-Salem."

"I mean a medical research facility. Do you know of one nearby?"

For the first time, the clerk looked up. He spit out his wad of tobacco and gave Matt a penetrating gaze. "What if I do?"

"I'd like to know how to get there."

The clerk went back to reading his rag but drummed his fingers on the counter. "Might be somethin' like that a few miles out that-a-way." He waved his hand vaguely in the direction southwest of town, then drummed his fingers on the counter again.

Matt took out his wallet and laid a ten-dollar bill on the counter. "Can you be a little more specific?"

The clerk stuffed the bill in his shirt pocket. "Ya take that street right over there and foller it a good ways out. Then, ya make a right turn onto a gravel road and foller that until ya cain't go no further."

Matt set another ten-spot on the counter. "Exactly how far is 'a good ways out'?"

"I'd say, oh, 'bout eight, maybe ten miles. The road got no street sign, got no houses, got no place to park your truck like a huntin' trail would. Jes' kinda leads off into the woods." He stuck the ten-spot into his shirt pocket with its companion.

"Much obliged for your help," Matt said wryly. "By the way, how's the food at the diner?"

"Best in the Blue Ridge, I'd say. Martha's got her own chicken farm, bakes her own pies. Everything's fresh as ya can get."

Matt crossed the street to the diner and sat in a corner booth. Before long, the waitress, a tall, middle-aged woman with bleached blonde hair and a broad smile accentuated by lipstick a few shades too red for church, came to his booth.

"Well, hello there, young fella. Don't see many strangers in here, least of all on a Sunday. Name's Martha. What can I get you?"

"I heard your eggs are to die for."

"Only way to get 'em any fresher is to hold a hen over the griddle an' give her a good hard squeeze."

"Great. Three eggs, over easy, and a cup of coffee."

"We got terrific homemade sausage, and the pie of the day

is blackberry. I picked 'em fresh yesterday."

"I'll take both, and I've got a question. Can you tell me anything about the research facility outside of town?"

Martha's smile vanished, and she looked around quickly to make sure nobody had heard. "Everyone's got their food. I can take a minute." She slid into the seat across from him and leaned in. "It's a strange place, is all I can say," she said in a conspiratorial tone. "Don't nobody in town work there, and nobody I know has ever been in there. It's only once in a great while anybody who works there comes to town. Kinda spooky if you ask me. I been told by people that got lost goin' down the road that leads to it that the whole place is surrounded by a barbed wire fence, an' they got armed guards at the gate shooin' people away."

"You know of any way I can sneak a peek at the place without the guards seeing me?"

Martha leaned closer. "The turnoff is eight miles out of town," she whispered. "If you go 'bout a half mile past it, there's a huntin' trail off to the right that leads up the side of the mountain overlookin' the place. Don't know if you'll get a good look through the forest, but it's the best I can tell you."

"One more question. Do you know where I can get Wi-Fi?"

"Sweetheart, does this look like a Starbucks to you? Unless you see a dish on their roof, I don't think anybody in town gets Internet."

"Hey, Martha," a customer yelled, "what's a guy gotta do to get a little service 'round here? Starve to death?"

"Oh, hush, Frank. I'll be right there." Martha got up and gave Matt a wink. "Be back with your food before Frank even makes up his mind what he wants to order."

***

"Anne, wake up. You're missing a beautiful day."

Anne opened her eyes to see a smiling Ruth, whose hands lightly shook Anne's shoulders.

"Guess I was more tired than I thought," Anne said, yawning and stretching in the recliner where she'd received her infusion. "How long have you been awake?"

"A few hours. I have been watching church services on the television. Those churches are enormous. I have never seen so many people. More than Charlottesville."

"Would you like to go to one of those churches someday?"

"No, I miss being on the mountain and talking about God and Jesus with Miriam and Isaiah. Charlottesville frightened me. Too many people."

"Someday soon, we'll go back to the mountain. But for now, we'll be staying here with Dr. Garaud."

There was a knock on the door. "Are you two decent?" Evan's voice rang out. "May I come in?"

"Come on in," Anne said.

Evan stuck his head in. "If you're both rested up, I'll show you around the compound. I know a great place for a picnic. Ready?"

***

For the first time, Anne got a decent overview of the property, which was deceptively large. The shape was roughly triangular, with the security gate at one apex of the triangle, the two-story laboratory in the center, and smaller satellite buildings behind the lab. Clearly, efforts had been made during construction to spare the old-growth pine forest that filled the compound behind the laboratory and shaded the buildings, which seemed designed to blend with the environment.

Evan took them down a wide walkway through the forest, covered with pine straw from the overhanging trees, and Anne breathed deeply of the aroma. The ground felt wonderfully soft and cushiony compared to the rocky terrain she'd climbed in Eden. As they strolled wordlessly along, Anne's ears picked up myriad sounds: the gentle crunch of their footsteps on the pine straw, distant bird calls, and the frantic hammering of a woodpecker. The tension melted from her shoulders. *I could get used to this.*

"How much farther?" Ruth asked, breaking the tranquility.

"Not much. Believe me, it's worth it," Evan answered. "Ah, here we are."

They emerged from the forest onto a grassy area the length of a football field, which ended in an abrupt drop-off about fifty feet from the forest edge and opened up into a spectacular panoramic view of the Smoky Mountains, seemingly stretching off forever into the mists of western North Carolina that gave the mountain range its name.

"It is so beautiful," Ruth exclaimed.

"Perfect place for a picnic, wouldn't you say?" Evan said, laying a red and white gingham tablecloth on the ground and setting it with china plates, crystal glasses, and silverware. "Sometimes, I come here just to watch the sunset over the Smokies. It's a magnificent view and incredibly peaceful. Don't get too close to the edge, though. It's a 250-foot drop to the valley floor." Evan gestured to the gingham cloth. "Have a seat. I've got burgers, coleslaw and potato salad for Anne and me, ratatouille and roast corn for Ruth, and honest-to-God homemade lemonade for everybody."

"What is ratatouille?" Ruth asked.

"It's a French dish made with summer vegetables, olive oil, and herbs," Anne said before turning to Evan. "Where did you get the recipe?"

"Traditional Garaud family recipe. It's got a few secret ingredients my grandmother made me swear never to divulge." He spooned some onto everybody's plates.

"He cooks, too," Anne said. "Evan, you never cease to amaze me. I can't believe this lab facility. How in the world did you get it built?"

"It wasn't easy. I happened across this property a few years back and managed to buy it on the cheap. The design and construction were the hard parts, especially here out in the sticks. I had to round up a bunch of venture capitalists to front the money, but once I told them about my major breakthrough in transplant technology — and I do mean major — they opened their wallets. In short, the lab is primed and ready to go. But Ruth seems less than thrilled with medical talk, so why don't you tell me about what's happening in Eden?"

Anne shared the long tale of the week's adventures.

"What did you think of Charlottesville?" Evan asked Ruth.

"I would rather stay here. It reminds me more of home," Ruth said with a telltale catch in her voice.

Anne touched Ruth's shoulder. "Don't worry. We'll get you home soon. But for now, we're safe here. Nobody can find us."

"Then how will Miriam know where we are?"

"If you're in Anne's hands," Evan said, "I'm sure she knows you're safe. Now, everybody dig in before the flies get to it."

***

Matt climbed high enough on the hunting trail to catch a glimpse of the compound through the trees, but it wasn't until he climbed onto a jutting rock ledge up on the mountainside that he got a good view.

Binoculars in hand, he scanned the well-camouflaged compound. He made out the lab building and some of the residential quarters, but much of it was well-concealed from above by tall pines. Around the periphery ran a razor-wire-topped chain-link fence, and multiple security cameras sat atop high posts set at regular intervals. Whatever was going on inside that compound clearly merited tight security.

Matt searched the fence, looking for any defect or gap he could exploit, but it appeared solid. At the western edge, he spotted a grassy field with a steep drop-off, the fence vanishing as it dived over the edge of what must be a steep cliff. He spotted one security camera, but its range was probably limited. After all, no sane person would try to breach the premises via the cliff. As he combed the field for other cameras, he caught sight of something that made him stop short: three people picnicking. But a stand of intervening trees blocked their faces. He reached into his backpack for the Winchester Magnum and scrutinized the field with his sniper scope. Much better. But what he saw almost made him drop the rifle.

He clearly made out Anne sitting alongside a man and a girl he could swear was Ruth, wearing jeans and a white blouse, but her hair was dyed ash blonde and cut in some disastrous punk style.

Matt refocused the scope. No question it was Ruth. Anne must have disguised her. *But who was this guy they were having dinner with?* He trained the scope on the mystery man but could only see the back of his head, and the sun was starting to set. In a few minutes, it would be too dark to make out his features.

Ruth stood and walked toward the cliff, then sat cross-legged a few feet from the edge as she watched the sunset. Matt refocused on Anne. She was smiling and saying something to the man, then she reached over and pulled his head toward hers. The man leaned forward and kissed her, allowing Matt a brief glimpse of his face. Which was more than he wanted.

For the second time, he almost dropped his rifle, both from the shock of recognition and incredulity over the kiss.

Evan Garaud. *Was Anne in love with him?*

Matt set down his rifle, slid down from the ledge, and sat on the dirt trail while the sun slipped behind the mountains. It took him several minutes to process what he had seen and even longer to process how he felt.

Long after the sky turned dark, Matt logged on to his satellite-linked cellular phone and dialed.

"Drisner?"

"Yes, Sid."

"I hope you have good news."
"You'd better sit down. This is a doozy."

CHAPTER XXV

"And finally, this is our game room," Evan said with a flourish. "Which ends our walking tour of the main building's living quarters."

Ruth and Anne stepped into a large room. There was a movie screen against one wall, a flat-screen TV against the opposite wall, and multiple game tables, including Ping-Pong, pool, Foosball, as well as smaller tables for chess, checkers and cards, and chairs for reading and socializing. Disconcertingly, the scattered group of teenagers engaging in all the available activities stopped what they were doing and stared at Ruth.

"Allow me to present our special guests," Evan began. "This is Ruth Morehouse and her guardian, Dr. Anne Mastik. They'll be staying with us for a while."

Several teens approached and said hello to Ruth, who turned to Anne with a pleading expression. "May I stay?"

"Of course. I'm going to finish the tour with Evan. You'd be bored anyway."

A lively cluster of teenage girls swiftly surrounded Ruth, her face beaming, and guided her to the game tables.

Evan introduced Anne to a stout middle-aged woman reading at a corner desk.

"Barbara is our chaperone," he said. "During the school

year, the staff's children attend boarding schools but come home for the weekends. When they're here in the common room, Barbara makes certain they're safe."

"I keep a careful watch on the children, especially the teenagers," Barbara said with a wink.

"Ruth's a sweet girl," Anne said. "She won't give you any trouble. But she's a bit naïve."

"I've worked with teenagers most of my adult life. Not much gets past me. I'll keep a special eye out for Ruth, I promise."

Anne turned to say goodbye, but Ruth was already engrossed in spirited conversation with a swarm of new friends. She was surprised to feel a tad snubbed by how easily Ruth separated from her.

Evan took Anne's hand. "Come. I'll show you the labs."

***

"I have to admit," Anne said as they strolled toward the laboratory wing, "I just got an inkling of what my mother must have felt when I left for college, and I've only known Ruth for a week. It must have been hard for her aunt to let her come with me."

"I'm sure she knew that you were the best hope for Ruth, who seems to be a singular girl, by the way."

Evan unlocked the lab area with his ID card. As the door slid open, Anne heard a faint hiss and felt a light breeze drawing her into the lab corridor.

"The entire lab is under negative pressure. Keeps the risk of infection down," he explained as they both donned sterile gowns, masks, and gloves. "We run the fans 24/7. There's nobody here now, so we can go into any rooms you wish."

The initial tour, looking through observation windows from the hallway, astonished her. In the middle of the western North Carolina woods, Evan had designed and built an advanced high-tech facility. In addition to a series of research laboratories, there were advanced technology MRI scanners, CTs for guided needle biopsies and lumbar punctures, and even a fully equipped surgical suite.

Evan stopped at a door decked with a bright yellow biohazard sign.

"And now," he motioned with a swaggering gesture as he opened the door to a small white cubicle, "my pride and joy."

Anne's face was tinged with unease. "I've never been taken to a biohazard facility on a second date before."

Evan chuckled. "That's not a warning. It's a reminder. This is a sterilization room. Put these goggles over your eyes."

Anne obeyed, and Evan pushed a large red button on the wall. A light spray enveloped them as Evan signaled Anne to turn around. As soon as the spray stopped, a green light flashed, and a door opened. They removed their goggles, and Evan led Anne into the lab.

Whatever she had seen from the hallway was a mere hint of the actual lab. In actuality, the complex contained a sequence of immaculate, fully equipped labs. Evan proudly pointed out the state-of-the-art equipment, culture equipment, temperature baths and 3-D printers.

"Are you doing human organ transplantation?" Anne asked.

"That's the next step. We've got a team that's ready to go. In fact, while Barbara is cueing up the evening movie for the kids, why don't we go outside and chat?"

Anne enjoyed the touch of crispness in the mountain breezes after sunset as she and Evan wandered together through the forest. She told Evan about the circumstances surrounding their escape from Eden, including Wainstock's subterfuge, the Amber Alert, and her concerns that someone was trying to kill off Ruth's family.

"I don't see why you went to Charlottesville," Evan said. "It would have been safer to come directly here."

"I was entrusted with a valuable historical document. I needed to give it to someone for safekeeping."

"What kind of document?"

Anne hesitated. "I'd rather not say." *Who knows how Ruth's new friends would react to* that *tidbit of news?*

"What about your job at UVA?"

Anne sighed. "That's also ancient history. I haven't contacted my chairman for days, and against his will, he's been holding down the fort. Worse, I'm a fugitive. I can't exactly saunter into the department and act like nothing's happened."

Evan grew visibly enthusiastic. "Then let me make you an offer. When we start doing transplantations, we'll need an Infectious Disease doctor with exactly your expertise. I can offer you the job right now, and I will beat whatever salary the university could offer."

"I...I don't know what to say. I'm flattered, but—"

"I know, it's a big decision. I don't expect an answer right now but consider it an option."

Right now, what other options do I have to consider?

***

Matt retraced his steps down the mountain from the rock ledge. The main hunting trail was easy to follow, but that would just take him back to the road. After a lot of trial and error exploring the labyrinth of side trails, he managed to find one that led to the cliff defining the western end of the compound. Taking advantage of the moonlight, he inspected the cliff face, losing sight of it as it plunged into the gloom of the valley below. He traced the security fence, ten yards in from where he stood and illuminated by a single overhead spotlight. It tracked down the cliff face for twenty yards before ending at a long projecting rocky ledge. To avoid the security camera, he'd need to climb down the cliff outside of the spotlight beam, scoot across in the shadow below the ledge, then scale back up the cliff to the grassy field. That drew his thoughts unwillingly back to seeing Anne and Evan kiss.

What a jerk!

He hid his stuff under a large fallen tree, then strapped his flashlight to his shoulder, tucked his Beretta into his waistband, and stuck its silencer and a small tool kit into his pockets. Down he went into the darkness.

***

Anne sat in front of Evan's fireplace, the flames casting a shimmering radiance, and sipped her Cabernet. "I still can't believe how you built such an incredible facility in the backcountry."

"Please, there will be time to discuss business and medicine later. This time is officially restricted to talking about Anne Mastik." Evan put his wine glass on the coffee table, picked up an iron poker, and stirred the dying logs, provoking a flurry of embers that spiraled up into the chimney and flared the fire back to life. The music was set low enough that it didn't interfere with conversation but loud enough that it could be heard over the crackling of the logs.

Anne shifted her legs to relieve the spasticity. "There's not much to say. I went to medical school with dreams of becoming a surgeon. Then I married with dreams of becoming a working wife and mother. Then I got multiple sclerosis, and BOOM! I had to think up a whole new set of dreams when the old ones flew out the window."

"I didn't know you'd been married," Evan said.

"He was a good man, took my MS in stride and accepted the physical changes, but he couldn't accept the emotional changes."

"Such as?"

"I had to prove to myself that I could do anything, that any offer of help was an offer of pity, and I resented it. But now I realize that Roger tried his best." Anne took a long sip of wine and stared into the glass before continuing. "He couldn't put up with my pushing him away, and I changed into a woman he didn't know how to love anymore." She wiped away the beginnings of a tear.

Evan touched her hand. "You do publicize your independence issues."

She gave a short laugh. "Then you remember our golf game."

"Our first date, and you fell down a hill. How could I forget?"

"Well, I'm changing, thanks to Ruth. Sometimes it takes a person really needing you before you realize how much you need them."

"Perhaps you could see it in your heart to need me as well?"

Evan leaned forward, and Anne closed her eyes. She felt the warmth of the fire against her face and could still detect the flickering orange-red light through her closed eyelids. For the briefest moment, Evan's head blocked the heat and light before the gentle pressure of his lips met hers. She placed her hand behind his neck and drew him closer as his hand caressed her thigh, then wandered to her waist and chest. She gave an involuntary gasp as Evan cupped her breast in his hand, wrapped his arm around her, and supported her as she lowered herself to the carpet. Anne cradled his head in her hands and welcomed the weight and warmth of his body on hers.

***

Matt gripped a handhold on the cliff face, his feet pressed into a gap for support, then glanced at the security fence. It would have been easier to climb along the fence itself, but the spotlight had forced him into the darkness outside its cone of illumination. Of course, if Regen had installed infrared detectors, he might find himself at the wrong end of a rifle when he reached the top of the cliff.

The moon crept over the cliff edge, allowing Matt to make out the dim shadows outlining potential handholds and footholds. Then he spotted a sapling growing out from the rock an arm's length away. He took one foot out of its supportive crevice and pressed it against a projecting rock to test its weight. Feeling secure, he grabbed the sapling and swung over to grasp it with both hands — just as the rock propping his foot broke loose and clattered down the cliff, crashing into the arboreal canopy above the valley floor. He reflexively swung his foot to a nearby ridge for footing, then grasped a thick clump of weeds jutting from a slit in the rock.

Using whatever means he could, Drisner continued his steady creep until he reached the ledge, whose smooth undersurface offered no grip while its projecting slant eliminated any footholds.

Matt gripped the leading edge and worked hand-over-hand, his fingers in the full illumination of the spotlight. After creeping out a foot or two, his feet lost their purchase, and he dangled freely above the valley floor. *No turning back now!* He continued inching along the ledge until his fingers touched the concrete footing of the fence post.

Halfway there and no alarms. Yet.

Shoulders and forearms burning and fingers half-numb, he finally worked his way around the ledge. A fortuitous indent in the rock at foot level allowed him to rest his aching arms while he made a critical calculation. On the one hand, he had to keep away from the spotlight's funnel, but with every second spent creeping sideways, the cramping aches in his fingers and toes worsened, and the risks of plunging to certain death increased. He took slight solace that, in the darkness, he couldn't see how far he would fall.

He worked his way ten yards past the fence when the guiding moonlight unexpectedly disappeared, leaving the cliff face in total blackness. A large raindrop struck his head, and a distant rumble of thunder reverberated through the valley.

End of discussion. Drisner scrambled straight up the cliff face as fast as his aching muscles would let him. Luckily, the geology turned more accommodating, and he got to within five yards of the cliff edge when, with a blinding flash of lightning and a simultaneous sharp crack of thunder, the heavens opened. Torrents of rain thrashed the mountain, making any handhold treacherous. In no time, a river of rain could rush out of the forest, cascade over the cliff face, and wash him into oblivion.

Jesus, I'm a sitting duck!

He jammed his foot as far as he could into a still-dry vertical crack in the cliff face and, clutching and scraping with his hands, inched his way up. On either side, water poured over the cliff edge and splashed over rocks that minutes earlier had been his pathway along the cliff face. Rivulets of water began trickling into the crevice when his fingers touched a thick tree root that had somehow meandered in. He pulled it as hard as he could, and it held fast. Another hard yank convinced him that it would support his weight, so he rope-climbed it to the cliff edge. But he didn't dare grasp the wet sod above, knowing it would disintegrate in his hand. Instead, he lifted his leg and crammed his foot into the crack, wedging it against the root, then heaved himself over the cliff edge onto the grassy field.

He caught his breath and moved on. No time to rest. The pouring rain likely hid him from the security cameras, but the next flash of lightning would light him up like a cockroach on a white kitchen wall. He sprinted across the field, legs aching, not stopping until he was several yards inside the forest. He dove under a low-lying cluster of pine branches to gain cover.

In the nick of time.

A distant pair of flashlight beams waved back and forth across the path leading from the main compound. Matt pulled a clump of pine straw over his head, drew his Beretta, and screwed the silencer onto the muzzle. Two guards approached, but their guns were holstered, their conversation casual, mainly curses about the difficulty of lighting cigarettes in a downpour.

Come on, guys, it's pouring. Take a breather, go back to the breakroom, and pour yourselves a nice hot cup of coffee.

Matt's legs cramped as he waited out the guards' cigarette break. After five minutes, evidently feeling their job descriptions did not require getting soaked, they retreated to the compound. Matt crumpled to the ground underneath his pile of pine straw.

So much for the easy part.

CHAPTER XXVI

A magical sensation of weightlessness lifted Anne as she walked arm in arm with Evan along the Morehouse farm. The sun warmed her face, and she no longer needed her legs as she and Evan floated a few feet above the ground. Ruth's voice called, and as she and Evan turned, Ruth floated toward them, her arms spread wide to embrace them both.

Then, with a brilliant flash of light, the entire mountaintop exploded like an erupting volcano, propelling them all into the sky.

Anne sat bolt upright in bed, her heart pounding and her breath coming in deep gasps. The rumbling aftermath of the thunder filled her ears. Lying next to her, illuminated by the fire's dying embers, was Evan's well-toned body. She reached out and touched him, seeking the reassurance of his strong arms. He stirred, opened his eyes, and grinned, but when he saw her expression, he reached out and grasped her. "What's wrong?"

"I was having the most wonderful dream when the thunder woke me," she said, and snuggled close to his body.

He wrapped his arms around her. "Then go to sleep and get back to your dream."

"I'd rather rest here in your arms." After a moment, she propped herself up on her elbow. "By the way, you never did tell me about your groundbreaking new research."

"It's one o'clock in the morning. You sure you want to hear about it now?"

"I won't be able to get back to sleep anyway," she said with a contented sigh as she caressed the hair on his chest.

Evan grinned. "You don't really expect me to discuss the fine points of biotech research while you're doing that?" He slid out of bed and walked to the dresser. "Our lab has perfected techniques for growing pure tissue cultures," he said, getting dressed. "Then we use organic scaffolding—made with 3D printers—to provide a framework for the tissues to grow on and eventually create a functioning organ part."

"That's incredible. Why didn't you tell me this earlier?"

His back to Anne, Evan stood in front of the dresser mirror and buttoned his shirt. "Because we didn't have the most critical piece of the puzzle until now."

"Which is?"

He brushed his hair as he looked in the mirror. "Ruth," he said.

"Ruth? You can't be serious. What's she got to do with this?"

Evan settled into a chair to put on his pants as if he hadn't just dropped a bombshell in Anne's lap.

"Five years ago, I was at West Virginia University, doing basic research on tissue cultures for transplants. Everything was humming along, but there were two major problems. First, tissue cultures grow very slowly. It was taking forever to grow enough tissue to cover even a small part of the scaffolding. Second, transplanted tissues trigger an enormous immune response in the recipient. Unless we use a ton of immunosuppressant drugs, we risk transplant rejection. But those drugs increase the risk of infection—or even cancer—and they tend to kill off the tissue culture cells."

"Of course, but what does this have to do—"

"We tried getting around it by cloning the patient's own

stem cells, but that takes too long. The patients would die of organ failure before we could grow the new organ. When you're in organ failure, you need premade tissues ASAP."

Suddenly, uncomfortable in her nakedness, Anne started getting dressed herself. "Evan, what does this have to do with Ruth? How do you even know about Ruth? I still don't get it."

Evan tucked in his shirt, then held up his hand. "Hear me out. While I was trying to sort out this puzzle, I received several blood specimens from a girl who had developed a peculiar infection. Her primary care doc wanted to know if she had some immune defect. Imagine my astonishment when we discovered a unique collection of mutations inbred into this girl's genes. Now, the chance of these specific mutations developing in the same individual is one in ten billion. Under normal circumstances, such a person would never survive to puberty."

Anne grew apprehensive. *I don't at all care for where this is going.* "I assume this girl is Ruth?"

"Exactly. Ruth has a cluster of mutations that allows for lightning-fast cellular growth. More importantly, she has other mutations that affect the antigen complexes on the cell surface."

"Meaning?" *Has this all been some sort of a ploy? What have I gotten us into?*

With rising excitement and increasingly frantic gesticulations, Evan continued. "Meaning that when Ruth's tissues are transplanted, they aren't recognized as foreign, making Ruth a truly universal donor — for blood, tissues, organs, anything! Once we culture her tissues, they can be transplanted into any human being with no risk of rejection."

God Almighty, he's really going off the deep end. "Evan," Anne said with forced calm, "you're talking about a human being. You can't chop Ruth up into pieces."

He gazed at her with a pitying look. "Don't be ridiculous. That would only give us a finite supply of tissues, with too high a risk of cancer in the transplants. We've got to take cells from the earliest stages of embryo development and modify them to grow quickly into whatever tissue we need. That way, there's no risk of transplant malignancy."

Did he just say what I think he did? "Oh, so you're only going to chop her *ovaries* up into pieces?"

Evan seemed to totally miss Anne's sarcasm as he gestured excitedly. "*Now* you're getting the idea. The critical factor is to leave her genetic material untainted. To fertilize her eggs with outside DNA would make her mutations useless. We're going to use the cloning technique I mentioned in my lecture — parthenogenesis — to develop her embryos *without* fertilization from an outside source. Just like that" — he snapped his fingers — "her genetic material remains pure and unadulterated."

Anne launched herself from the bed and stormed over to Evan, her face inches from his. "You can't just cut the ovaries out of a fifteen-year-old girl. She has the right to determine what is done with her body."

Evan dismissed her concerns with a wave of his hand. "Ruth is too young to understand the ramifications of our research. That's why I need you to convince her of its importance."

"This is lunacy. Think of the cost to this girl. She'll never have children of her own."

Evan rolled his eyes. "Don't you get it? Ruth's embryonic cells will save millions of lives. She's of incredible value to humanity. She'll be saving so many lives. You can tell her that she'll be world-famous."

The words shot into Anne's head almost as if from a gun: *And from the womb of this last woman shall come the salvation of humanity, and she shall be called blessed above all other women on earth.*

"No," Anne said, breaking into a cold sweat as she shook her head. "It's wrong. It's all wrong. That can't be what it means."

"What the hell are you talking about?" Evan muttered.

"I will not be a part of this," she screamed. "I will not allow you to destroy Ruth's life."

"Anne, don't you see? I care deeply about Ruth. I was orphaned at an early age, just like her. Shunted from foster home to foster home, ignored, belittled. I know what that's like. But I will make my mark on the world, and so will Ruth."

This man is deeply disturbed. How could I not have seen this sooner? "Ruth will never consent to this, I will never consent to this, and her aunt will never consent to this."

As if a mask had been drawn from his face, Evan's look became stony, his eyes icy cold. "What Aunt Miriam will or will not consent to is irrelevant. She's dead." His voice had gone flat and emotionless.

The shock almost knocked Anne off her feet as everything became crystal clear. She cried as she beat her fists against his chest. "You killed her, you lousy son of a bitch! And you killed Isaiah, didn't you? And you murdered her parents too. All so you could get control of this girl."

Evan grabbed her arms and threw her on the bed. For a long, terrible moment, there was nothing from him but a pitiless glower. "You have no proof. Lillian disposed of the fruit for me. And yes, Isaiah and Miriam had to go in case I couldn't entice you to bring Ruth to me."

"Lillian? Oh, not you! Did you kill her too?"

"Of course," Evan said offhandedly. "She had outlived her usefulness."

Anne realized she was looking at evil incarnate. "You're a monster," she shrieked. "You're an absolute monster!"

Evan's face turned crimson. "You, of all people, should understand what I'm trying to accomplish. Think of what an infusion of nervous tissue into your spinal cord might do. You could walk normally again. We could cure any number of diseases rather than watch people die horrible, prolonged deaths. The Morehouses were doomed. For generations, their genes condemned them to early death from infection and cancer.

Ruth's genetic material is beyond priceless. I must—I will— have her ovaries."

"You can't force Ruth to stay here. You've kidnapped her."

Evan sneered. "Correction. *You* kidnapped her. This has worked out better than I dreamed. I knew Ruth was sick and needed expert intervention—not that incompetent Matt Drisner— so I planned on convincing you to go to Eden, but Drisner did the job for me. It proved so much safer to have you bring Ruth here than to rely on that drunk, Lillian, to help me kidnap her. Now, everything is untraceable." Evan grabbed her wrist and pulled her from the bed. He spoke caustically, his face contorted with rage. "Don't make her mistake, Anne. I hope you'll join my research team, but if you won't, I have alternatives. I will do this, with or without your cooperation."

Anne yanked her arm away and glared at him. "What are they worth, Evan? What's a pair of ovaries worth to you? You clearly can't support this lab on your own. It will take years before it turns a profit, and your venture capitalists want a quick return. What's the real angle?"

"I have several interested parties lined up. Biotech companies, overseas research facilities, and even a few foreign governments. As soon as I can guarantee the viability of Ruth's embryos, the bidding will begin at ten million dollars each. The facility will be paid off in a few weeks, and everything else? Pure profit."

Anne took a step forward and stared directly into Evan's eyes, her rage building to where her legs almost wouldn't support her. With all the force she could muster, she spit in his face.

Evan wiped it off with the back of his hand. "I take it that was your final answer."

"You murdered everyone who was dear to Ruth. I will never allow you to do this."

Evan pressed a button on his desk, then opened a drawer and withdrew a white envelope. "I had this removed from your luggage. It's the letter Miriam wrote to authorize your guardianship of Ruth. Since you won't agree to help, this is of no use to me." He threw the envelope into the fire.

"No!" Anne screamed. She raced to save the letter, but Evan threw her to the floor. He picked up the iron poker and prodded the envelope further into the flames.

Anne staggered desperately to her feet, her mind reeling. She saw Evan's ID card on the coffee table near her shoes. While his back was turned to her, she quickly picked it up and slipped it into her bra.

As soon as she finished, the door opened, and two security guards stepped in. Evan continued to poke the ashes of the envelope, ignoring Anne.

"Escort Dr. Mastik back to her room and lock her and the girl in there." Evan finally turned and leered at Anne, a sardonic smile twisting his lips. "We have to prepare for Ruth's surgery tomorrow."

***

Matt crept through the saturated underbrush, constantly on the alert for approaching flashlights or footsteps. At 1:45, vibrations from his cell phone alerted him to a call from Sid.

"I need an update, Matt."

"I'm on the property," Matt whispered. "It shouldn't take long to find the girl."

"You've got three hours, that's it. The SWAT extrication has to start before dawn if we're going to catch them by surprise and minimize casualties."

"That's not giving me a lot of leeway."

"This is turning out to be a hell of an operation. It's gotta stay on schedule. Get the girl to a safe extraction point. Got it?"

"Yes, sir."

With the storm over, Matt headed to the compound, staying in the woods and paralleling the path to avoid further patrols. He reconnoitered the main building, hiding in the trees as much as possible.

Floodlights bathed the entire front of the building. Much too exposed, and the doors had electronic smart card readers. The back was safer, but the only way in was by transom windows set much too high for climbing. Matt's gaze followed the tree branches as they arched over the roof.

Looks like the best way in is up.

***

Ruth sobbed inconsolably as Anne held her. Anne had shared the bitter truth that Miriam was dead, although she'd hidden Evan's identity as the murderer of Ruth's family.

Anne had already tried the suite door, but the security guards had locked it as soon as she stepped in, and there was no inner security lock on which she could use Evan's card. The only windows were small transoms set a few inches below the cathedral ceiling, at least fifteen feet up. She'd even grabbed a paperweight from a desk and thrown it at a window, but it had bounced off without even chipping the glass.

This was no guest suite. It was a well-appointed prison cell designed for a specific prisoner: Ruth Morehouse. Evan must have been biding his time for years—until Ruth reached an age where her eggs were viable. And to keep anyone from coming after her, he had killed off her relatives, doing it at intervals to avoid suspicion. Meanwhile, he'd constructed his facility and advanced his research until all he needed was Ruth's embryos. He had tricked poor Lillian into doing his bidding by playing on the affections of a lonely, vulnerable woman, killing her when she was no longer useful. He'd even poisoned poor Artemis, the only witness to his comings and goings.

Am I next? Is Ruth? Because once Ruth's ovaries were removed, she'd also be expendable.

"Anne, what shall we do?" Ruth cried.

"We need to figure a way out of here somehow." She searched in vain for any weak point, any chink or crack that she could exploit for escape. Finding none, she sat down next to Ruth and held her close. "Somehow," she finally said, trying desperately to keep the hopelessness out of her voice.

CHAPTER XXVII

Matt stole across the roof, exploring possible entrance points into the building. There were two separate wings. On the north side were immense heavy-duty negative pressure fans blowing gales of exhaust into the air along with small vent hood exhausts. The only way off the roof was a steel access door. He tried the handle. Locked. No surprise there.

The south wing was more promising. It appeared to be residential, with brick chimneys that surely led down to fireplaces. An updraft of warm air seeped out of the largest chimney. On the side of the building, a dim light shone out of transom windows, but he couldn't make out any details of the room.

A sharp bang sounded from the southernmost end of the building like something hard had hit a window. He raced to where the noise had come from and leaned over to look through the transom windows. The lights were on, but the angle was wrong, and he couldn't see down to floor level.

Pressing his ear to the chimney, he made out two muffled female voices. One sounded like Ruth, crying loudly, and drowning out the other. *That's all I need to hear. There's only one way in.*

He sprinted back to the access door, pulled out his tool kit, and selected a pair of lock picking tools. Forty seconds later, the dead bolt snapped open. Then he maneuvered a credit card under the latch bolt and slid it back. He paused inside the doorway and strained his ears for any sound before feeling his way down the dark staircase.

The main hallway was lit only by red EXIT signs. In the center, a single revolving security camera was fixed to the wall, just below the ceiling. It slowly swept back and forth, covering the hall. Matt timed a full circuit of sixty seconds. He took off his shoes and waited until the camera turned away. Hugging the wall, he stealthily edged his way down the hallway until he was directly under the camera. He held his breath as its arc swept by him, then raced to the south end and rapped on the door.

"Who is it?" Anne's voice said from inside.

"It's Matt," he whispered. "Open the door." He heard Ruth squeal with delight on the other side of the door.

"Matt, is that really you?" Anne whispered frantically.

"Yes. Now open the damn door."

"I can't. They locked us in."

Matt examined the electronic lock. His credit card trick wouldn't help, and the security camera had reached the other direction and was starting to sweep back in his direction. There was only one option. He took out his Beretta and silencer.

"Stand back. I'm shooting off the lock."

"Wait! For God's sake, don't do that. I've got something better."

Anne slid Evan's purloined ID badge under the door.

Matt rolled his eyes. *How the hell did she…? I don't think I want to know.*

As soon as the door opened, Anne and Ruth wrapped their arms around him and burst into excited tears. Matt pushed them back into the room and put his finger to his lips.

"Turn off all the lights," he whispered. When the room was dark, he propped the door open with his shoe and checked his watch. Fifteen seconds to spare.

"How did you find us? How did you get here?"

Anne and Ruth peppered Matt with questions until he put his fingers to his lips to silence them.

"I'll explain everything later, I promise. But right now, I have to get you two out of here. In less than an hour, a Federal SWAT team will be crawling all over the compound, and we need a safe place to meet them."

"What's the SWAT team for?" Anne asked, puzzled.

"Her," Matt answered, nodding at Ruth.

Anne cocked her head. "Wait a minute. What do the Feds want with Ruth?"

"Probably the same thing Garaud's interested in."

"Her ovaries?"

"I don't know the details. I'm just the agent assigned to protect her."

"Agent? You're a doctor!"

Matt shrugged. "I'm a man of many talents."

Dr. Matt Drisner, Man of Mystery, huh? Little did I know.

"Three years ago," Matt said, "Ruth was declared a top national security priority, and I was sent to Eden to make sure she stayed healthy. When you left town, it set off alarms all over the National Security Agency, but I managed to track you two down, and my boss is sending a SWAT team to extricate Ruth. Now that her family is gone, she needs to stay in Bethesda for her own safety."

"They can't legally do that, can they?"

"They've invoked the Inventions Secrecy Act. If an invention or discovery is deemed critical to national security, the government gets control of it. Or, in this case, her."

Anne's eyes blazed. "Matt, you may not be aware of the details, but I am. Once Ruth's condition is discovered, everyone will want a piece of her. She's like the goose with the golden eggs, and we all know how that story ended. If the government gets its claws into her, they'll stick her away in some secret facility, steal her tissues, and rob her of her right to have children. And what happens when she's no longer of use? With no family, she'll be discarded like a used lab rat."

Matt grabbed Anne's arm. "We can discuss this later. We've got to get Ruth to a safe place. Now."

"Anne, do not let them take me away," Ruth cried.

Anne grasped Ruth tightly. "Nobody is taking you anywhere. Whatever happens, you're staying with me." Myriad thoughts shot through her brain at once but above them all, she heard Miriam's last words to her: *You may do anything you need to protect her. Absolutely anything.*

I need to calm down. The time has come, and there's only one thing to do.

"I can get us into the clinical wing," Anne said coolly to Matt. "Perfect place for the SWAT team to meet us. I'll get a flashlight."

***

With a little timing and a lot of luck, Matt sneaked them by the security camera. By the light of Anne's flashlight, they made their way to the main laboratory entrance, where Anne used Evan's proximity card to enter. She then led them down the corridor to the first tissue culture lab, opened the door with the card, and signaled to Matt.

"You lead the way," she whispered. As Matt passed her, Anne lifted the flashlight and crashed it down on his head, knocking him unconscious.

Ruth gasped. "What did you do that for? He was trying to help us."

"No, he wasn't," Anne said, checking his pulse, breathing, and pupils to make sure he wasn't seriously hurt. He was knocked out cold but probably wouldn't be for long.

Anne took Ruth to an operating suite, locking the door behind them. Ruth started to protest, but Anne put her hand over Ruth's mouth. "Listen to me. I was hoping to save you from all of this, but I have no choice. I don't have the time to explain everything, but they want to take out your female organs for transplant. Once they do that, you can never have children." Anne removed her hand.

"I heard what you said to Dr. Drisner before, but I do not understand."

Anne hesitated. "We may have misinterpreted the prophecy."

"How? I want to have children. I must have children. That is what the prophecy is about."

Anne looked into Ruth's eyes. Never had she been so torn. *Do I tell her the complicated truth that by fulfilling the prophecy, she may save millions of lives, perhaps even cure my multiple sclerosis, but by doing so, she'd have to give up her dreams and be condemned to a life of fear and loneliness? How do I ask a naive fifteen-year-old girl, raised alone on a mountain with the hopeful expectations of generations of forebears, to make a decision that may destroy her — especially after I swore an oath to Miriam and Isaiah to care for her? Most of all, what of Ruth's words: "To be chosen by God is to suffer"?*

"Please, please, don't let them do that to me," Ruth said with tears running down her cheeks. "All my life, I have been told that it is God's will I must have children." She broke into uncontrollable sobs.

The whir of helicopter blades pulsed in the distance, and something large and motorized, probably a troop transport, sounded like it had just crashed through the compound gates. Alarms blared, and strobe lights flashed throughout the lab.

"We don't have much time," Anne said as she led Ruth through the operating suite to a storage room.

"What are you doing?"

"Trust me. This is the only way. Stay right here, and don't move."

She ran into the storage room and came out with a wrapped procedure tray and several pairs of sterile gloves and set up the tray on a Mayo stand.

"Let me tell you all about the prophecy," Anne said as she ripped open the sterile wrapping and donned a pair of sterile gloves. "'If you foreswear eating of any part or product of any animal.' That was to keep you free of infections carried by animals or animal products like milk or eggs. That's why you got sick when you ate Mary Beth's contaminated chocolate ice cream." Anne cracked open a vial of local anesthetic and drew it into a syringe. "'You shall live apart from other nations so that you will remain holy to your God.'" Anne set out the contents of the tray. "That was so you didn't get any communicable diseases carried by humans." She found a bottle of antiseptic solution and squirted it into a small well in the tray. "'Then know that at the end of times, your bloodline will die out, all but one woman,'— that's you—'and from her womb shall come the salvation of humanity.'" She paused and looked at Ruth, "And that is why we're here. Because as you are, there will always be people who will stop at nothing to hunt you down, for good or evil, to steal what's inside your body. But there is one last requirement in the prophecy—that you shall abstain from getting blood."

Outside, the helicopters grew louder, and excited voices clamored outside the building. Anne lowered her pants below her waist, exposing her hip bone, then changed her gloves.

"They are here," Ruth wept. "They will find us. Then what will they do?"

"When they find us, it will be too late. The prophecy said to abstain from getting blood, but guess what? We're going to disobey that one. I'm going to give you a bone marrow transplant. I'm going to take *my* bone marrow and inject it into *your* bone marrow. Because of your special immune system, you shouldn't have any reaction. But my white blood cells will go all over your body. Once that happens, you'll no longer be a universal donor."

"And they will leave me alone?"

"They sure will."

"But if you give me your blood, will I still be able to have children?" Ruth asked.

"Of course," Anne answered. "But I don't know if they'll be the salvation of humanity."

"Then go ahead. I will take that chance."

Anne scrubbed her hip with the antiseptic and took out the biopsy needle, whose hub was covered by an innocuous-looking T-shaped handle of green plastic. Protruding from that was the needle itself, four inches long and as intimidating as any needle imaginable. The tray had only enough anesthetic for Ruth, so Anne would have to jab this thing into her hip bone with full force and try not to scream.

Anne felt for the point of her pelvis where the skin of her abdomen attached directly to the tip of the pelvic bone, then moved her finger to where the bone was only thinly covered by muscle.

This is not going to be pleasant.

Anne stuck a roll of gauze between her teeth and bit down, then counted to three.

She thrust the needle through the muscle. It plunged into the outer layer of bone and stopped, the gauze muffling her scream. She pressed down hard on the plastic handle and twisted the needle, stifling her groans until the bone gave way, allowing the needle to enter the soft inner marrow.

A wave of dizziness enveloped Anne, and she broke out in a sweat, almost passing out from the pain. She grabbed the flimsy Mayo tray for support as Ruth ran to her, but she waved Ruth off and took the gauze out of her mouth. "I'm okay. Just need a moment to catch my breath."

As the dizziness passed, Anne grabbed a large syringe and screwed it onto the hub of the biopsy needle that protruded from her hip like a dart. She pulled back on the plunger and watched the syringe fill with dark maroon bone marrow. When the syringe was full, she twisted the needle out of her bone with one last sharp cry.

Ruth held her arms out in front of her and shook her head. "I cannot do that. I cannot do that."

Anne replaced the biopsy needle with a fresh one from the tray. "Don't worry. I have medicine that will numb you. I swear it won't hurt."

Ruth started to cry. "I cannot do that. I cannot do that."

Now directly overhead, the chopping blades of the helicopters were deafening, and loud voices clearly shouted threatening orders. The SWAT team would find them in minutes.

Anne grabbed Ruth by the shoulders and leaned down to her level. "Listen to me. We've got to do this right now. You must trust me. I will not hurt you. Do you hear me?"

Ruth was sobbing too much to speak but nodded yes.

"Good. Now pull your jeans down a little bit and turn around." Ruth did as she was told, wiping the tears from her face.

"I'm wiping you off with a sterilizing solution. It's going to be cold."

Ruth gasped involuntarily as Anne sponged the cold liquid over the back of her hip.

"I'm going to numb up the area. It's a tiny needle, smaller than the ones they used back at the hospital. It will sting a little. Is that okay?"

Ruth sniffed and nodded again. She gave a whimper as Anne injected lidocaine all the way to the bone. The heavy tread of boots thudded on the roof directly over their heads.

"The worst is over. I'm going to put the biopsy needle into your hip bone. I want you to relax and take deep breaths." Anne moved to Ruth's side so she could see her. "Do you trust me?"

Ruth wiped her nose on her sleeve, smiled weakly, and nodded. "I trust you."

"Good. Then here we go."

Anne pushed the biopsy needle through the muscle until the point rested against Ruth's pelvic bone.

"There will be a little pressure now. Are you ready?"

Ruth grabbed the operating table in front of her to steady herself. "Yes, I am ready."

With a hard thrust, Anne pushed the needle through the outer layer of Ruth's pelvic bone. Ruth gave a brief gasp but continued her deep breathing.

"Are you all right?"

"I am fine. Do what you must."

The door to the operating room burst open, and Evan stood in the doorway, half-dressed and wild-eyed, holding a gun. He looked at the bone marrow tray and knew instantly what was happening.

He walked toward them, gun aimed at Anne's head. "Get your hands off the syringe. Now. Or I'll kill you and put a bullet right through the girl's belly." He smirked, "Then we'll see how many kids she can have."

Anne raised her hands, leaving the full syringe jutting from Ruth's hip. Her legs were so stiff she could barely hold herself up, but she managed to step in front of Ruth to protect her. "Nothing you can do now, Evan. There's a government task force overrunning the facility. Apparently, you're not the only one who knows Ruth's secret."

Evan sneered. "In that case, I have no use for either of you."

Matt stormed in, gun drawn and blood dripping down his face. "Drop it, Garaud! The lab is surrounded. There's nowhere to run. Drop the gun and give yourself up."

Still armed, Evan started to pivot, but as he did, a shot rang out. He thudded to the floor, a circle of blood expanding rapidly over his chest. Meanwhile, Matt stood stiffly in firing stance, his face impassive, smoke streaming from the barrel of his Beretta.

SWAT team officers swarmed the suite, weapons drawn. Anne put her hands down and turned to Ruth, but an officer tackled her before she could take a step. In the same instant,

Ruth reached behind her own back and grabbed the barrel of the syringe.

"Everyone, stand down!" Drisner shouted. "Nobody move! Ruth, stay where you are. Don't worry. We'll get the syringe out."

Pinned, Anne couldn't move, but she saw Ruth's eyes scanning the room. Ruth's fingers gripped the barrel of the syringe so hard that her knuckles turned white. Her other arm tensed as her hand balled into a rock-hard fist.

Ruth looked down at Anne, her brow creased, and her lips drawn tightly together.

Anne felt a twinge of hope. *I know that look. I saw it many times on Miriam, and on Ruth before she carried me to the stream. Something is about to happen.*

Staring straight ahead, with a distant gaze that seemed fixated far beyond the men surrounding her, Ruth took a step back. Then another. And another.

"Stay where you are, Ruth," Matt ordered. "Do not move."

Several officers advanced toward Ruth, but before they could get close, she raced backward, still gripping the syringe, until her body hit the wall. With a guttural scream that seemed to come from deep within — so loud and penetrating that it filled the room and stopped the SWAT team in their tracks — Ruth thrust her hip backward, pressing the syringe against the wall and pushing the plunger in to the hilt, which forced Anne's bone marrow into hers.

Chaos erupted as the entire contingent of SWAT officers mobbed her.

Ruth looked down at Anne one last time, and smiled. "It is done," she mouthed softly.

CHAPTER XXVIII

Three Days Later

"Calhoun County Family Court, the Honorable Judge Stephen R. Solomon presiding, is now in session," the bailiff's voice rang out. "All rise."

Wearing an orange prison jumpsuit, Anne pushed herself clumsily from her chair, her steel arm and leg shackles adding weight to the neurologic shackles she'd carried for years. Her attorney, Angelica Stanton, stood beside her. Tall, tastefully coiffed, and nattily attired, she presented an elegant, professional appearance.

Out of the corner of her eye, Anne caught sight of Ruth standing alongside the public attorney representing her. Ruth made a quick sidelong glance at Anne, a fleeting smile flickering across her face.

"Be seated," the bailiff said as Judge Stephen Solomon walked in and sat down behind the bench. Short and bespectacled, with a ring of silvery white hair, his countenance projected a no-nonsense air.

"Would the attorneys please identify yourselves?" Judge Solomon said.

"Angelica Stanton, attorney for Dr. Anne Mastik."

"Linda Bryford, public attorney, representing the legal interests of minor female Ruth Morehouse."

"Timothy Waldman, attorney for Dr. Marcus Stendahl and Reverend Lucius Wainstock."

"The issue we have before the court today," the judge said, "is the guardianship of one minor female, Ruth Morehouse. Ms. Bryford is requesting that Miss Morehouse, who is without a legal guardian, be made a ward of the state." He straightened his glasses and continued. "This request is being contested by three individuals: Reverend Lucius Wainstock, pastor of the Church of the Righteous Disciples in Eden; Dr. Marcus Stendahl, a physician and neighbor of Ms. Morehouse; and Dr. Anne Mastik, also a physician, each of whom is applying for guardianship. Are there any corrections or clarifications to this summary?"

Waldman stood up and made a brief vain attempt to button his suitcoat over his protuberant belly. "Only that Dr. Stendahl and Reverend Wainstock are applying together for joint guardianship, Your Honor," he said.

"Ms. Bryford," the judge said, "does Miss Morehouse have any living relatives?"

"No, Your Honor."

"Your Honor," Waldman said, "may I add that Dr. Mastik is accused of surreptitiously checking Miss Morehouse out of a hospital against medical advice and transporting her to a medical research facility administered by the now-deceased Dr. Evan Garaud, who is thought to be the responsible party in at least two of the deaths in Miss Morehouse's family?"

Anne raised her hand to object, but Stanton pulled it down and shook her head.

Judge Solomon slammed his gavel. "Then let's get moving."

***

"Do you swear to tell the truth, the whole truth, and nothing but the truth, so help you God?" the court reporter asked Reverend

Wainstock once he'd settled himself in the witness stand.

"As God's love guides me through every moment of my life, I do so swear."

Timothy Waldman stood up, nodded politely at Judge Solomon, and addressed Wainstock.

"As I understand it, Reverend Wainstock, you broadcast many of your Sunday services."

"I endeavor to spread the light of the Word of God to those who still live in darkness."

"Do you get paid for this service?"

"Only by the contributions of those whose lives have been changed as they now see themselves free to pass through the Gates of Heaven and dwell in Paradise for all eternity."

"How do you know Ruth Morehouse?"

"She and her family have lived on top of Eden Mountain for as long as anyone can remember. But they live in the darkness of the soul that comes from rejecting the redeeming grace of God, which came with the death and resurrection of our Lord Jesus Christ."

"Are you married, Reverend?"

"I have been living in wedded bliss to the same woman for forty years. We have three grown children and four grandchildren."

"Would you please tell the court why you are applying for guardianship?"

"This young girl's previous guardians, who are now sadly deceased, endangered her immortal soul by keeping her isolated on a mountaintop and instilling her with Satan's lies and half-truths, disparaging the true message of Christ by the Apostle Paul. In addition, I believe they neglected her pressing medical issues, which is why I am applying for joint guardianship with Dr. Marcus Stendahl, a physician well-known and highly respected in our community."

"That is all, your Honor."

"Ms. Stanton, your witness," Judge Solomon said.

***

"Reverend Wainstock," said Anne's attorney, "did I hear you say that your services are broadcast on the radio?"

"Yes, on Sundays. I have plans to broadcast a weekly Wednesday sermon starting in a few months."

"How many watts of transmission power is your station?"

Wainstock chuckled. "I leave that to the engineers. The only power I need to know is the power of the Lord."

A twitter arose from the courtroom, and Stanton smirked.

"Quite appropriate, Reverend Wainstock," she said. "For the record, I'd like to introduce Exhibit A, a Federal Communications Commission application by Reverend Wainstock, dated March 25, 2003, for a transmission tower for his radio broadcast. Perhaps this will refresh the Reverend's memory." Stanton approached the witness stand and handed the paper to Wainstock.

Wainstock put on his reading glasses. "I see the tower transmits at 1000 watts."

"How far does your tower transmit your services?"

"As I understand it, about 75 miles."

"That's not terribly far, Reverend. And that's on a clear day, isn't it?"

"We're deep in a valley, surrounded by mountains."

"How far would a 10,000-watt transmitter go?"

"I…I'm not certain how far…." Wainstock stammered.

"Objection!" Waldman exclaimed. "Relevance."

"Your Honor," Stanton said forcefully, "I am trying to establish that Reverend Wainstock has an ulterior financial motive for seeking guardianship over Ms. Morehouse."

"Objection denied. Proceed, Ms. Stanton."

Stanton returned to Wainstock, who was dabbing his forehead with a handkerchief. "How far would a 10,000-watt transmitter broadcast if positioned on top of Eden Mountain?"

"Objection," Waldman said. "Reverend Wainstock already testified that he knows nothing about the technical aspects of his broadcasts."

"Your Honor, I believe Reverend Wainstock knows more than he admits about the technical aspects." Stanton held up a small sheaf of photocopies. "I would like to offer in evidence, as Exhibit B, a recent petition to the F.C.C., signed by Reverend Lucius Wainstock and requesting permission to build a 10,000-watt transmission tower on the top of Eden Mountain for the purpose of broadcasting not only radio but televised and online services as well." She spun to Wainstock. "Now, please answer the question, Reverend Wainstock. If you would like to refresh your memory again, you can review this yourself."

Wainstock's face flushed, and he shifted uneasily in his chair. "That won't be necessary. From its current position in the valley, a 10,000-watt tower would broadcast about 250 miles. It would cover the entire state of West Virginia and adjacent portions of Virginia, Maryland, Pennsylvania, Ohio, and Kentucky."

"And if it were on top of Eden Mountain?"

Wainstock read carefully from the document. "It is anticipated that by repositioning the transmission tower to the top of Eden Mountain, this will expand the transmission range to between 500 and 750 miles."

"So, at minimum, having the transmission tower on top of Eden Mountain, on the Morehouse property, would extend the range of your radio and televised broadcasts to most of the United States east of the Mississippi River. Is that correct?"

"Yes, that is correct," Wainstock acknowledged.

"No more questions."

***

Linda Bryford stood up. She was a head shorter than Stanton and a bit more matronly in appearance. She flipped through the pile of papers in front of her briefly before conducting her cross-examination. "Reverend Wainstock, I understand that the

Morehouse family were believers in the divinity of Jesus."

"Their beliefs are false doctrines, creations of Satan designed to lure them from the one true faith," Wainstock said. "They believe that Jesus Christ, our Lord and Savior, was born of the sinful relations between a man and a woman, not begotten of God. It is only by bringing this poor, misguided child into the true knowledge of salvation through the sacrifice of Jesus Christ" — Wainstock closed his eyes and continued in a slow, measured voice — "begotten of the Father, of one substance with the Father, who came down from Heaven, was made incarnate, suffered on the cross and was buried, then rose again on the third day."

Anne rolled her eyes. *Pompous ass!*

"I see you know the Nicene Creed," Bryford said. "Do you know when it was written?"

Wainstock beamed. "Three twenty-five A.D. The Year of Our Lord."

"That was almost 300 years after the death of Jesus and about 250 years after the death of Paul. What do you think happened in those two or three centuries?"

"I really don't know."

"May I introduce into evidence as Exhibit C a copy of the King James Version of the Holy Bible?"

"Objection!" Waldman shouted.

"Ms. Bryford," Judge Solomon said, "I do not wish to bog down this hearing with extended theological discussions of the Bible."

"Your Honor, I simply wish to point out that even in the Bible itself, there is evidence of fundamental conflicts between the beliefs of Paul, whose teachings Reverend Wainstock follows, and James, the brother of Jesus, whose teachings my client and her family follow."

Before Waldman could object further, Wainstock pulled himself up to his full height in the witness stand, his voice shaking with fury. "They are wrong!" he screamed, his face crimson.

"They denied Him, and her parents will burn in Hell for their heresy." He pointed a tremulous finger at Ruth. "So will she if she does not see the light of God's truth."

Linda Bryford turned to Ruth, who sat weeping in her chair, then she spun back around to glare at Wainstock. "No further questions, Your Honor."

***

Timothy Waldman stood as his client, Dr. Marcus Stendahl, took the stand.

"Dr. Stendahl," Waldman began, "you're a neighbor of the Morehouses, aren't you?"

Stendahl appeared poised and confident in the witness chair. "I've lived on an adjacent piece of property downhill from the Morehouse homestead for about ten years. My family has been living on that mountain for several generations."

"Did you know the Morehouses personally?"

"Not really. They pretty much kept to themselves, though I recently had a professional relationship with Ruth Morehouse."

"What was the nature of that relationship?"

"She was in septic shock. I had to put in a temporary pacemaker because she was going into complete heart block."

"By doing this, would you say you saved Ruth Morehouse's life?"

"Definitely. Her heart stopped as I was putting in the pacemaker."

"I see. Dr. Stendahl, I believe you recently learned that your daughter, Mary Beth, was a close friend of Ruth Morehouse. Is that correct?"

"Yes. As I understand it, they have been friends for most of the ten years we've been living on the mountain. From what Mary Beth told me, they would meet in a clearing in the woods between the two properties."

"Did you oppose those meetings?"

"No. Frankly, until a few days ago, I wasn't aware the two

girls even knew each other."

"Do you oppose this friendship now?"

"Not at all. Ruth is a charming, intelligent, thoughtful girl who's been a positive influence on Mary Beth. That's why I believe Ruth would feel very comfortable living with our family."

***

"Dr. Stendahl," Angelica Stanton began, "you stated that you had placed a temporary pacemaker into Ruth Morehouse's heart. Was it you who inserted the device?"

Stendahl shifted. "Dr. Mastik did the actual insertion. I instructed and guided her."

"That's peculiar, isn't it? Why didn't you do it yourself?"

"The girl's aunt, Miriam Morehouse, insisted on Dr. Mastik performing any procedures on her."

"Even though both you and Dr. Mastik told Mrs. Morehouse that you were very experienced in this dangerous procedure and that Dr. Mastik was, shall we say, a novice? Wouldn't you say that was an unusual position for a child's guardian to take?"

"I would say so."

"Why did she take that position?"

Stendahl glanced at Waldman, who shrugged his shoulders. "She said that Dr. Mastik was the only person she trusted to touch her niece."

"Interesting. Thank you, Dr. Stendahl. That will be all."

***

Linda Bryford again scanned the papers laid out on the table in front of her. "Dr. Stendahl, you stated that you've lived on Eden Mountain for ten years. How did you come across your property?"

"There had been a large parcel of land on the mountain owned by the Donnard family, which was my maternal grandmother's maiden name. When she died, she willed part of the property to me, one of her two surviving grandchildren. She had previously given a neighboring portion to Artemis Donnard, her other surviving grandson, and a cousin of mine."

"That is the late Artemis Donnard, isn't it?"

"Yes. He died a few weeks ago."

"How large is your property, Dr. Stendahl?"

"Three hundred acres."

"How large is the late Artemis Donnard's property?"

"About the same, maybe a little larger."

"What are the boundaries of each of your properties?"

"My property runs from the Morehouse property to the base of the mountain. I don't know how far Artemis's property extends."

"That's odd," Bryford said. "I had a look in the Eden Courthouse records, and seven years ago, you are recorded as having requested the records of all Donnard properties on Eden Mountain. Those records list the size and location of both your property and Artemis Donnard's. Your Honor, may I introduce this document as Exhibit D?"

Stendahl reddened. "I...may have investigated it back then. That was a long time ago."

"Did you also look up your grandmother's will at that time?"

"I...may have."

"Yes, or no?"

"Yes, I believe I did."

"Then, you are aware that in the event of Artemis Donnard predeceasing you, given that he has no survivors, his property would pass to you or your survivors?"

"Objection," Waldman called out. "Artemis Donnard died intestate. His property and estate are currently in probate."

"Let me rephrase the question. Pending probate, you may end up owning all the real property on Eden Mountain except for the Morehouse homestead."

"Yes, I recall reading that," Stendahl said nervously.

"Are you also aware that several large real estate

development corporations want to build a ski resort and condominiums on Eden Mountain, and the only thing holding up their plans is the refusal of the Morehouse family to sell their homestead?"

"I have heard rumors to that effect."

Bryford paused and stared at Stendahl. "How much would your property be worth if that resort were built?"

"Objection. Conjecture."

"Sustained."

"I withdraw the question. No more questions, Your Honor."

***

After being sworn in on her own Bible, Ruth fidgeted in the witness chair, hands clasped and resting on her long linen skirt, her bleached blonde hair contrasting with her olive skin and dark eyes. Linda Bryford sat behind the desk, giving Ruth a moment to settle down.

"Ruth, this hearing is to determine who will be responsible for you until you come of age to legally make your own decisions. Do you understand that?"

"Yes, ma'am."

"You are not on trial today. You have done nothing wrong. Do you understand that as well?"

Ruth shifted nervously. "Yes, ma'am."

"Good. I have only a few questions. Did you ever read or see a letter your aunt wrote authorizing Dr. Mastik to be your guardian?"

"No, I did not."

"Did your aunt or uncle ever tell you they wanted to make Dr. Mastik your guardian?"

"No. Anne…. Dr. Mastik…told me that was their wish. She said they made her promise she would always take care of me."

"But you never heard your aunt or uncle say those words,

correct?"

"Yes, ma'am. That is correct."

"When Dr. Mastik took you from the hospital, what was your understanding about what would happen?"

"She said she was bringing me to a friend of hers who had a hospital where we could hide, and I would be safe and get the medicines I needed."

"And after you were better?"

"That we would go back to Eden Mountain so I could live with my Aunt Miriam again." Ruth brushed away a tear.

"Did your Aunt Miriam ever tell you that Dr. Mastik could make all medical decisions for you, even on a temporary basis?"

"No, ma'am, not that I remember."

"No more questions, Your Honor."

***

Tim Waldman stood up and swept loose strands of his thick, graying hair back with his hand. "Ruth, what religion do you consider yourself?"

"Ebionite."

"For those who don't understand that term, could you please explain it?"

"We believe that our Lord Jesus, born of a man and a woman, preached the imminent coming of the kingdom of God, and a person could enter that kingdom by living and acting in a righteous manner according to the Laws of Moses. We believe that God chose Jesus to be His Son and to be the perfect sacrifice for the sins of humanity because of His perfect righteousness."

"So then, you would consider yourself a Christian?"

Ruth looked puzzled. "I do not know that word."

Waldman looked flustered as if prepared for any answer but that one. "You do believe that Jesus is the Christ?"

"I do not know that word, either."

"Do you believe that God anointed Jesus? That he is the Messiah?"

Ruth nodded. "Yes, sir."

Waldman looked relieved. "So, when Saint Paul called Jesus 'the Christ,' he meant 'the Anointed One,' so the two mean the same thing."

Ruth's forehead creased. "I do not hearken to the words of Paul."

"But you do believe that Jesus was divine."

"Only after his death and resurrection."

Waldman paused, then seemed to land on an idea. "Ruth, did Dr. Mastik ever discuss your beliefs with you?"

"Only to ask what foods I could and could not eat."

"Why did she ask that?"

"She thought it might be important for my health."

"As any physician should ask. But did she ever ask you about your belief in God?"

"No, although we did discuss the contents of the scroll."

Waldman turned to Judge Solomon. "Your Honor, the other attorneys and I have all agreed that the issue of the scroll is not directly relevant to the matter at hand and would be an unnecessary distraction."

"Taken under advisement. Proceed with your questioning, Mr. Waldman."

Waldman turned back to Ruth. "Did Dr. Mastik ever offer her own religious beliefs?"

"No, sir."

"You never discussed religion or God with Dr. Mastik to any significant degree?"

"No, sir. I did not."

"No more questions."

***

"Ruth, did you ever feel threatened by Dr. Mastik?" Angelica Stanton asked.

"Oh, no. Never."

"How about when you were in the hospital? Did she ever

make you feel in danger?"

"No, ma'am. I felt very safe."

"And when you and Dr. Mastik were on the run?"

"Anne protected me many times. I was frightened when we were locked up in Dr. Garaud's compound, but Anne comforted me."

"What about when Dr. Mastik performed the bone marrow procedure on you?"

"I trusted her. Completely."

"Ruth, this hearing is to decide whether your guardianship will be entrusted to Dr. Stendahl and Reverend Wainstock, or if you will become a ward of the state and placed in a foster home, or if Dr. Mastik will be your guardian. If it were up to you, which would you choose?"

Ruth's face brightened for the first time, and she smiled at Anne. "I would never, ever leave Anne. I have given her my word."

"Did your aunt and uncle ever say that they wished Dr. Stendahl or Reverend Wainstock to be your guardians?"

"They never would have said that. They did not trust any of the townspeople, especially Reverend Wainstock."

"Why not?"

"They thought everyone in town coveted our property, and they felt they were all Paulists."

"By that, you mean...?"

"That they were led astray in their understanding of the teachings of Jesus by Paul."

"Thank you, Ruth. No further questions."

***

"Calling Dr. Anne Mastik to the stand," the bailiff called out.

Anne stood up, her hands and feet still bound.

Angelica Stanton shot up from her chair. "Your Honor, may I request that Dr. Mastik be allowed to take the stand unshackled? She is not violent, nor is she a flight risk. She has a neurologic disorder, and the shackles impede her balance and mobility."

"If neither Mr. Waldman nor Ms. Bryford has any objection...."

Both attorneys shook their heads. The bailiff unlocked Anne's shackles, and Stanton helped her to the witness stand.

"Dr. Mastik, how did you become involved with Miss Morehouse's case?" Stanton asked.

"I was consulted by Dr. Matthew Drisner as an expert in Infectious Diseases. Ruth had a severe infection in her blood stream by Listeria, a bacterial infection that is unusual in someone with a healthy immune system. She needed to be hospitalized, but the family had refused to consent."

"Did they listen to you?"

"It took some doing, but I convinced them there was no alternative to hospitalization."

"We have heard Dr. Stendahl testify that Ruth's aunt and guardian, Miriam Morehouse, refused to have anyone else touch her niece but you. Is that true?"

"Yes."

"For that reason, you stayed with Ruth and Miriam, in Ruth's room, for several days, taking her vital signs, personally regulating her IV fluids, drawing her blood samples, and even performing necessary medical procedures on her."

"That is correct."

"Was there any time that Miss Morehouse's aunt and uncle discussed their plans for Ruth's guardianship?"

"Her uncle Isaiah was quite ill, but on his deathbed, he made me promise that I would always take care of Ruth. And while Ruth was in the ICU, her aunt Miriam also made me swear that I would always take care of Ruth." Anne's eyes met Ruth's. "That is my intent."

"Thank you. No further questions."

***

"Dr. Mastik," Timothy Waldman said, "are you married?"

"No, I'm divorced."

"Did your husband beat you, abuse you, or have extra-marital affairs?"

"Heavens, no."

"Then why did you get divorced?"

"After I contracted multiple sclerosis, strains developed in our marriage, and we grew apart."

"You grew apart. Did you seek marriage counseling?"

"For a while, but it didn't seem to work."

"All told, how long did your marriage last?

"About five years."

"I see. Do you have any children, Dr. Mastik? Any nieces or nephews?"

"I do not."

"So you divorced basically because you and your husband fell out of love, and you've had no child-rearing experience."

"That's not what I— "

"One last question. You said that Miriam and Isaiah Morehouse made you swear to always take care of Ruth. Were there any witnesses to these assertions?"

"No."

"Did you tell anybody about them?"

"Yes, Lillian Petrillo."

"Who was recently murdered."

Anne shifted uncomfortably. "Yes."

"Do you have any written documentation to support your claims?"

"I had a note written by Miriam, but it was destroyed."

"By whom?"

"Dr. Evan Garaud."

"The man who allegedly murdered Ruth's uncle and aunt and attempted to kill you and Ruth but was himself shot and killed, is that correct?"

"Yes," Anne said quietly.

"A man you chose to have sexual relations with the night before, is that correct?"

"Objection!" Stanton shouted.

"Question withdrawn," Waldman said. "Dr. Mastik, you told the court there was another copy of Miriam's note at the Morehouse property."

"It was placed for safekeeping in a cleft in a large granite outcrop."

"May I inform the court that Federal agents have been over every inch of that homestead, including the outcrop in question, and no copy of that note—or any other documentation of Dr. Mastik's claim—has been found?"

"Then someone must have taken it. I saw Miriam put it there."

"I would like to introduce as evidence Exhibit E a written affidavit from Dr. John Buckram, Chief Medical Officer and Chief Executive Officer of Eden Community Hospital. It states that only one day after Ruth Morehouse was admitted, he attempted to have her transferred from the Intensive Care Unit to a different floor, but you argued against this, saying it would be injurious to Ruth's health and well-being. Do you recall that conversation?"

"Yes."

"And yet, two days later, you appealed to Dr. Buckram to let you transfer Ruth not just to another floor but to a different hospital over a hundred miles away."

"Ruth's medical situation had stabilized, and I felt she would be better off at an academic facility to evaluate her complex underlying immune disorder."

"I suppose the timing of this proposed transfer had nothing to do with Dr. Stendahl and Reverend Wainstock applying for guardianship earlier that day?"

Anne squirmed in her seat. "It did not."

"Dr. Mastik, when you took Ruth out of the hospital,

did you intend to bring her to the medical facility of Dr. Evan Garaud?"

"Yes. He had offered medical care that Ruth couldn't get anywhere else."

"But you testified that you had previously wanted her transferred to University Hospital."

Anne reddened. "That was no longer an option."

"And why was that?" Waldman asked sharply.

"Because of a court order against moving her, which I did not feel was legitimate. Neither did her aunt, who notified the police officer of her concerns."

"But nonetheless, there was a court order."

"Yes, there was."

Waldman put his hands on the table. "Dr. Mastik, were you having an affair with Dr. Garaud?"

"Objection—relevance!" Stanton exploded.

Waldman turned to Judge Solomon. "I mean to demonstrate that Dr. Mastik's motives may not have been as selfless as she claims."

"Overruled. Continue."

"Dr. Mastik, were you or were you not having an affair with Dr. Garaud?"

"I had only met him once, at a conference, and we spoke several times by phone. I wouldn't call that an affair."

"Did you ever have sex with Dr. Garaud?"

"Once. In the research compound. But I discovered afterward that he had murdered Ruth's family and intended to harm her. I felt totally betrayed and disgusted."

"I need to clarify one last issue. Immediately prior to your rescue from Dr. Garaud's compound, you performed a medical procedure on Ruth. A bone marrow transplant, is that correct, Dr. Mastik?"

"Yes, it is."

"Can you describe the procedure, please, as it was

performed by you on Ms. Morehouse?"

"Under sterile conditions, I inserted a special needle into my pelvic bone and withdrew a specimen of my bone marrow."

"What consistency is bone marrow, Dr. Mastik?"

"It's like a thick paste."

"I imagine you had to use a fairly large needle to penetrate through the hard bone and withdraw a thick paste."

"That's right. I anesthetized Ruth's skin and muscle with local anesthetic and inserted the needle into her bone marrow — "

"So you had to push this large needle into her pelvic bone?"

"Yes, but because of the anesthetic, she only felt a pressure sensation."

"I see. And then?"

"At that point, pandemonium ensued, and Ruth actually performed the injection herself."

"How could Ruth possibly do that?"

"She backed into a wall and used it to push the plunger in."

Waldman paused and briefly rubbed his chin before continuing. "Under normal circumstances, why would a patient receive a bone marrow transplant?"

"For a variety of blood disorders."

"What would these include?"

"Aplastic anemia, leukemia, lymphoma — "

"For the sake of brevity, I won't ask you to list all of the indications for a bone marrow transplant. Can you tell me the medical indication you used to justify an invasive, painful, and potentially dangerous procedure without having tested for donor compatibility?"

"Ruth's immune disorder."

"Which is called…."

"It is a unique disorder that hasn't been named yet."

"So you can't give me any research study, journal article,

or other scientific or medical evidence to warrant doing this procedure on Ruth Morehouse, which could potentially have exposed her to a life-threatening reaction?"

Anne cast her eyes down. "No, I cannot."

Waldman turned to the judge. "To summarize, Your Honor, Dr. Mastik claims verbal authorization for guardianship of Ruth Morehouse, but the only people who can testify to this are dead. She then claims the existence of a written document confirming this authorization, which conveniently was destroyed by a man who is also dead. She maintains there exists a copy of said documentation, but it appears to have vanished into thin air. Finally, Dr. Mastik has demonstrated instability in her past marital relationship and denies any experience whatsoever in child-rearing or Christian education. May I remind the court that she is currently charged with transporting Ruth Morehouse out of a hospital in the middle of the night, an action that even she has indicated was against best medical advice, and she subsequently committed assault on a minor by performing a bone marrow transplant without permission and without pressing medical need. It is our belief that giving guardianship of Ruth Morehouse to this woman would cause the child irreparable harm and that the best recourse for this unfortunate young girl is a dual guardianship under Dr. Marcus Stendahl, who can provide for her parental, financial, and emotional needs, and Reverend Lucius Wainstock, who can attend to her spiritual needs, rather than be thrown to some unknown foster home as a ward of the state."

Waldman sat down with a smug grin.

Anne stood up, her legs shaking so much that she had to support herself on the rails of the witness stand to keep from falling as she faced the judge. "May I address the court, Your Honor?"

"Go ahead, Dr. Mastik."

"I have done some unwise things in the past several

weeks, and some of them may, in the court's eyes, seem to have been reckless and ill-advised. But Isaiah and Miriam Morehouse trusted me to safeguard Ruth and keep her away from toxic influences in Eden." She looked directly at Ruth. "I have always done what I felt in my heart was best for Ruth and what her family would have wanted me to do."

Angelica Stanton rose to her feet. "May I request a recess, Your Honor?"

"Granted. Thirty minutes for lunch."

***

"I hate to say this, but things are looking bleak," Stanton said to Anne as the two sat in the gallery after everyone else had left the courtroom.

"But you heard what Ruth said. She wants me as her guardian."

"The judge will take that into consideration, but the deck is stacked against you."

"You can't let Stendahl and Wainstock be her guardians. They'll steal her property, and Wainstock will brainwash her against everything her family believed in."

"In West Virginia, having a child get a proper religious upbringing is an important criterion for guardianship. Since there are no other Ebionite families available, the judge will choose the closest thing, which is a traditional Christian upbringing, which you can't give her." Stanton reached over and touched Anne's hand. "Look, I know this is hard for you, but it's in the judge's hands, and there's nothing I can do. I'm certain that in your mind, you did the right thing, but in the eyes of the law, what you did was illegal and may have endangered Ruth."

"But these are accusations. I haven't been to trial yet. Aren't I innocent until proven guilty?"

"That's why Waldman wants Matt Drisner to testify, and when he testifies that you assaulted a Federal officer, even if you haven't been proven guilty in a court of law, Judge Solomon will view your guilt as a *fait accompli*. The judge will assume that, at the very least, you'll have your medical license revoked, you'll be fired from your job, and you won't be able to practice medicine in Virginia. Probably not in any other state, either. It's likely you'll be jailed on a felony charge of kidnapping and reckless endangerment of a minor. And if they become Ruth's co-guardians, Stendahl and Wainstock could also sue you for medical assault. How could you possibly care for Ruth under those conditions?"

Anne wiped away a tear. "I wish Miriam were here. Whatever I did was what she would have wanted me to do. She would set everything right."

***

Matt Drisner and Sid Antonucci sat together in silence in the witness waiting room. Throughout the proceedings, neither had said a word. But the recess was ending.

Antonucci broke the silence. "Now that you've been briefed on the girl's genetics, you're good with testifying?"

Matt sneered. "Do I have a choice?"

"Drisner, you spent the last five years of your career trying to protect that girl and her family, and your doctor friend out there screwed up the whole project."

"But if she hadn't helped, the girl would've died."

"From the standpoint of Operation Gene Pool, she might as well have died."

"What the hell did you just say?"

"It's true. Once she got the bone marrow, her immune system was contaminated. She's worthless as far as any tissue cultures are concerned."

"Would it have been better to have Garaud send her eggs to every foreign research facility willing to cough up ten million dollars?"

Antonucci waved away Matt's objection. "Garaud was running a mom-and-pop operation. We could have shut him down with the Inventions Secrecy Act, no problem. But the girl, she was critical, and now the whole project is canceled."

Matt started to speak but thought better of it and held his tongue.

"You've got to nail Mastik," Antonucci continued. "If she loses guardianship, she doesn't have a leg to stand on in Federal court. She'll learn that she can't screw around with the Federal government and get away with it."

"She did what she thought was best for Ruth."

Antonucci lifted a brow. "You're not sweet on her, are you?"

"I've seen how she interacts with Ruth. Those two have a real closeness. I can see Anne's point when she says she did what she thought was best for Ruth."

Antonucci stood, angrily pointing his finger at Matt. "You listen to me, Drisner. We had big plans for that girl. She was one in a million—no, one in ten billion—and now, two thousand years of inbreeding all goes down the drain. We're putting that bitch away, and you're going to help us do it because your job is on the line. Capisce?"

"Dr. Matthew Drisner, please take the stand," the bailiff called out.

Matt stood and headed toward the courtroom. "Perfectly clear," he said over his shoulder.

"Would you tell the court your name and occupation?" Tim Waldman said.

"Dr. Matthew Drisner. I practice Internal Medicine as well as hospital medicine in Eden Community Hospital."

"Who is your employer, Dr. Drisner?"

Matt glanced at Sid, who nodded at him from the gallery.

"The Federal Bureau of Investigation," Matt said.

A collective murmur filled the air and then faded after Judge Solomon banged his gavel and called for order.

"Why would the FBI hire a physician to practice in an out-of-the-way place like Eden, West Virginia?"

"The government had...an asset there."

"Please tell the court what you mean by 'asset.'"

"Five years ago, the National Institutes of Health received blood samples from a physician in Eden for evaluation. The patient had developed an unusual infection, usually seen only in people with impaired immune systems."

"This patient being...."

"Ruth Morehouse."

"What was the result of this evaluation?"

"We found that Ruth had a unique set of genetic mutations that rendered her cells essentially invisible to other immune systems, while additional mutations enabled her cells to multiply very rapidly under certain conditions."

"Dr. Drisner, I'm certain this would make a fascinating lecture at a medical conference, but for the sake of us laymen — I beg your pardon, lay*persons* — could you please tell the court why the NIH and FBI found these findings so significant? In plain language, of course."

Antonucci nodded again.

"In simple terms, Ruth would be a truly universal donor for any transplantable organ and in theory, could provide an inexhaustible supply of those organs."

"And Ruth's unique set of mutations were considered important by our national government?"

"Critically important."

"For reasons of national security?"

"Yes."

"When Dr. Mastik kidnapped Ms. Morehouse — "

"Objection," Stanton said. "Dr. Mastik has not been tried on kidnapping charges. Mr. Waldman's statement is prejudicial."

"Mr. Waldman, please restate your question," Judge Solomon said.

"Certainly. When Dr. Mastik removed Ms. Morehouse from the hospital and brought her to Dr. Garaud's facility, were her actions deemed to be against our nation's security interests?"

"Yes. The National Security Agency had invoked the Inventions Secrecy Act regarding Ruth's genetic material."

"Which is why you tracked her to the research facility in Gethsemane, North Carolina?"

"Yes." Drisner felt the perspiration building up under his shirt.

"And that is why you, with no small amount of risk to yourself, entered the grounds of the facility with the intent of rescuing Ms. Morehouse."

"Correct."

"And that is why the Federal government sent an entire SWAT team to extricate Ms. Morehouse from the facility." Waldman's voice was building in intensity.

"That is correct."

"And while you were performing your duties as a government agent, Dr. Mastik struck you on the head with a heavy object, resulting in a temporary loss of consciousness."

"Yes."

"And those are the reasons why, as an official agent of the Federal Bureau of Investigation, you subsequently had Dr. Mastik arrested."

Matt was sweating profusely. He could see Antonucci smiling.

"That is also correct."

Waldman's voice had reached an almost theatrical level as he slammed his fist repeatedly on the table for emphasis. "And when you arrested Dr. Mastik, you knew that she had no legal right to withdraw Ms. Morehouse from the hospital, no legal right to transport her across state lines, and no legal right to expose her to an invasive and potentially dangerous medical procedure which would render useless her unique genetic makeup that the

United States Government sought so desperately to protect."

Matt glanced at Antonucci, who silently mouthed, "Do it." Then Matt caught a glimpse of Ruth clutching Linda Bryford's arm as tears streamed down her cheeks. He noticed Anne in her orange jumpsuit, stoically staring straight ahead as she grasped Angelica Stanton's hand.

Matt glowered at Waldman. "That is not correct."

The courtroom erupted. Judge Solomon repeatedly banged his gavel to restore order. Matt glanced at Antonucci's shocked face, then quickly looked away.

Waldman stepped closer to the witness stand. "Could you clarify your statement, Dr. Drisner?"

"It is my understanding that Dr. Mastik is the properly authorized legal guardian for Ruth Morehouse."

Waldman's face turned pasty white. "On what do you base your understanding? You do realize that any unverified conversations between Dr. Mastik and members of Ruth Morehouse's family must be construed as hearsay and are inadmissible."

"I base my understanding on written documentation." Matt pulled a white envelope from his suit pocket and held it up. "I have the missing copy of Miriam Morehouse's guardianship letter."

CHAPTER XXIX

Eight Years Later

The long, tiring drive from southwest Virginia to Eden had worn Anne out, but when she saw the familiar flat top of Eden Mountain looming in front of them, her anticipation picked up. Even Jinx, her Labrador retriever, woke up and paced back and forth in the rear seat.

"You miss being on the mountain, don't you?" Matt asked her as he turned his pickup onto the familiar steep road.

"Very much so. It's hard to explain the calm and tranquility I felt there during those five years as Ruth's guardian. You'd think I'd have been bored, but farming has its own rhythms and rewards. When you're working in the fields, there's lots of time for thinking. Especially since I had to get Ruth up to speed academically."

"She was lucky to have you as a teacher," Matt added.

"Homeschooling Ruth to high school level was hard work, but she was a great student. In the evenings, she would do her homework until it was too dark to see the pages. Then we'd sit by the fireplace and talk. That was when we *really* got close."

The paved road gave way to the rugged dirt trail leading to Artemis's shack.

"Ugh," Anne said with a grimace as she bounced in the passenger seat. "After all this time, you'd figure someone would have graded this road."

"If you prefer, we can go back to the main road, and you can climb the path to the mirror tree clearing." He put his hand on her leg and squeezed it playfully. "We almost had our first date on that path."

Anne stroked his hand tenderly for a few seconds before lifting it up and placing it back on the steering wheel. "Both hands on the wheel, please. And thank you, but I'll pass on that route today." She looked around wistfully, thinking back to that trail, which she and Ruth had descended every day so Ruth could catch a ride to school with Mary Beth. It had been awkward at first, but eventually, Marcus and the entire town had come to grips with the idea that there would always be a Morehouse atop Eden Mountain, especially after Ruth married Bo Overmeier, her high school sweetheart, three years ago.

"How did you ever let me entice you to come to Galax?" Matt asked, referring to the southwest Virginia town where they had shared an internal medicine practice for the past three years.

"Dropping the assault charge against me helped a whole lot," Anne said with a laugh. Then her tone turned serious. "You risked a lot when you brought out Miriam's letter at the hearing. That gave me a whole different perspective." She crossed her arms and stared straight ahead. "Of course, I was pretty pissed that you had stolen it in the first place."

"I didn't steal it," Matt protested. "I was...holding onto it. For safe keeping. Besides, I'd think that driving from Galax to Eden twice a month to see you—for four years—would be sufficient atonement."

Anne softened and held Matt's hand between hers. "Forgiveness granted. By that time, I was ready, and so was Ruth. Besides, she had Bo. Their wedding was the perfect excuse for me to move out."

"And their baby?"

"The perfect excuse for me to return. For a little while, at
any rate. Ruth will probably need my help once the baby arrives,
although Bo is a real sweetheart. Deliver a calf? Easy peasy.
Shoe a horse? No problem. But change a diaper? No way. He'd
probably drop the baby."

"Speaking of weddings," Matt said as he felt Anne's
engagement ring pressing into his palm, "when do we start
seriously planning ours?"

"Not until after Gary and Lara get married this fall. Gary
deserves to be happy, and I want to be available for anything he
needs from me."

Matt parked at the familiar clearing by Artemis's cabin.
"Well, here we are," he said, stepping from the truck and letting
Jinx out of the back seat.

Anne got out and took in an eyeful of Artemis's shack. Still
standing, probably more out of habit than structural integrity. "I
didn't think it was possible, but it looks even more decrepit than
when we last saw it."

"You think they cleaned out the empty bottles yet?" Matt
said with a wink.

"Oh, please. That was so disgusting."

"I suspect the police went over it with a fine-tooth comb
after I gave them the evidence of his murder. But the property
lost a lot of value when Ruth made it clear she was staying on the
homestead."

Matt stepped onto Artemis's porch and pushed open the
door, its rusted hinges groaning in protest. "Care to take a look
inside? For old time's sake?"

"No! We came to see Ruth and Bo. Grab the suitcases, and
let's get going."

Though the walk proved difficult for Anne, especially in
the heat, she felt strengthened by her excitement and anticipation.
After a few minutes, she and Matt reached the old bronze bell,

still hanging from the ancient branch that had supported it for decades. Anne picked up a rock, probably the same one Artemis had used ten years ago and struck the bell three times.

"Bo, come quickly!" Ruth's voice squealed from inside the cabin. "Anne and Matt are here."

Upon hearing Ruth's voice, Anne ran the remaining few yards as fast as her stiffened legs could carry her. At the same time, Ruth burst out of her farmhouse at full speed. The two women embraced in a mixture of joyful screams, laughter, and tears while Jinx barked and jumped around them.

"I missed you too, Jinxie," Ruth said, kneeling to give him a hug. "It is so nice to not worry about infection," she said, happily submitting to Jinx's licks.

"I hate to break up the party," Matt said as he dragged their suitcases forward, "but I sure could use some help here."

Bo Overmeier, a powerfully built giant of a man with shoulder-length blond hair and a beard reaching to his chest, strode over and gripped Matt's hand, giving it a single hard shake. "Good to see you again, Matthew. May God's grace be on you. We're so glad y'all could come." Making it look no more strenuous than picking up a pair of kittens, Bo lifted both suitcases. "Come on in. I've got iced tea in the refrigerator. West Virginia mountain-style iced tea, if you know what I mean," he added with a wink as he led Matt inside.

"Refrigerator?" Anne said as she and Ruth strolled arm in arm toward the house.

"And electric lights, an electric stove, and satellite television." Ruth pointed to the windmill electric generator that stood at the highest point of Eden Mountain, next to the granite outcropping that had hidden the scroll. "All part of the deal I made with Bo to get him up here. Otherwise, we would have to live on his family's farm in the next valley. I love them, but...."

"I know. You and Bo needed to be together, just the two of you. That's why I left. How's married life?"

"It has been wonderful. Bo is as gentle as a lamb, but I have never felt so completely safe as when I am with him. He meets all the requirements for love that you taught me. Every single one." Ruth patted her protuberant belly. "Plus some that you did not mention."

"Tell me, how is the future salvation of humanity?"

"Stop that, Anne Mastik," Ruth bellowed. "I will not hear that from you. Besides, the bone marrow you gave me broke the prophecy. Come a month from now, I will be blessed with the most beautiful baby in the whole world. God will have to choose someone else to save humanity because I will have none of it."

Anne laughed. "You've always had your aunt's determination." Her tone turned serious. "Do you ever wonder what Miriam would have thought about what we did?"

Ruth walked in silence for a long moment, her eyes misty. "I miss Aunt Miriam. Sometimes late at night, I lie in bed and think of her and Uncle Isaiah and Abbah and Imah, all looking down at me from heaven. I do not know if they approve of what we did, but I do know what they would have thought of the alternative. Then I remember Aunt Miriam always saying that whatever happens is God's will. I never understood what she meant, but now I believe that, in some way, everything that happened had its purpose. Perhaps someday we will know that purpose."

Ruth helped Anne up the steps, and the two women, followed by Jinx, stepped out of the summer heat into the coolness of the farmhouse.

***

At the same moment that Anne and Ruth were strolling to the farmhouse, Dr. Peter Jones's secretary buzzed him on the office intercom.

"There's a call on line two from the Department of Comparative Religion at Hebrew University. I think I heard him correctly...is the name Dr. Reuven Shimowitz familiar?"

Dr. Jones's face brightened as he picked up the phone. "Reuven, *Shalom aleichem.*"

"*Aleichem shalom* to you, Peter. How's the family?"

"Everybody's doing great. How are the girls?"

"Zipporah is a sophomore at Technion University, and Leah starts medical school at N.Y.U. in July. I tried to convince her to stay in Israel, but you know how kids are."

"Sure, sure. Time flies when you get old, doesn't it?"

"I'd love to *schmooze*, but I'm calling about something important. Do you remember the lecture you gave in Jerusalem on the Gospel of the Ebionites?"

"Of course. Afterward, your wife made the best brisket I've ever tasted."

"I'll let Rivkah know. Anyway, can you tell me the backstory of the scroll?"

"Sure. It's crazy. For two thousand years, one family had possession of a jar holding an ancient parchment. The family entrusted it to a physician, who brought it to me for safekeeping, no questions asked. It took ages to unroll, but it's clearly authentic. Most of it was an Aramaic copy of the lost Gospel of the Ebionites, but at its introduction was an apocalyptic prophecy by James foretelling that...let me remember the exact words...*at the end of times your bloodline will die out, all but one last woman. And from the womb of this last woman shall come the salvation of humanity, and she shall be called blessed above all other women on earth.*"

"Did you examine the jar?"

"Yes. The jar is from Qumran, and I mean the real deal. In one of the unoccupied old houses on the family's property, I found boxes of handwritten documents that traced the family tree all the way back to Salome, the sister of Jesus."

"How did they get from Palestine to West Virginia, of all places?" Shimowitz asked.

"The whole community fled to Pella before the First Jewish War against Rome, like James told them to. The community wandered around for over a thousand years, from the Arabian Peninsula to North Africa to Spain. During the Inquisition, they fled to Amsterdam and somehow found their way to America."

"Well, I've got a story that will knock your socks off. I've got a second copy of your scroll."

Dr. Jones nearly fell from his chair.

"Peter, you still there?"

"Sorry, I was a little dumbfounded."

"Believe me, so was I."

"How did you get it?"

"A few decades ago, a Messianic family immigrated here from some isolated mountain community in the Caucasus region where they had lived for a thousand years. They were in Syria and then Persia for a thousand years before that. Anyway, they claimed Israeli citizenship as Jews under the Law of Return, which caused a big *tsimmes* at the time because Messianic Jews are excluded from the Law of Return. But the Israeli Supreme Court ruled that they were Jews because—now get this—they could trace their Jewish lineage—unbroken—to late Second Temple times, and they followed the biblical laws to the letter. In fact, they had documentation that they were descended from Shimeon, another brother of Jesus."

"So, both of our families were *desposynoi*?"

"Yes, descended from the house of David through Jesus's family lineage, yours through a female line, mine through a male line. But that's not all. My family brought with them an Aramaic manuscript in a sealed clay jar identical to yours, traceable to the Qumran region."

"I can hardly believe it."

"They donated it to Hebrew University six months ago, and we've been unrolling it and translating it since then."

"And it's the same as my Gospel of the Ebionites?"

"So far, word for word. It even looks like the same scribe copied it."

"What about the prophecy?"

"It's there, in Hebrew, identical except for a single word. Instead of instructing the believers to flee to Pella, James told them to flee to Antioch, in Syria."

"You're saying that two separate groups of *desposynoi* followed the same prophecy, each convinced that they were responsible for the salvation of humanity, but neither community knew of the other."

"Exactly. James hedged his bets hoping that if one group didn't make it, the other would."

Dr. Jones pondered the revelation. "Reuven, a month ago, I learned that the last survivor of the family was pregnant, but since she received a bone marrow transplant, she can no longer fulfill the prophecy. What about your group?"

"That's the other reason I called. My group has died out, too, and as of a year ago, only a single childless couple remained. The husband died four months ago, leaving behind his pregnant wife. She delivered a baby girl by C-section at the Holy Family Hospital in Bethlehem two months ago."

"A Messianic Jewish woman giving birth in a Palestinian Moslem hospital run by a Catholic charitable order in the city of Bethlehem. That's incredible! Why there?"

"High-risk pregnancy, and this was the closest hospital with a neonatal intensive care unit."

"Why was she high risk?"

"Make sure you're sitting down because you're not going to believe this. It was her first pregnancy — and she was seventy-three years old! Her husband was seventy-seven when he died."

"Reuven, you said she *was* seventy-three?"

"Sad thing. She died in the hospital a few days after delivering."

"That's tragic. How's the baby doing?"

"The baby's doing well. But the strangest thing happened. Before the mother died, she absolutely insisted that her obstetrician adopt the baby. Of course, the obstetrician was taken aback, especially since she was unmarried, but she fell in love with the baby and agreed to adopt."

"She?"

"I know, I know…*a woman healer sent by God.* That's in our copy too."

Jones was flabbergasted. "My God, Reuven! In the Bible, Abraham's wife was one hundred years old when she gave birth to Isaac. Rachel, Rebecca, and the mothers of Samson and the prophet Samuel were all barren for years before they gave birth."

"And Elisabeth, mother of John the Baptizer, was barren until old age," Shimowitz added.

"It sounds like after the girl in West Virginia was excluded from the prophecy, your woman became the last, but she couldn't get pregnant until she actually fulfilled the prophecy and became 'The Last.'"

A long silence fell on both ends of the line.

Shimowitz finally broke it. "He maketh the barren woman to keep house and to be a joyful mother of children."

"How unsearchable are His judgments, and His ways past finding out. For who hath known the mind of the Lord? Or who hath been His counselor?" Jones replied.

"Praise ye the Lord," said Reuven Shimowitz.

"Amen," answered Peter Jones.

Without saying another word, both men hung up.

Gil Snider is a practicing neurologist, born and raised in Brooklyn, New York and medically trained at the University of Michigan. The proud father of two grown sons, he and his wife Judy reside in Virginia Beach, Virginia. He is a member of Hampton Roads Writers, an associate member of the International Thriller Writers and has published "Brain Warp: A Medical Thriller". He has been featured in multiple articles and interviews, listed on his website www.gilsnider.com.

Made in the USA
Middletown, DE
17 July 2023

34899438R00187